MW00649378

Midnight in Silverton
American Gothic

Fiction

Adam Copeland

For
Jennifer
may your adventures
never end

Adam
Copeland

11-19-22

Other Books by Adam Copeland

Echoes of Avalon

Ripples in the Chalice

For Mom.

We'll dance again someday soon.

This is a work of fiction. Events portrayed herein did not occur. At most, certain scenes were loosely inspired by actual events. Permission was obtained from real persons to use their likeness as characters portraying themselves. Likewise, permission was obtained from individuals whose likeness partially inspired fictional characters. All other characters are entirely fictional, and any resemblance to persons living or dead is coincidental.

Copyright © 2020 by Adam Copeland
ISBN 978-0-578-72404-1

All Rights Reserved

Printed in the United States of America

Editing performed by Sarah Cypher:
https://threepennyeditor.com/

Cover Design by Cheri Lasota:
https://www.authorsassembler.com/

Cover Art by Lori Rodrigues:
https://www.silverstreamstudio.com/

Acknowledgments

"White Rabbit"
Words and Music by Grace Slick
Copyright ©1966 Irving Music, Inc.
Copyright Renewed
All Rights Reserved. Used by Permission
Reprinted by Permission of Hal Leonard LLC

"My Body is a Cage"
Words and Music by Win Butler, Regine Chassagne, Tim Kingsbury, Richard Parry, William Butler and Jeremy Gara
Copyright © 2007 EMI Music Publishing Ltd.
All Rights for EMI Music Publishing Ltd. Administered by Sony/ATV Music Publishing LLC, 424 Church Street, Suite 120, Nashville, TN 37219
International copyright Secured All Rights Reserved
Reprinted by Permission of Hal Leonard LLC

American Gothic

American gothic fiction is a sub-genre of gothic fiction. Elements specific to American Gothic include: rationality versus the irrational, puritanism, guilt, the uncanny (das unheimliche), ab-humans, ghosts, and monsters.

—Wikipedia

Pseudo. adjective: being apparently rather than actually as stated : sham, spurious distinction between true and pseudo humanism. Synonyms: affected, artificial, assumed, bogus, contrived, factitious, fake, false, feigned, forced, mechanical, mock, phony (also phoney), plastic, pretended, put-on, sham, simulated, spurious, strained, unnatural.

—Merriam-Webster Dictionary

Table of Contents

Prologue

"How does it start?" Homer asks.

"On a bridge," I answer and open my eyes. "There is a mystery and choices to be made."

I hesitate over that response, mulling its veracity. Also that I'd answered in the present tense. That seems to be a theme now. Choosing. Choosing as I go.

And searching. Searching for answers, self.

"Excellent," Homer says, satisfied.

I look beyond him to the scene around us. Where has the pub crowd gone? The room is dark, illuminated by the ghostly light of neon bar signs and natural candlelight at each table. The wall clock is encircled by a purple neon tube that spells out "Mac's Place."

The ceilings fans are interconnected by belts that crisscross the ceiling and blow a gentle breeze on me and make the candles shiver. As a result, I feel colder than I should, damp, though when I hug myself and rub my upper arms, my shirtsleeves are dry.

I reach for my drink, a whole pint of amber-colored beer. My wrist drags in a puddle on the table, and I raise my forearm to stare at the wet fabric, then the pool that caused it with fascination. Odd. Something tugs at my mind.

Sitting across the table from me, Homer says, "A bridge is a good start. Very symbolic."

He's just finishing consulting his pocket watch. He snaps it shut with a crisp motion, and what light exists in the room glints off its case as he returns it to his vest pocket.

I like Homer's vest. I like his style—a neat three-piece suit, but he wears a cravat instead of a modern tie. The collar of his plain white shirt hugs the tie so stiffly that I'm not sure whether he is wearing his suit or whether it is wearing him, holding him upright.

Doesn't matter, I like it. Nothing wrong with a bit of starch in a man's back. It suits the solidity of his demeanor, its conviction. And though his suit is plain gray, I like that too. Nondescript. Reflective of a man who knows how to say what he means, without the distraction of a flashy wardrobe.

That's why I trust what he has to say, even if his truths can be harsh.

I agree that bridges can be symbolic, but add, "I have to admit, though, that I didn't expect it to start like this. I pictured this happening toward the story's middle."

"Best laid plans," Homer says. His handlebar mustache turns up when he smiles, causing its phalanges to rise alongside his hawkish nose like a bird taking flight.

I smile back.

"What's important is to just keep at it," Homer continues. "Even when it gets hard, when it seems like all aligns against you."

A voice from my right adds, "Yes, just keep at it." Oh, Stephen is there, even though I'd lost track of him. "One word after the other. One foot in front of the other. It's not going to do itself. I believe it was Ray Bradbury who said, 'You must stay drunk on writing so reality cannot destroy you.'"

Suddenly, Stephen is sitting to my left. I shake my head clear and stare at him in his new seat. I also suddenly remember that Stephen hates the use of the word *suddenly* in narration— my use of it, not only once in this paragraph but twice, embarrasses me. I hope he forgives me.

He slouches forward over his drink. He is the opposite of Homer. More relaxed. Laid-back and contemporary in his blue jeans and black Ramones T-shirt. The pub's thin light reflects off his round spectacles. Streaks of gray have started to appear in his signature long black hair. Up close, he is kind of a creepy-looking bastard, but the mischievous glint in his eye shows that it's just a performance, and he is not the least bit dangerous. The consummate outsider. Which I can also admire. Or, at least, relate to.

"I think Ray would like you," I tell him. "You both had such similar things to say."

"I know, I liked him," he says, taking a drink of his diet soda. I don't begrudge him the fact we're in a bar, and he's drinking a soda because he's a recovering alcoholic.

"I promise you," Homer says, "it will become more difficult as you go, but don't let that deter you. The truth is important. It must be said."

He picks up his teacup, sips once from it, and returns it to the saucer. Both are gold-trimmed and painted with a vine motif. The china rattles perceptibly.

I look to my right at the table: a glass pint mug sits there now. Clark's beer awaits its owner's return. Unlike my drink, Clark's is very yellow, most likely Olympia. (Clark has no time for all these faddish microbrews.) I am grateful I'm not the only one drinking a beer.

I take a pull of my amber brew and consider my companions. Despite their differences, there is a resonance. After all, Homer, with his center-parted hair combed through with pomade, coupled with that mustache, could pass for Edgar Allen Poe's doppelgänger: a complement to any creepy bastard.

I consider their advice on my tale. If nothing else, I can put one foot in front of the other. I do have some convenient strengths. Am I not often accused of going on and on? Saying too much? Doing too much? For once, it's a strategy. And in the end, eventually, it will mean something.

I sigh heavily (at least it's not *suddenly*), thinking about meanings. I've been searching all my life for purpose. That will be the challenge. It will be my undoing if I'm not careful. I need these wise souls. So long as they speak plainly and don't go on like the Mad Hatter's Tea Party, I might be okay.

The sound of a coin making its way through the circuitous route of a jukebox draws my attention to the back wall. Beneath a gallery of black-and-white photos of musicians, a glowing Wurlitzer radiates rainbow pastels into the ghostly atmosphere.

Clark stands before it on the dance-worn hardwood floor. Satisfied with his selection, he returns to the table. Despite broad shoulders and big working hands, he still manages to look like an impostor in his gray work shirt and wool pants held up by suspenders. The five o'clock shadow darkening his lantern jaw does nothing to hide his movie-star good looks. If anything, it enhances them. He sweeps a dark forelock out of his eyes with one hand and seizes his pint with the other.

As Clark takes a drink, Peter Gabriel's voice fills the room from the jukebox:

My body is a cage

that keeps me from dancing with the one I love

but my mind holds the key

"Things reveal themselves like they were meant to be," I say distantly, listening to the music as Peter's voice drones on, drifting about the room, an errant spirit trying to find its way out.

"Art imitating life," Clark adds. He would know, the actor playing at being a logger.

I incline my head, murmuring, "...but my mind holds the key."

My body is a cage

that keeps me from dancing with the one I love

but my mind holds the key

I'm standing on a stage

of fear and self-doubt

it's a hollow play

but they'll clap anyway.

"Don't lose yourself," Clark warns. "Do what you must, to move forward, but don't get caught up in someone else's truths. Find yours, then..." He leans forward and holds my gaze. "Find your way out."

"Hear, hear," Homer says, raising his teacup.

"I'll drink to that," Stephen says, and he and Clark raise their glasses.

I feel fortified by their companionship and goodwill. I raise mine, touch theirs, and take a drink.

When I do, I look over the rim of the glass and note over the bar there is now a flat-screen television playing the news. An anchorman is talking into the camera. The sound is off, but the news ticker at the bottom announces two local women have been murdered, and a third is missing.

"Looks like there is more than one mystery to be solved around here," Clark says.

I set my glass back on the table, dragging my arm through the puddle again. It's much bigger now. Concern grips me as I stare at my wet sleeve, accompanied by an irrational fear that the wetness might spread and overcome me. There is a throbbing in my temples. My heartbeat accelerates. A sound invades my ears.

Peter Gabriel is drowned out by the new sound over the loudspeaker above the music stage near the jukebox. Static? No, not quite. Electrical, though. A crackle. An electrical crackle, but somehow muffled. Somehow near. Somehow far.

Something drops on my sleeve. I look at it. A drop of moisture. Followed by another.

I look up to the ceiling just in time to see another one coming, just before it lands in my eye.

Chapter 1
Splash

Her arms flail. The water splashes. The cool dampness had awakened her only long enough for a single scream of desperation, which was cut off in a choking gurgle as gloved hands at her throat forced her head beneath the chemical-scented water. Her hands push, pull, punch, slap, and scratch at the gloves and forearms covered in a coarse long-sleeved shirt. But the gloved hands holding her throat, pressing their thumbs into the softness of her flesh, are as solid and immovable as the surface pressing against her back. Even as her hands turn to weak, messaging pleas, the assailing hands remain an iron grip. Emotionless, dutiful in purpose.

Though only a few inches of water separate her face from life-giving air, it may as well be a mile, for it's all the same when the moment comes: an involuntary gasp that takes in water, releasing a bubble from her mouth. The terrorized eyes, bulging in shape, flatten in spirit and stare into nothingness. The struggling body goes limp. The arms flop with a final splash.

She is sanitized. She is released. She is better off.

The gloves and long-sleeved shirt will be discarded.

Chapter 2
The Bridge

Something is coming.

But that notion strikes me as wrong.

Something? Shouldn't it be *someone?*

I wrestle with the distinction, almost right away lose my train of thought. What am I doing here? What am I waiting for? Was I waiting at all?

I assess my surroundings: I'm standing on a footbridge. It's the wooden one that straddles the creek at the park. The smell of creosote surrounds me, emanating from the railroad ties repurposed for the bridge platform. Ironically, when I am on railroad tracks, I think of this bridge. It's been part of my life for as long as I can remember, and now I stand at its center tonight. The city's well-lit swimming pool behind and above me, up a flight of stairs, casts contrasting shadows in the trees and brush that line the creek bank. The shadows dance gently in a warm breeze.

The waters below get caught downstream at a concrete berm before spilling over like a miniature Bonneville Dam, complete with a fish ladder on the far side. The dam, the fish ladder, and adjacent pavement walkway have all buckled and shifted with age, pushed up by decades of tree roots that reveal what true power looks like: slow, deliberate, patient.

In my father's time, it must have looked a little different. He played here as a child, just as I had. Did the concrete slabs jut up as far? Did the fish ladder lean as much as it does now? Has it changed perceptibly even in my lifetime?

No, I'd been thinking about something else. Why am I here again? I was waiting, but why? The park's darkness doesn't answer. The bridge narrows ahead of me, terminating in darkness, crowned by evergreens boughs. Despite the night hour, sweat beads on my skin and flecks my shirt like a constellation of stars. I sway on my feet in rhythm with trees and shadows, keeping pace with the creek-song.

I blink, shake my head. I almost have it—the memory of why I'm here.

"It begins," I murmur. "For real." I lean heavily against the rail and look down into the water. Lamplight shows rocks on the shallow side in every shade of brown with hints of ochre and black, like the surface of an eggshell. A large trout darts among the rocks. The creek is partially shallow here, partially deep. One step forward, and you can see the creek-bottom, a floor of water-smoothed stones ranging in size from my fist to my head. One step back, and the bottom drops off to a dark chasm.

A noise at the stairs startles me.

My heart races, and I crouch like an animal.

Nothing is visible, but still, I think, *Something is coming.* I feel its presence.

The stairs are more railroad ties embedded in the bank, and my eyes follow them up to the swimming pool parking lot. I can't see up there, but it doesn't matter. I can feel the presence vanish.

I should move on, get out of here.

Before turning my back on the scene and entering the park, I cast a glance at the mechanical structure on the pool-side bank, extending down into the water. Brambles and blackberry vines cover its upper portions, and its lower part disappears into the water with a small rocky grotto behind it. A distressed chain-link fence also extends into the water to keep the inner workings safe from swimmers or to keep swimmers safe from it.

I never knew what that thing did. It always scared the hell out of me as a child, making me think that if I swam too close to it, the gears and pistons would fire up, creating a vortex of water that would suck me in.

It wasn't a relic of a bygone industrial age when mills lined the creek, grinding wheat into flour, but still served some function, and had for the past fifty-some years. I always assumed it was how the city pool got its water. It growled away in the shadow of the bank, and even at night, I can make out its chipping turquoise paint. No wonder, I think, that they put a fence around it. Kids swimming in the creek would find that color inviting, drawing them with its playful color like Pennywise the Dancing Clown.

I reach the park, where it is darker. Smaller lamp posts up ahead light the asphalt road to the parking lot. I pass playground equipment, war memorials, and a well-manicured lawn between an army of sentinel trees. To my right, buildings and converted homes line the creek bank, now serving as art museums and gathering places.

The solitude works its calming spell, and I drop my fear and the struggle to remember my errand. The sound of the creek rushing over the dam and fish ladder subsides, giving way to a cricket symphony. Soon I pass through the park's signature, double-arched gateway of concrete and riverbed stones, a larger version of the rocks I saw in the creek. A bronze plaque announces this place as Coolidge & McClain Park. The stepped arches still please me, though not my mother, whose distress I caused by climbing all over them.

Outside the grounds, a tranquil residential street leads to town. Old houses, classic houses, charming homes. Yellow slivers of life light windows despite the late hour. At the corner to my left, a stone cottage convinced my sister and me Snow White lived there with the Seven Dwarves.

I jump up on the sidewalk and continue on my way.

Like the creek path, the sidewalk and concrete steps to each home buckle with age. Every other house has a sprinkler system hissing away, adding cool moisture to the warm night. I thrust my hands into my pockets. When I do, I feel the reassuring presence of my car keys, but also something else. I withdraw the long stringy object from my pocket and see my rosary that usually hangs from my car's review mirror. I grunt in surprise at the glossy dark beads and silver crucifix before returning it to my pocket, the gesture only momentarily breaking my stride.

Where am I going? It's late, but not too late. What should I do?

I can't shake the feeling I need to be somewhere. Doing something. But focusing on the questions only pushes the answers further away.

The street ends at a tee where a car launches from the stop sign and continues to town. I take a right and follow it at my own pace.

The town ahead is all stone, brick, and iron. A motorway bridge crosses the creek downstream from the park. The car that left the stop sign ahead of me passes over it, stops at the first intersection, then turns right at the stately historical building there. These bigger, antique homes surround the Eden house, now a bed and breakfast, which anchors the left side of the intersection. The Parkinson house sits opposite. They give way to two-and three-story commercial buildings at the bridge.

As I cross, I pause to admire the view, how the mortared stone foundations reach the waterline. The balconies of the various businesses extend over the creek. The meandering stream chatters around the stones. A dozen paces from the motorway bridge is another bridge for pedestrians, covered and extending from a small park with a small war memorial. The public restroom building displays a mural of Santa and Missus Claus.

As I leave the quaintness and come to the intersection, pain lances my skull. I stop, squeezing my eyes shut, and press my palm into my forehead, trying to massage the agony away.

It passes in its own time, and for some reason, I look back toward the way I've come. Wet footprints on the bridge sidewalk chase me to where I stand. Pain grips my head again, and I squeeze my eyes harder this time, determined not to cave in. Finally, the pain recedes, and when I open my eyes again, the footprints are gone.

Chapter 3
Break

"Break," Stephen says.

"What?" I say.

"You need to break from the current narrative," Stephen suggests, leveling those creepy eyes at me. "Don't always stay in the linear. You'll get stuck in the narrative, unable to move on, and the overall work will suffer for it. It's okay to jump around."

"Precisely," Homer agrees, consulting his pocket watch again. "Consider the standalone cartoon cell. It is a complete work, a narrative that stands entirely on its own. It needs no immediate context. A powerful thing when utilized correctly."

"Right," Clark adds. "It conveys a complete unit of meaning, uninterrupted like a movie scene. The movie scene is encapsulated, delivering its necessary information to the audience, so the rest of the story can move on. I don't know about going completely 'non-linear,'" he casts a glance at Stephen, "but I do see the value of occasionally diverging to focus on a particular and powerful—or just useful—scene to keep things interesting."

Stephen gives a shrug that says *agree to disagree*. "If you get caught up trying to shoe-horn the story by the numbers, the story may never finish. This story needs to finish."

Nodding, I take a drink of my beer and ponder my following words carefully.

Chapter 4
The Tomb

The congregation silently flows out of the church like a dark and tenebrous river, moving slowly and with a purpose to the parking lot. One service a year ends like this. There is no parting music. No one speaks. No one rushes in the dim lighting of the church sanctuary. Still, you can hear the rustle of the funereal fabric of the congregants' best Good Friday garments in the darkness. Candlelight casts the auditorium-like seating in dancing shadows, which makes the chamber feel cavernous.

At the conclusion of Mass, I had stepped away from my pew and immediately stood back against a wall, letting my fellow parishioners shuffle by. I was in no hurry to join the madhouse which would be the parking lot. Best to wait a bit and let the jockeying cars thin out.

Pausing like this, however, allows me to ponder more than what is probably good for me.

I am tired, and it has nothing to do with the late evening hour.

I'm not just tired; I'm feeling dead inside. The Good Friday Mass punctuates the feeling with its observance of the crucifixion and the subsequent shroud of death that separated us from Christ while he lay in the tomb.

I glance to the wall above the altar. Even the spot where the image of Jesus on the cross normally resides is left bare under a spotlight, emphasizing his absence and reminding us what the darkness of doubt is like so we can appreciate Easter morning all the more.

Right now, that morning is looking further off than ever. Furthermore, when it does come and the cross returns to its place, I'm not certain it will drive away this growing feeling inside me.

This feeling that, until recently, had been kept at bay by the trappings of my faith: the cool touch of holy water, the engulfing aroma of incense and chrism oil, the glow of candles, the gold glitter of the chalice, and the murmur of recurring familiar prayers. Even the crashing chorus of Handel's *Messiah* and the goose-bump inspiring *Ave Maria* had acted as insulation against doubt. Coupled with the roughness of cracked leather-bound books in my hands that smelled of time and history, these things propped up my faith. A faith that provided answers and offered order and structure to my universe. For the longest time, these things, these tangible things, had been enough to satisfy the intellect of a man with a degree in chemistry.

But now, these things that appealed to the senses were not enough. As I grew older, I learned that touching something wasn't the same as feeling it. Touch had taken me as far as it could, leaving me at a precipice looking out into the darkness, waving frantically, trying to connect with something just out of reach.

All that waving has left me exhausted.

The departing crowd jostles me, breaking my reverie and gently turning me about so that I'm facing one of the long windows that intermittently line the walls of the church. I don't mind, and thrust my hands into my pants' pockets and patiently wait. When I do, I feel the rosary in my pocket and, out of habit, start thumbing through the beads as I stare at the reflection in the glass. Not my reflection, as I have no interest in looking into that sad and tired face, but the few lights in the sanctuary behind me that speckle the glass like a constellation. I focus on the largest, which is the illuminated vacancy above the altar.

I'm reminded that in the Catholic tradition, as stated in the Apostle's Creed, when Jesus' body lay in the tomb, his soul descended into Hell where he broke its gates. There, he ministered to the righteous dead, offering them salvation.

My hand grips the rosary tight in my pocket.

Perhaps that is why I'm feeling particularly empty inside tonight. Jesus is less here than usual, ministering to those who need him most.

"What about me?" My whisper is almost a shout, and I withdraw my hand to clutch the fabric at my chest. When I do, the rosary comes with it, still entangled among my fingers. "Am I not dead inside? Am I not dead enough?"

I feel guilty for asking. I feel silly, really. Pretentious and melodramatic.

Just the same, I try to envision Jesus here with me to answer. When I do, I successfully see his reflection in the glass as he stands behind me. He's not answering, though. Instead, his head merely tilts to the side, and there is a slightly sad, slightly bemused look in his eyes.

"I..." I start to say but realize I don't have any words that don't sound petulant. So instead, I let my heart do the talking.

It doesn't just speak. It screams. Of smothering emptiness. Of longing. The desire for more. For answers beyond the intellect, beyond knowledge. It calls for the need for "feeling." For something to wrap the soul around. A tangible intangible. A...

Okay, now my heart is just babbling.

My hand at my chest claws deeper into the fabric of my shirt as if it might dig its way to my heart and give it a good shake so that it will make more sense. It doesn't work. It just hurts.

"I don't know what I'm trying to say exactly," I explain to Jesus. "But could you say something? No? Well, if not, could you at least touch me?"

The corners of Jesus' sad smile turn up just a hint more, and he reaches out and grasps my shoulder. When he does, I startle as I actually feel something.

I spin around, my heart pounding.

"Whoa! Sorry young man, didn't mean to scare you!"

Jesus is not there. In his place is an older couple I recognize, smiling. Their white hair floats like clouds against the backdrop of darkness. The crowd is almost gone.

"We just wanted to say how much we enjoyed your scripture reading tonight," the woman says, continuing in her hushed tone to maintain the reverence of the night. She withdraws the hand used to gain my attention.

"Yes," the man adds, also in a hush. "We've always admired your turn as a lector at the ambo. You speak with such passion! Such fervor! It is so good to see faith in action!"

"Thank you," I say, deflating. I feel like a fraud. And not just because I can't remember the names of this couple.

"Will you be speaking at any of the other Holy Week services?" the woman asks. Her face is earnest, and the smile lines around her kind mouth bunch up.

"I, uh, no, I won't be."

"Ah, that's unfortunate." The man's eyes are downcast below his bushy eyebrows but then brighten. "Next week, maybe?"

I shift on my feet, smooth out my disrupted shirt while watching the last of the crowd disappear from the sanctuary. I feel like an empty bicycle inner tube. My spine feels about as rigid as one.

"I've actually been thinking about taking a break, going to visit my folks for a while," I suggest.

The woman pats my upper arm. "Well, family is important. You do what you have to do. We'll certainly miss you."

I smile, genuinely moved by their kindness, and we make a few more passes at small talk before they too exit the church. I linger a little longer, making one final glance at the empty spot above the altar and the reflections in the windows, looking for something.

Before I leave, I pause at the exit where an art collection is displayed for Holy Week. A painting in Greek icon style utilizing simple two-dimensional characters and shapes on a field of gold leaf catches my eye. It is a scene of Jesus swathed in a shroud in the tomb. The Devil, basically a shadowy smudge with head, arms, and legs, menaces outside the tomb at the stone that blocks the entrance. The two points of red that make the Devil's eyes drill into me.

Chapter 5
The Crossroads

I sway on my feet, just now realizing my eyes were closed again while I was deep in thought. My head doesn't hurt this time.

Wait. What? Was I in pain?

The sound of clicking grabs my attention, and I open my eyes.

Along the sidewalk comes a white and brown Collie, its toenails ticking on the pavement. Off-leash and ownerless, it pauses at my feet, assesses me, then heads past the street signs marking the intersection of Main and Water. It goes down South Water Street. Flapping above, suspended across Main, is a banner sign that says, "Homer Davenport Days! Joins Us the First Friday, Saturday, and Sunday of August!"

I teeter there for a little while longer at the crossroads in front of the historic Ames Building. Maybe I should follow the dog, but then I hear music coming from the opposite direction. Jaunty, upbeat bluesy music. It is enticing—and when I look down South Water again, the dog is gone. At least now I know where I'm going.

I head north, up Water Street to the center of town. Memories wash over me with a thousand bits of trivia. Maybe *this* is where the story begins. With a stage. What is a story without a stage? What is a rocket without a launchpad?

My hometown. Even though I don't live here anymore, it's still home. Always was, always will be.

Silverton, Oregon.

Smalltown, USA, complete with a Main Street that could have been painted by Norman Rockwell with glowing highlights added by Thomas Kinkade. It is a place that could have been written into existence in the pages of Bradbury, Tolkien, King, and even Poe and Lovecraft, and of course, Davenport.

It's the sort of place that has regular visits by Santa Claus, and the moon, when full, seems a bit bigger here than in other places. Maybe not a-bunch-of-kids-in-Halloween-costumes-riding-bikes-with-an-alien-in-the-handlebar-basket-across-the-moon big, but generous.

Unfortunately, because of the infamous Oregon rain, those spectacular moons, fat with purpose, rarely get to preside over a Halloween night as kids in damp bedsheets, perspiration-soaked plastic masks, and smeared makeup gallop across the local cemetery on a dare.

Likewise, Santa's visits are rough on his sleigh runners because the snows come but once a year, and what day that happens is anybody's guess. White Christmases in Silverton are as rare as unicorns, but we never give up hope.

Decorative cartouches surmount many of the buildings, stating in plaster, "Nineteen-oh-something-or-other" as the building's commissioning date. Large windows display everything from art to baking goods to antiques and jewelry. Someone somewhere has a model train circulating through a Christmas Village steeped in wispy cotton every holiday season. Every Fourth of July, and indeed any holiday requiring a flag, the streets are bathed in red, white, and blue. Telephone poles line the streets like looming giants, joining hands by yards of drooping phone and power lines. Beneath them are shorter brethren, the parking meters, reminding all motorists that this is a place of rules. Their teardrop heads with cyclopean glass eyes and red-arrow pupils maintain an unblinking gaze that reminds visitors to pay their dues and not overstay their turn, making room for another worthy visitor. With their shape and ubiquitous presence, you'd be forgiven if you thought they grew like fronds rather than set there by the city elders.

No cobblestones, though. Here, on the West Coast, we started with muddy streets, skipped cobblestones, and went straight to concrete and asphalt.

To my right is the "Wolf Building," named for its architect, restored recently to its historical glory and painted yellow with an original advertisement from the turn of the century prominently painted and lovingly restored on the wall. A castle-like turret juts from one corner, topped by a cupola rimmed by colorful stained-glass windows. A wolf-shaped weathervane perched atop the cupola waits for a breeze strong enough to give meaning to its life. It would have to wait a few more months until the weather turned. Wasn't that true of all of us, though? Always having to wait for our meaning in life—usually, when the weather turned.

To my left is a long line of businesses whose balconies overhang the water. I pass the Wine Bar. People gaily chat inside, taking sips of rubies and topaz from crystal balls. The scene looks inviting and warm, but the music from further down the street is more alluring. As I walk, steel trapdoors in the sidewalk creak under my step. In all my life, I've never seen the delivery hatches in action. Rumor has it the whole underground of Silverton interconnects by tunnels accessed by these trapdoors, not unlike Portland's more famous Shanghai Tunnels. My shoes make a duller sound when I step on the purple, semi-translucent cubes embedded in the sidewalk. These often accompany the iron hatches, forming a grid-work that allows daylight into the cellars. All I know is secondhand from friends who've had to hustle beer kegs and boxes for a living.

Soon I come to the intersection of Oak and Water. The Palace Theater dominates one corner, with ample space underneath the bright marquee. This week, it's a double feature: *Gone with the Wind* and *Alice in Wonderland*. A girl in a pillbox hat sits in the glass-and-gold filigree cage of the box office situated between two double glass doors. Wooden cabinets display the gaudy movie posters, giving the establishment a carnival atmosphere.

It is a place where both Ray Bradbury and Stephen King would feel at home. So many of their stories are set in places very much like Silverton. In fact, not too far away is another town not so different than this one. In Brownsville, cameras rolled to make the film *Stand by Me*, based on a King novella called *The Body*. In the same vein, the facade of Silverton's Ames Building will look familiar to outsiders. The reason is both extraordinary and straightforward: It was the scene of a bank robbery some years ago—a fake one carried out by Bruce Willis while Billy Bob Thornton waited outside as a getaway driver. Yep, that's right, one of the opening scenes in the movie *Bandits*.

It wasn't the worst movie in the world, but it was no *Stand By Me*.

Heat still radiates off the street and the town's yellow, red, and white brick walls like a pizza oven. Oregon's long summer days don't relinquish their hold, not even after dark. Likewise, in winter, the wet cold seeps into the town's marrow till spring. But that would come later. Right now, the summer night sky stretches above like a black velvet mantle twinkling with jewels. The moon is shy tonight, so the Milky Way pours from one side of the horizon to the other. Big Bear and Little Bear waddle along.

Yes. This is home. Where I was born. When I die, I hope to be put to rest here.

The pain stabs my head again, this time at the base of my skull. I reach back there and rub the spot. When I release my hand, I half expect to see blood on it, but I don't.

No, I'm not dead yet. But something is troubling my mind, something that needs a resolution while I'm still haunting Silverton on this side of the grave.

A chorus of motorized thunder comes from further up Water Street, accompanied by blinding lightning. The earth shakes, and the windows vibrate, threatening to shatter. The engines become deafening. The headlights are blinding. I have to squint as the dozen or so Harleys blow through the stop sign. I catch a glimpse of beards, long hair, and brown leather vests. On the back of each vest is an evil cigar-chomping skull wearing a cowboy hat. The skulls stare back at me with malicious intent. "Regulators" arcs over the emblem.

The last rider to pass gives me the finger.

Once they've blown through the intersection where I encountered the dog, it isn't long before they are out of sight and earshot.

The music is still calling me. It draws me back to the here and now, shifting from the jazzy, upbeat tune to the opening moody guitar riffs of Jefferson Airplane's "White Rabbit."

"Time to get this show on the road," I mumble and turn to a door with a handle fashioned from a baseball bat. The opening instrumental of "White Rabbit" yields to the opening lyrics.

One pill makes you larger

and one pill makes you small...

"Five-dollar cover," the doorman says. He's a youngish guy. Scruffy and looking like a musician himself. He has a knit cap on his head shaped like a mouse, with a pair of white cloth mouse incisors centered on his forehead. A wedge of yellow fabric cheddar cheese covers each ear.

"No problem." I scan the place while I reach for my wallet.

It's a single large room with a polished wood bar to the left with an elaborately carved liquor shelf behind it, worthy of a Western. Tall round tables occupy the center, a dance floor to the right with an area that could nominally be called a stage. The area is partitioned off by a barrier reminiscent of a communion rail. Behind it, a woman with shoulder-length brown hair croons into the microphone.

Lighting mostly comes from neon beer signs, table lamps, and a little illumination from a digital jukebox. Even the stage lights are currently only blacklights, casting the band in ghostly purples and whites. Behind the group, the backstage wall is a mural imitating vintage advertisements. Two cherubic women pucker Cupid-bow lips against the letter-work: "Mac's Place—The Finest in Musical Entertainment." There is much more to the mural, something from the region's main tourist attraction, Silver Creek

Falls, but most of it blurs in the dark. Only the two cherubs glow in the blacklight.

The place is packed, though not many are dancing. Waitresses steer through the tables with drink trays held high.

"Who's playing?" I ask as I place the money in the doorman's hand. I squint at the singer. Something about her is familiar.

"Laura Booke and the Time Keepers," he replies, then adds while waving the five-dollar bill, "Thanks."

"Laura? No kidding?" Now I recognize her.

I meander my way to a brass bar railing where people line up to place orders.

The bartender, a pixie of a girl, approaches and says, "What can I— Well hey, Mister Famous Writer Guy, long time no see!"

"Hey, Carrie," I say, smiling, happy to see a friendly face. "And it's just me. Not so famous."

"You're famous to me. I liked your books. Working on any now?" she asks, her Flapper-Girl haircut bouncing with enthusiasm. Her long tattooed arms work the taps, filling glasses.

Am I? "Yes," I say at last.

"Cool! Is it a sequel?"

"No. Yes. No... I'm not sure. It's a mystery to me." *My mind holds the key.*

"A mystery? That's kind of different for you, isn't it?" She frowns. "Well, I'd probably read it!"

"No, it's..." I trail off when she becomes distracted by a more demanding customer. I turn my attention to the stage. Laura is going full Grace Slick with a rousing:

Feed your head!

Feed your head!

The finale comes, and the crowd erupts into applause and cheers. Then, the stage lights come back on, and Laura announces the band is taking a break.

I shake my head at the word.

Break?

Why is that significant?

My head aches again. I squeeze my eyes shut.

"Here you go," Carrie's voice infiltrates my thoughts, and the pain drains away. I turn, and there is a frosty pint of amber beer waiting for me on the edge of the bar between the brass hoops.

"Er, thank you," I say. I reach for my wallet.

"I got this one," she says. "Just give me a cameo in your next book, and we'll call it even."

"You got it," I reply with a wink and take a sip.

I search the room for a place to sit. Unfortunately, the place is busier than any weekday night should be.

"There might be seating out on the deck," Carrie suggests. "It's Homer's Week, so every high school class is in town for reunions. Is that why you're in town?"

I frown because I don't know. "Sure."

That explains why many of the faces in the crowd look familiar. More than usual, anyway.

Carrie moves to help another customer.

I see a blonde head of hair in the crowd turn toward me. The woman detaches herself from her table and comes my way.

Chapter 6
Break

"It's imperative to break from the narrative when you come to a difficult spot," Stephen says. "Not necessarily difficult in writing, but important enough that you need to take a step back before you draft it. To get it right. Because somethings do hinge, and if not properly oiled or screwed in, it just won't swing right."

Stephen turns to his soft drink and stabs at the bobbing ice cubes with his straw.

Homer is busy with a sketchpad in the crook of his arm, making grandiose swipes of the charcoal while occasionally looking up at me. Otherwise, he has no contribution to this conversation.

Clark does. "Sometimes, you have to swerve from the script. Improvise. Ad-lib. Be spontaneous and let natural creativity flow."

"Listen to the Muse?" I say, swirling my beer.

"Or Muses," Clark says.

The amber in my glass swirls like a miniature maelstrom.

Chapter 7
Mac's

The blonde woman pauses before approaching.

I understand why when I sense someone else coming up to me.

"Hey Laura," I say to the singer as she approaches.

"Hey yourself," she replies. "Imagine seeing you here."

"I'm from here, originally," I explain. "What are *you* doing here, besides singing, I mean."

Laura flags Carrie down and places an order for a Jack and Coke.

"That's right, you're a Silverton boy. And us? We're just here to play a gig. Pays well."

"Silverton? I thought your stomping grounds were more in the Portland area." I take a sip of my beer.

Laura gestures with her chin to the end of the bar, where a sandy-haired man with reading glasses looks over some paperwork by lamplight. I don't recognize him, but it's obvious he's comfortable, like he belongs here. With his sleeveless denim jacket adorned with many patches, he looks like a veteran roadie. He's maybe in his late forties, but the lines on his face would suggest he's been around the block more than a few times.

"Boomer Johnson invited us down," Laura explains. "Boomer is pretty big in the Portland music scene. That's how I know him. I guess he and Cisco, Mac's previous owner, go way back. So, when Cisco announced he's going on sabbatical, he tapped Boomer to take over his businesses here in Silverton."

"Get outta here." Shocked, I take another look at the stocky stranger. "Cisco's an institution around here. I can't imagine him not running Mac's and his other places, let alone letting someone else run his empire."

Laura shrugs as she takes a little glass concoction from Carrie as she passes by. "When you need a break, you need a break. Which works out great for Boomer, because though he knows the music side of the business, he wants to learn the bar management and catering side of things."

"He does seem to know good music," I agree. "That was a great cover of White Rabbit. But, now that I think about it, this is the first I've heard you guys play. I've always meant to, hearing you talk about it when I had lunch at Bugatti's."

"Hey, speaking of which, we haven't seen you around a while. What's up with that?" She flicks her tongue around the little red straw in her drink, eventually succeeds in trapping it for a suck.

I take a deep breath, just short of a sigh. "Long story short, I no longer have a day job, so I won't be seeing you too much at your day job anymore."

Her eyes get big. "Wow, I'm so sorry to hear that. Day jobs come in handy. I love this..." she gestures to the stage, "...but I also like my insurance, so I don't mind waiting tables. Any prospects?"

My next deep breath is a sigh. "Nope. Turns out nobody is in a hurry to hire someone who hated the only work experience he has and dreams of becoming a writer."

"Or a singer. Yeah, I hear ya." She makes a face. "So, what happened? You were with that outfit for a long time. Something to do with chemicals and the paper mills there at the Falls?"

I swirl the beer in my glass, stalling. "Yeah, I was a sales and service rep for a chemical company. Called on both West Linn Paper and Oregon City Paper..." My mouth moves, and I wince at the memory. My stomach tightens. I expect that mysterious pain in the back of my head to come, especially over this topic, but it doesn't.

Laura sees my struggle and sets a gentle hand on my forearm. "Don't sweat it. You don't have to tell me. I know how it goes."

I tear my gaze away from my swirling beer and look into her face, grateful. "I promise I'll come to the restaurant sometime and tell you all about it. A visit will do me good. I hated my job, but I loved the location of those mills, straddling Willamette Falls like that." I brighten up, seeing an opportunity to change the subject. "I especially liked West Linn Paper. Did you know that the only way for boats to get up and down the falls is by way of the locks next to the mill? I had to cross over them by a little footbridge every time I made a sales or service call. The gates on the locks are still wood planks. You believe that?"

Laura patiently listens to my slight detour into trivia as she sips her drink, bobbing her head. "I did not know that. Cool. And, oh, hey, if you don't make it to Bugatti's, chances are you may see us here again. We've become regulars."

She points to the wall above the jukebox. I squint in the dim light and see an eight-by-ten glossy of her and her band among the other black and white pictures.

I'm impressed. "Good company, right next to Curtis Selgado and Bob Zany."

She makes a face and turns to look at the photos, noisily draining her drink. "Bob Zany? Ha, I didn't even notice. Who's Bob Zany?"

"Comedian," I say. "Saw him on MTV. Funny guy. Never realized he'd been here."

"Well, like I said, Boomer knows everyone." Laura sets her empty glass on the bar, and the ice rattles. "You heard he got some greats acts to perform up at the Oregon Garden, right? Like Joan Jett, Three Dog Night?" It's my turn to bob my head as I work on my drink and listen. "Well, anyway, I gotta get back to it. Nice seeing you again! Stop into Bugatti's when you get a chance."

"You bet," I say. "I miss the tiramisu too."

Laura laughs. As she leaves for the stage, she says over her shoulder, "More like the pretty waitresses. You weren't fooling anyone."

"Touché," I say.

The blonde woman has been lingering, and now she moves in.

"Hey there, remember me?" she asks, tilting her head back at me. She's very short.

I do remember her. This is something about Silverton that perhaps small communities all over the world have in common. If you grow up in one, chances are you know many people and have known them for a very long time. I know several hundred people, dating back to kindergarten or thereabouts, and still know them.

She is one of them. She looks like a watercolor paint-by-number version of Marilyn Monroe condensed to Mini-Me size. Okay, that's not fair, but I feel huge next to her. She has blue eyes and natural blond hair helped along to platinum by a bit of pharmacy magic. Maybe a little too much makeup, which she doesn't need. A dress with a plunging neckline I can't avoid from my vantage. A pink feather boa wraps around her neck and trails down her arms, where she spins one feathery end in her hand.

"Gwen, of course, I remember you," I say. "It's been years, I think."

"I'll say. Probably not since school," she agrees. "I haven't even heard you were around."

I grimace. "I've had a demanding day job. I was usually just in and out for the holidays."

"Day job?" Her brow furrows at my choice of words but then gives over to astonishment. "Oh, that's right! You've written some books! I remember seeing them in the window of Books'N'Time. How's that going?"

"About as well as my day job." I shrug. She looks at me, expecting me to elaborate. I relent. "Which is to say, not very well."

"Aw, you poor baby, you just need to have some fun and relax," she says, making a pouty face. "Come sit with us. There is room at our table. There are some people from your class with us. You know how Homer's Week is: just one big class reunion. Doesn't matter what class you were in. Everyone gets together."

She takes my non-beer hand and tugs me toward a table full of people having a good time.

Chapter 8
Death of a Salesman

The red emergency light swirls, flashing like crime, like wreckage, like shouts of alarm.

I've always known the light was there, in its red casing sitting on top of the jumble of metal, plastic, and rubber that comprised the starch delivery system. But never once had it come to life. In all my years, I never imagined it would. It's meant for catastrophic failures. For failures involving chemicals like the one being used today. Which is highly corrosive and dangerous to anyone within twenty feet. We need help.

But I'm mesmerized by the flashing light. It's not registering yet what's happening.

I'm exhausted. I can't think straight. I can't see straight. This is my third 6 a.m. in a row performing mill outage service at three different mills from Springfield, to Albany, and to here, Oregon City. Paper mills run twenty-four-seven. Once you manage to get a proper roll spooling at the end of a football-field-long paper machine, you do whatever you can to keep it that way, without a break, as long as you can to maintain profitable efficiencies. If you don't, your competitor down the road, or over in China, will. But you do have to go down, at least one day a month, to perform maintenance. To make changes, to oil and lube, to clean, and so on and so on. That one-day-a-month is very hectic—a narrow window to do a lot. Superintendents and mill managers spend the whole month strategizing how to implement that one day. To do it just right. They put as much effort into their planning as generals going to war or NFL coaches preparing for Sunday. Everything has to be just right. Run smoothly. Nothing can go wrong. Or there will be hell to pay.

The light flashes in my face. Red. The color of hell. The color of the Devil.

I can only hear my heartbeat in my ears. Everything else sounds muffled as if coming from far away under a wet blanket. I'm aware of people running around me. New people are arriving every second with panicked looks on their faces.

One man is at the eyewash, hunched over, sticking his face in the flowing water of the twin arms that rise out of the plastic yellow eyewash bowl. Another man, wearing signature mill attire —canvas Carharts and a flannel—rubs the back of the man with his face down in the eyewash. His mouth is moving, saying something. He glares in my direction.

My arms dangle at my sides. A wrench dangles from my grip. Blood trickles down my pinky and makes small ruby drops on the concrete. The wrench slips out of my hand and joins the blood drops with a clatter. Sweat drips down my temple. Some gets in my eyes, making me blink, but it barely registers.

I'm also vaguely aware that my cargo pants and the lower half of my polo shirt—my signature sales/service rep attire—are soaked with something white and sticky.

The light whirls red. An alarm is sounding, rattling like a metal pipe beaten on the inside of a trash can. The alarm, the voices, the shouts, the rushing eyewash fountain water are all muffled. A thousand miles away.

The starch delivery system.

The system provides an ingredient to paper to give it specific desirable properties.

The system delivers hot, liquefied starch at tremendous volumes and pressure to a machine the size of a football field.

It needs a thorough cleaning on that one day of the month, during that narrow window of time.

One of the mill personnel is supposed to do it. But, in reality, it falls to the supplier of the highly corrosive, dangerous chemical that circulates through the system.

Sometimes, that supplier is exhausted. Can't see straight. Can't think straight. Because he's been that way for months, if not years. Not being a good fit in your job leads to constant harassment from coworkers and customers, leading to depression. Depression leads to poor sleeping. Poor sleeping, coupled with little sleep, leads to...well, hell.

The red light flashes in my eyes.

Sometimes mill personnel rush just as much in that narrow window of time as their managers. Occasionally they offer help. Offer to drain the system quicker but don't know the proper way to open the filter housing to relieve pressure.

In that case, a supplier might say, "Hold on. It's like this..." and push the mill worker back. The supplier would then stick a wrench through an eye-bolt on the filter lid. Turn the eye-bolt. It could then thread up and release the tension that holds it to the filter housing. Or it could explode, almost taking some fingers with it. Almost. Or it can gouge you pretty good, causing you to bleed onto the concrete.

Shit. Through the hypnotizing red light, some truth leaks into my brain. The pressure relief valve at the bottom of the filter. I forgot to open it. I forgot the procedure. Protocol. Familiarity breeds contempt, and so does exhaustion.

There are other considerations, as well.

Sometimes, the customer, in their rush to be more productive, more efficient, wants to use a more aggressive chemical. Even when it's not recommended, sometimes they insist.

The spray could have gone in any direction. It could have squirted in my face instead of my crotch and belly.

It didn't. Most of it went into the face of the mill worker.

He's got safety glasses on, as does everyone who is within one hundred feet of the paper mill, but it still gets him pretty good on the forehead, cheeks, and lips.

Hydrofluoric acid cleans the holy living daylights out of anything stainless steel. The face is a more delicate surface.

My gaze shifts to the wall behind the starch system. The blue 55-gallon drum of hydrofluoric acid sits there with all its hazardous material labeling mocking me, telling me, "I told you so."

World-ending tension builds in me like a compression spring. My mind wants to retreat in on itself. Provide justifications. For instance, the acid was diluted and somewhat neutralized by circulating through a starch system for a couple of hours. What else? My mind wanders further, grasping at bits of information and bringing them to the forefront to distract me.

The wall behind the drum is roughly mortared stone. It's the original foundation of the Oregon City Paper Mill. Probably older than Portland itself. Probably laid when the last of the ox-drawn covered wagons trundled into the territory. Relatively modern concrete and iron girders sit atop it. The trusses are painted green. The paint is probably lead-based. A ridiculously complex network of pipes, tubing, and wiring fills the basement rafters where the starch unit resides, next to legions of vacuum pumps and other arcane equipment. Special wrapping encases some of the piping, making it look like the sort of plaster cast used to set people's broken limbs. Stenciled in red on the casts are the words "Danger: Contains Asbestos."

Yeah, that's how old this place is. It is dim, dripping, full of dangling chains, and a forest of piping with steam wafting from dark corners. I'm pretty sure it served as the inspiration for the interior of the USCSS *Nostromo*, the corporate cargo ship in the movie *Alien*.

Movies. More trivia.

This place has actually been in movies. Benicio Del Toro and Tommy Lee Jones fought a duel to the death just outside this wall on the shore of the Willamette River. Episodes of *Grimm* and *Leverage* filmed here as well, and...

Someone yanks my arm, spins me around.

Dave Davidsen, the plant manager, is angry on the best of days. Today he is livid. His red alcoholic's nose pulsates, the spiderweb of red veins circulating among the acne craters in the skin is ready to burst. His broad face isn't faring much better. A sufferer of shingles, his face is about to melt off. His black eyes are drilling into me.

He's old, he's about as tall as pop-culture history says Napoleon Bonaparte was (which goes a long way to explaining Dave's attitude), but he's stocky as hell and aggressive as a badger. He has two or three pending harassment complaints lodged against him with the union on any given day. But he's an old-school papermaker. Lots of experience. Very knowledgeable in the papermaking craft. Despite his faults, he's just what a struggling mill needs.

All in all, it's no surprise that he's pushing me, then punching me.

He's yelling at the top of his lungs. I can't hear what he's saying over my pounding heartbeat and the wet blanket thrown over my soul.

One last hard shove to my solar plexus, and I've had enough.

Before I realize it, he's on a knee, holding his mouth. Blood trails to the floor in a long saliva-thick stream.

I hold up my fist and stare at it quizzically. There is more blood there now. It's not all from when the lid blew off.

Chapter 9
Mac's

Gwen leads me to the table. She pulls out the one empty chair that had been hers and offers it to me.

"Nah," I say. "You go ahead and take it back. I'll stand behind you."

"Suit yourself," she says and sits down and leans heavily into me.

Most of the faces are familiar, some from as far back as kindergarten.

"Hey, hey, man, how you doing?" Dylan says to me. He's still very blond, no gray yet, but his body has filled out since high school. That's to say he looks like an average person now. He'd been thinner than me back in school, which was pretty damn close to a broomstick. We were both on the wrestling team, and people used to say that when we wrestled, it was a miracle we didn't literally tie each other up in knots.

Sitting next to him is his wife, Bailey. She's filled out too since school. That's to say, she looks more like a soccer mom now and less like a cheerleader.

They've been together so long friends referred to them as "The Firm" because "Dylan & Bailey" sounded like a law office.

Also, at the table, I see the top of a man's head bobbing over his drink as if he were already long drunk and ready to pass out. His hair is pale and dirty, not quite as bright as Dylan's. Finally, after a few more exchanges of pleasantries between me and Dylan and Bailey, as I'm just getting settled in enough to wonder how I look to them, the man's head snaps up.

Our eyes meet.

Chapter 10
A Death in the Family

In my 1980 Plymouth Horizon, I turn into the parking lot of Silverton Union High School. It's a gray day, but at least it's not raining. A chill fog hides most of the neighborhood around the school and the baseball fields beyond the chain-link fences. The stadium is a looming outline in the haze.

The parking lot is mostly full, and I creep along. I turn the radio down as if muffling Def Leppard's "Pour Some Sugar on Me" will help me concentrate on the search for an empty spot.

"We're going to be late," I mumble. I'm more thinking out loud rather than making a conversation. It sounds a lot more accusing than intended.

"Sorry, man. I appreciate you coming out to pick me up, though," Jodi says from the passenger seat.

"It's okay." I whip the steering wheel around to maneuver into a parking spot that appears. "Though if you'd stop crashing your Mustang, neither of us would be constantly late like this. What happened this time?"

Jodi shrugs. "Biffed it in a ditch."

"Why's that?"

Jodi shrugs again. "Driving too fast?"

I smile, shaking my head. It was a wonder Jodi has lived to be sixteen years old.

I wrench up on the e-brake, making that ratcheting e-brake sound, and switch off the engine. Def Leppard disappears altogether. We exit the little multi-tone blue economy vehicle.

"You should get a real car," Jodi suggests, slamming the door behind him. His breath comes out in white puffs.

"You mean like your Mustang held together by duct tape? No thanks." My white puffs evaporate almost as fast as they come out of me. We head for the orange-red brick school. The place looks like a prison on sunny days. In the fog, it looks like a haunted prison. "I'll stick to nerdy four-doors that are cheap to fill with gas. Besides, haven't we had plenty of fun in it?"

Jodi shrugs then laughs. "Remember last weekend when we had like, what? Six of us crammed in there. Wendy Watkins was practically sitting on Cortlund's lap in the back seat. Trying to give him a personal massage, if you know what I mean."

"Nuh-uh!" I retort. "Is that what he was complaining about? I thought he just wanted out to take a leak." We pass through the back courtyard, the teacher's parking area, and enter. Murky-sweat cigar smoke assails us from the janitor's lounge. At least one of the old-timers likes to start his day with a good stogie.

Jodi laughs again. "Nah, man, he was totally freaking. Wanted to trade places with me."

I shake my head at the memory of the girl who was mostly hairspray and eyeliner.

"Well, I guess that's what we get for picking up strange girls in front of the Palace on a Saturday night."

The inner double doors lead into the corridor outside the locker rooms. The cigar smoke gives away to body odor and Cramergesic sports cream. Concrete floors and wood paneling seem to radiate murk. A chain-link wall separates us from the weightlifting area. Only the light from the training room illuminates the space. We can hear the ice bath humming as it circulates water. A susurration of activity in the PE locker room means people are already getting ready for gym class. We're a little late, but Jodi stops me.

"Hey, you gonna cut weight this year for wrestling?" he asks.

I know where he's going with this. Soon cross-country season will be over, and wrestling will start for both of us. There are only so many positions on both the varsity and junior varsity teams. Wrestling is popular at Silverton, and Jodi and I are about the same size. The same weight. We'd rather not compete with each other for the same spots. Throw in the fact that most of our crew is about the same size, too, not to mention that Jodi's brother was in the mix, and it makes for complicated, sometimes frustrating, dynamics in our group friendship.

"I don't think so." I stroke the little yellow fabric image of two wrestlers on the giant orange S of my letterman jacket. "I've lettered. I'm ready to go the challenge route to get a position around my normal weight. Starving myself last year sucked. Kinda freaked my mom out, too, to be honest. I didn't have any weight to lose, yet she still let me cut weight to make the team because she knew how important it was to me. No, not this year."

Jodi looks disappointed or maybe concerned.

I stab his letter—the CC symbol with an arrow through it—with my index finger. "You've lettered, so you're golden. Don't sweat it."

"It's not the same," he says.

I understand what he means. You don't participate in a sport to *not* letter. You letter in everything that you do, as many times as you can. After you get your letter and the little icon for the sport you did it in, you get a gold bar for every year after that.

Jodi looks at the three bars crowding my S, along with the wrestlers, the CC, and the winged foot for track and field.

"You'll probably get a spot without having to cut. You know how it goes; the chances of anyone staying in the same weight class all season is slim. People get sick, injured, move up or down a class. There will be plenty of opportunities. It's a long season." Jodi brightens as I go on. "The same thing come spring in track. Before you know it, you'll have all your letters, and also probably a captain's patch or two, and you'll look like a dictator from a third-world country."

Jodi laughs. "El Generalissimo Jodi!"

I laugh too and slap him on the upper arm of his jacket. The cream-colored leather makes a good smacking sound.

I have to admit, we do look pretty good in our jackets. Which is the whole point, I guess. A tangible reward for efforts—blood, sweat, and tears—representing our school in the athletic arena.

Teenage gladiators. Knights of a modern age in our leather-and-wool plate armor.

And there was blood, sweat, and tears, literally.

We turn to the locker room and quicken our steps. The room is a labyrinth of little orange cages that serve as lockers for gym class. Boys crowd the room in various stages of puberty and undress and are engaging in spirited horseplay. Lots of chatter. Lots of towel snapping.

Jodi and I start to peel our jackets off, but Mr. Berger steps out of his office and gives a blow of his whistle.

"All right, enough of the grab-ass and get out to the gym!" he turns to me, and his tone softens. He even calls me by name rather than "Shakespeare" or "Professor" and invites me into his office.

Jodi and I turn to each other and make a face. Coming a little late doesn't merit a lecture. But I tentatively step into his office and get hit with a wave of cheap cologne.

"Shut the door, please," he says, and I know something's wrong when he says, "please." He never says please. Or thank you.

His bulk slumps into his office chair. His dad-bod bulges underneath his white polo shirt. He toys with his metal whistle with one hand and absentmindedly strokes his comb-over with the other.

"I just wanted to say how sorry I am," he says. "If you need to skip class, I understand. I'll write you a note."

I'm confused.

The morning newspaper is unfolded on his desk. The headline reads *Silverton Man Shot*. I recognize the victim's name in the subtitle.

I can't seem to exhale. Instead, I'm sagging against the door handle because, at the moment, it's all that's holding me up.

Mr. Berger's stern face slackens, and for once, he looks more paternal than mean.

"Oh shit. You didn't know."

Chapter 11
Mac's

"Hello, Jodi," I say.

Jodi has wavy blond hair but could pass for Mr. Spock's cousin. His ears aren't pointy, but his face is long and sharp, and his eyebrows angle down to the bridge of his nose. The angle steepens when he sees me. However, the resemblance to Spock ends at the fact that he's short, stocky, and has freakishly blue eyes.

"Well, well, well." His voice is somewhere between a slur and a sneer. "Guess they'll let anyone into this place."

I bristle and tense up. The table falls silent.

"Apparently," I say, "if you're here."

"Whoa-oh!" Jodi retorts. "Look at this guy! Full of witticisms!"

His big teeth amplify the malice in his smile. He's always had these unusually long and pointy canines too. His glassy gaze drifts from me, and he grasps for his beer with long Nosferatu fingers, misses initially, then manages a good grasp on it and takes a drink.

Another person joins the table.

Chapter 12
Break

The arm in the jukebox flips the 45. The record spins, and the speakers send out an initial moment of muffled static. It competes with the white noise that's been in my head all along.

I have it. I recognize that sound now. Maybe. That sound you hear when you drift to the bottom of a swimming pool. That crackling noise in your ears when there are no other sounds. The crackle in the quiet before your friends start to jump in.

Also, it sounds like...I can't put my finger on it, and just when I think I got it, the static escalates as if to override my other senses, and the stabbing pain grips my head again. I squeeze my eyes shut.

"Clark, be a good fellow and put something on that contraption that is more agreeable," Homer suggests.

"Right," Clark agrees and shoves his chair out to the sound of wood scraping on wood, and makes his way to the jukebox.

"Happens to the best of us," Stephen says, rubbing my shoulder.

"I swear I can see it perfectly clear when I'm not trying," I insist, opening my eyes when the static leaves. A quarter is rolling its way into the guts of the jukebox. Vaguely I realize it's not the static I'm talking about. It's the story. "But when I look directly, there are gaps."

"So don't look directly into the sun," Homer suggests. "Look at the shadow it casts."

Stephen sings. "*...but mama, that's where the fun is....*"

Homer looks at him quizzically.

Music starts to play. Manfred Mann starts up. Homer leans in and listens, and before long, he is nodding along.

"Excellent suggestion," Clark says when he returns to the table. "Taking a break is sometimes necessary, but looking at something from the corner of your eye can be just as revealing."

Chapter 13
Mac's

The newcomer takes the last empty seat at the table between Bailey and Jodi. He notices me for the first time.

"Hey, hey, big guy, how's it going? Long time no see," he stands just enough to reach across the table with a hand the size of a paddle.

We shake vigorously.

"How you doing, Jeremy? I thought you and Mr. Cheerful here were still in Iraq."

Jeremy glances at Jodi, whose head dips so far over his glass his hair is almost in his beer. "Nah, we've been back for a while now," he explains.

I raise my glass. "Well, glad you made it back okay. And thank you for your service."

He returns the toast.

"Hear, hear," Bailey says, raising her drink, followed by Dylan and Gwen. Even Jodi comes to long enough to join. Cheers all around.

"Yeah, these two have been running a side business for me," Dylan explains. "They perform landscaping and property management out of my hardware store in Molalla."

I do a double-take. "*Your* hardware store? Last I knew you were the manager. You say you're a partner in the store now?"

Dylan brightens with a big smile, and Bailey explains before he can say anything.

"He's the sole owner now. He bought the store when the franchise went under. Now he's got all kinds of things going on, like contracting and," she gestures to Jeremy and Jodi, "landscaping outfits. Soon he'll have a chain and franchise all his own."

"Yep," Dylan proudly agrees, "I'm calling it Willamette Valley Land and Craft."

"'W-V-L-C,'" Bailey announces.

"Congrats," I say, earnestly impressed.

"It's only temporary for us," Jeremy says, giving Dylan a wink. "Soon, we'll buy out our share and become independent landscapers."

"More power to you," Dylan says. "By then, Todd will be up to speed and can take over."

At that, Gwen tosses her feather boa further over her shoulder. "Not likely."

"Hey now," Dylan says. "Just because he makes a lousy ex-husband doesn't mean he's a not decent employee."

"Which amazes me," Gwen retorts. It's friendly mostly. "He can't pay his child support on time. Can't pick up his kids on time. Can't drop them off on time. But boy, if I'm late with anything..."

"Well, I'm just saying he's doing all right at work," Dylan replies.

"Which means he should be able to pay." Gwen looks like she's gearing up for a tirade, and judging by looks on the faces of those at the table, it's a familiar one. So I give her a nudge.

"Hey, I didn't even know you were married and had kids."

She tilts her head back, showing her big eyes, big nose, big cheeks, big...

"Divorced," she corrects. "Three kids. I'm not surprised you didn't know. I bet you barely even remember me."

"Of course I remember you!" I can feel my shoulders knotting.

"Yeah, what do you remember about me?"

I pause, mind grasping at information, trivia, random things, trying to put a chronological order to it. She raises her eyebrows at me.

"Well," I start, shifting on my feet. In my memory, I grasp the sound of the school secretary's voice over the PA system while Joe Berhorst and I struggled to make a coconut cream pie in home-ec. Finally, the content of the announcement clicks home. "In

January of your sophomore year, you got third place in your event at the Wilsonville swim meet."

There, how do you like them apples? I look about the table, smiling and standing straighter. Turns out to be a damn good apple. Gwen gives me a strange look, somewhere between impressed and WTH?

"Ah no, no, no," Bailey almost yells, wagging a finger at me. "You can't use that super-weird memory of yours. That doesn't count."

Gwen looks confused. Dylan and Jeremy are laughing as they take drinks of their beers.

"Yeah, that's right," Bailey explains to her. "I remember in Mr. Bruekner's physics class you aced the stand-up quiz. Mr. Bruekner said you were the first ever to do that."

"Huh?" Gwen says.

"Yep, this guy didn't have to take the final exam because he won the physics class stand-up quiz Mr. Bruekner put on every year," Dylan clarifies. "Everyone in the class starts by standing, and Mr. Bruekner goes from person to person, asking a question that might be on the final exam. If you got it wrong, you sat down. If you got it right, you stayed up. He went around and around the room until there were only two people still standing. If the first of the last two people answers the last question wrong, then they sat down. If the second of the last two people got it wrong also, then the first person stands back up. It keeps going until one person is left standing."

"I take it handsome here won?" Gwen interjects.

"Yep," Bailey says, "and then some. Not only did he answer the final question, *he recited the entire paragraph on the page where the answer was found,* and *the page number.*"

"What do they call that?" Dylan asks. "A didactic memory?"

"You mean eidetic," I reply. "Same as a photographic memory, which I definitely don't have. I just have a...weird memory. I can't remember everything I come across. There are just some things I just can't seem to forget. It actually sucks. Turns out people get really pissed when you remind them of the crappy stuff they did or the things they promised to do but never did. And it isn't something I can turn on. If it were, I would have had better grades in high school and college. Unfortunately, you can't get a degree in trivia."

Gwen looks back up at me. I shrug, and she puts her fists on her hips and huffs indignantly. "So that's all I am to you? Trivia?"

"Oh no," I assure her. "There are plenty of personable memories too."

"Like?" she challenges.

I stare at her for a moment, then say, "Like your laugh. I remember your laugh. At Robert Frost Middle School, I was playing on that concrete culvert pipe on the playground near the chin-up bars—"

"Hey, I remember that thing!" Dylan interjects.

I continue without a beat. "You were hanging from the chin-up bar, the lower one. You had a white shirt with red V stripes on it. You had a perm too. You were laughing that silly giggle-laugh of yours. Then you fell off the bar and landed hard in that sawdust that was made of giant chunks of wood which you could hardly call sawdust..."

"I remember that too!"

"You started to cry, and I remember thinking how funny it was, well not funny ha-ha, but funny-peculiar, that your laughing and your crying kind of sounded the same. It was kind of sweet."

Gwen's mouth drops, and her eyes go soft. She looks like she might cry.

"Aw," Bailey says.

"Aw, it's bullshit!" Jodi declares, erupting from his stupor over his drink. "Screw your memory! You're just stating the obvious! You're all fucked-up in the head! Always have been!"

Everyone at the table shifts uncomfortably, frowning.

"Take it easy, man," Jeremy says.

Jodi shakes off the cautioning touch. "You remember, don't you? His moods? His getting sick at practice and competitions because of those medications he was on?" He turns to me, his eyes almost turn black in the dim light. "You still crazy? Still taking drugs? Still seeing things?"

The table grows uneasily quiet except for Jeremy's low-key attempts to defuse him.

I stare right back at him. "To answer your questions: Never was, no, and, yes."

Jodi's response is a confused sneer.

"I was never crazy," I continue. "Long story short, I had food allergies that caused a chemical imbalance that caused insomnia, which caused what's known as sleep paralysis, which results in *seeing things* in a sleep-walking-like state. And yes, for a while back in school, I had antidepressants to deal with it, and the results were crappy."

"I'll say." Jodi sneers again. "You're still crazy, aren't you? I'll bet you heard all that nonsense from some woman psychologist or some bullshit. You don't have food allergies or 'clinical depression,' or sleep sassy-frass or whatever the fuck that was. You're just plain crazy. Messed-up in the head because your wires are crossed because you're a mongrel. A half-breed."

"A what?" Gwen says, increasingly confused by the conversation.

"Half-breed!" Jodi declares, words slurring as he leans in closer to her to make his point. "You didn't know that? He's part injun. A damn prairie nigger!"

"That's enough of that," Bailey cuts in.

Jodi turns to unleash his bile on her, but Dylan starts to stand. That shuts him up.

"I gotta take a leak," he declares and pushes away from the table and lurches into the crowd, almost knocking over one of the waitresses' drink trays.

"Well, that was fun," Jeremy says, eyes flaring. "Good times, good times."

"He's not going to be a problem, is he?" Dylan asks.

"No, he just has a few drinks in him. I'll keep him under control," Jeremy replies.

"I mean for the bigger picture," Dylan clarifies. "You sure you want him as a business partner? I depend on you guys to make *my* business work."

"Look, he has a few issues. Don't we all," Jeremy looks at me. "But I can tell you, back in Iraq, there wasn't anyone more in the world I'd rather have my back than that guy. Everything is going to be fine."

"Does he have a gun on him right now?" Dylan asks. "There are rednecks, and then there is Jodi. He likes his guns."

Jeremy shrugs. "He feels safer with one. But like I said, I trust him with my life. Drunk or sober, he's more qualified with a weapon than most people. He's licensed to have it on him. I can promise you this is a non-issue. Haven't we've done good work so far and brought in clients?"

Dylan raises his drink, satisfied.

My stomach is in knots. A riot of emotions bouncing inside my head. I mentally wrangle the feelings, stuff them in a box. My stomach gradually loosens as the conversation turns to something else.

"Soooo, let's talk about something more positive." Bailey addresses me. "So? What have you been up to? Write any more books?"

I wish I could just go sit at the bar and listen to the music. "Not really. I, uh, am out of a day job. Kind of focusing on finding something that provides health insurance."

"Aw, man, sorry to hear that," Dylan says. "Had I known that a few months earlier, I would have given you the position I gave to Gwen's ex."

"Yeah, but then she wouldn't be getting her child support," I respond. "Can't have that." I also add internally, *And I don't think my pride would allow the charity.*

"Well, you look good," Jeremy adds. "What you doing to keep in shape?"

"Hot yoga, believe it or not," I reply.

Jeremy laughs. "Yuppie motherfucker." I shrug and laugh too, then he continues, "We need to get together, really catch up."

"Oooooh, I don't know about *thaaaaat*."

"What's that all about?" he asks in mock offense, raising his hands.

"Because, seems to me, every time we get together, things... happen," I say.

"'Things?' What do you mean, *things*?"

"Oh, I don't know, sirens, strippers...midgets...you know... *things*."

Laughter erupts around the table.

"Midgets?" Gwen almost shouts.

"Actually, they were dwarves. Turns out they don't like to be misrepresented," Jeremy corrects.

"Dwarf strippers? What the hell did you guys do?" Bailey asks.

Jeremy waves her off. "No, no. Not dwarf strippers, dwarves and strippers, two separate things, and besides these days, I think the proper term is 'Little People' and... You know what? It's a long, sordid story not fit for a lady's ears."

"Now I really want to know," Bailey insists, then looks at me. "We'll have you over for dinner. You'll spill the beans."

"Sure, you bet," I reply.

"You still living in Vancouver?" Jeremy asks.

"Yep," I respond. "Beautiful Vancouver, Washington."

"How long you down for?" Bailey asks.

I frown. My head hurts. Why *am* I here? When did I arrive? "I'm...not sure."

"Staying for Homer Davenport Day's for sure, right?" Dylan says.

"Y-yes," I say. "Maybe longer. "I can look for a job from a computer. It probably would be good to spend some family time. Seems with my old job I was on the road too often."

"Your folks still out on Oak Street?" Jeremy asks.

"Yes."

"Say hi for me. Always loved them."

I smile and touch his glass with mine.

"How did you ever write books if you were on the road all the time with a day job?" Gwen asks.

My head still hurts. They may have been impressed with my weird memory, but it isn't helping right about now. It seems to be doing the opposite. I'm feeling out of sorts. Out of time. Things aren't adding up. Like my chronology of events is somehow out of whack. But how? Why? If I had an average memory, I wouldn't be feeling this odd, disembodied experience with such detail. So literally. Maybe Jodi is right. Perhaps I am crazy.

A stabbing pain explodes at the back of my head.

The next thing I know, Gwen is rubbing my forearm. "Are you okay?"

"Yeah, I'm fine." I laugh it off but am rubbing my head. I haven't spilled my beer, but I'm holding myself steady on the back of her chair. I misdirect by answering her earlier question. "I guess having no life pays off when you have a lot of me-time to work on hobbies. That's how I get books done."

"You never married?" Bailey asks.

"Nope, never met anyone I was willing to be divorced from," I laugh. An uncomfortable, forced laugh, but still a laugh. The table buys it, though—they burst out in genuine guffaws. I think I came up with that one on my own.

"You'll find the right ex someday," Jeremy assures me.

"Yeah," Gwen adds, still rubbing my forearm.

"How about you? You ever find someone?" I ask him.

"Nope, though a little girl managed to steal my heart," he replies, pulling out his smartphone and swiping at the screen. Eventually, he finds a picture and hands the phone to me.

A little blonde girl of about five or six smiles from the photo with missing front teeth.

"You're kidding me?" I smile and hand his phone back.

"Yep, I'm a daddy."

"She can't be yours. Much too cute."

49

"She is. She's my world."

"Where is she tonight?"

Jeremy looks downcast, plays with his beer glass. "Aw, she's with her mother in Salem. I get to see her every other weekend."

"I'm sure you make the best of it. I'm sure you're a great dad, too," I say. "And I can't wait to hear the stories when she's a teen and starts dating guys like you."

Laughter at the table erupts again.

Jeremy bobs his head. "Yep, karma. Coming for me hard, I'm sure."

"What else is new in Silverton?" I ask.

"Same old same old," Dylan says.

"Yeah, boring stuff, like the city council promising to update our hundred-year-old water system," Jeremy states.

"Which I hope they don't do," Dylan adds. "I've contracted with the city to perform maintenance on the irrigation and fire hydrant systems. Things are falling apart faster than I can put them back together. Which is very profitable for me." Dylan smiles at Gwen. "That's what I'm mostly keeping your ex busy with at the moment."

Bailey takes a drink of her daiquiri. "Boring. You know what isn't?" Her eyes widen alongside the little umbrella in her drink. "We have our very own serial killer now."

"Really?" I say. "A serial killer? You must mean Salem, not Silverton."

"It's not true," Dylan says in a teasing fashion, looking at his wife. "A couple of girls have turned up dead, floating in Silver Creek, but the deaths are unrelated."

"Two girls from the same small town, about the same time? Another missing? That's the definition of serial killing," Bailey counters.

Dylan laughs. "Pretty sure it's not. The only thing those girls had in common is that they came from rough backgrounds and had rougher boyfriends. Just sad is all."

"It's all that damn meth going around," Jeremy says, shaking his head. "It's a plague. And it's gotten worse since those Regulators have shown up in town. I don't think it's a coincidence."

"Yeah, I saw them," I say, remembering the rumbling biker gang and parting middle finger. "Though I don't recognize them. I thought the Gypsy Jokers were the local biker gang."

"They were," Dylan explains. "For whatever reason they've moved on. Regulators are here now, really trying to make a name for themselves. They're really into dirty businesses like meth. Which is unfortunate, because kids these days are really into it."

"Sad," I say.

"Sad," the table agrees.

"What's really sad is nobody is doing anything about those poor girls," Bailey says, making listless stabs at the slushy ice in her drink. "The fact that someone as close as Vancouver hasn't heard anything about their deaths is what's sad."

"And they never will, because one was a Mexican immigrant and the other was a former prostitute," Jeremy agrees. "People don't seem to care unless the victim is rich, blonde, and comes from a good family."

Dylan's face goes hard; any jovial sentiments that had been there a moment ago disappeared. "That is messed up. Maybe that needs to change. Maybe society needs a good lesson."

"This town needs an enema!'" Jeremy declares, making his best Jack Nicholson Joker impression. It's not very good, but we get the reference and give him the laugh. Dylan is smiling again. He's smiling so much I'm reminded how big and perfect his teeth are and how bright blue his eyes are. He was always a happy-go-lucky guy, and I envied him for it.

Jodi returns to the table, bumping it hard enough that the drinks almost slosh out of their glasses.

He snatches up his beer, drinks the remainder of it in one long pull, and slams the glass on the table. This time the drinks about the table do slosh out, and quite a bit splashes onto Gwen, causing her boa feathers to wilt.

"Hey, you lummox, watch it!" Gwen half rises from her seat, shaking her wet hands.

Jodi, swaying on his feet, regards her with a contemptuous stare and leans into her face. A bead of moisture on his lip flicks off when he says, "Not my fault you can't control your drinks any better than you can control your men."

My gasp joins the chorus at the table as Gwen's eyes widen and her jaw drops. Her entire head trembles as she struggles to retort, and color rises in her face. When she can't find her voice, she whips Jodi's face with the wet boa which clings to his cheek with a stinging "slap" noise.

Jodi's eyes flare, and his face turns red all over, not just at the developing welt on his cheek. Chairs screech on the floor when people rise from their seats when he raises his hand to strike her, but I'm the one closest to act.

"I don't think so," I growl as I snatch his threatening arm at the wrist.

He turns on me, yanking his arm free. His eyes do that thing when they almost turn black, and his lips contort in hatred.

Before I know it, he socks me pretty good in the stomach.

The white-hot pain is shocking. Stomach pain is a special genre. It is a deep-rooted, lingering pain that you have plenty of time to contemplate while you wait to get your breath back. It's made all the worse by the fact that you don't expect it, not as an adult. As a kid on the playground, you might expect it from the schoolyard bully or downtown from regular bullies. Life sucks when you're a kid and learn life lessons from those encounters, but adulthood has rules. Certain things just don't happen. Getting sucker punched is one of them. So, feeling a deep, gurgling, internal-organ-rearranging punch to the gut that doubles as a shocking slap to the face is an outrage.

And not a little embarrassing. Doubling over in pain and falling to the floor in a public place is its own kind of pain. My humiliation radiates from my face like a fire siren.

I ball up on the floor next to my glass and the remains of my drink.

"Hey, knock that off!" Boomer shouts from his perch at the end of the bar. He's staring over the rim of his reading glasses in a fierce paternal fashion. He then turns to the side and jerks his head in our direction.

A giant of a man wearing a "Staff" T-shirt turns in our direction and lumbers toward Jodi. His bushy beard is big enough to have its own zip code.

As the behemoth approaches, he holds out his hands and says, "Dude? Really?"

"I was leaving anyway," Jodi growls, puffing out his chest. Then, with his arms partially cocked to each side, he swaggers crookedly to the exit. His cowboy boots are loud on the wood floor, even over the murmuring crowd.

Conversations in the room return to their former hum. The drama is over.

Gwen and Jeremy help me off the floor. I do my best to brush it off and look unflappable, but truth be told, the shock of adrenaline is still coursing through my body like liquid lightning. I hope my hands aren't shaking too much.

Gwen is thanking me, clinging to my arm. Her grateful eyes say much more. Her boa is tattered and missing about three inches at one end. The redness of her own face is slowly receding just as quickly as the drama lingering in the air.

"Sorry about that, man," Jeremy says.

"What a dick. What is his problem anyway?" Bailey asks.

Dylan gives Jeremy a hard stare. "Do I need to ask again?"

"I promise he isn't going to be a problem. I got it under control," Jeremy reiterates. "I'll talk to him. I guarantee his on-duty work ethic will be perfect. I can't guarantee his off-duty behavior, though."

Before Dylan can comment, the gigantic bouncer stops at our table, no longer pursuing Jodi.

"My man," the bouncer says to me in a sing-song fashion.

Before I can look up, Jeremy identifies him. "Bubba! How you doing? Didn't know you worked here too."

I should have recognized him when Boomer sent him over, but I was too busy gasping like a fish out of water. "Hey dude," I say, taking the giant hand extended in my direction. It swallows mine, almost crushing it. I try not to wince. "Good to see you."

Matt "Bubba" Mathews has grown into his name. Six-eight and north of three hundred fifty pounds, he is hard to miss unless you are curled up on the floor in a fetal position. He could have been a pro footballer, but he still walks with a limp from one of the bad-luck events in his life.

"You too," he says. When smiling, he has a babyface. "Hey, I'm still waiting for the movie of your book."

"Yeah? You and me both." I straighten up and take a rattling test breath. I should consider myself lucky that Jodi socked me in the diaphragm and not in the ribs. It's just my pride that is bruised.

"I would read the book," he confesses, "but it just doesn't have enough pictures."

I laugh, knowing that's not entirely true. Matt is plenty smart. It's just that my book isn't his cup of tea. Apparently, it's not a lot of people's cup of tea.

"How long you in town?" he asks.

"A while," I say, no longer fighting the sense of disembodiment. It's starting to look like I'm meant to be here. Might as well take the ride.

"Cool," Bubba replies. "I'm throwing a kegger, and you're invited. I think you'll know almost everyone there. Like these guys." He jerks his thumb at Jeremy and Dylan.

"Does that mean Jodi will be there too?" I ask crestfallen.

Bubba pauses, then makes a sweeping gesture with a finger. "Er...yesssss, now that I think about it. But don't worry, that guy does NOT dictate who's welcome at my place. Say you'll come."

I can't refuse. Besides, I know there will be plenty of people there I'd like to see. Matt always did throw great parties at Chez Bubba. But, as I start to agree, some escalating voices and a pushing match at the pool table nearest the stage grabs Bubba's attention.

"Great," he says to me with that big furry smile. "Looking forward to it. I've got to get back to work. Take it easy, man!"

With that, he moves toward the pool table, the crowd parting before him like the ocean before a container ship.

"Dudes? Really?"

Once our group recenters itself, Gwen asks, "I thought you and Jodi were good buddies a long time ago."

"Yep," is all I can manage, rubbing my stomach.

Gwen sucks the last from her rum and coke. By now, all the red is gone from her face. "What happened? Why does he have such a chip on his shoulder?"

"I honestly couldn't tell you. Best I can tell, our friendship died of a thousand little cuts over time." I puff out another test breath and decide I'm going to live. "As for the chip on his shoulder? He's had that long before I met him. Probably started when his daddy named him after a girl so he'd grow up tough, always fighting anyone who made fun of it."

"So, you're really going to be around for a while?" Dylan asks. Carrie arrives with a tray full of little shot glasses filled with green liquid. "Going to make this your base of operations while you look for work? And hey, what's this?"

Carrie distributes the shot glasses. Jeremy pays her. Sneaky bastard, I didn't even see him place the order.

"I believe so," I reply. "I can be oppressed by unemployment just as easily here as in Vancouver."

"All right, dammit, enough about fighting, exes, and serial killers!" Jeremy declares, holding up one of the shot glasses. "Lighten the mood already!"

"Cheers to that!" Bailey agrees, snatching up a shot.

We grab the rest.

"Here is to the return of a friend, and may it be a good summer!" Jeremy announces.

We clink glass, and down go the green pills.

Let's go down this rabbit hole, I muse.

On the music stage, Laura and her crew square off to their mics. First, the bassist starts into a familiar, upbeat rhythm that promises a rousing good time. Next, Laura breaks into a tremendous rendition of The Doors' "Roadhouse Blues."

Chapter 14
The Stage

"And now the stage is set. All the pieces are in place," Homer states. He takes a long sip of his tea.

"And the players are in position, the cameras are ready to roll," Clark adds.

Stephen pours himself another glass of diet soda from the pitcher on the table. Clark pours me another beer. It's going to be a long night.

"Let the games begin," Stephen says.

"It's time for some more music," Homer announces. "Clark, be a good fellow and put something on."

Chapter 15
Oak Street

I'm standing in front of a swirling pole. A meter-tall glass cylinder the color of a candy cane lights up the sidewalk. The barber's pole in front of Gary's Barber Shop, kitty-corner from both the Palace and Mac's Place, is currently the only thing alive. Even the Palace Theater is closed for the night. Its multitude of carousel lights has gone dark.

The pole's spiraling colors hypnotize me in their endless turns to the gentle hum of electricity.

"You know why they're those colors, don't you?" a raspy voice asks.

I turn to the bench near the barbershop. Some potted plants next to the seat obscure a pile of rags that moves.

"Hey, Willy, didn't see you there," I say to Silverton's only official homeless person. At least I think he's homeless. He's been a fixture in the community for as long as I can remember. A likable fellow, though a little scruffy in appearance, who often offered a tidbit of local history or trivia in exchange for some change. But, strictly speaking, he never begged. Seemed to me he didn't need the money, just wanted an excuse to approach tourists to take them on an informal tour. Likewise, I've never seen him sleep outdoors, though the glow from his campfires often flickered from underneath bridges. He was a mystery.

"When you're in my situation, you do tend to be invisible to people," he says. "But you caught me on a good day. I'm allowing you to see me." Willy pulls back some as if seeing *me* for the first time, looking me up and down. "Or maybe you're here with me now. The running boy."

A moment of disorientation washes over me that has nothing to do with alcohol.

"Pardon?"

"You're that runner fellow," Willy explains. "If I had a dollar for every time I saw you running, I'd be rich."

"Ah," I say, understanding dawning on me. "That was high school. Between cross country and track and field, I was always running around town. Running for wrestling too, when I was struggling to make weight."

Willy nods sagely. "All that running, surely you must have gone to the Olympics. How'd that go?"

I laugh. "I ran a few years in college until the cartilage in my knees gave out, then life had other plans for me."

"And what were those?" Genuine curiosity sparkles in his dark eyes.

My laughter dies. "I'm still trying to figure that out."

Willy grunts, and though his gaze wanders elsewhere, my senses tell me he is still very present. An awkward moment of silence hangs between us, then the ache at the back of my head flares, and my hand in my pocket clenches the rosary tight.

Willy sees me. Willy knows me. Maybe he has answers. The idea is just crazy enough to be true.

"Do you know why I'm here, Willy?" I ask.

Willy stands. There is the sound of a glass bottle tipping on the concrete and rolling away. He starts shambling off, trying not to make eye contact, but then pauses.

"Quantum entanglement," he says over his shoulder. "You're neither here nor there. Entanglement also implies tangled—like in a net or web. Weaving patterns. The thing about webs is either you're weaving one or caught up in one. Or is it String Theory? Is it still a theory, though, when you pluck the string on a cello, and it makes music? Perhaps dark matter holds you in bondage at the bottom of a black hole, preventing your information from escaping the event horizon."

He turns his head completely to me. If he's amused by my confoundedness, I cannot tell. He gestures to the barber pole.

"The red stands for fresh blood," Willy says, turning back around and shuffling in the opposite direction. "The blue, also for blood, but from the vein. Once upon a time, barbers were the surgeons. And the white is for shaving cream."

"Willy," I call after him, still hoping for a plain answer, "why am I here?"

Willy is silent for so long that I almost don't think he will respond, or if he does, he'll be too far away for me to hear. But he does. And I do.

"You're lost," he responds. "Just like I was once. Now look at me."

He disappears into the night.

I stare after the spot where he vanished, then the barber's pole flickers and crackles with electricity, settling back into its hypnotic pattern.

"Okay then," I say and move on myself. I'm on Oak Street. One end of it. The other end is home. I put one foot in front of the other.

The crickets rule the night. Flying insects float about the lamplights like a carousel of fairies. The even sidewalks of downtown start to give way to the uneven, root-buckled slabs of the outer neighborhoods. Green-spiked orbs litter the path. When you step on them, they burst and spit out a wet, unripe chestnut. In a few more months, the spiked balls will turn brown and hard and stick to the soles of your shoes if you're not careful. I know from experience that "chestnuts roasting over an open fire" isn't just a holiday myth—they're delicious.

The corridor of chestnut and walnut trees opens up, and the path turns uphill. A metal rail runs along the left-hand side. Businesses have long ago given way to homes, the newest ones probably built in the sixties. Those that upslope to the right are more like from the fifties, surrounded by well-kept yards.

Once upon a time, Eric Doolittle and I knew the best secret path through those shrubs and flowerbeds paralleling the street. It was never good enough for boys walking home from school to take a straight path home. Our route was longer, more adventurous, and entirely ours.

A car swishes by. Coming, going. There are only a few on the road tonight.

Oak Street winds up the hill to a corner where Hill Street disappears into darkness. Doctor Davies's house sits back, surrounded by an iron fence painted yellow and backed by a dense hedge. Of course, it's not Doctor Davies' house anymore, but neither is the Eden house or the Parkinson house. Others live in them now, but you had to call them something because the edifices were so distinctive. Every generation had its own names, I guess, but the earlier terms have dissolved into history.

Oak Street straightens out, and a lone traffic light at the top of the hill blinks eternally yellow, suspended from a sprawling pair of spider legs over the intersection like one of the tripod machines from H.G. Wells's *War of the Worlds*. To the right of it, on the corner, is the Circle K mini-mart.

I pass by and continue. The space between homes widens, accommodating bigger yards, more trees, a small field here, a forested copse there. The scene gradually becomes more rural, but there are still street lights. Eventually, I step off the road onto the lawn behind one of the last lights on Oak and approach the shadowed house. A pair of apple trees keep watch over the single-story home. In the dark, you can't tell the color, but I know it's green. A darkish green, green like the skin on the stalk of wild grass on the edge of a pond.

I know this because it's home—my home.

This late at night, the doors might be locked, but I know how to get in.

But I'm still drunk from my encounter with Dylan, Jeremy, and the others. I sit on the side of the house where the lawn slopes toward the neighbor's yard. There is a drainage ditch across the way that separates their property from the next one over. I guess you can't call it a drainage ditch because it has water flowing in it year-round. You can't call it a creek or a brook either because it's tiny. Now that I think about it, I never knew what the hell that thing was. I just knew that it flowed across the field behind the house and emptied into Webb's Lake. Which wasn't a "lake" either, just a large pond.

I digress. I'm only now realizing that my mind wanders off to little corners of data and information when it is trying to protect itself. But what's got me stressed? Yes, the unemployment thing. That must be it. Maybe that's why I'm home. I'm running away from my troubles. Running home to Mommy, hoping to hit the reboot button.

My mile walk from downtown has done little to sober me up. Instead, I feel enlightened, aware of the little nuances that would have escaped me before. Eyes adjusting to the darkness, I listen to the breeze rustling the limbs and leaves of the tree next to the house. It's a peaceful sound. But, the longer I listen, I hear a whole different universe. Frogs, for instance, croak in the field behind the house and—wait—is that the yip-yip, followed by the eerie howl of a coyote?

I strain to listen, but it's gone.

Alcohol brings down the walls of my inhibitions, and beyond those walls lies open fields of freedom, strange wisdom, horrible truths, and future entertainment—and, because I'm safe at home, sitting unobtrusively, I make no poor choices. I've never done any other kind of drug, but I imagine the appeal. Perhaps that is why it is so easy to get lost in that strange country and never want to come out. I hope I never find out. The land of Bacchus is enough for me.

I glance one more time at the streetlight and the insects floating about it, then lay back on the lawn, stretch my arms out behind me and stare up at the night sky.

Frogs and stars. Yes, they do nicely.

The stars' icy twinkle plays like a crystal orchestra. The Milky Way splashes across the sky to the sound of a cosmic waterfall, gushing through Heaven's gates. A falling star streaks across the sky, making the sound of a bowstring sharply pulled across God's cello. The tune is bittersweet and lonely, but it is beautiful. And tonight for me, the night's only audience, the song is only for me. There will never be another like it.

I close my eyes. Howls follow me into sleep.

Chapter 16
The Palace

I'm sitting in the Palace Theater.

The expansive room is dim, with just enough illumination coming from the Art Deco sconces. Looking down the slope of seating, I see that Homer and I are the only ones in the building. We're seated about dead center. My feet shift on the floor, making sticky noises. The upholstered seats are comfortable. There is a drink holder in each position, but we've left our beer and tea back at Mac's. The smell of buttered popcorn lingers in the air.

An usher appears, emerging from one of the side entries like a groundhog. His head swivels around to survey the theater. He uses the flashlight with its red-cone lens cover to push his pill-box hat back a bit. When he swings the flashlight up, the light beam travels over the brass buttons of his red uniform, and they briefly glitter in the dark.

He disappears behind the wall that separates the theater from the ramp leading to the lobby. Not long afterward, the red velvety curtains part with a raspy whisper, revealing deep darkness, a portal to countless worlds.

A cone of light shoots out from the projector booth and illuminates the screen, dancing with dust motes. I look over to Homer, and in the flickering silver light, he looks like a Sears catalog picture from 1901, advertising hair tonic.

The projector rattles as images start to play out in black and white.

Rotating on the screen is a cheesy model airplane attached by a wire to a cheesy model Earth. The film is marred by streaks and random artifacts. When it starts with fanfare music, the sound doesn't fare much better with its static and gaps. In huge, block font appears the text "RKO World News." More words appear with the names of producers and crews who contributed to the piece.

The music dies down, and the images shift.

"This is more like it," Homer says at my side, straightening out his vest. "None of those alien and abstruse entertainments Clark has been playing on the music machine."

"I think those have been for my benefit," I say. "They aren't exactly from his era, either."

Homer tugs on his vest. "Quite so. That is very good of him. Though I thought you might benefit as well from this. You seem quite fond of a good flicker show. Talkies, no less."

"Quite so," I agree, smiling.

Text in sprawling signature font spreads across the screen: "Ripley's Believe It or Not!"

A tinny announcer's voice speaking in a clipped Mid-Atlantic accent narrates the moving images of smiling people standing around a dog. The footage is jerky as the people stroke the animal affectionately and turn to the camera to smile. The dog sits there on its haunches with its tongue hanging out.

"In August 1923, while on a family road trip in Indiana, Frank and Elizabeth Brazier, with their daughters Leona and Nova, were visiting relatives in Wolcott, Indiana. Unfortunately, their two-year-old Scotch Collie/English Shepherd mix dog, Bobbie, was attacked by three local strays and ran away. After an exhaustive search, the heartbroken Brazier family could not find Bobbie and reluctantly continued their trip home to Oregon, expecting never to see their dog again.

"However, much to everyone's surprise and delight, in February 1924, six months later, Bobbie returned to Silverton mangy, dirty, and scrawny, with his toenails worn down to nothing. He showed all the signs of having walked the entire distance, including swimming rivers and crossing the Continental Divide during the coldest part of winter. During his ordeal, he must have crossed close to 3,000 miles of plains, deserts, and mountains in the winter to return home, an average of approximately fourteen miles per day. Since his return, the little fella has become quite the celebrity, winning him the title of Bobbie the Wonder Dog!"

The footage shifts to a group of men in suits and top hats. They have an abundance of Homer-esque mustaches and enough hair tonic to fill a swimming pool. Bobbie is sitting on an Ionic pedestal, looking unphased, as a man wearing a sash slips a ribbon over Bobbie's neck with an oversized skeleton key dangling from it.

"Yessiree, Bobbie the Wonder Dog has been given the keys to several cities for his demonstration of devotion and stick-to-it-tiveness and has been honored with a jewel-studded harness and collar by the Portland Humane Society. Why rumor even has it that Hollywood has come calling!"

The music escalates to an epic scale before the newsreel shifts to another story.

"You see," Homer states. "You can always find your way home, no matter the odds."

I'm not sure what to believe, but I feel it's important to show some appreciation for Homer's generosity, and I throw a smile in his direction.

My smile falters when I see the screen. Up there, the images have changed to modern things. Though still in black and white, and that jerky old-timey film with streaks and blemishes, there are police officers in contemporary gear and uniforms carefully combing their way through the brush of a wilderness area, poking here and there with sticks.

The announcer's voice returns, still in that affected Mid-Atlantic enunciation.

"Authorities have had no luck finding any clues to the death of the latest woman in the Silverton area. However, investigations into her being a victim of domestic violence have received criticism. Locals believe that her strangulation is linked to another in recent months, and not to foul play at the hands of an estranged boyfriend, as the police suggest."

Homer's eyes squeeze shut, blocking out the scene on the screen. When he opens them again, it's to consult his pocket watch.

And just as quickly, he snaps it shut and stuffs it in his vest pocket.

"We should be getting back," he says.

Chapter 17
Home is Where the Heart Is

The sound of methodical crunching arouses me from my slumber.

Upon opening my eyes, my first impression—a question—is why is that deer sideways? Then, it slowly dawns on me that I'm sleeping on the lawn and a pair of deer munch on fallen apples.

Their long jaws work slowly but loudly, sliding sidewise as they masticate the fruit. A lot like their distant cow cousins, as a matter of fact. There is something pleasant, even magical, about sharing a space with wildlife. No matter how many times deer visit my parents' yard, they are always welcome. It is peaceful and sweet to see them going about their day, cohabiting on the edge of civilization, making the most out of a home's apple trees. And the plum tree. And rose bushes. And tulips.

Good thing we never grew a garden.

Their heads jerk up, and they bolt into the neighbor's yard, leaping the drainage ditch and disappearing out of sight. I am not sure what disturbed them; it couldn't have been me, as my pounding headache prevents me from moving. I wish I could, though, because under the soft grass is bumpy earth.

I turn my head, and the sky above me is a perfect blue. The sort of sky I've learned to appreciate because I know sooner rather than later it will be fall, then winter and the long melancholy days will be upon me.

A face comes into my field of view, smiling.

"Hello there, stranger," she says. "You know there's a bed inside, right?"

"Hey, Mom," I croak. My throat is dry and sore. Did I puke? I don't remember. "I know, but it was just so beautiful last night, I couldn't resist sleeping outdoors. The universe was singing to me."

My mom doesn't like getting her picture taken, so she probably wouldn't like me describing her for the whole world, either. So I won't. Suffice to say that she's my mom, she's beautiful, and that's all I've got to say about that.

"I'm sure the pink elephants were trumpeting too." She holds out her hands to help me up. I struggle to a sitting position, can't manage much more than that, so I decide to pull her down to my side.

She adjusts her bathrobe to get comfortable.

"You're lucky the neighbors called us and not the police about the dead body on our lawn," she says.

I grunt.

Now that I'm fully awake, I see that it's not just morning but closer to noon. There is plenty of traffic on Oak Street. This far out of town, it's closer to becoming Cascade Highway. I hear a lawnmower growling in the backyard. I have no idea how I slept through all this.

"Don't see your car, so you must have done the right thing and walked from town. When did you get in?"

I have to think hard. My head hurts, and not just from the hangover. I try hard to piece this puzzle together. This time, no random trivia comes to mind to insulate me from the pain.

"I'm not sure," I say truthfully. "But I think I'm here for a while."

"Longer than the weekend?" she asks. "Are they sending you to Springfield or Albany this time?"

I swallow hard and know she sees my sheepish look. More like a pained, embarrassed look. Shame, really.

"I lost my job."

"Oh, sweetie." She surrounds me in a hug. "What happened?"

"The 'official' narrative," I explain, "is that I failed to follow proper safety protocols while flushing a piece of equipment. Someone also got hurt. Almost seriously hurt. But that all was just a pretext for finally giving me the boot. They've hated me for years. I was, normally, doing a great job as a service representative, but not so much as a sales rep. I couldn't get customers and coworkers to like me."

My mother shrugs. "You never did like taking shit off people. And honey, you know you can't help it if people just don't know how to deal with your 'brusque.'"

I make a funny face while tilting my head. I can feel her looking at me, feel her knowing there is more to the story.

"Don't make me ask for it," she says.

I keep bobbing my head. "I, uh, kind of punched a customer."

She raises her eyebrows. "How brusque of you. You have legal troubles now too?"

I snort. "No. The guy was practically assaulting me already. He has a long history of it, so his people chose to overlook it, so long as my company promised to can me."

"But you can get another job with another chemical company, right?" she asks.

It's my turn to raise my eyebrows.

"Right," she says. "You've hated the whole sales rep thing for a long time now. You're a trouper to have lasted so long."

I place a hand over my heart. "I'm eternally grateful to Uncle Jim for helping me get my foot in the door, but I was never cut out for it. It paid well, and it made it possible for me to travel the world, but I ended up not wanting to get out of bed in the mornings. No amount of money will change the fact that my soul is shriveled up, and I'm glad to be done with it."

Her face is all sympathy as she tousles my hair. "You'll find something better."

I shrug. "I have no idea what I want to do. The only experience I have that looks good on a resume is a whole lot of what I just got the hell out of."

"Writing? You can do that full time now," she says.

"I've got a couple of books out there already," I explain. "They haven't made me rich or famous, let alone pay for health insurance. I don't know anyone whose writing pays the bills. So I'm going to need something to hold me over."

By now, her fussing has completely tangled my hair. "You'll figure it out. Until then, you're always welcome here."

Tension drains out of my body, feeling like I just latched onto a life preserver.

"Well, I've got more bad news," she says. "Rooney is back in town."

Shit. I absorb all the unpleasantness that is Rooney, then finally look at her and see a diluted version of the feeling mirrored there. "How is that even possible? I thought he was banned from Silverton for life or something like that."

"No, not for life," Mom explains. "Just twenty years. His lawyers argued it was unconstitutional to inhibit his freedom of movement or something. We've got the newspaper article if you want to read it."

I wave the idea away and snarl. "Lawyers! Unbelievable. How is it possible to shoot an unarmed person in the back of the head, with witnesses, and only go to jail for *one* year?"

"You were young when it happened. It was complicated."

"I was in high school, not so young that I couldn't understand."

"You have to understand your cousin Johnny ran with a tough crowd," she goes on. "He was kind of an intimidating guy. I guess he used to beat Rooney up. Real bad, like nearly killed him a couple of times. So when they had their last confrontation, and Johnny turned to go into the house, Rooney assumed Johnny would get a baseball bat. Rooney claimed he had no choice but to shoot him. I know it's bullshit, but it didn't help that the prosecuting attorney did not have his ducks in a row. Rooney should have gotten more than a year in prison but didn't."

"I bet if Walt had been district attorney at the time, things would have been different," I say, referring to a friend of the family from when mom was a legal secretary for the county.

"It was before his time," Mom explains.

"At least the judge banned him from Silverton. I just didn't expect twenty years to go by so fast," I say, placing my forearms on my knees and hanging my head between them. "How does Dad feel about all this?"

Mom rubs my back. "He's understandably upset. But he's confident Rooney will screw up again soon and either end up back in prison or in the graveyard. Let karma take its course. It's inevitable, especially since he is running with the Regulators now."

My head shoots up. My stomach ties into knots and panic sweeps over me when I remember how belligerent they seemed. But the rider who gave me the finger had been fat and old. As far as I knew, Rooney was a scrawny meth-head-looking piece of shit not much older than me. Also, Rooney probably couldn't pick me out from a lineup either. Still, I didn't like the thought that Rooney had ridden right by me last night.

"We just wanted to give you heads-up," Mom continues, "so you're not caught off guard should you come across him."

I shrug. "We don't exactly travel in the same circles."

"And what about your circles?" Mom asks, brightening. "You going to go visiting while you're in town?"

The idea is immediately cheerful. "Yeah, I got all kinds of invites last night. Your favorite son's going to be a social butterfly. Oh, by the way, I saw Jeremy last night."

Mom beams. "What's that scoundrel up to?"

"Mostly being a scoundrel," I say, "and working for Dylan over in Molalla at the old hardware store. I guess Dylan is the sole owner, and he's contracting landscaping services."

"Well, good for them," Mom says.

"We're supposed to get together soon," I say.

Mom scoffs. "Don't believe it. Talk about a butterfly."

"Yeah, well, he *is* a scoundrel."

"And if you do go out with him, stay away from those midgets."

"They were dwarves."

72

"You know what I mean," she says with conviction. "Come, get up. There's coffee inside."

She stands and helps me up, and we enter the house.

When people visit for the first time, they're usually first struck by the fact the doorknob is set dead center of the door, then they note the authentic long bar with four comfortable barstools, followed by the concrete disk of a fireplace set in the center of the room, speckled with thumb-sized agates of every color and shape. Above it, hanging from the ceiling extends a black metal cone that serves as the chimney.

Those were the essential elements of the room, which hadn't changed for over forty years, making for a comfortable abode of a retired couple, hosting many a family holiday event. And an occasional wayward, lost soul of a son. I stand in the sunlit room while Mom pours the coffee in the kitchen. The smell is tantalizing. The lawnmower is still making its rounds in the backyard. Tension drains out of my body.

A few other items haven't changed in generations.

On the room's window side is a museum's worth of Native American art hanging on the wall—most in vacuum-sealed shadowboxes. Tattered woven mats, a grouping of obsidian arrowheads, paintings with motifs from our Klamath tribe. Between the windows hangs a truly ancient three-by-three-foot parchment made from tree bark, rubbed to subtle softness and stained with berry juice to depict repeating images of fish, cattails, and leafy wocus rice fronds. Grandpa had found the treasure in a cave back on the reservation. It rests on a moisture-resistant mat, all set behind glass in a distressed wooden frame that could itself be a remarkable museum piece.

I move to a deep shadowbox holding a glass bottle ingeniously wrapped in woven grass and painted in a pattern of blue-black stars. Next to it, a grainy black-and-white photo from a news clipping shows my great-great-grandmother in traditional dress. Her smile lights up her weather-worn face. I smile too when I read her name in the caption along with, "—noted Klamath basket maker from around the turn of the 19th century."

I tense up as a stab of discomfort courses through me abruptly. It's not the mysterious pain I've lately been feeling at the back of my head. There is no mystery about this pain, which comes as the voice of Jodi sneering, "Prairie nigger."

I squash the inner voice and rub the bridge of my nose as I squeeze my eyes shut.

"Your father is almost done with the lawn," Mom says, mercifully disrupting my reverie when she returns with the cup. She holds the cup out to me. "I'm sure he'll be happy to see you."

I take the hint. "The yard looks good. Benefitting from retirement." I make a face when I sip the coffee.

"Sorry, we don't have any of that foo-foo stuff you like. There is some sugar in the kitchen—"

"It will do me good to drink some straight black coffee. I drank enough carbohydrates last night to last me a lifetime."

The lawnmower sputters to a stop.

"You better go see your sister too while you're in town," Mom adds.

"Yes, Mom," I say and open the sliding glass door to the deck and backyard.

The deck is treated cedar planks occupied mostly by metal-work deck furniture from Home Depot, and a bulky item I know is a barbecue under a frayed white tarp. An old hot tub sits at the far end, but it's been long-dead and mostly now a breeding ground for mosquitoes, despite its sun-bleached lid.

The grass is green and freshly cut. A multitude of colorful flowers decorates the bark-dust region between the deck and lawn. And across the yard is a single room guest house slash shed, painted the same light green as the main house. And like the main house, a trellis spans one end of the building to the other, supporting wisteria vines in full bloom, dangling bluebells that only whisper in the wind, never chime. A cherry tree sways nearby. A fence is behind it, separating the property from the development beyond what once used to be a horse pasture.

My father is stiffly dismounting an unfamiliar riding lawnmower.

"Oh, so now you get a riding lawn mower," I say as I approach my dad. "Couldn't be bothered to get one when I was ten, huh?"

Dad looks up and smiles in surprise.

"Hey, you," he says while laughing at my remark. Then, he reaches out to hug. We hold each other for a long time. Then, when we release, I take him in.

He's short. My mom's short. Which is odd because both my uncles on my father's side and my aunts on my mother's side were giants. I often lamented that if they hadn't been the runts of their families, I might have been taller.

He is jolly in shape and curly-haired, a real-life Bilbo Baggins with kind gray eyes. "When did you get in?"

"Last night?" I say.

He misses the rising inflection.

"Well, let's have some iced tea." He sticks his thumbs in his suspenders and hobbles to the deck. "I need a break."

I sit at the deck table while he pulls a couple of plastic store-bought sweet iced tea bottles from the old refrigerator near the sliding glass door. The old General Electric workhorse is older than me and shows no signs of giving up. He sits opposite me, handing me a bottle.

Dad wipes his sweaty brow. Little bits of grass cling here and there to his forehead and stubble. "Seen your sister yet?"

I shake my head. "Not yet."

We talk for a good long time. I spill the beans about my job situation. He talks about Rooney and karma. The sun beats down. A hummingbird does an amazing anti-gravity act near the candy-red feeder hanging from the eave. Dad has kind and supportive things to say. Maybe that's why I'm here—it just had become too painful to be *out there*.

When I say as much, Dad assesses me. "Sounds like the Coyote has been harassing you a great deal lately."

"If you mean an entity from native folklore is haunting me, sure, why not," I reply, trying not to sound dismissive. I take a drink of my iced tea. "It makes about as much sense as anything else."

Dad is quiet for a beat. A corner of his mouth rises just a hint as he maintains his gaze on me.

"Right, folklore," he says.

"Well, why would a god of Native American legend bother to harass people?" My sister and I had grown up hearing about the trickster god, but I'd never delved into it as an adult. "Doesn't he have something better to do?"

Dad smiles. "Why does the Devil of Christianity tempt people? Why does God let him?"

Seeing that I'm not satisfied with the answer, Dad chuckles before taking a drink of tea and launching into an explanation.

He touches his temple to indicate something more ephemeral. "When people have become so beset by life, whether by their own choices or set down a path by their environment, their spirit becomes weakened," he starts. "The Coyote plays many roles in legend, and one of them is to act as an antagonist. Those who suffer in life are beset by the Trickster. If you're strong, you will survive his antics and come out stronger."

Intrigued, my bottle pauses at my mouth. "And if you're not?"

Dad sighs, and he seems to deflate just a little in his chair. "Many a person of the First Nations has fallen victim to alcohol, drugs, violence, mental illness...all the woes of white men that accelerate suffering. The Coyote's final task is to lead them to the underworld. Your cousin Johnny was probably the last victim of the Coyote in the family, like his father before him." He is quiet for another beat, and I contemplate his words, feeling rather small myself in my chair. "But I'm sure you'll be fine; you're strong. Just going through a rough patch."

He is quiet for more than a beat this time, and my bottle finds its way to my mouth.

"You know, I think I did hear coyotes howling last night as I lay on the lawn," I point out after I swallow.

"Well, there you go," he chuckles. "Seeing him coming from a mile away is half the battle."

I chuckle too and finish off my iced tea. Mom comes out, and as she is placing a vinyl record on the ancient portable turntable near the barbecue, she looks over her shoulder and says, "Hey, you want to give your son a ride downtown to find his car?"

"Sure thing," Dad agrees, guzzling the last of his iced tea. "Ready?"

I rise as Mom slips back inside.

Before entering the house, I hear the record skipping on the turntable and look down at it. The needle seems caught on a burr and keeps repeating the opening static before the first song. A chill runs down the back of my neck, and an aversion that is beyond the expected annoyance at the scratchy sound overcomes me, and my hand shoots out to nudge the needle into a new track. Relief comes in a flood when Willie Nelson's crooning fills the air.

Inside, Dad puts on a blue veteran's baseball hat with the US Navy logo for the USS *Tattnall*. He grabs his keys, and soon we're retracing my steps in his little white pickup.

When we come to town, we have to drive in circles because of Silverton's street plan. One-way streets are going around in a loop downtown. We don't see my car, and I'm starting to wonder about my head. Not just the pain in the back of my head but the state of its contents.

"I was definitely at Mac's," I say. "And something about the park rings a bell..."

"The park?" Dad makes a face. "What could have been going on at the park? Nothing is booked for another week."

We pass the Branstetter Building—new structure, old-timey brick architecture—for the second time before taking a left at Park Street to circle back downtown.

"You going to make it to the Rez this year?" Dad asks.

I grunt. Not sure I want to answer that. The annual family gathering at my cousin's ranch outside of Chiloquin is usually a pleasant experience. Though few family lived on what used to be the Klamath-Modoc Reservation, we gathered there regularly, usually on Labor Day weekend, to maintain roots. But this year would be different. This year I would have to repeatedly explain why I was out of a job and hear all kinds of advice on how to get back in the saddle. Right now, I just wanted to crawl under a rock and die.

"Probably," I finally reply. "Unless a new job situation prevents it."

"There'll be a pow-wow dance going on in Chiloquin that same weekend," Dad adds, casting a glance at me. "Want to go?"

I shift uncomfortably in my seat and play with the chrome of the glovebox handle. "Sure."

We're quiet for a while again, then Dad says, "You know, your godfather and I are putting on a showing of *The Saga of Sylvie Creek* at the theater during Homer's. He would like it if you stopped by to see it, I'm sure."

I smile. "Does the playwright get his cut for the use of the source material?"

Dad chuckles. "No, not really."

"You ever think about writing more plays, going big time?" I ask. Dad had majored in theater at Mt. Angel College back when it still existed. He had dabbled in writing plays, creating a little fun piece with a fellow actor friend using local place names for characters. I know his love is for acting and not so much writing— the complete opposite of me. You couldn't get me on a stage at gunpoint.

Dad shrugs. "You know the difficulties of publishing. At some point, the fun drains out of it."

Enough said.

"I'd be happy to see Uncle Norman," I reply. "It's been a while."

I had many "uncles" growing up. Uncle Norman, my godfather, the man with a penchant for pipes and fedoras, was probably the single biggest reason for my love of movies and all the film trivia crowding my head. It was our thing.

We pass the Palace Theater and Mac's as we head down South Water Street, passing the little yellow blockhouse that used to be the police station. For the longest time, I thought the only police station in the world that was smaller than Silverton's must have been a phone booth on a small Caribbean island. But now, the police had moved into City Hall. Then we pass the library and the Silverton Museum. Next to the museum is what used to be the town's train station way back when lumber was still king. Not in its original location but moved to augment the museum.

Just when I think that is just the sort of trivia Willy would approach tourists about and give them an impromptu history lesson, I see him on the sidewalk doing just that.

As we pass, I mention my encounter with Willy the night before, especially his nonsensical statements regarding scientific theories.

"Good old Willy," Dad chuckles. "You can take the engineer out of the university, but you can't take the university out of the engineer."

My lips screw sideways. "Really? He was an engineer?"

"Yep. He was in my high school class. Brilliant individual. Dual degrees from the University of Washington in physics and engineering. Had a good job at Boeing."

Shocked, I scrunch down in my seat to get a better look at the scruffy-looking man dressed in near-rags receding in the sideview mirror.

"Good Lord, what happened to him?"

Dad shrugs. "When his mom passed away, he took it very hard. William was the sort of guy who was very driven. He always put a lot of pressure on himself to succeed while trying to solve the world's problems. He was going to be an entrepreneur that invented the next big thing that saved the planet and saved people from themselves." Dad pauses, thoughtful. "But he couldn't save his mom from death, I guess." He turns down Wesley Street to the city swimming pool. "Technically, he still lives on her property in that big old house above the reservoir, but he doesn't seem to care to stay there. Instead, he spends more time under bridges in and around town."

As Dad slows to a stop, I'm still thoughtful, pondering the mystery that is Willy. A mystery I had never considered asking about because I was too busy making the wrong assumptions about him.

I look up, and sure enough, parked there in the parking lot as if I had planned to go for a swim was my little black Suzuki SX4.

"I have no idea why it's here," I muse out loud.

"Must have been having a really good time last night, huh?" Dad says.

I rub the back of my head. That noise that sounds like the crackle at the bottom of a pool buzzes in my ear.

Maybe I did go swimming last night, I think.

"I got it from here, thanks," I say, opening the truck's door. "I'll see you back at the house. I'll probably go visit Sis first, though."

"Your sister will like that, but she's working the evening shift in the kitchen up at the Abbey just so you know," Dad says. "Maybe you'll want to wait until you join her for Mass at church?"

I freeze as I exit the truck, then decide to re-seat myself. The door creaks back-and-forth idly in my right hand.

"I, um, am taking a break from going to church," I finally confess.

His only response is to tilt his head a little sideways, allowing me just enough room to gather my thoughts for an explanation. Which I do.

"I guess you can say I've been struggling with—things. I feel like I've been spinning my wheels in the mud, and the harder I spin them, the deeper I sink. I just need a break." Then, feeling more explanation is in order, I add, "It's like this, I think: back in college, I beat my head so hard against a wall studying for calculus and organic chemistry that my grades started to actually suffer. It wasn't until I decided to just let go, goof off for a while, that they improved. Aced a couple of tests, really. I'm hoping that is what happens here."

Dad's lips form into a sympathetic half-smile. "I'm sure it will. Catholics call this the 'Dark Night of the Soul,' but like you say, it will pass." He pauses, and his half-smile turns full as he puts the truck in gear and the engine revs a little. "Though I've always been impressed that you and your sister found your own way to the Faith, I can't help but wonder if by giving it Catholic context, you've made these dark moments worse. Kind of like feeling more guilty than necessary for kissing a girl just because the church said you should feel guilty."

I laugh, feeling a bit of darkness evaporate. "Well, the Coyote can't have all the fun." I step out of the truck and shut the door, then ask just before he pulls away. "How about you? You miss going to church at all?"

He lifts one of his hands from the steering wheel so I can see the back of it and the faint spider-webbing of white scars there. Though he's still smiling, it's a little strained when he says, "I don't miss the nuns."

After he's gone, I stand there staring at the staircase and railing leading down to the bridge. It crosses the creek to the park. My head hurts more. The sunlight is killing my eyes, reflecting off the light-colored concrete parking lot with white-painted lines. I hope my sunglasses are still in the console of my car.

Chapter 18
The Rez

It wasn't the dim light of the dawning day filtering into the tepee that woke me. Instead, something cold and damp had dropped on my face, followed by wetness flowing over my cheek.

I sit up in my sleeping bag, sputtering and swiping at the thing on my face. Something heavy plops into my lap, and a husky chortle of a laugh greets me at my side. Crouched on his haunches near me is Cousin Johnny struggling to contain his laughter by pushing his fist into his scruffy mustache.

Something croaks and moves in my lap. I jump when the bumpy toad leaps away and disappears through the gap between the tepee and pine needle-strewn ground. This, of course, only causes Johnny to laugh all the more.

"Hey, that thing peed on me!" I cry, wiping my face with the edge of the sleeping bag.

"Yeah, it did," Johnny whispers a laugh. "I didn't see that coming."

When I continue to protest, he shushes me by placing one finger at his lips and points around the interior of the circular enclosure at the other bulging sleeping bags. Each one contains a snoring cousin.

Johnny leans in and hisses in my ear. "You wanna go fishing? We'll have better luck in the morning."

I nod vigorously. Anything to make up for my deplorable showing yesterday. My whole life coming to the reservation, I seldom had luck fishing. So I struggle out of my bag in the biting cold, trying not to wake anyone. Even though it's Labor Day weekend, I'm sure there is frost on the ground in the shade. In the sun, it's probably already scorching hot. Contrasts in the Klamath Falls area are as unsubtle as being on the moon.

I fumble my boots on, sucking air between my teeth when the cold leather hits my feet. Eventually, with teeth chattering and breath coming out in puffs, I stumble out the flap of the tepee held open by Johnny.

He looks perfectly warm in his red-and-black-striped flannel jacket. His mop of curly blond hair probably holds a lot of heat in too.

My eyes sting at the abrupt brightness. Like all good Indians, Uncle Gordon has set up his tepee so the door faces the rising sun. It's rising like a fat egg yolk through the forest of slim pines. As we walk to the camp side of the tent, I note our shadows against the canvas, elongated across the painted image of an eagle.

My father's people—my people, the Klamaths and Modocs—were not tepee-living people. It's just that the tepee became a universal symbol for all Native Americans and a heck of a lot easier to erect and dismantle each camping trip than the historically accurate wickiups of earth and branches.

The camp is mostly still asleep. A city of firepits and small, bright, nylon tents weaves among the big pine trees. The watercress-filled brook disappears downhill into the forest, and our campfire is just now coming back to life, tended by, God bless her, Aunt Cathy who has always made sure we were fed and taken care of. She moves about the fire with her hair up in a bright red handkerchief, preparing sizzling bacon while listening to a softly playing radio. Wolfman Jack's signature husky voice announces the Eagles' new song, "New Kid in Town."

Mostly older and beat-up trucks, cars, campers, and trailers round out the scene. You'd think refugees were escaping civilization after an alien invasion, but nope, it's just the annual family get-together back on the Rez.

Yellowed pine needles litter the ground, forming a carpet over the forest floor. When I was real little, I was convinced the bundles of two to three four-inch strands ending at dark, pitchy match-heads were actually miniature torches. Like the sort villagers used when chasing Frankenstein's monster or the Hunchback. Looking around the forest floor, I figured that had to have been an awful lot of villagers.

The smells of pine, sage, and wood smoke fill the dry air. It always takes at least a day for my nose to adjust to the dusty environment. Later, when returning to Silverton, it usually means blowing dirty boogers for days.

Our feet kick up dust and pine "torches" as we approach the giant ponderosa, which guards all the fishing gear at its base. Sure enough, there is frost in the shade, and the sun's rays slowly start to warm me up like a microwave oven wherever it touches me.

Johnny crouches down and opens an ancient relic of a tackle box. It's dented and scuffed and lets out a rusty squeal, and though its paint is faded, you can tell that at one time it had been the same shade as a Radio Flyer wagon.

At the noise of the tackle box opening, Aunt Cathy looks our way. "Breakfast will be ready soon, and people will be leaving for hunting not long after, so you better hurry back if you want to join them. Better yet, hurry back with some fish so I can cook them up too."

"Sure thing, Aunt Cathy," Johnny calls over his shoulder.

As he takes stock of the tackle box, not the least of which is its dirt-filled Styrofoam container of worms, I fiddle with the tree's bark. We grew up calling them "puzzle trees" because their bark flakes off in layered sheets, which in turn are comprised of little pieces that fit together like jigsaw pieces. I dare you to stand next to one sometime and not feel the urge to play with the bark.

"It's awfully nice of you to take me fishing this morning," I say, casting my eyes to the ground and kicking at a pumice stone. The Swiss cheese-like rock bounces along, light enough to almost float away on the air. Being the youngest, I usually feel like a pest tagging after my older cousins. Of course, it didn't help any that I never caught anything, which made it seem like a waste of a fishing pole.

"It's no problem, little man," Johnny says, scrutinizing a pair of hooks and not me. "I don't want to go alone."

"It's not because you feel sorry for me?"

He pauses with his fussing with the tackle. "Nah, not at all. Let's go."

He shuts the box, grabs a pole leaning against the tree, and starts down the dusty road leading out of camp. I snatch a pole and rush to keep up with his long-legged gait.

As we head down the pumice-dirt road, our feet send up little puffs of whitish dust. Johnny whistles tunelessly, easily carrying the tackle box and pole. I first look up at him, glad he invited me along, then I look around, noting not for the first time how different things are here on the Rez. Though sprinkled with gray-green sage, the forest floor is nowhere as cluttered as the woods back home. You can actually run through these woods, unlike the briar-thick mess in the Willamette Valley.

And here, the climate was so dry. Back home, if you left the trail for any reason, rain-soaked fronds reached out and caressed you until you were soaking wet—a matter of moments. I loved the green of Silverton, but it came with a cost. *It rained. All. The. Time.*

These thoughts raise a question. "Do you know why we live in Silverton and not here?"

Johnny stops his whistling, takes a while to respond. "The Rez isn't always a perfect place. Dad says it's rough on people, I guess. Not always a lot of jobs. Causes people to drink a lot. Dad says it causes people to..." His bushy eyebrows bunch up as he strains to remember the word. "Despair."

I try to fathom what it was about a place that could cause people to *despair.* I say as much to Johnny.

He's quiet a long time, then struggles to explain. "Dad says it's like this. If you live in a giant box, and there are no jobs or nothin' much to do in the box, you kinda go crazy after a while. Add on top of that the people who live outside the box are doing everything they can to keep you from feeling welcome outside the box, then all you know is the box, which is driving you crazy." Johnny looks down at me to see if I understand. I don't. Not really. Not yet. But I nod anyway. "Grandpa recognized all this, and I reckon he didn't want Dad or your dad or Aunt Cathy and the rest to go crazy—to despair—so he packed them up and went far away. Went to Silverton and went to college nearby and used his GI Bill to make things better for the family. Understand?"

I do, and I say so, but just the same ask, "Did they make Grandpa feel unwelcome? The people outside the box, I mean?"

"I reckon so. Though he rarely complained about it."

We walk on in silence for a while.

"Speaking of drinking a lot," Johnny says, smiling with a mischievous grin. "I heard Cousin Don is coming in today from Chiloquin."

I laugh too. He's our relative who still lives on the Rez in town. He is big as a bear, with long thick gray braids. He looks like a dime-store Indian.

"Remember that time he got so drunk he took a nosedive right into the dirt at the campfire after dinner?" I ask. "I thought that sort of thing only happened in the movies."

Johnny laughs his throaty chortle. Unexpectedly, though, he turns serious and looks at me. "That's why we don't live here. You don't want to dirt dive, do you?"

I shake my head, the laughter gone out of me as well.

We're fast approaching the end of the dirt road, coming to a red metal gate. A barbed-wire fence extends on either side of it forever. Beyond the gate and fencing is a green grassy flat land with a river snaking through it. It's the only splash of real green in the whole area, a swath of grazing land running for a couple hundred yards on either side of the river for miles. Black and brown splotches browse in the grass. The occasional swish of a tail indicates they're cows.

Johnny tugs on the gate. It was open the day before. It's chained shut now.

"Cousin Don," I say. "He's the one who calls me the Swede, right? Because of my hair?"

Johnny snorts. "Yeah, that was his idea. But you got it easy. When I was your age and my hair was longer, and I tried to braid it, he called me Swiss-Miss." He grins. "No, no dirt-diving for you. I heard you're pretty smart. Probably even going on to college. Me? I'm joining the army in a couple years. I'm going to be a Ranger."

My mouth drops. "Cool!"

The gate is clearly labeled, "No Trespassing." It is basically a bunch of pipes welded together, just spaced enough to keep big animals from getting through, but it wouldn't stop small animals like goats, sheep, and young humans. Johnny wastes no time bending over and slipping through the gaps, taking care not to get the box and fishing pole tangled.

On the other side, he looks at me while I'm nervously still staring at the warning sign.

"Well, you coming or not?"

I shake my misgivings and follow. We leave the road on the other side of the gate and head out into the grass. It is like sword grass you'd find at the beach, clumped in little hillocks. Cows lift their heads at us while chewing their cud but decide we're not a threat. So they go back to nosing their way through the landscape. Grasshoppers scatter before us, and dragonflies do an occasional fly-by.

We approach a bridge of wood boards lying across a pair of logs straddling the river. The river is probably less than thirty yards across at this point and flows at a lazy pace. After that, it gets broader downstream, boiling over rocks for good white-water rafting. Here, it is quiet, deep, and dark.

We sit on the weather-worn boards and dangle our feet over, with boot soles a good couple of feet above the water. Johnny rummages around for the container of worms and threads a fat nightcrawler onto his hook. He hands the container to me. I find one I'm happy with and stab the hook through its veiny body. It squirms silently, and I repeat the process until it's impaled twice. I won't be losing my bait this time.

Meanwhile, Johnny has already expertly cast his line to the far riverbank. The sinker makes an audible plop, and the yellow-and-red bobber does its job, marking the spot.

It takes me a few tries to get my line near his without crossing it, but eventually, I get the job done. We sit quietly, watching the bobbers float, the dragonflies hovering and zooming, as the sun rises higher in the sky.

After a while, I ask, "Where'd you find the toad? That was a big one."

"It crawled out from a hole near the campfire. I guess the heat made it uncomfortable," he replies.

More time goes by. The day gets hot. Johnny takes his flannel coat off to reveal the tank-top T-shirt he's wearing, which in turn shows his assortment of blue-ink tattoos whose specifics I'd eventually lose to memory. He also takes a cigarette, grips it between his lips, and lights it with a Zippo, cupping the flame in his palm. He squints through his first drag.

After another long quiet stretch, I ask, "Can we be here? The sign said no trespassing. And the gate was closed."

Johnny scoffs as he reels in his line. "Heck yeah, we can be here. Our people were here long before the rancher who bought the grazing land decided to put a fence around it. Besides, nobody *owns* the river. We can fish here."

His hook, sinker, and bobber rise from the water, and after making sure his worm is still firmly attached, he casts it back out with a *zzzzzz* of the reel.

"I don't have a fishing license, do you?" I ask.

Johnny laughs. "Heck no, don't need one. Not here, not anywhere, really. Just do what you want, I say."

"But our dads and Uncle Gordon still need to get deer license sto hunt deer, even on the Rez. All they have to do is show their tribal ID, but they still need a license, though."

"Bunch of malarkey, all these rules." Johnny tugs on his line and stares inquisitively at the bobber. "Just like that stupid rule the tribe has that me, you, and our brothers and sisters aren't officially members of the tribe because we're less than twenty-five percent Indian."

"Blood quota," I say, remembering the word bandied about the campfire during heated conversations among the grown-ups.

Johnny gives a sharp nod as he tugs on his line again. "Yep. Rules. Rules are stupid. Rules are made for breaking."

He sits straight up, excited. His bobber is going crazy, and he starts reeling. Soon, a twelve-inch dart is flopping at the end of his line as he pulls it out of the water and brings it to rest on the boards. He snatches it with a hand, grips the slippery body, and wrestles the hook from the gasping mouth, which is only snagged by its single barb at the jawline. He then whacks the fish's head on the wood, once, twice, and it stops moving.

Grinning, he hoists it up so we can take a good look. I marvel at the sleek creature. Its silvery underside is divided from the dark topside by a freckled band of rainbow dots. It's a beautiful trout—one of the bigger ones I've seen.

He throws it in the tackle box and sets to re-worming his hook.

My bobber is doing nothing except floating.

"What if the rancher shows up, tells us to leave?" I ask after Johnny has cast his new line.

"Screw him. It's nobody's business to tell me where and when I can fish with my cousin."

"Really?"

"Heck, yeah. Fight him too, if I have to. I'll fight anyone who tells me what I can and can't do. Live free, die hard, I say."

I smile and tug on my line. Nothing happens. A long time passes. Maybe an hour. Johnny catches another fish, though not as big as the first one.

I check my line several times. The worm is always there, looking limper and limper.

Eventually, Johnny checks the sun, his watch, and my bobber, and then looks over his shoulder in the direction of the camp.

He lights another cigarette and appraises me. "You got a knife?" he asks. The cigarette wags on his lip.

"Me? No. Why?"

Johnny reaches into the pocket of his jeans and pulls out a folding knife. The case is plastic but stylized to look like carved wood. He unfolds it to reveal a long blade with an upswept tip. He brushes the edge against his forearm. Blond hairs shave away effortlessly, collecting in a pile, demonstrating its sharpness.

"Whoa!"

"You want it?" he asks.

"Well, yeah."

"Tell you what." He stands and throws the knife far into the grass. "If you can find it, you can have it."

"Wow, really?" I stand, shocked at the turn of events. I run into the grass, searching among the little hillocks. It doesn't take me that long. I grab it up, admiring it as I walk back, happy with my new prize.

When I return, Johnny is pointing to my bobber. "I saw it move. You might want to check it."

Heart beating fast, I take a seat and pick up my pole where I had set it down. I crank on the reel and feel a heavy drag. Eventually, a fish comes out of the water, dangling listlessly at the end of the line.

When I get it in my hands, it is not moving. The hook in its mouth has no worm, and it is obvious the hook has been forced entirely through the jaw.

I look over to Johnny, trying not to show my disappointment.

He winks at me. "Love you, little man."

Chapter 19
The Grotto

I do a walk-around the car. Nothing seems out of order. I fish my car keys out of my pocket with the rosary still entangled in them and beep the lock open.

At least I had the good sense to lock it, I think. *So, there's that.*

Inside, nothing is out of order here either. I hang my rosary in its usual place on the rearview mirror, grab my sunglasses from the console, and sigh with relief when I put them on. Polarized is the way to go. When I start the engine, the radio blares at me. It's playing Peter Gabriel's "My Body is a Cage." Something about the song strikes a memory, but it darts away like a fish in the stream. I turn the radio down to average volume and leave it on.

I shrug the odd feeling off, let down the e-brake, and steer my little all-wheel-drive back to South Water. Before I get very far, I'm passing the *Criterion* mural on the side of a building. Silverton is famous for its murals. This is one of the older ones, depicting bicycle racers in action. I have an idea and pull over to a row of parking meters along the street and turn off the engine. I fish around in the console and find my stash of pennies. I blow the dust off them and exit the vehicle.

One of the other things Silverton is famous for is its historic parking meters. The original tear-drop-on-stem devices with cyclopean glass windows still function only with pennies, nickels, and dimes. This or that politician has constantly threatened to replace them with actual revenue-generating devices. Still, the quirky beacons of yesteryear have always charmed tourists and managed to live another day.

I pump three pennies into the thing, twisting the bubble-gum machine knob after each one. That will buy me 45 minutes. Plenty of time for what I have in mind. Maybe. Or maybe I thought something similar last night when I parked my car, then: *"I'm only going to break into the pool and take a quick dip at midnight?"* Next thing you know, I'm sprawled on my parents' lawn.

Anyway, I get across traffic and slip down a stairwell situated beneath the *Criterion*. A sign hanging from the corner of the building announces the Creekside Grill & Grotto studded in light bulbs. An equally studded arrow points down the stairwell.

At the bottom is a glass door that opens into an underground mall of shops. An electric fountain gurgles near another door across from the stairwell. Next to it is a sandwich board with the day's specials written in chalk. Large windows open up into the restaurant, the eponymous grill, and even from here, I can see the windows on the far side of the seating leading to more eating space on a deck and a drop off to the creek below. Mostly trees and sunlight fill the view beyond.

I bypass the main door and chalkboard and head to a pair of swinging glass doors inside. "Grotto Bar" is etched in the glass. There I dodge around a wheelbarrow full of painting supplies sitting on the mall-side of the door. It's full of pails of various sizes, tarps, and brushes of all sizes, all splattered with paint as if a child had been left alone with the equipment. I find a seat at the little bar in the small room; in fact, the bar at my parents' house is bigger.

However, this one is colorful, lit up by sunlight streaming in from the creek-side windows that ignite various fun-looking bottles. If the bottles themselves aren't colored, then the liquid inside them is, and furthermore, sitting on under-lit glass shelves makes the scene as festive as a Christmas tree for hardened drinkers.

The scattering of tall round little tables is empty. The bartender has her back to me, and what a back it is. She has a healthy physique covered by a black, backless blouse exposing a giant ochre tattoo of an owl in flight. The owl's wings are spread up and over her shoulders. The owl's big eyes stare at you. Its talons extend down beneath her waistline.

"Cool ink," I say.

She whirls around, holding a hand to her chest. The blouse is sleeveless, exposing her shoulders, and its collar is gathered at her throat like a turtleneck. The owl's wings continue over her shoulders and extend down each arm to her forearms. She gives a nervous laugh.

"I'm really not normally a fan of tattoos," I confess, "but even I have to say that is a really cool one."

"Well, thank you," she says, sweeping back a stray lock that has escaped her ponytail. "What can I get you?"

"An iced tea?"

"You're not very adventurous."

"It's not even noon yet."

"People don't find their way down here to drink just an iced tea," she teases.

"Okay, fine, twist my arm," I say. "What do you suggest?"

"Well, we have this new concoction called a Blue Lamp Special." She gestures her willowy arm to the blacklight dry erase board on the wall. A somewhat artistic rendering of a bulbous-shaped glass filled with blue liquid topped with an umbrella is drawn in neon marker, along with the drink's name and the price.

"Er, sounds good," I say.

Pleased, she goes about making the drink.

"Hey, is Lori in by any chance, or maybe Manny?" I ask.

Before she can answer, the very person I'm looking for walks in from the corridor connecting the Grill to the Grotto. Lori is tall and looks about ten years younger than her age—and her presence explains the mystery of the wheelbarrow. Her straw-colored hair is tucked up underneath an English driving cap, and paint splatters her coveralls. Her bare shoulders are white like a true Pacific Northwesterner.

"Hey there," she greets me as she continues on her way to the back of the bar. "How you been?"

"Actually, I was hoping you could tell me," I say.

She gives me a slantwise look but smiles anyway. "How so?" She pours herself a glass of water from the tap.

"Was I in here last night by any chance?"

She laughs in mid-drink of her water, spluttering. "What? You don't remember?"

I shrug, making a face.

"Wow, good time last night?" she says, tipping her hat back. Her eyelashes are black and huge, almost like Raggedy-Ann doll eyes. She has a bit of an overbite. Very cute.

The tattoo girl is smiling at our exchange as she puts the final touches on my drink.

"I don't know entirely," I explain. "I remember how it ended but can't remember how it started. I found my car, and this is the only place I can think of that would have brought me down this way. It would be funny, except this has never happened to me before. Honestly, it's kind of disturbing."

She's not smiling now, eyes big with surprise and some concern. "Wow, *weird*. Usually, it's the other way around."

"I know, right?"

"I didn't work last night, so I don't know if you came in," she admits. "I didn't even know you were in town. Did you see him last night, Clea?"

The tattoo girl places the Dr. Seussian drink in front of me. "No, but my shift ended early." She spins to the digital server monitor, stabbing at the screen with her finger.

Lori leans over the corridor-side of the bar and shouts down the hall. "Hey Manny, come here for a sec, would ya?"

A tall, thinnish African American fellow arrives. Salt and pepper are scattered in his temples and mustache these days, and he has a kind face and a kinder voice.

He smiles in recognition. "Hey partner, how you doing?"

"That's what we're trying to figure out," Lori answers for me. I have just taken a slurp of the radioactive slushy, and the overwhelming flavor is syrup, with only a little bit of alcohol bite. I'm not digging it. Nevertheless, I give Clea the thumbs up.

Manny is laughing either at the drink or Lori's remark, but he catches the undercurrent of concern. "No, no, I didn't see you come in," he says, "but I was working the restaurant side. So you might have."

Clea fills a tray full of drinks and heads for the corridor.

"You staying for a little while?" she asks.

"Um, I guess," I say.

"Cool." She winks and continues on her way.

I watch her as she leaves. The muscles in her back undulate beneath the skin, causing the owl to ripple.

Lori also watches her but leans on the bar towards me on her elbows. "You know she was flirting with you, right?"

"Wha—? Nah..." I say, making a face. I take another run at the drink, determined to finish it. "She's just friendly. And probably wants a tip. Which I'm going to give her."

Lori shakes her head. "Why aren't you married?"

"Because I'm ugly?"

Lori rolls her eyes. The giant eyelashes flutter. "No, really."

"Because...I'm ugly on the inside? Hell, I don't know." The blue drink is no longer blue, sucked down to the point that its residual crushed ice catches the light in the glass bowl.

"You'll find someone," Lori says.

"I used to tell myself that twenty years ago." I meant that more tongue-in-cheek, but I turn thoughtful. "Unfortunately, my being unmarried is a symptom of something greater."

Lori's head tilts a little to the side. "What would that be?"

"That's the million-dollar question." I suck one last time on the straw but stop when the sound becomes annoying.

"Look at me," Manny says. "By the time I thought I would never find true love, I had no idea she was just being born."

He and Lori beam at each other. It's adorable. It also makes me feel awkward.

"Well, my love, have to get back to the restaurant," Manny says.

"Okay, I'm headed out soon. Clea's got the bar."

"Nice to see you," Manny waves to me as he turns to the corridor. "Hope you find your answers."

I wave back. "My mind holds the key..."

I freeze. *Where the hell did that come from?* Manny and Lori don't seem to notice. But just in case, I plaster on a smile and gesture to her paint-spattered coveralls. "Mural painting?"

"Touch-up," she replies. "City contracts me to keep them in shape."

"But you made a bunch of them, right?"

"Yep, six."

"Cool," I say, genuinely impressed. "I can say I knew you when."

"And I can say I knew you when, before your books really took off," she replies as she moves around the bar to the door where her wheelbarrow full of paint supplies waits for her.

She grabs it by the handles and maneuvers it into a glass shaft in the mall's center outside the Grotto door. She also steps inside the chamber, shuts a metal gate, pushes a button, and begins to rise.

"Stop by again," she calls out before disappearing into the ceiling. "And it wouldn't kill you to flirt back with Clea."

"It might!" I shout at her feet.

"What might?" Clea asks, coming through the corridor.

I gulp. Hold out the empty glass. "Another drink might kill me."

Chapter 20
The Salesman

I return to my car and open the hatchback, figuring I might as well take care of some other business. A large Rubbermaid container full of books, book-sized easels, pens, and miscellaneous literature is nestled inside the tiny compartment. My travel bag is there too. I open it and find my toiletry kit and some spare clothes. I don't remember packing it.

A sharp pain hits the back of my head.

Trivia. I need some trivia to distract me from the pain, but nothing comes to mind. The only thing going for me is that I'm slightly buzzed from the couple of Blue Lamp Specials I just chugged. Clea talked me into another one, but that was about all the talking we did. My introversion kiboshed anything else.

I rub my head with one hand and pull out my beloved canvas mailbag from deeper inside my storage compartment. Got it at Barnes & Noble. I fill it with several paperbacks from the Rubbermaid container. Next, I take out a handful of business cards from a small cardboard box labeled "Vistaprint," also in the Rubbermaid. These I place in the mailbag's side pocket. Satisfied, I slip the bag's strap over my neck and shoulder and let it dangle across my body. I lock the Suzuki and walk towards the center of town.

Right away, I see two of the town's famous murals.

To my left, incorporated into the fence separating the sidewalk from the drop-off to Silver Creek, is a collage of Bobbie the Wonder Dog. It comprises an image of the Collie, reproductions of newspaper clippings, and a map of the Western United States with a dashed line to signify the route he must have taken to reach home. Next to the fence is a replica doghouse too. I stare at Bobbie for a moment. For some reason, it lessens my headache.

Ahead, the entire side of a brick building depicts a nostalgic scene of a couple standing outside a 1920s car. The man is holding a picnic basket in one hand and kissing the woman's hand with his other. In the background is a covered bridge up a country road. I recognize the bridge. My cross-country and track coach sent our team many times over Gallon House Bridge as part of a six-mile circuit from the high school.

I don't see Lori, so she must be at one of the many other murals in town.

As I'm walking, Willy is shuffling my way. He has two tourists in tow, interpreting the murals and architecture, regaling them with trivia for a small fee, and it reminds me that he's probably forgotten more trivia than I'll ever know.

As our shoulders brush, we exchange a glance. His dark eyes, lined on either side by wrinkles, stare out at me from underneath scruffy gray eyebrows. His beard stops moving for a moment—the sight of me stalls his discourse. He picks up again as soon as we pass.

I can hear the male tourist lament about getting a warning from the police for having been driving in the wrong direction on one of Silverton's one-way streets.

"It *is* Silverton," the woman points out. "I told you it's a quirky little place."

The man isn't having it. "Why on earth does a town this size have one-way streets? It's the stupidest thing I've ever heard."

I hope you brought pennies, I think, *and were able to pay your parking meter.*

I walk farther into town, and just after the Palace Theater on the right is a large display window with books and clocks. Stenciled in the window is the name Books'N'Time. I enter.

You know how you enter an environmentally controlled office building and immediately feel the difference in the atmosphere? How the temperature is different? How even the pressure is different, making it difficult to open the door? That's Books'N'Time. Except it's not the temperature and barometric pressure that is altered; it's something else. Maybe it's the smell of countless paperbacks and rare books. Perhaps it's the sound of dozens of vintage clocks ticking away. Maybe it's just that vibe any decent bookstore or library has. A kind of magic. Perhaps it's the clocks that make time more visceral, like something you can feel on your skin or get tangled in your hair.

Chuck is sitting at his booth near the entrance when my arrival jingles the door. He tilts his head toward me to look over his reading glasses. Sunlight glints off his silver hair.

"Long time no see."

"Hey, Mr. Chuck," I say. "How're things?"

"You know, so-so," he says, "but I can't complain. Sold some of your books, you know."

"I figured you might have. A couple cousins threatened to buy copies, and it sounds like they made good on it," I say. "Ready for a couple more?"

"Sure, sure," he replies and opens a ledger and taps on the screen of his iPad.

"The usual? Two?"

"Sure."

I dig in my mailbag and produce two of the voluminous paperbacks. Part of the reason I have trouble selling them is that they are the size of cinderblocks. Not many people want to invest time and money in a 500-plus page book from an unknown author.

I set them on the counter, and he hands me some money. It's not a lot—enough to pay for the printing and shipping costs and a little more. But selling to people like Chuck isn't really about profit. It's about visibility and networking. You never know who might pick up your book in this or that store. Plus, in Silverton, it's a good place for people who know me to easily stop by and grab a copy if they want.

"How are my friends doing?" I ask with a head-jerk to the shelf labeled "Local Authors."

"Some do quite well, others..." He shrugs. "But I thank you for helping me connect with them. Even though they're mostly Portland authors, they're still Oregon. You'd be surprised at how many people come in here, see that shelf, and realize that they too can fulfill their dream of becoming a writer. It's really inspiring."

"You're very welcome," I say. "It's the least I can do for the kindness and support you've shown me. I send people here every chance I get."

"Wish I could do more for you," Chuck says. He plucks a pen out of the cup and reminds me I need to sign the copies of my book. We go on talking for a while. I ask about a few classics. He doesn't have a copy of Washington Irving's *The Legend of Sleepy Hollow*, but he can get it. I say, sure, why not? He places an order, and I can pick it up in a few weeks. This effectively gives him his money back for the books I just sold him, but that's okay. It's more about community.

I leave with a promise to be back in a few weeks for the Irving book.

Farther up the street, I cross at the intersection. Once upon a time, there had been half a dozen gas stations within a stone's throw of downtown. They are still there, but they no longer serve gas. The buildings, still obviously gas stations in structure, have been converted to other kinds of businesses. The one I now pass, Le Pooch, is a pet groomer. It must be doing well because it has outlasted some of the other businesses downtown by years.

Past Le Pooch is an open lot occasionally used by food trucks. At its far side is a two-story brick building painted red with white trim. It is almost a perfect square of a building, and between its upper- and lower-story windows is a sign that looks like it would be more at home over an old-time cowboy saloon. But it advertises flowers, not whiskey or sarsaparillas. Inside the windows are all sizes and shapes of floral bouquets, both living and preserved for interior decorating.

When I enter, the bell above the door rings like a cathedral bell. The inside is spacious, and like the bookstore, has its own vibe. Flowers both living and deathless fill the mostly one-roomed bottom floor, accenting the antiques. Neatly arranged are wicker baby strollers, Singer sewing tables (some still with the vintage machine attached), giant teddy bears, Nutcrackers, dolls, boxes of brass and glass doorknobs, door knockers, drawer handles, coat hooks, and more. All emanate a dusty, lived-in scent into the flowers' perfume. If in Books'N'Time you could feel time flow, here it comes to a standstill, freezing the past in place.

Refrigerated cabinets line the walls. Through illuminated glass doors, arrangements wait for weddings, funerals, high school dances, and apologies.

I love this place. Everyone in Silverton loves it. Virtually every boy for the past three decades has come here to get their prom corsage. The big red building has been a fixture since before I was born, and I once wrote a short story based on it: a curio shop dealing in everyday magic has a brush with real magic—very *Twilight Zone* but in a sweet way.

To the right is the sales counter. Somewhere under the mountain of flower pots, houseplants, memorabilia, books, candy, and tourist literature is probably a desk, possibly an antique itself. There is a vintage brass cash register, but also an iPad for sales transactions.

Among the books for sale are two coffee-table photography books centered on Silverton and its surrounding countryside. Another picture book is devoted purely to the murals. In addition, there are some fiction and nonfiction paperbacks. One of those is mine. The Silverton Flower Shop has the distinction of being the first store ever to sell my books.

Behind the counter is Norma Jean. She is busy arranging flowers in a vase. Her steel gray hair is short and curly. Gold-rimmed spectacles sit on the bridge of her nose. She wears a checkered apron with frills.

All in all, she looks like Missus Claus. Everyone in Silverton loves her. She has been as much a fixture as the building.

"Hello, Miss Norma Jean," I say when the bell toll falls quiet.

"Hellloooo there!" she says with a giant smile.

"How are things?" I ask.

"Peachy! And you? Long time no see!"

"Yeah, the day job has been he...heck," I say. "Kept me away for a long time. But now, that's over, and I have more free time. So I can get back to reconnecting with folks."

Norma Jean purses her lips in sympathy. "Well, I hope that is a good thing, darling."

"It is," I'm quick to say. "Speaking of reconnecting, I just wanted to check in with you." I reach down to the one remaining copy of my book, pick it up, and blow the dust off it. "Aaaand I can see I don't need to replenish the inventory."

Norma Jean smiles sadly. "We sold quite a few that first year, but since then..."

I understand. "It's a familiar story. I just need to write more books."

Her eyes light up behind her delicate glasses. "Are you? Writing more, I mean?"

"Er, yes, I am." *I am?* "Though it's a completely different kind of story. Reaching a broader audience. Not so much to do with dragons, knights, and damsels in distress."

"I hope it still has magic," she says.

"Oh, it will. I mean, it does. And mystery." *What the hell?*

"Splendid! I can't wait to see it!" She claps a little clap. "I love mysteries."

Me too, I think.

I look around. There seems to be an unusual amount of flower arrangements in various stages of preparation.

"Looks like business is going well," I observe.

A shadow falls over Norma Jean's normally amiable countenance, and she doesn't seem to notice that she bunches up her apron with her hands.

"So many funerals lately," she laments. "So many pretty girls much too young to be put in the ground. It's a sad sign of the times, where the value of human life just isn't what it used to be. It all started when people stopped saying 'please' and 'thank you,' stopped holding doors and pulling out chairs for one another. After the Great Depression and World War Two, people understood the value of life. Now, all people seem to care about is reality TV."

I find myself following her words closely, leaning in.

"Do you think it's what they say, a serial killer?" I ask.

She realizes she's wadding up her apron, stops, and smooths it out. "Doesn't matter. Even if it is, you catch one, and there's another to take his place. Evil has always been among us, growing like a weed, but we no longer seem to care to weed it out. Just let it grow out of control, and we wonder why our flowers get choked to death."

She reaches to a rose in a vase, caresses the petals, then throttles the stem between thumb and forefinger. She stops when she notices me watching.

"But enough of that." Sunshine returns to her face. "So when is your Aunt Catherine coming to visit again? Such a sweet girl, and she sure could cut a rug!"

I laugh, respecting her desire to change the subject. "The 'girl' is retired now and might be here this coming Homer Davenport Days for her class reunion. I can't swear to that, but she and her family usually come up from Eureka for it."

"That would be fantastic!" Norma Jean says. "Tell her I said hello!"

"I sure will," I promise.

I stay for a while and talk about family, the town, the shop. Connect. Network. Be human. A tall order in most circumstances, but this is what my book does for me. Its legacy is to make me get out and be the salesman I could never be peddling someone else's chemicals. It's just that it's such a damn shame my books could never make me the kind of money the chemicals did.

After a while, I wave my goodbyes, and the bell is tolling again.

Directly across the street is the Silverton Inn. Much love went into the creation of the hotel and restaurant. It's a handsome twenty-first-century building of wood and glass imitating Old World European architecture. Like the Wolf Building, it has a castle turret at one corner with a pennant fluttering at its peak. The place has come a long way since its days as the Nordic Motel. A running joke used to be that the Nordic charged by the hour. It kind of looked like it did, no matter the truth. But now it's this shiny tourist attraction.

The venerable Eugene Field Elementary School is across the street from the inn, forever painted in dark mustard. My parents went to school there. I went to school there. At least one of my nieces went to school there. People have been going to school there since the 1920s. The hitching post on the corner, a concrete obelisk with an iron ring, is older than that. I'm pretty sure it smells the exact same inside even now—dry wood and crayons melted on the steam radiators. Not surprisingly, many of my first memories live in that building.

But business does not take me in that direction, and I return to downtown. Soon I'm passing shop windows filled with arts and crafts. I stop at one festooned with crystals, dreamcatchers, and Native American art. Inside is a painting depicting an Indian warrior in a bison headdress centered among images of wildlife, one of which is a coyote.

Oddly, the coyote image doesn't remind me of my conversation earlier that morning with dad, but rather of a time in high school when I sat in my Advanced Placement History class. We were preparing for the PSAT exam. My pencil hovered over the bubbles next to the ethnicity question at the beginning of the packet. Particularly the bubble next to "Native American."

"Why does it ask for our ethnicity?" I had asked Miss Morgan.

She looked up from her podium at the head of the class and responded, "It's like the census: it gives the test makers a better idea of who is taking the test. Also, it helps scholarship providers allocate funds to underprivileged groups."

"Why, you looking to get a free hand out?" Billy Dade in the seat next to me asked. His fat bully-face made his tone all the more mocking.

"Don't you?" I returned. "Maybe you should check the 'inbred' box."

Billy puffed up in his football jersey and opened his mouth to say something, but Miss Morgan cut him off. "Gentlemen, the test has started, and you're running out of time. I suggest you get to it."

Billy reluctantly turned his eyes back to his desk.

Despite my clever response, I still felt the sting of Billy's words and my classmates' eyes on me. Stalling, my pencil hovered a little longer over the "Native American" bubble, then I filled in the one next to "White."

I shake the memory and continue to Silverton's Odd Fellows building, a stout redbrick edifice occupying the entire corner of Main and First. Its distinctive triple-chain-link symbol pops out from the brick. My dad says that there is almost always an Odd Fellows building in every little town in Oregon. They serve as relics of a fraternal order like the Masons or Elks, which has gone the way of many things in America—live music, dances, and municipal semi-pro athletic leagues—things relegated mainly to black-and-white in the history books. Before telephones, television, and then the internet made it too convenient to stay home.

The upper stories of the Silverton Odd Fellows building are now residential, and the lower part is now commercial and partitioned out to various businesses. The corner business is a Radio Shack. I enter and find in the center circular kiosk among the shelves a bespectacled fellow with black hair, beard, and mustache. I cringe when I think of him as "fast approaching middle age" because he is not much older than me. In fact, we share the same birthday.

He stands to take my hand. "Well, look what the cat drug in. How's it going?"

"It's a loooong story, Jason," I say. "So long, in fact, I won't bore you with the details. I just stopped by to say hi and check on the status of my books. I know you're busy. Being a store owner has many more responsibilities than just being a store employee."

Jason waves me off. "Bullshit. Well, I mean, yeah, it has waaay more responsibilities, and I *am* busy, but I haven't seen you in forever. You got time for lunch?"

I'm shocked. My jaw drops, actually. Usually, Jason has no time for anything. His refrain is, "I have to get home to my wife." I'm not about to say no.

"I've got all the time in the world. Which is part of my long story. Ready to go now?"

Jason shoots me an odd look. "My help will be here shortly. Why don't you get us a seat at the Gallon House, on the patio? I'll be there soon."

Again, I'm flabbergasted. "Yeah, sure thing, I'll go do that."

Jason's smile glows approval, and I back out the glass door as he turns to a customer at the counter.

I walk a few blocks north to the Gallon House, passing what used to be the First National Bank. A few years back, it was quickly joining the photographs in history books, belonging to the class of bank that had a caged room with the giant safe door swung open to reveal a room full of safe deposit boxes. An ornate wood counter with tellers in stalls waiting to assist the next client. It was the kind of place I always expected to be robbed by note: one slipped across the counter, "This is a robbery, don't act funny." But like many buildings in Silverton, it's been repurposed to some other business. I have no idea what.

When I arrive at the Gallon House Pub, named after the Gallon House Bridge in the mural elsewhere in town, I'm reminded that not all change is bad. It had always been a tavern just a hair's breadth above seedy—low key, unassuming, comfortable for loggers, truck drivers, farmers, and old-timers.

My own father used to occupy a barstool here. Legend had it that the windows had been blacked out to prevent wives from doing drive-by snoopings, perhaps with my mother among them.

Now, under new ownership and an infusion of money, the place has joined the twenty-first century and attracted a younger crowd. The windows are now mostly glass roll-up garage doors and a patio with parasols where the parking lot used to be. The inside has a new speak-easy motif complete with imprints of newspaper clippings from the Prohibition era. The Gallon House also has the ubiquitous digital jukebox and flat-screen monitors displaying keg icons—what they have on tap and how much. Their technology and marketing are giving Boomer a serious challenge to his empire of classic pubs and roadhouses. But Boomer still has the music.

Inside, the waitress descends on me and directs me to a tall table on the patio. I take my seat and am looking directly at the building across the street. I guess my Uncle Charlie used to live in the upper-story apartments, which led me for a long time to believe that only sketchy characters lived there. "Never worked an honest day in his life," Mom used to say about the tall, quiet man who perpetually wore sunglasses. Evidently, Uncle Charlie was a professional gambler and carried a razor in his boot and a .38 in his waistband.

When he wasn't living in shady upper-room apartments in downtown Silverton, he lived in my room at our old house on Quarry Avenue. I remember sneaking into my room for clothes late in the mornings while he snored away in my bed (because Uncle Charlie was out all night, apparently doing sketchy things). While quietly pulling the particle-board drawer out of the dresser, I would fixate on the pink-and-white false teeth staring at me from a glass of water. It rested between the bottle of Karate aftershave and the aftershave in the green glass bottle shaped like a trout with the detachable plastic fish head. Somewhere in my developing child-mind, I understood that he had lost his teeth in a fight with angels. For the longest time, I was confused. Finally, my older sister clarified that he had lost them in a fight with the *Hell's* Angels. Even that turned out to be wrong, though. When I was older, Dad laughed at the childish story, saying, "No, he lost his teeth because he never brushed them."

Still, there was no doubt about one thing. My high school teachers knew Uncle Charlie as "Meat Hook." Something to do with his right hook punch and the way his adversaries dropped like a piece of dead meat.

"He was quite the troublemaker," Mr. Bowerman once said to me in the school office while I was submitting a doctor's note. He said it with a sneer that tipped his ridiculous mustache to the side. "He was a real piece of work."

I had leaned forward over the counter and made deliberate eye contact with the man. The leather of the sleeves on my letterman's jacket creaked. The medals from track and field jingled. Then, fortified with the fact I had already been accepted by my college of choice with my near straight A's, I sneered right back.

"Beats being a douchebag."

Not sure how to respond, Mr. Bowerman had walked away with a scowl.

Uncle Charlie had been Johnny's dad. Now they were both gone.

Without warning, Jason drops into the chair opposite me, grabbing a menu from the center of the table among the condiment dispensers. He opens his mouth to talk, but before he can, a wailing sound fills the air, coming from far away to the south. A droning wail that rises and lowers in pitch, cycling a couple times. I take the moment to gather myself again and put on a cheerful face.

"The Germans are attacking," I say.

Jason laughs.

The siren is short-lived and is gone, not to return for another 24 hours.

"You ever think it's odd that Silverton has an air raid siren rather than a tolling bell or music chime? Hell, even Mt. Angel has a glockenspiel *and* a church tower."

Jason agrees as he skims the menu. "We need a proper clock tower."

"That's right," I add, also looking at a menu. "Marty McFly will never be seen racing down the streets of Silverton in a DeLorean at 88 miles per hour."

Jason laughs again. The waitress arrives and collects our orders.

"Seriously, you're on the city council," I grumble. "Can't you do something about that?"

"We've got more pressing issues to deal with," he says, shaking his head. "Besides, where would we put it?"

"Good point."

"You not having a beer with me? You too good for me?" I ask when the waitress returns with our drinks and free chips and salsa.

He makes his signature chortle. "I have to get back to work after lunch. My help is only there for a couple hours, then I'm on till close."

"Yikes, man, you ever take a break?"

He sighs heavily. "No. Work is work. How about you? How's work for you?"

I cringe, even though I knew this moment was coming. I tell him the news about my job situation. Like most reasonable people, he is sympathetic and wishes he could help. Still, people's life problems and career problems generally belong to those experiencing them. We can only watch from the sidelines and be supportive. If we're lucky, a relief pitcher might come in and give us some breathing room.

I tell him I'll be okay.

"How you doing for money?" he asks. Not invasively, but with an eye for financial things. Jason was always good at that.

"I'm currently siphoning off my former 401(k) I rolled over into a money fund," I explain, "and that will last me a good long time, but it's, you know, my future. My retirement. This can't go on forever. It took me a long time to build that up, and now it's evaporating like gallium in my hand."

"I actually got that reference," he says, digging into the chips and salsa. It's hard for me to watch him eat with his hands. He has big hairy fingers. "I understand using your retirement up. I put much of my money into the franchise. I'm turning a profit now, but it didn't happen overnight. I imagine your books will be the same. Speaking of your books..." He sucks on his fingers, making slurping noises. My face crinkles as I take a drink, threatening to spill beer out of my mouth. "I'm sorry that I don't have better news for you. The copies I have on the counter are still there."

"No problem," I say. "I expected as much. I'm grateful that you have them there. Thanks, man."

We change the subject, talking more about mundane things. Like how our families are doing. How his moonlighting as a councilman is going.

"Politics is politics," he says to the latter. "But somebody has to do it."

"I still think it's funny that people our age are the ones calling the shots now," I say. "It makes me realize that all the politicians running things when we were growing up must have just been people too. They went to grade school. Went to high school. Put their pants on one leg at a time. Probably played marbles or pogs or whatever kids did in those days."

Jason chortles.

"Any dirt you can share?" I ask, only half kidding.

Jason stalls by taking a long drink of his soda. He looks over his shoulder before answering. "Well. I can tell you that there is some debate on whether more investigation needs to go into the murder of those girls."

"But Silverton doesn't have 'detectives' exactly," I say. "What do you think happened?"

"Exactly," Jason confirms. "We rely on the county for much of our investigative resources. Unfortunately, so far, we've been hearing crickets regarding these girls, all 'coincidentally' drowned in chlorinated water. Also, little to no help with the troubles we've been having with meth and the Regulators. It's no coincidence, I think, that the victims are all women. I'm sure they're connected. Drugs and sex trafficking go hand in hand. We're not that far from Interstate-5, a direct pipeline between Vancouver, B.C. and Tijuana. We're a hub for illegal activity. Nobody would suspect a sleepy little town for being that, which is precisely why it is."

I stiffen at the name of the biker gang; the rest only superficially registers in my mind.

"Any progress on resolving any of this?" I ask.

Jason levels a serious gaze at me and shakes his head.

When he does, with his beard and glasses, he reminds me of someone. So I see an opportunity to lighten the mood.

"I ever tell you that you kind of look like Stephen King?" I ask.

He takes a sip of his soda and bobs his head. "Yes, you have. And when we were younger, you said I looked like Kenny Loggins."

Chapter 21
Koi

It's hot. It's impossibly muggy. Neither of these things should be happening at night. But I wasn't in Kansas anymore. In fact, I wasn't in any state anymore.

My eyes don't even need to be open to know that. I could close my eyes and feel the impossibly moist air on my skin soaking into my shirt, weighing it down with sweat. I could hear it in the language all around me. The casual conversation was not even English.

But it is the smell most of all. *That* smell that came with every Asian country I'd ever been to. I could never identify it. Never found its source. But there it was, always, in every Far East country I'd been to—Thailand, Hong Kong (a country back then), and now Singapore. Part fish market, part fruit market, all enhanced and freighted by the humidity. It is a strange smell to my Western senses. But, I wonder, do Asian people visiting the West have a scent they just can't put their finger on when visiting? Do their heads swivel wildly about in a cab in New York or Dusseldorf, trying to figure out just *what* that smell is?

When I open my eyes, the scene hits me like a neon light between the eyes.

Many cars are fighting to make gains on a narrow street, using no rules or laws that I can discern. People packing the sidewalks, wearing everything from the new and chic to peasant garb from the turn of five centuries ago. All ages. All dark-haired, dark-eyed. From the ugly to the beautiful. And the neon. Colorful pennants, banners, and paper lanterns crisscross the space above the noisy traffic. Above it all is the night sky. There are no stars up there— just tiny bits of darkness in between the skyscrapers.

I've gotten away from all the commotion and am sitting on the edge of a giant fountain. A gargantuan marble mer-lion gushes water from its mouth, projecting it into the harbor. At the water's edge, colorful koi come to me like tame dogs. Orange, white, and velvety black carp so big and so distinctly colored it's hard to believe they're real.

"They want you to feed them," Jade says next to me. She disturbs the water, and the koi come to her. She pets them. Their big sucker-mouths pucker expectantly but only gasp the empty air. "Had I been thinking, I would have got us a bag of treats for them while we were still in the market."

I reach down and pet the fish myself, amazed at their trust.

"Wow," I say, "we have koi ponds back home too, but they don't come to you like this. I guess they're too used to raccoons coming after them."

Jade's sharp eyebrows knit together over her nose. My attention is drawn to her eyes, which are covered in blue contacts. But, of course, it was what I noticed first about her online profile; blue eyes on a darker-skinned Asian face. Picking her out of the crowd at the airport was easy when she picked me up—that and how tall she was. One spindly arm continued to agitate the water, collecting more koi about her finger.

"Raccoons?"

"It's an animal, like a...like a...well, like a raccoon. Kind of like a little panda. They have little people's hands. We call them bandits because they have a mask over their eyes. They eat fish," I explain.

She smiles at my explanation. I love how much she loves my stories.

"Isn't it too cold where you live to have koi ponds?"

"Sometimes," I say. "But koi are very resilient. When it snows and their ponds freeze over, they drift to the bottom of the pond and hibernate. They just slow way, way down, almost like they're dead..."

I freeze. Something nags at my mind. *Almost dead. Play dead.*

"That's amazing," Jade says, looking at the koi as if seeing them for the first time. "They don't get a chance to do that here."

"Well, you have other kinds of fish that do equally amazing things here," I point out, rubbing a red spot on my cheek. "Like fly. Our fish don't fly and smack people in the face."

Jade giggles at the memory of not too long ago when our tour boat on the harbor got caught in a school (flock?) of flying fish. Tourists got pelted left and right by their spiny wing-fins. I did, too.

"Yes, and we have other amazing things. Come," she says, standing and extending her arms to help me up, "I'll show you soft shell crabs. They're delicious."

"Ew. If you say so."

Chapter 22
Corpse Pose

My eyes are closed again. I'm lying down on a moist towel and mat. It's forty-five percent humidity and 104 degrees Fahrenheit. Exactly. I'm in nothing but stretchy shorts—moisture beads on my body. A rivulet pours down my side, tracing the line of my ribs.

The yoga instructor in front of the studio announces after the long moment of silence, "Breathe out... Relax... Slowly sit up... Turn around..."

I finish the sentence for him by singing, "*Bright eyes. Every now and then I get a little bit lonely, but you're never coming around...*"

The yoga instructor slaps his forehead audibly, and the class giggles.

"Okay, enough of that. Everyone, come to rest on your stomachs and place your hands just underneath your shoulders. Your elbows should stick out like a grasshopper but close to the body. Your legs are straight. Tight. Zip them up like one leg. There is only one leg. You have a cobra's tail. Now, raise your chest..."

He continues with the instruction. It's easy for him to say because his mostly naked, scrawny, hippy-ass self is standing on the pedestal at the head of the room. He's sweating too, but only because the place is so humid that anyone would be after forty-five seconds.

I strain as I try to raise my chest as high as possible, but all the previous poses have strained me to my limits. You wouldn't think that putting yourself in a stress position for a minute at a time in these conditions would be that difficult. But try bending over and attempt to stick your head up your butt, for real, and hold that position for a good minute, and you'll see how much you sweat at just room temperature. Now add ninety minutes. 104 degrees. Forty-five percent humidity. And twenty-five more very uncomfortable postures after another.

In the last ten seconds of the pose, Brent counts off the time: "Six... Seven... Eight... Nine... Nine and a half... Nine and three quarters..."

So far into the class, his instruction is annoying and distracting. I struggle to breathe. My lower back feels like Legos coming apart. I'm reminded of all my neck and shoulder problems from a lifetime of scoliosis. Yet, I remind myself the pain is worth it. Before the moisture destroyed it, I had an athletic wrist monitor that showed that I was burning just as many calories and experiencing as much cardio as the boot-camp-style Crossfit classes I used to take. And slow as it may be happening, my health issues, my alignment issues that have dogged me all my adult life, are starting to reverse themselves. At the very least, they stopped advancing in the wrong direction. Give me another thirty years, and maybe I'll correct my thirty-some years of lousy posture.

At the wall where it meets the ceiling are scrawled words of encouragement. The one right in front of me is "Preserver." It sounds mocking.

I'm confident the posture's minute was up long ago.

I know this because right about the minute mark, in this pose, Cobra Pose, I experience the same recurring phenomenon.

It feels like the back of my skull opens up, and fluid drains out. I get light-headed, my eyes roll into the back of my head, and random memories come to me. Well, one in particular. A memory I hadn't recollected for at least a decade. And now it happens almost every time I do this pose.

I had met a girl online and went to visit her in Singapore. Though we are in touch and remain friends, that trip had been mostly unremarkable. We didn't pursue a relationship for many reasons. But now, with Cobra, I recall smells and tiny nuances that had escaped me.

I look over at Brent and glare, hoping he notices and ends the damn pose.

He notices alright, but his scraggly beard turns up in a smile, and his eyes behind those Coke-bottle glasses squint with mirth. With that bushy head of hair and beard, he looks like the Lorax.

"Relax," he finally relents.

Collectively the class groans and flop to their mats, roll over and perform Corpse Pose.

"The hardest pose of all," Brent asserts. "To lie perfectly still and keep your mind focused and alert, yet calm your breath and control your tension is the hardest thing to do. Whoever said being dead was easy?"

I gag, tasting something slimy. My tongue swells as if reacting to shellfish. That was the other thing Cobra did to me. Not just give the sensation of smell, but also taste.

"Does our resident wordsmith remember Singapore again?" he asks.

"Yes," I admit.

"Yoga will do that," Brent explains to the class. "You are increasing the flow of blood and oxygen to parts of your brain little used, stimulating the tissue there, releasing not just memories, but stored sensations and emotions. It is not uncommon to experience feelings that are completely out of context. Or experience taste. What is it you always taste?"

His voice is directed at me now.

"Some kind of seafood," I reply.

"Some people experience sensations long after the class is over. Some people wake up in the middle of the night, performing a pose in bed. Alice over here woke up doing Full Lotus the other night, didn't you, Alice?"

An older lady's voice comes from among the rows of corpses.

She says, "My husband says I drew up all the bed covers, and they were hanging off me like laundry on a clothesline. That's how strongly I was engaging the pose in my sleep."

"Yes, the mind and body are amazing things, capable of doing such things unconsciously," Brent says. "It makes you realize what is good in life."

I roll my eyes behind my eyelids.

"What else is good in life?" he asks.

No one answers. I feel him standing over me. I look up and see his giant spectacles peering down at me.

"What is good in life?" he asks again.

I clear my throat and do my best Arnold Schwarzenegger impersonation while quoting from *Conan the Barbarian*. "Destroy your enemies, see them driven before you, and hear the lamentation of the women."

Chapter 23
Jewels

"That's it," Stephen says. "It's incredible, isn't it? How it all comes together. Every little experience would have something to contribute, even if you didn't think so at the time."

"Yes, you should be more appreciative of everything at every moment," Clark adds. "Live in the moment. Relish it! Collect the moments like jewels in a crown."

Homer scribbles feverishly on the pad, not even looking at the page, just staring at me as he draws.

Chapter 24
Sis

It is a short drive to Mt. Angel from Silverton. Five miles. Five minutes.

Five minutes is not long, but it is enough to get lost in my thoughts and feel my stomach knot up. I reach up and nudge the rosary hanging from my rearview mirror and set it to swinging. When I do, I look in the mirror and not just imagine Jesus sitting in the back seat; I see him.

"How do you think she'll take the news? About my break?" I ask him.

His only response is an enigmatic smile before turning to gaze at the passing countryside. I hadn't expected an answer, but still, I had hoped for one.

I pass a gurgling fountain upon entering town, then turn onto College Street and head east.

If Silverton was an example of Americana, painted in pastel Mediterranean colors, then Mt. Angel displayed Bavarian Old World charm. Gabled buildings. More wood and plaster, less brick and metal. All daubed in earth tones. There are four clock towers (counting the one in the Abbey). Each reaches higher into the sky than the last, starting with the stout frontier-era train station turret, then the colorful glockenspiel, then St. Mary's church spire that threatens to pierce the moon when it passes over.

There isn't enough time to admire them. I have to see my sister.

It's a short trip to the far edge of town. There, I take the road that winds through tall evergreens. Unlike most other brushy forested areas in the Willamette Valley, the slope of Mt. Angel is primarily open in between the trees, almost as if manicured by woodland gnomes. Green moss carpets the forest floor. The place already exudes peace and tranquility.

Along the road are little Bavarian huts—slender, upright structures with shingled roofs. Open in the front, a rail separates visitors from the interior containing a Station of the Cross in the form of a museum-worthy painting. People visit several of the fourteen stations, praying or contemplating the image therein even as I pass.

The tranquility of the scene causes the knot in my stomach to loosen up. Doing so reminds me of a knot in the first place and why, which ironically causes the knot to return.

My flip-flopping stomach persuades me to pull to the side of the road with what feels like an anxiety attack. My car comes to rest next to one of the huts. I think it's the 5th Station of the Cross, but my mind is too far elsewhere to confirm that.

My grip squeezes on the wheel in rhythm with each of my deep breaths. I'm vaguely aware that Jesus is still in the backseat.

I close my eyes and take an extra-long breath. When I open them again, the landscape is glowing more emerald than before, slashed here and there by yellow sun rays piercing the canopy of evergreens.

The strangulation of the steering wheel continues as I speak.

"Sis won't be angry. She won't judge," I reason out loud, whether to myself or to Jesus, I'm not sure. "She'll be disappointed, I'm sure, but won't say so."

Sis probably won't be disappointed either, but guilt's ability to magnify things makes me feel otherwise.

I'm speaking, of course, about my sister. Sis. The woman who had helped set me on my spiritual journey precisely because of her lack of judging and preachiness.

In the past, I had assumed to become Christian meant you had to be preachy and judge-y. The very things that had always pushed me away from God.

Not so with my sister. You would have thought that the wild woman with a rebellious streak would have been perfectly suited to become the *Annoying Christian*, but she hadn't. Instead, despite fundamentally remaining the same headstrong and tough person, she never beat you over the head with her faith. Instead, she demonstrated daily without words the peace she had found.

That is what had impressed me most: that she had found God while remaining herself. She cemented this notion with a single illuminating sentence while gripping my wrist with that strength of hers coupled with an almost challenging gaze. "There are as many different roads to God as there are people. Yours will look completely different. Never forget that."

That had pleased me. That had been my foot in the door in my own search. But now here I was, stuck halfway in that door while it closed on my body, crushing it like an intruder.

Another deep breath, then my breathing is almost back to normal.

It's not just a confession that I'm here for today. I've just been away for far too long. I've neglected my family. Time to reconnect. It will be good to see the girl who used to hold me down and punch me in the arm until I cried, "Uncle."

But first, I will have to tell her about the break. My desire to catch my breath before continuing my climb to the summit.

Under my grip, the steering wheel is undoubtedly strangled to death by now.

Enough thinking. Enough soul searching. Time to get moving. Nothing ever happened by sitting still.

"Well, let's get this show on the road," I say, again out loud and to no one in particular. As I put the car in gear, I glance over at the hut by which I've parked. It is indeed the 5th Station of the Cross. In the painting, Simon of Cyrene is carrying the cross for Christ. Simon had started out unwillingly, but by the end, he was a changed man.

I draw the deepest breath yet. "I may not currently have enough faith to carry the cross for you," I address the rearview mirror, "but apparently, I have enough to be your chauffeur."

Jesus joins me in a smile as I pull away from the shoulder and continue on my way.

Before reaching the top of the hill, I turn and follow the asphalt to a parking lot along the embankment. I park near one of the concrete staircases leading up to the church.

I run up the stairs, two at a time, and catch my breath at the top. From here, Mt. Angel Abbey looks like a mountaintop college campus. Which it is. A seminary, or school, for those pursuing the vocation of priesthood in the Catholic Church. It is also a monastery, home to an order of Benedictine monks, who manufacture soap and—like all good monks—beer.

Much like the town below, coming here is much like stepping into Europe. I pass two buildings and enter a central promenade that leads to a basilica with an open-air belfry. As I approach, the huge bells come alive, a cacophonous barrage with no discernible tune other than to announce to the world that it was "time."

The sun is low in the sky. In winter, it would be completely dark. As it is, there is plenty of daylight left. I make my way through an open-air atrium upheld by squat, rose-colored marble columns. I mount the few steps and pass through the columns to the double doors inside, then into the basilica's narthex. Here is another set of double doors flanked on either side by glass windows into the church.

I dip my hand in the holy water font next to the door and cross myself. The moisture blooms on my shirt just below my collar bone.

The light inside is dim except for in the choir section. Modern electric lights illuminate the rows of wood seats on either side of the altar area at the front of the church, where the rows face each other. Men in dark robes and cassocks are filtering into those pews from the sides, taking up seats, preparing books before them.

The church is high-vaulted with giant wooden crossbeams. Marble walls and pillars flank a balcony area with an ornate railing. I could describe this place for pages and pages. Suffice to say, it is beautiful. Serene. Holy. Even people of a different faith, or no faith, can feel it. The place is special.

Yet, the pews host only a handful of people. Some are on the kneelers praying. I approach one of them in particular. My sister is wearing a traditional lacy mantilla that covers her head. She's also wearing a heavy cotton shirt buttoned along the side of her chest.

I genuflect in the direction of the tabernacle and take a seat next to her. Aside from an acknowledging head-tilt in my direction, she does not break the reverence of her prayer. When I return the gesture, I notice that against the wall, the wrought iron votive stand is overflowing with candles, spilling along the floor like flowing lava.

Soon, the bells stop their tolling, and movement among the men in the choir has calmed.

One young man in studious glasses stands, holding a book before him, and begins to sing. His opening note is long and vibrant. There are no accompanying instruments, only the song in Latin. The acoustics magnify and enrich his gift. His brethren follow suit, creating a chorus that pulls darkness from my chest and replaces it with scintillating light.

Some in the congregation join in singing, such as they can, following the pamphlets collected from the narthex. I could have grabbed one myself from beneath the schedule board of the Liturgy of the Hours, but I'm perfectly aware of my voice and its limitations.

The chant rises and falls, vacillating between a cloudburst and a drop of rain threatening to drip off a leaf.

The Liturgy of the Hours is the culmination of the monk's duty to praise God continuously. It is not just song but prayer. The times of day devoted to this prayer, like clockwork, ushered in by the bells, have names that are just as beautiful as the songs themselves. Vigils, Lauds, Vespers, and Compline. Now it is Vespers. I always felt like the word sounded like "whispers," and it wasn't hard to imagine the Holy Spirit was here doing just that, flowing about the room like an elemental force.

When it is over, the men in robes quietly melt into the shadows at the head of the church.

The people in the pews stand and migrate to the door at the back.

"I heard you were in town," Sis says.

We hug.

She is shorter than me. Brown-haired. Brown-eyed. Darker of complexion. *She* looks like an Indian. And she is beautiful too. More maternally beautiful nowadays, less the rocker chick she used to be in high school. When most girls tried their best to look like Madonna, my sister effectively pulled off the Pat Benatar look. To this day, if I come across some guy from high school who leers at me and asks, "How's your sister doing, man?" I'd reply, "Fuck you. That's how she's doing. Fuck you very much."

These days, however, in her mantilla, she looks more like *the* Madonna.

"How's it going, little brother?" she says a little sadly. "Besides the obvious, I mean. I heard about your work."

The knot in my stomach winds to its tightest. After a deep breath, I grab one end of the knot and pull all at once, like ripping off a scab. It unravels, and everything spills out of me in a rush.

I tell her about the emptiness that peaked on Good Friday. The frantic waving into the abyss. The exhaustion. The need for a break. I even use the calculus and organic chemistry example. When I finish, I involuntarily give a little bark of a nervous laugh.

"Sooo, that is pretty much what's occupying my thoughts these days," I add after her only response is a slightly tilted head and a sympathetic smile. "Other than that, I'm fine. The good news is that I finally have that time I always wished I had to spend with family and friends. I plan on making the most of it."

"That's the spirit." A fuller smile blooms on her face. "You're very welcome to come by the house. Your nieces and nephews will be happy to see you for more than a day at Christmas and Thanksgiving. We're having dinner soon—come then."

And just like that, my existential crisis is a non-event.

"Er, I'll be sure to do that." I scratch my head.

"In the meantime, I'll be praying for you," she adds.

"Thanks, I can use all the help I can get."

Absently mindedly, I genuflect and move toward the narthex. Sis does the same. This is not going how I imagined, and I'm not quite ready to dismiss it as a non-event.

I turn to the altar and the crucifix above it. In this particular church, how they're positioned, both seem miles away at the end of a long aisle between the choir seating and organ.

"You ever question why he does what he does?" I ask. "Like, why would I spend all those years in that job, terrible at it, but not finally given the boot until recently? What was the point? The purpose? You'd think I'd know what it is by now."

"Have you asked him?" she asks.

"All the time."

"And?"

I turn to her and smile sadly. "He's not very talkative." She raises a finger, but I cut her off. "I know, I just have to 'listen,' or, 'He works in mysterious ways,' and so on."

"Actually," she says, laughing, "I was going to deploy, 'Everything happens for a reason.' He wouldn't give this to you unless he knew you could handle it. Have you tried visualization prayer? I find it helpful."

"What, like picturing him right here, having a conversation, that technique?"

"Yes, that, or inserting yourself into the scene of scripture as you contemplate it," she adds. "Like imagining yourself at the foot of the cross."

"I can see him just fine," I say, a little bit more angrily than I intend. "He's right here." I wave to the altar area, and sure enough, there is Jesus staring at me.

"Then what's the problem?" she asks.

"The problem is the guy never says anything," I say in exasperation, my voice rising to echo in the building. "It's kind of creepy, really."

She laughs. "Well, it's good to know you don't have any trouble with doubting his existence. That's all you need, really. Trust me, the rest will fall into place when it's time."

"Yeah, you're probably right."

I read between the lines of what she is saying—*You're overanalyzing*—and decide to let go for now.

We walk to the door and soon are standing outside near the rose-marble columns.

While there, six Mexican women pass us to enter the church. They wear mantillas like my sister. They are stout women, and their weather-worn faces bear distinct ethnic features of indigenous people. Yet, it's not just the sun etched in their faces that catches my attention. It's the magnitude of sadness in their eyes. Sadness from a well so deep it has never seen daylight. I almost gasp at it.

"Family of one of the murdered girls," Sis whispers after they have passed. She crosses herself. "They've been coming every night since the poor girl died, lighting candles every time."

I remember the lava flow of votives. Shame rises in my face when I realize there are people in this world genuinely suffering, and my issues are ridiculous by comparison.

"What do you think?" I ask distantly, thoughtful. "Is it like they say? A serial killer? In Silverton?"

Sis shrugs, removing her mantilla and replacing it with a baker's hat from her pocket, the same color as her shirt. "Serial killer. Angry boyfriend. Mugger. There is no lack of evil in the world." She changes tone, clearly wanting to change the subject. "Can I get you a coffee or something before I go back to work?"

"Yeah, sure, I'd like that," I reply, snapping out of my reverie.

We walk to one of the nearby buildings. She punches in a code on the keypad to the door and leads us inside.

The interior looks like most any older college. Lots of dark, oiled wood. Classrooms and faculty offices. She takes me to a staircase that winds down. It reminds me of something out of Hogwarts. At the bottom is an expansive cafeteria populated by many round tables and chairs. On the far side, large floor-to-ceiling windows catch the twilight.

"Make yourself comfortable," she says. "I'll be right back with the coffee."

She walks past the buffet area and disappears into the kitchen through swinging doors.

I meander over to the windows and take in the incredible view. From here, you can see the Willamette Valley in all its glory. The emigrants on the Oregon Trail called their destination God's country for a reason. Farmland rolls in every direction, flaunting every shade of green. Some fields are still being plowed for crops, creating rich plots so dark they are black. Tonight, it looks more like God's quilt. At the foot of Mt. Angel are row upon row of wire strung across tall wood poles as if telephone poles were holding a convention. Dangling from the cables, however, is a jungle of vines. Hops. Destined for every domestic beer bottle in America.

My sister returns with a cup of coffee. I take the little ceramic mug, and she joins me with her own. She touches my cup with hers.

"Welcome home, little brother."

Chapter 25
Break

Stephen sets the notebook down, being the last to have read my next scene.

I wait patiently, eventually raising my eyebrows at Stephen as he sucks on the straw to his diet soda, making a slurping sound. His brow is furrowed in thought.

You can do better than that," Stephen admonishes.

"I agree," Clark concurs. "You have better imagery and metaphors in you."

Homer nods. "Draw from something personal. That always creates the best realism."

"Okay, fine," I grouse, and take a drink of my beer, then pick up the notepad.

I turn a new page, click on the pen, and begin writing.

Over the speaker comes the Muslim call to prayer.

Chapter 26
The Tapestry

The call to prayer comes haunting and beautiful, echoing all over Marrakech.

The sun flattens as it sets, spilling like a red egg-yolk over the horizon. Even down here in the bazaar, the redness finds its way into the winding and twisting mud-brick alleys. A vehicle could barely pass through here. Only the occasional power line or streetlight gives any indication that this isn't thirteenth-century Morocco but the dawn of the twenty-first.

The wind infiltrates the bazaar as well, kicking up dust that harasses us as we move along. The air blows hot. It is still over a hundred degrees, but it is a dry heat—the sort of dryness that would keep a mummified pharaoh in pristine shape for millennia. I love it.

Our guide comes to a door studded with iron bolts and a little cage about a peephole. He knocks with a large iron ring. The wood is polished by time and sandstorms.

I hug my traveling companion, Jade, turning my back into the wind to guard her against the sand. The three of us wait only a bit, then a little slide door opens behind the cage. Our guide exchanges a few words with an unseen attendant.

The little door slams shut, and the big door laboriously opens. Our guide motions us to enter.

Inside is a frail man in a robe and fez. His heavy mustache can't hide his smile. He bobs his head, greeting us in the language that has followed us all about the streets all day.

I don't know Arabic, or Berber, but I do say, "Merci beaucoup, nous sommes trés enchanté être içi."

The man's eyes widen, and he bobs his head again. "Trés bien! Trés bien!"

He gestures up the stone stairs in the narrow hall to daylight at the top. Our guide urges us on so the old man can shut the door behind us.

At the top is a big room with expansive windows opposite the stairwell. Before I enter, I stop to kick my khaki boots on the last step to knock the dust off. When I do, their metal buckles jingle.

Clay pillars hold up the ceiling, and alternating blue and white tiles create a pattern on the walls. Tapestries and carpets of every shape, size, and color fill the room, and the cushions on the floor are just as diverse. A hint of jasmine fills the air. Near the window, activity is revolving around what looks like some sort of loom. Though no lamps are lit, the room catches the red sun coming through the windows. I can see much of Marrakech from this height: a sea of square tan buildings, bathed in red, bristling with a forest of TV antennas and power lines. Had we come a few hours earlier, the sky would have been the most brilliant cobalt you've ever seen in your life.

"Please, sit, sit," our guide says in heavily accented English. The jolly short man is unwrapping his scarf to reveal his trimmed beard and mustache set in a cherubim face the color and texture of polished mahogany. He gestures to a pair of ottomans next to an ornately wooden table on short legs.

My companion removes her face covering as well, sneezing at residual dust. She blinks her eyes clear, enough to disturb her blue contact lens a few millimeters, revealing a slice of the dark iris beneath. A colorful headscarf protects her hair, and for a moment, she could be from almost anywhere between here and the farthest edge of Asia. More than once, children would come up to her to practice their English. They would ask her if she was related to Bruce Lee. After that, she covered up to deflect the assumption.

She takes a seat, and I join her as I remove the scarf from my face and take off the aviator sunglasses with side leather shields. I let them dangle around my neck by their cord. Our guide joins us as a woman comes from another room and sets the table with china and silverware. Soon she is pouring hot tea, and the smell of mint supplants the jasmine in the room.

We touch cups with each other and our guide.

"As I promised, soon you will see the best carpets in all of Marrakech," our guide says, his smile still vast and frozen in place.

"How's that grab you, Jade?" I say to my companion. "Isn't this more interesting than staying in Paris? Though we could always go back if you like."

"No, no," she says, taking a sip of her tea. "This your vacation. Was your turn to choose."

"You have to admit, the shopping is better here."

She smiles and nods enthusiastically, my adventure companion.

I turn to our guide. "And this is where they do it? Where they make the rugs? By hand?"

"Yes! Yes!" Big smile.

"May I watch?" I gesture to the women at work.

"Yes! Yes!"

I pick up my teacup and saucer and approach the women at work while sipping my mint delight.

There are three women. One, covered in a traditional veil and robe, must be much older than the others because her posture is stooped with age. She ferries basket after basket of dyed wool to a spinning wheel where a pre-teen girl expertly feeds the wool from a basket into the wheel that turns it into thread. No headdress or veil covers her short black hair, shiny as raven wings. Her big brown eyes follow her work, but she spares a glance to smile at me.

The woman at the loom is middle-aged. She is handsome, wearing a headscarf and dark kohl around her hazel eyes. Her skin is medium-brown, lighter than her daughter's, and her forearms ripple with muscles and pop with veins as she deftly throws a wooden shuttle horizontally across the "V" of threads strung between a pair of wood frames. The wooden shuttle is attached to the filament produced by the spinning wheel.

Every time the weaving woman throws the shuttle, she steps on a pedal, and the wood frames came together to the sound of *whoosh! clack!* The transient thread becomes entrapped in the "V" threads, growing the piece of fabric.

I watch intently, amazed at the colors and attention to detail. The weaving woman knows or trusts that the spinning girl will change wool color, incorporating it into the gradually emerging pattern.

Whoosh! Clack!

I strain my eyes, trying to decipher the images. This is no basic repeating pattern but intricate images that tell a story. There is a newborn baby, a toddler, a young man, and...

Whoosh! Clack!

...a face. A familiar face. Mine.

Whoosh! Clack!

The old woman approaches the thread strung between the spinning wheel and the loom. Hunched over, she reveals a pair of coarse iron shears. She touches the moving thread from underneath with her free hand, letting it glide over her wrinkled hand. By doing so, she stops its wild bouncing and can bring the shears to bear on the thread. She inserts the fabric line into the "V" of the metal instrument, and as the thread passes through, it catches on the lower blade and begins to fray ever so slightly.

The old woman looks up, and her veil falls away, revealing a blind eye and toothless, grimacing smile.

Whoosh! Clack!

I stagger back and drop my teacup and saucer. They shatter on the floor.

Chapter 27
Break

"Ah, much, much better," Homer states. "I knew you had it in you. It often takes us a few stabs at it, yes?"

Stephen and Clark murmur in agreement.

"I usually draw rough-cuts several times before settling and sending it off to the editor," Homer elaborates, then sets his teacup down. "Speaking of drawing." He reaches under the table and reproduces his tablet, and commences to swipe away with the piece of charcoal.

"What are you making there that is so important?" I ask.

He winks. "All in good time, all in good time."

I raise my glass to take another sip of beer. A drop of water splashes in it before it reaches my mouth.

Chapter 28
Daisy Chains and Dandelions

I am quick to take my sister up on her offer for dinner and, a few days later, find myself driving into a hillside neighborhood not all that far from Mom and Dad's.

Driving along, I slow to a crawl to examine a new housing development rising where once was a copse of oak trees. Not just any housing, but those "tiny homes" crammed into as small a space as possible. My head wags sadly at the thought of the missing trees I used to play among, and I move on.

It is suppertime, but the summer sun still rules the sky.

I park at the curb in front of an old two-story house on the downhill side of the street. Despite its age, the pale-green house is in good shape and exudes a lived-in quality, which is not surprising since it's been home to generations of my brother-in-law's family.

I descend a few brick steps, and as I pass through a creaky gate, a Labrador mix announces my arrival with languid bark.

"Hey, Strider." He snuffles my pant leg. I bend over and give him a good rubbing: the toll to enter. Satisfied, he wanders off, and I continue to the front door. Scattered about the patchy yard is an army of dolls in various stages of loved, Legos, Nerf footballs, and broken pieces of giant chalk. The chalk has done its work on the sidewalk between the gate and porch, creating a wobbly hopscotch grid.

A tuxedo cat sits on an old birdcage on the porch. She stops licking herself long enough to give me a once-over.

"Nice to see you too," I say before knocking on the door.

My sister's voice invites me in. She's in the kitchen across the living room, setting a pot down on the kitchen table with giant gray oven mitts. She's swapped her chef's uniform for a traditional apron.

Sis points her chin up and calls, "Boys, girls, your uncle is here."

Cattle stampede overhead and rumble down the stairs.

I don't have to wait long. Six children of varying ages between four and twelve flow from around the corner, squealing with delight. Four girls, two boys. They're all jumpers, skinned knees, and missing front teeth. There are some dark-haired children in the bunch, but mostly they are blonde, with yards of cornsilk between them.

"Gunky! Gunky," they cry, holding up their hands.

I bend down and hug as many as I can in a single embrace, squeezing.

I feel their glow, and their joy and the pain in the back of my head dissolves away, forgotten. Satisfied, for now, I relinquish them and stand to take a good look at them. Then, with a cacophony of giggles, they dance a circle about me, holding hands, swirling faster and faster until their feet lift off the earth, and they become a daisy chain of angels floating near the ceiling.

My heart is full.

As Sis ladles juice over a roast in the oven, she says, "We'll eat when Rod arrives. He should be here soon. Sarah knows you're in town but couldn't make it tonight. She's all grown up and working now, don't you know?"

I stand on the aged-polished wooden floor of the living room beneath a chandelier of yellowed crystals, taking in the family's worn furniture. Madonna and St. Patrick statuettes, rosary beads, and portraits of Jesus and Mary adorn the walls and shelves, sharing space with Disney DVDs and Harry Potter books.

Sis stands at the back screen door, holding it invitingly ajar, causing the spring to creak in protest.

"No, let's go to the backyard while we wait; it's a lovely day." She exits, letting the screen door slap behind her.

I take the hand of the nearest niece and follow Sis out, trailing the daisy chain of children. After the last sibling bounds through, I catch the door and keep it from clapping hard against the frame. Passing through the kitchen, aromas are replaced by the smells of freshly cut grass and dandelions as I step into the warm sun.

Sis is already sitting in a lawn chair next to a wooden cable spool. It has been turned on its side and repurposed as a table. It's an old spool, but much care went into sanding and polishing its surface to make it a fashionable piece of lawn furniture.

The children spread out—some to the elaborate treehouse, some to the full-size basketball court, some to the lush grass. I smile at all this play and take a seat next to my sister.

Surely Sis and I were this carefree once. I vaguely recall it. It was a long time ago. Before we had to grow up to sales jobs, punching customers in the face, and murdered women in the creek.

"What are you thinking about?" she asks.

"Hmm?" I say.

"You have that look on your face. You went to that place you go to." She leans toward me with her chin on her fist and a smile on her lips.

There are two tall glasses of iced tea on the table. I don't recall how they got there. Beads of moisture collect on their sides and slip down the glass. As I watch the bead fall, I feel a similar sensation of falling, as if drifting with a crackling sound. Are those screams I hear?

"Oh, I guess I was just thinking about when we were kids. We played like this," I respond, shaking the drifting feeling away. "I think sometimes that is why you had so many children. How can you be unhappy when there is this much happiness going on around you?"

Her smile wavers just a fraction, but her eyes never leave me, probing. "Maybe I like that there is never a dull moment, and there is plenty of love to go around."

"We had plenty of love, with just the two of us." I shrug, sipping at the tea.

"You can never have too much of a good thing," she counters, then asks with her eyebrows coming together in concern, "Are you unhappy, then?"

I try not to groan. I didn't come for a pity party. Or to be lectured. But what is family good for but talking?

"Well, yeah, of course I am." I shift uncomfortably in my chair. "The whole unemployment thing and what we talked about at the Abbey has got me down."

"No, I mean besides that," she says, still smiling, though a bit sad now. "That will all pass. I mean, are you unhappy in general?"

My chair-shifting turns to full-on fidgeting. "Hell, I don't know. I guess my current situation is like having a compound fracture..."

Sis's frown deepens at the analogy.

"...having a bone sticking out of my skin kind of distracts from whether I'm running a fever, you know?"

She smiles, understanding the analogy now, but keeps pressing. "Having a family of your own might help. If you have seven kids, you don't have time to notice your own fevers or compound fractures."

I'm careful to shunt my scoff towards humor rather than scorn. "If I had a family right now, that would be just one more thing to worry about. Besides..." Right about then, little Casey climbs into my lap and looks up at me with a big smile. "Why start a family when you have enough for both of us?"

"Whatcha talkin' 'bout?" Casey asks, stroking my clean-shaven face.

"Grown-up stuff," I explain. "Boring stuff. You wouldn't like it."

"Gunky, are you going to stay the night? We're going to sleep in the treehouse."

"That sounds stupendous. I just might have to consider that."

"Say yes! Say yes!"

"Maybe Gunky will let you know after he's done with the tall-people talk," Sis says gently, but with no room to argue.

I look up at Sis and give her my best sad frown. When I return my gaze to Casey, I do a double-take. It's not Casey lying in my lap; it's Mayana now.

She groans with disappointment and crawls off my lap. "Oh, okay."

She bounds into the grass to play with Casey.

I'm still staring at them with a mystified smile, wondering how they pulled off the switch-a-roo so cleverly without me noticing, when Sis picks up her last train of thought.

"What about Jade? Minerva?" she asks.

I fidget again. Retake a drink of iced tea.

"Jade and I email each other happy birthdays. That's about it anymore," I confess. "Minerva should be here visiting her family come the holidays. I'll probably see her then. Have dinner or something."

Sis is pitying me. I know it. I feel the lecture coming on.

"That's not what I mean," she says. "Why didn't you start a family with one of them?"

I rub the back of my head. The pain has ebbed a little, but a new pressure builds in my skull. "I dunno. My relationships seem to suffer from my inability to embrace *anything*. It just never seems to work out. It never seems quite right. Then again, I'm not sure if there is a 'right.' Wouldn't know it if it hit me in the face. How did Mom and Dad know it was right? How did you and Rod? Maybe God has something else in mind for me."

I resist the inclination to look over my shoulder to see if Jesus is there with an answer. I dismiss the urge, because of course, he isn't, and even if he were, he'd have no audible answers.

"Or," I add, taking an agitated sip of tea, "it's this memory of mine. Prevents me from having normal relationships."

Sis frowns. "How's that?"

"I can't forget. Every little negative thing anyone has ever said and done in a relationship feels like it happened the day before.

The hour before. It's hard to forgive people when you're still stewing over what they've done to you," I explain.

It's Sis's turn to scoff, and she takes a sip. "So stop dwelling on the negative."

"Ah, but don't you see? It's a universal rule that it's much easier to destroy than to create. Human nature gravitates toward the negative, despite our best efforts."

Sis rolls her eyes, sets her drink down, and sits back in her chair with her arms crossed. "I think you're over-thinking, not over-remembering," she counters. "You know, Eva is back in town too. Helping her folks with the restaurant. Maybe you should—"

"Maybe we should talk about something more cheerful," I interject, putting on an exaggerated smile. "Let's talk about mental illness."

Sis bursts out laughing.

"I know, okay," I admit, "but at least it changes the subject."

She gently kicks a rubber ball back to the children. "What do you want to know?"

"There is a...history in the family, yes?" I start, rubbing the back of my head. "You're older. Maybe you remember. What it was like, I mean. How it looked. How it...manifested."

Her expression falls. More blank than concerned. Thoughtful, maybe.

"Yes, I suppose. Certain family members struggled with schizophrenia. It was pretty obvious when they were having an episode. High energy. Almost frantic. Emotional over some detail. It could be annoying but harmless, or it could be quite scary."

"Scary?"

She jiggles the ice in her glass, paying it a little too much attention. "Aunt Sharon, before she passed, would grip us by the wrists and shake us, telling us not to eat cheese because the government had poisoned it. That sort of thing."

I quietly ponder that. I don't remember. Then again, I was very young when Aunt Sharon had lived with us that time. Like all the women in the family, she was pretty, with the long black hair of a Native American woman, straight as a board, and parted down the middle. The rest is a blur.

Or maybe not. A walk in the countryside with her and Dad. She stopped to look at a dead tree, and then she was in tears.

"Do you think you are seeing things?" Sis breaks my reverie. Her tone is serious, but she is careful to add just the right amount of non-judging in it.

I look at the glass of iced tea. At Casey and Mayana.

"No, no," I'm quick to say. "But I've been experiencing... oddities."

"I thought you worked out the things caused by your sleep deprivation by changing your diet. It's been a long time, hasn't it, since you walked or saw things in your sleep?"

"Yes," I say, taking a sip. "No sleepwalking that I know of. Nothing I'd call an episode of sleep paralysis. But the hours I was putting in at work and the stress I was under were causing other things, I think."

"Like?"

"Memory lapses, which is odd for me, because you know, my memory normally does the opposite of that."

"Mom told me about your work. The fight you had. That kind of stress would do all kinds of things to anybody's brain." Sis rests her chin on her fist, scrutinizing me.

"Yeah, maybe. But I'm missing entire *days*."

Sis is quiet for a while. Her face shows no emotion other than loving attention. "That's why you're here, isn't it? To get some rest? To be at home. To reboot. I bet in a short while you'll be back to normal. You'll see. As for the other question you're not asking out loud, the answer is no."

"What question is that?"

"Are you crazy?"

I sit for a while.

"You are a creative type, remember?" she reassures. "Your mind handles things differently. I imagine it especially handles stress and trauma differently. It will all work out."

Or maybe I *am* crazy.

As if reading my thoughts, she reaches over and touches my hand. I grip it back.

"I guess I should thank Dad for the imagination I inherited from him," I say, putting on a brave grin. "Like 'ghost poop.' Remember when he told us that?"

She laughs. "Yes. For the longest time, I actually believed that Styrofoam packing peanuts were ghost turds."

Chapter 29
The Feather Boa Constrictor

I stare at the computer screen, listening to the dial-up screech in the background. It's driving me crazy. Mostly because I know once I make the connection, loading web pages will be just as slow, making my tasks excruciating.

"Did you get it working, honey?" Mom calls from the other room.

"Sort of. I mean, it's trying," I call back.

"That's more than we've been able to do for a while," she replies.

I glare at the screen, willing it to go faster, but it doesn't care. The little computer-and-telephone-wires icon in the center of the monitor maintains a sad-face icon next to it. I lean back in the creaky old office chair and stare at the ceiling, then around the room. The old bedroom, which had alternately belonged to Sis or me, is now a storage room full of cardboard boxes, book-filled shelves, furniture, piles of tax documents, and an old exercise bike. The desk, chair, and computer are relatively new additions. Placed here when the reality could no longer be ignored, and even my parents had to acknowledge the internet age.

I reach the shelf above the computer for a thick paperback, sandwiched between a homemade ceramic ashtray and a dog. The ceramics were some of my finer work from fifth-grade art class. The book is *Dhalgren* by Samuel R. Delany. One of Father's books. I've always meant to read it but was always intimidated by its size. I thumb through the pages, then glance back at the sad face icon.

At this rate, I just might have time to read this after all.

The sad face turns happy, and the browser opens to the local phone company. I sit up in the chair and put the book back.

"You know you guys can get internet through your cable provider, right?" I shout.

"It's just as crappy, trust me," Dad responds from somewhere else in the house.

"How about Dish?" I ask.

Mom chimes in. "Worse. Plus, some bizarre things happen, like a continuous live feed from the International Space Station, and nothing else for hours at a time."

"Really?" My voice sounds more dubious than I mean it to. "That doesn't seem possible."

"Tell me about it," Dad says. I hear the refrigerator door open.

"You should get that fixed," I suggest, shoving a pile of documents on the desk to better position the keyboard.

"Sure thing, Mr. Money-Pants." I can hear Dad's snort from here. "It wouldn't matter. It's Silverton. Things are wonky here."

You can say that again. I tap away at the keyboard. Sure enough, it's slow going, but I can access the various job search sites I'm registered with. I have no new messages. Not real ones, anyway. Plenty of spam from agencies promising to find you just the right job, but for exorbitant fees. The headhunters I've been working with are frustratingly absent, so I write a couple of them with the same kind of message: *Any news? What's the status of that one job posting at XYZ Company?* Etc., etc.

None of the places I've applied to have responded. Not even so much as a thank you for submitting my resume. So I scan the job boards. Nothing sounds appropriate for my qualifications.

Qualifications. I know I don't have any. I spent the last ten years squandering my hard-earned chemistry education as a sales representative, never developing the actual chemistry aspect, just floundering at something I deplored inside the golden cage of a decent salary.

I click through the titles and categories. But, since losing my job, reality has settled in, and I realize that a bachelor's in chemistry is not that helpful in life. Even a master's is just a stepping stone to a real career that requires a doctorate.

Slumped under the weight of it all, I switch to another job search site. Log in. Browse the "Science & Technical Services" category. Lab technician. *Maybe later, when I'm truly desperate.* Crime scene clean-up technician. *No.* Waste treatment operator. *Hell no.* Water softener outside sales. *Definitely no.* Pharmaceutical Sales. *Tempting, but still no. It's a trap.*

A post catches my eye.

Tesseract Chemical Industries data analyst, the post states, followed by an appealing salary figure.

I click on it and read the job description, and my heart leaps. I can do this. I reread the blurb and qualifications, making sure I didn't miss something. It has great benefits from a reputable company in the Hillsboro area, or as the media likes to refer to it, the "Silicon Forest." I read it correctly. I can do this.

I click on the application link.

However, I sit back in my chair and groan when the link opens up on a multiple questionnaire page with a worksheet. I hate these. It's not a simple matter of uploading your resume, which I was hoping for, but more like writing multiple essays to answer the employer's questions and restructuring your work history into the format they require. Basically, you're reinventing the wheel for over an hour...just so you can get ignored.

I sweep my hair back, roll up my sleeves, and dive in. I copy and paste parts of my resume into what fields I can on the application. Education and work history, mostly. I select from drop-down menus my relevant skills. Excel, Word, technical writing, foreign language... I pause when entering "French." Again, something I've always kicked myself for. I should have taken Spanish. Nobody cares about French.

I shake the thought off and continue.

I come to the essay questions and groan again.

Why do you think you are qualified for this position? What are your best qualities? Where do you see yourself in five years? Describe how you resolved a confrontation with a coworker. What do you want most out of life?

"Are you kidding me?" I shout.

I sit back in the chair, chewing my knuckle.

It's like they somehow looked inside my head and knew all the wrong things to ask.

"Okay, fine," I say, sitting up and hovering over the keyboard like the Phantom of the Opera over an organ. "I've written entire novels. I can do this."

The keyboard clicks away. And I lie. Lie like a bastard.

Half an hour later, I hit "Send" and sit back in the chair, sweating, my stomach in knots.

I use the bathroom, get a drink of water, and go back to the computer. And spend much the day in the same fashion. Most of my research leads to dead ends. I apply to a couple more jobs that I already know I don't want, but I apply anyway to make it feel like I made *some* kind of progress.

When I disconnect from the internet, shut off the computer, and stumble in the family room, I'm exhausted. Mom is behind the bar. Dad is snoozing in his comfy chair.

Mom asks, "Why are you sweating?"

"Well, I have to pedal really hard to keep the internet going on that computer."

Mom rolls her eyes. I join her behind the bar. She's pulling an orange juice from the mini-fridge.

"It's not that bad," she says, pouring the juice into a glass. "Besides, don't you have a laptop?"

"Not anymore. That stayed with the job, along with the company car, company gas card, and expense account."

I lean against the bar, bracing myself and staring into the reflection of a glass as if it's a magic mirror capable of showing me my future. Instead, it's blank except for my own face.

"Sweetie, you need to take a break. Drink?" Mom holds up a bottle of vodka just before pouring it into her juice.

I wave the offer off. "I'll take a break. Maybe go for a walk. Go downtown. Dunno."

"Any luck with the job hunt?" Mom asks, taking a sip of her drink.

I sigh. "Turns out nobody wants you if *you* don't know what you want."

She rubs my back when I place my face into the folds of my arms on the bar.

"Maybe being home for a while will give you some perspective," she suggests.

I look up, nod. "I think that's why I'm here. That and being at my house in Vancouver left me in a rut. I needed a change of scenery. There's nothing I can do there I can't do here for job searching. It's all internet these days." I smile. "Even slow internet."

My attention freezes. *My house.*

"It's on the market," I say distantly.

"What is?" Mom asks.

"My house," I reply, remembering. "I'm selling it. I've got debts to pay. Plan on downsizing. Leaving my options open for future employment. Looking to reboot, since going back into sales is not an option."

I'm both alarmed and reassured at the sudden memory about the house. Alarmed that I had even forgotten, but reassured that the Lego piece has fallen back into place, giving hope that maybe other memories will too.

Mom makes a sympathetic mom-noise, continues her back rubbing.

"How are you doing for money?" she asks.

I give her the same answer I gave Jason, drawing on my 401(K), but now that I have had time to think about it, the truth of it hits me again. "That's my retirement. My future. Just evaporating before my eyes."

"You didn't qualify for unemployment?"

I shake my head. "Face-punching customers is not a qualification for unemployment benefits."

There's that word again, *qualifications*. Life is all about "qualifying" for something. I feel pressure building up like steam behind my eyeballs.

I tap the surface of the bar like a drum set. Dad startles momentarily in his sleep but doesn't wake up.

"That does it," I say. "Taking a break. Going to town."

"You have fun, honey."

***

I consider walking to town but change my mind at the last moment and drive.

As I roll into town, I come up behind a truck pulling a specialized trailer. It is essentially a flat box, low to the ground, peppered with holes all over the top. Each hole is used to hold a flagpole, and currently, about half of them are American flags. Boy Scouts are walking along with the slow-moving trailer, plucking out flags, and inserting them into slots on the sides of the parking meters.

When I was their age, I once performed the same task, preparing for holidays and Homer Davenport Days.

I turn down another street to park. Then, after inserting my obligatory pennies, I start my way to Mac's Place.

Inside, it feels different in the daytime, even though it's still murky. Daylight suffuses the room from the front windows, giving a pastel glow. The polished wood bar, floor, tables, and liquor shelf shine brighter, and the crowd is a different sort. Old-timers. A TV plays quietly. The jukebox plays a forgettable song. Even the ceiling fans are languid.

I take a seat at the bar. The bartender, an unfamiliar woman with long brown hair, hurries behind the counter on another task.

"Excuse me," I say. "I'd like a pint of your finest, cheapest beer...when you get a chance."

She doesn't respond. I politely wait a while but then resort to clearing my throat loudly. Before I can up my game to get her attention, I feel a tap on my shoulder.

I turn to see Gwen.

"Hey, handsome," she says. "What a surprise to see you here."

I look all around, being slow and obvious about it.

"Wait," I say, leaning in close to her and whispering in a conspiratorial tone. "You mean you can see me?"

A confused look crosses her face but melts away as realization dawns on her. Her lips, covered in bright red lipstick, widen into a smile. A bit of lipstick is smeared on her big teeth.

"You're so funny!" she shouts and buffets me with her signature feather boa. It's pink and matches her low-cut blouse. A black mini skirt rounds out the outfit.

"What are you doing here already?" I ask, blowing an errant feather off my lip.

Her mascara-laden eyelashes flutter as she looks around and says, "I was supposed to meet some fellow moms for a girls' night out, but I'm not seeing them. I probably got the night wrong again. But that's okay. I get to see you! Buy a girl a drink?"

"Er, yeah, I'd love to if I could get the bartender to pay me any attention..."

Gwen places her fingers in her mouth and gives an ear-piercing whistle. I flinch. I touch my Gwen-side ear and move my jaw as if trying to free an air bubble lodged in my ear canal.

"Oh, hey, Gwen," the bartender says. "What can I do for you?"

"Handsome here would like to get us some drinks," Gwen replies.

"Sure thing," the brunette says and levels an expectant gaze at me.

"Um, a Henry Weinhard's and a..." I look to Gwen.

"Sex on the Beach."

"...Sex on the Beach," I finish.

"I'll get to it as soon as I can," the brunette says and leaves.

"Take your time, as long as you're quick about it," I call after her back, only mildly trying to hide my sarcasm.

Gwen hears it, though, and sweetens it— "Thanks, Natalie!" Then, she takes a seat on the stool next to me.

"Girls night out, huh?" I say.

"Yeah." Her big, expressive face looks fragile. "I need to hang with my tribe. Commiserate. Get some advice. That sort of thing."

"On what?"

"My ex," she explains. "He keeps coming around and taking the girls when he's not supposed to. Every *other* weekend, you know? That's when he's supposed to have them. Not when he feels like it. He throws a fit every time I point that out. Makes a scene. The neighbors want to call the cops on *me* because *he's* throwing a fit."

She waves dramatically with her boa for emphasis.

"Isn't there some sort of law against that? If rules are rules, shouldn't he get in trouble for taking them on days that aren't his?"

"Ah, sweetie," she replies, looking down her nose at me. Not maliciously. Probably not even intentionally, but nose-gazing just the same. I'm sure I deserve it. "The wheels of justice turn slowly, especially when he is a world-class liar, and I have no proof. And he has a temper. Which just leaves me with commiserating as my only solace."

I notice the mobile phone she has set on the bar. It's bedazzled with sequins and lined with fuzz.

"You can record video with that, right?" I ask.

"Heck yeah, I can."

"The next time he comes over," I suggest, "hit the record button and prop it against something when he isn't looking and remotely record the conversation. Videos automatically date and time stamp, so a judge won't have a choice but to do something. Especially if he makes threats at you."

Her eyes widen, and she snaps her fingers. "Yes! I like it!" She leans back on her stool, bobbing her head. "Very 007. I knew writers were clever, but that's great. What about you? What are you doing here?"

"Oh, me? I spent all day on the computer looking for work. I needed a break."

"That's right, you're out of work. How's that going?"

"Terrible. I've—"

"Hey, what do you think?" She places her hands on her hips, shakes her head, and turns in profile to me.

"About?" I say, confused.

"My hair, silly, don't you like what I did?"

I scrutinize her head. She's still blonde as the day I first saw her in elementary school.

"I'm sorry, it must be the lighting in here," I say. "I'm not seeing it."

"Silver," she says, giving me a playful moue of disappointment. She buffets me again for good measure with her boa. "I got silver highlights."

"Oooooh," I say, blowing another feather away. "I see now. Yes. Very nice."

"Not that I need it," she adds. "I'm plenty blonde still. Not a lot of gray yet, unlike some of the girls around here."

"I know what you mean. At my ten-year reunion, there was so much premature gray!"

"I wonder why that is..."

"Probably something in the water," I joke. "Like the Reidman Sisters. Remember them? How their hair turned orange because of the iron in their well water?"

"Wouldn't that turn their hair gray too?" she asks, eyes narrowing as her thoughts deepen. "Iron is gray, isn't it?"

Our drinks arrive.

"Mmm, well, elemental iron is, but iron ions contribute a red color, like the hemoglobin in our blood." I take a drink of my beer.

She stares blankly at me, then her countenance falls. "You're making fun of me, aren't you?" The sadness in her voice is almost heartbreaking.

"No! No!" I'm quick to say. "I'd never do that!"

She hovers over her fruity drink and sucks on the straw. "You think I'm dumb."

"No, I..." I'm flustered, feeling like a complete heel.

Just when I don't think this can go any more south, she shouts, "Gotcha!" A mischievous smile cracks through her fake pout.

It's my turn to stare blankly.

She laughs her famous giggly laugh. "I'm fine, silly!" Then adds, "By the way, iron supplements will turn your poop black after it's come in contact with the hydrochloric acid in your stomach."

"Geez!" I say and take a gulp of my beer.

She grabs my knee and gives it a squeeze and shake. Her laughter is raucous. I fidget away, somewhere between ticklish and perturbed.

"That wasn't very nice of me," she says. "I'll make it up to you. Or maybe you can make it up to me after that whole lecturing thing. Either way, let's dance!"

I look around the room. A gap-toothed patron looks back at me.

"Dance?"

"Not here, silly!" she explains. "Up at the Garden. They have live music tonight. Have you been to the Oregon Garden?"

"Not for a while," I confess. "Not since I organized a writer's retreat there for my writer's association."

"Well, good, then you know the way. Let's go, Professor!" She downs her drink with impressive velocity.

***

It's a quick drive to the opposite side of town, heading out Cascade Highway.

The entryway to the Oregon Garden is on the left, marked by a large log archway with letters leaving no doubt as to where you are. There is no gatehouse or gate, just a paved road leading uphill to the various places within the Garden, where you have to pay admission.

"You see the Frank Lloyd Wright house over there?" Gwen points out a wooden structure barely visible through the trees that evoke rectangles and laminar lines. "The Garden just acquired that recently. Not too many of those around!"

I remember hearing in the news about the Garden Trust's purchase of the building.

"Over there is the grassy amphitheater," she says, rolling down the window and letting the warm wind whip her hair and boa about. "I saw Joan Jett there last summer! Good times!"

She undoes her seatbelt and all but climbs out the window and shouts into the wind.

"Hey, be careful there!" I call over the noisy open window.

"Oh, don't be such a stick in the mud!" she admonishes me, settling back in. "I don't get out much, and you don't have to be at work tomorrow, right? So live a little."

I shrug.

After a sea of blackberry bushes, we come to the end of the road. At the top of the hill is a sizable wood-and-stone lodge. We park facing the Garden against a black iron gate. The Garden slopes away from the resort, framing a glorious red sunset and much of the Willamette Valley. We can't see much of the flowers for which the Garden is famous in the creeping darkness, but we can hear the fountains playing away. The splash of water is alluring.

I glimpse a far corner of the property where a particular gazebo sits, but the shadows already swallow it whole. Gwen takes me by the hand and drags me to the resort, passing under the carport and through the main double doors. The bright reception is like any resort's, staffed by a pair of pretty girls who smile at us as we enter. Straight ahead are hallways and stairs.

Gwen directs me to the left through another door. Inside is the lounge, which is all wood, stone, and glass. A large fireplace takes up the center, surrounded by comfy couches. Round dining tables make a semicircle about a dance floor in front of a small stage in the corner. People are setting up speakers and microphone stands there. The room is abuzz with a large crowd.

"I love this place in the summer," Gwen says. "There are always weddings going on. Always a party up here."

She cuts through the crowd, pausing here and there to chat when she recognizes someone she knows. She clings to my arm and introduces me as her famous writer friend from school.

Eventually, we get to the bar. She looks at me expectantly.

I suppress a sigh and reach for my wallet.

"Two Henry's, please," I say to the bartender.

"Oh no," Gwen says to the bartender, overriding me. She turns to me and shouts over the buzz of the crowd. "We need to loosen that tight ass of yours. You need to have some fun. And that is a nice ass, by the way."

"I think I had too much fun the other night..."

"Whiskey!" she shouts at the bartender, who sets two shot glasses before us with a hint of a smile.

After he pours, Gwen holds them up for us. I reluctantly take one.

"Cheers!" she says, touching glass.

Chapter 30
Zia the Magnificent

"As much as I'm enjoying this, we better be going," Zia says as she sits up and struggles to pull her corset back together. The garment quality is much superior to the other corsets I've seen worn by some of the women among the eclectic mix of writers at the conference. This was custom made to fit and no mere costume piece.

The sleek velvet strains under the hooks. The lace undulates and ruffles along her neckline. Her skin glows in the shade of the gazebo.

"Really? We've got plenty of time," I say, diving to her throat, kissing and nibbling.

She laughs and weakly pushes at me. "Seriously, we have to go."

"Seriously, I'm much too be-spelled by your skin," I insist. I slowly kiss my way down her throat to her cleavage, savoring the perfect skin, the shape of her curves. She relents for just a moment, drawing in a deep breath, but then lets it out.

"You have a class in about five minutes." Her words come out in a sleepy moan.

"They'll manage without me," I say into her bosom.

She giggles and succeeds in pushing me off this time. "You're the one giving the lecture, remember?" she laughs.

I sit up. "Right. That."

She manages to get the last of the hooks on her corset in place, and she adjusts her curves, making ripples. I'm mesmerized. She reaches up and squeezes my jaw, drawing me in to give a long kiss. When she finally disengages, she sighs.

"And I've got to prepare for my class. I guess we're both multitasking this weekend."

I straighten my tie and pull at the bottom of my vest. I disentangle my pocket watch chain from the lace of her skirt. I'm almost mortified. It would be a shame to tear her dress. It really is a beautiful piece of work. Black and lavender, velvet and lace, paired with classy fishnet stockings and heeled boots. Her chestnut hair cascades around her shoulders. And she knows her effect. With her green eyes (real, not contacts), she catches me staring at her again.

She makes one final adjustment and looks around. "I do like the venue you chose for the Writer's Retreat this year. Very nice."

Indeed, the Oregon Garden hasn't failed to enchant the group of writers I've gathered for an opportunity to rub shoulders, exchange ideas, and sit in on lectures. Not to mention, get some actual writing done among the acres of grass, trees, giant thistles and sunflowers, gurgling fountains, and the occasional wildlife. A small herd of deer nuzzles the manicured grass near our own little "retreat."

"I grew up near here," I explain. "The Garden wasn't here when I last lived in town. It was just a field and private property. Sometimes I come up here just to walk around in wonder that it's actually here."

The deer startle and bolt. The garden tram trundles along the concrete path some distance away. The passengers in each car lean out to gawk at the retreating deer and take pictures. Soon the tram and the deer are gone, leaving only singing birds and lazy insects.

"So that is how you knew about the most secluded gazebo in the garden." She winks.

I look at the white lattice structure up and down. "Actually, this is where my niece had her wedding photos done."

Zia pulls a face. "Wow. I wonder how she feels about you defiling her memories."

I lean in and growl into her ear. "What she doesn't know won't hurt her. Though I don't think I'll ever look at those photos the same way ever again."

She laughs and pushes on my chest. "What's your lecture on again?"

"Dammit, right. My talk is 'The Power of Imagery in Your Prose'...I think."

"You think?"

I shrug. "I'm kind of winging it."

Zia rolls her eyes. "God, I hate people like you who can just pull out a great speech." Her voice dips into a sing-song rhythm as she descends the first set of stairs. "Which is precisely why I have to get back to my room and prepare for my speech."

I join her in the descent. "What's yours on?"

"'Spiritualism in Your Writing,'" she replies.

"Ah-ha, that's right. If I'm not mistaken, you're also reading palms during the next break after lunch."

"Correct."

"That's your day job, yes? Reading palms?"

"Tarot mostly, but palm reading too."

I pause on our walk back to the resort and conference center. "Can 'Zia the Magnificent' give me a quick palm reading? Let me know how my speech is going to go?" I ask, holding out my palm.

She playfully takes my hand into hers. She rests my hand face-up on hers, which is gloved in lace, then traces the lines of my palm with a finger. She's a long time scrutinizing, and her brow furrows. The concern looks real.

"What is it?" I ask, a little unsettled by her silence.

"That doesn't make sense," she murmurs more to herself than to me. "This isn't possible." She looks up at me. Her eyes are dead serious. Dead afraid. "It says you're dead. Have been for a while."

Chapter 31
Mill Town

Whoosh! Clack!

I wake with a start.

I'm staring up into the frilly canopy of a bed.

My head hurts, but not the usual hurt. This is a good old-fashioned hangover. My mouth is dry.

I turn my head slowly, looking around my environment.

I'm in a bedroom. A woman's bedroom. Everything is some shade of pink, from the wall color to the bedspread. To one side, a vanity mirror and desk are overflowing with makeup, perfume bottles, wig stands, feather boas, and a whole lot of only God and women know what. Numerous DD-sized bras dangle from the edges of the mirror. With most of its drawers open and overflowing with clothes of all sorts, a dresser is surmounted by dusty trophies. Some are from swimming competitions. Some are from cheerleading. Above them on the wall are orange and black pom-poms and many photos. A banner above them all states, "Silverton Union High School Silver Foxes! Go! Fight! Win!"

Virtually every space on the floor is covered with clothes. The edges of the room have them stacked in neat piles. The rest of the floor is under there somewhere, lost under a solid rug of recently worn clothes. The walls are covered in artwork with a definite fetish for unicorns and Marilyn Monroe.

Eventually, I start putting the clues together. I'm aware I don't have a shirt on. I never sleep without a T-shirt, unless...

"Oh, boy," I groan. I look under the covers and examine my state. "Oh no." I lay a hand across my forehead.

I look over to Jesus, sitting at the vanity mirror. He's playing with one of the perfume bottles, squirting it and taking a whiff. His face scrunches up.

"I know, okay?" I say out loud.

Jesus doesn't seem to listen. Just keeps trying out the perfumes.

I sit up and begin searching. Oddly, I find my socks on the nightstand. When I extract them from the tangle of items, I pick up a bottle and read the label. I recognize the prescription typed on the white pharmacy sticker plastered to the amber container. Long ago, before I had resolved many of my health issues through diet, I had taken this same one—anti-anxiety meds. I return the bottle and note the others, recognizing the various antidepressants and painkillers.

I put on my socks, find the rest of my clothes. As I lean over to pull up on my pants, I note the pictures next to the pom-poms. Many are vintage high school portraits of Gwen, Bailey, and others, arm-in-arm in their cheerleader uniforms.

Outside the bedroom, kitchenware bangs. A television is on. I smell bread burning.

When I come out of the room after getting fully dressed, I'm blinded by the brightness. I cover my eyes like Nosferatu. But, before I do, I catch a glimpse of the house. Every inch is covered in something. Whether laundry, children's toys, or what looks to be an incredible amount of arts-and-crafts materials. Boxes and boxes of them. The carpet, what I can see of it, is seventies-brown and worn. The smell of musty wood corroborates the guess. It's a wonder I can take notice of that detail because the smell of a litter box announces that there is at least one cat about.

I hover outside a living room occupied mostly by an ironing board and a sectional couch covered in laundry. The only other decorations are a picture of a velvet Elvis and a velvet Matador fighting a bull. A girl, about ten perhaps, plays a video game on the TV. My first impression of her is her bright red hair, freckles, and overalls. I take a seat next to her in the only clear spot on the couch.

The swirling images of a First Person Shooter game make me nauseous. The sounds hurt my head. I squeeze my eyes shut, give my head a good shake, and look at the girl.

"How are you doing, partner?" I ask.

The girl, a thinnish gal with straight hair on one side of her head and almost shaved on the other, seems to be so engrossed in the game she at first doesn't take notice but then turns to me with such a suddenness it takes me aback. She gives me a beautiful thousand-watt smile that penetrates like a laser. Then, just as quickly, she turns back to her game as if I weren't there.

I'm saddened by the withdrawal of the smile, but a noise from the kitchen distracts me.

A dish drops; bacon sizzles in a pan. "Oh, drat!" I hear Gwen's voice in the kitchen across a dining room. She pokes her head around the corner. "Good morning, sleepyhead!"

This woman doesn't do anything quietly.

"Come join us. Breakfast is about ready."

I stand and look at the girl. "You hungry, buddy?" I ask.

She continues clicking away at the console in her hands.

"Okay then, put 'er there." I put my fist out for a fist-bump. To my surprise, she bumps me with her tiny fist and goes right back to clicking away.

The dining table is completely covered with boxes of clear orbs that look destined to become Christmas ornaments someday, glue bottles, jars of various colored glitter, and multiple other craft items. Two other girls, blondes somewhere between seven and nine years old, sit at a play table. They are giggling up a storm, pouring pretend tea from a plastic teapot. One is dressed up in a ballerina outfit, the other in what looks like a little girl's version of a Holly Golightly dress complete with long-sleeved gloves and oversized sunglasses. Unfortunately, the plates of burnt toast before them are not pretend.

"Will you join us?" one asks.

"Of course," I say and take a seat at an available little person chair. It is sturdy plastic and holds my weight.

"Would you like some tea?" the little Miss Golightly asks, with an exaggerated British accent.

"Why yes, thank you," I reply.

She pours me a generous helping of the imaginary brew in the cup in front of me. I take it and make a good show of enjoying it. They giggle.

Sunlight streams through the windows of the dining room and kitchen more intensely than in the living room. My eyes really hurt now, making my headache worse.

"Say, do you have another pair of those I can borrow?" I ask the girl with the sunglasses.

She reaches under the table and produces a giant pair of sunglasses in white-kitten frames. I put them on and feel instant relief. Gwen arrives, sets a plate of bacon on the little table, and takes a seat at the last available little-person chair. She is in a purplish bathrobe, and her hair is disheveled. She has no makeup on and is looking more human than the boa-wearing starlet she was last night.

"How'd you sleep?" she asks, taking a piece of bacon and chomping on it with her big teeth.

"I'm not sure. I think I was dead," I answer.

Her quizzical look melts into a big smile. "You're so silly!" she says, and pinches my cheek, almost knocking the sunglasses off. "And who were you talking to in my room?"

"Jesus, I think," I confess. "I'm thinking about having him as a character in my next book."

Gwen's lips screw up as she takes that in. "Wouldn't that be a sin or something?"

"Probably," I say. "Copyright infringement, at least."

Gwen calls me silly again, but this time I dodge her cheek-pinching.

"How'd we get here? I didn't drive, did I?"

"Oh no, we got a ride," Gwen explains. "I always get rides since I don't have a license. I can't walk more than a mile before someone I know stops to give me a ride. Which comes in handy getting the kids to school."

"You don't drive?" I ask, picking up a piece of bacon. It's not in much better shape than the toast.

"No," Gwen confesses, sounding like it's not her favorite topic. "Not since the accident I had at my last job. The pain meds I take now cause occasional seizures. So, no driving for now."

I play with the bacon, trying to find a part that my stomach would agree with. Finally, I give up and set it back down.

"I know I'm not the best cook," Gwen defends, "It's not my forte, but I do my best, and I make up for it in love. Don't I, my sweets? Mwah! Mwah!" She leans over and kisses the girls on their heads, and they giggle and beam at their mother.

"The food's fine. I'm just not feeling well is all."

"Well, I'm not surprised," Gwen says. "You drank quite a bit last night. Sounded like you needed to blow more steam off than I did!"

I have vague recollections that corroborate her story, in addition to images of lots of dancing and Gwen performing karaoke on stage, doing a decent rendition of Madonna's "Material Girl," and me...

"Oh, God, did I karaoke?"

"Heck, yeah! You did a mean 'Lion Sleeps Tonight.' I had no idea you could hit those high notes!"

I clench my fists and look to the heavens, praying to vanish from this earth. I didn't need further evidence as to just how much the wheels had come off. Gwen laughs and rocks back and forth in her little chair.

The front door bangs open.

A man enters, wearing a khaki button-up service shirt. He has dark cargo shorts and several pouches attached to his belt, the sort that holds a folding knife and radio. He's short, wiry, and has a crooked, close-cropped blond mohawk.

There are people in this world who exude intensity. If it weren't for the fact he was so little, I might have felt intimidated.

"Todd!" Gwen shouts. "What are you doing here? You can't just barge in when you feel like it!"

"I'm here to pick up my girls, and it looks like not a moment too soon either." His face contorts into a caricature of indignation. "I see you've brought home another one of your man-whores. I can't believe you expose my girls to that sort of thing!"

"You're one to talk!" Gwen rises from her seat and approaches him, leaning over in attack mode. "You don't live here anymore because of who *you* went home with. Besides, what I do with my life is my business now. And none of this matters because you're not supposed to be here. AT ALL! Not until next week."

"What's a man-whore?" the ballerina asks.

"Me, apparently," I answer and take a drink of imaginary tea.

Gwen and Todd continue with their argument. Even though it appears to tread familiar ground, it's escalating. I look at the girls, and they seem genuinely unaffected—they continue with their tea, burnt toast, and mangled bacon. The fact they exhibit the occasional giggle shows maybe this is normal? Between shouts, I can hear the sound of the video game continuing on its merry way.

"If you ladies will excuse me," I say and stand.

I walk into the kitchen, go to the fridge, open it, and find what I was hoping for. I extract a beer and exit the back door.

The sunlight outside the house is even brighter than in the dining room, and I'm thankful for the sunglasses. I sit in a weathered lawn chair in a yard in desperate need of landscaping from scratch. I lean back in the chair, rest my ankle on top of my opposite knee, twisting off the bottle cap, and taking a long drink.

I know where I am. Mill Town. In the heart of it, evidently.

Once, long ago, on the edge of Silverton, there had been an enormous lumber plant called the Silver Falls Timber Company. It was a vast operation that played a significant role in the 1940s war effort. The laborers who had worked there lived across the street in affordable housing laid out in a grid, forming its own little town within a town. Mill Town.

Most industrial towns have such an area. When I called on the paper mills in Longview, Washington as a salesperson, there was a similar neighborhood, "The Highlands." And like Mill Town, it had a reputation. It hadn't been true, if ever, of Mill Town for a very long time, but it was still the wrong side of the tracks in some people's minds.

Across the cracked asphalt, a dog barked. Sport utility vehicles of every make and age lined the street. The houses were older and maintained, but all needed a little TLC. The wooden fences dividing the lots were weatherworn, buckled, and missing boards. This was the one place during years of running cross-county that I'd been bitten by a dog.

A white pickup occupies the gravel driveway, and its engine is still hot and ticking.

I see painted on the side, "Willamette Valley Land and Craft" in big green letters. An orange logo accompanies the text, a pie chart shared by a wrench, a water drop, a shovel, and a fire extinguisher. It looks like Dylan's business is very diverse. He didn't just take a bite out of the industry; he took the whole pie.

The door to the house bursts open, and the younger girls, carrying tiny backpacks, bound down the steps, followed by the inflamed Todd.

"Get in the truck!" he shouts.

The girls comply, still giggling and oblivious to the grown-up's anger.

The strutting rooster of a guy approaches me in the yard, fists clenched, causing the veins in his wiry little arms to stand out. "I oughta whoop your ass just for being here."

I'm struck by the fact that he is considerably younger than Gwen and that he looks very much like a weasel.

"Not with that haircut you're not," I reply, looking up at him calmly.

His expression relaxes for a moment as he tries to figure out what that is supposed to mean, and before he can gear up to verbally assault me, the door to the house bursts open again.

"Hey! Look!" Gwen shouts, stalking forward with her fuzzy-lined smartphone like a gun. "Smile, you're on camera!"

"You better put that down before you get yourself hurt!" Todd shouts back, stabbing his finger at the device.

"Go ahead! Try! I dare you to attack me while I'm recording!" She takes a stand in the yard, her bathrobe slipping down around one of her shoulders.

"Hey, you two," a neighbor shouts from across the street. He's holding a garden hose, watering his lawn. "This isn't the trailer park. Knock it off."

"Old man, why don't you shut up before I come over there and break your hip!" Todd responds.

"Oh yeah, I definitely got that!" Gwen taunts.

Todd raises his hand like he's going to hit her. My stomach tenses and I lean forward in my seat.

The neighbor shouts. "Hey, do I have to call the police again?"

Todd lowers his hand and waves her and the neighbor off, scoffing. He shoots me a final glare before jumping in his truck and peeling out of the driveway with a spray of gravel.

The girls wave from the open window of the truck. "Bye, man-whore!"

I wave.

Standing, I approach Gwen, who is readjusting her robe. She is cursing up a storm.

"I'm sorry you had to see that," she says.

I struggle to find the right words now that I've witnessed evidence to the extent of the situation. "I'm sorry there isn't more I could do."

"Well, you just being here is probably the only reason he didn't hit me, so there's that."

I feel lame, but try to add some levity. "Us man-whores are good for something."

She smiles apologetically.

Placing the empty beer bottle in a glass recycling bin near the door, I ask if I can do anything.

"No worries, I've already put you through the wringer with my drama," she responds, cinching up her robe even more. "I have to admit, though, you did handle that well. Most guys would either become super-macho and make matters worse or run away altogether. You were..." she squints at me, searching for the right words, "...scarily calculating."

I'm not sure if that is a compliment, and her tone implies that maybe she's not sure herself.

"The man who can't control himself is not a man," I reply, trying to explain my actions or lack thereof.

She bites her lower lip as she scrutinizes my face. "Yeah, but too much control is like bottling up steam. Where does that steam eventually go?"

I take so long thinking of a proper response my focus glazes over, and the answer eventually presents as a puzzled shrug. The moment of awkward silence stretches on, and I genuinely wish I could find just the right words to make the world a better place for her. Nothing comes. Some writer I am.

I feel the need to say something, to fill the silence, so ask, "How come he only took the younger girls, not the redhead?"

She sighs and wipes her eyes. Her voice is quiet. "Different father."

I feel further deflated, and after another pause, say, "Look, I gotta go. My parents are probably wondering what happened to me last night."

I give her a hug and turn to leave.

"When you picking us up?" she asks.

I freeze. "Pardon?"

There's naked disappointment in her eyes. "Davenport Days starts today," she says. "The kickoff parade is soon. You said last night you'd take us. Well, just me and Zoë now..."

"That's rrright." I swallow hard. "Well, I do need to let my parents know where I'm at and get a ride back to my car. It's still at the resort, I'm assuming?"

"You assume correctly, Professor."

"Okay, I'll see you in about an hour," I say. "My folks' place is only a ten-minute walk from here. Shouldn't be too long getting my car after that."

As she goes inside, her wobbly smile reminds me of a trampled flower.

It's not until after I get home that I realize I'm still wearing the kitty-sunglasses.

Chapter 32
The Parade

Dad's truck makes a wide turn in the resort parking lot and comes to rest near my Suzuki.

"I don't mind making a habit of this," Dad says, laughing, "but seriously, if you ever need a ride home, just call me. Doesn't matter what time."

I venture a weak smile as I get out of the pickup's cab.

"Oh, by the way," he adds through the open window as he pulls away, "Me and your godfather will be putting on a showing of the *Saga of Sylvie Creek* around four o'clock today. You're welcome to bring your friend."

"Yeah, might do that," I say, waving goodbye as he drives off.

I'm back in Mill Town within the hour, picking up Gwen and her girl, wondering how this all happened. I decide not to dwell on it too much and just enjoy it. She has dressed for the outing in her trademark style: a frilly off-the-shoulder white summer dress with red polka dots, giant plastic pearl earrings, cat-eye sunglasses, and high wedge heels that make a *clump-clump* as she approaches the car. Of course, she wouldn't be Gwen if she didn't have a feather boa. Today's is glossy black. The transformation from this morning is amazing. There isn't a hint of the tragic divorcee with the weight of the world on her shoulders, just a movie star ready to hit the town. She wears the role like armor, and I can't blame her. Instead, I focus on my role as a dutiful escort for her and her girl.

"I thought we could get brunch and ice cream at Boedie's before the parade starts," I suggest. "Everything is going to be outrageously expensive near the festival."

Gwen agrees with a squeal and a clap, and we're off to Boedie's, the single-story restaurant at the tip of the island formed by Water, C, and Front Streets. It hasn't changed much over the years: same red roof, same drive-through, same flat sandstone façade, and the same covered parking area. It is one of the few places you can still be served at your parked car. We eat with our trays hanging from the windows, scarfing the greasy burgers and fat crinkle fries. Zoë puts her Gameboy down long enough to enjoy her food in the backseat. I suppress the obsessive-compulsive discomfort at the mess she makes.

People are already starting to line up along Water Street, awaiting the parade that would soon spill from the high school parking lot and move up the street. Spectators set up lawn chairs and blankets in the grassy median. It is a perfect day for the occasion. Not a cloud in the sky, and the air is a friendly seventy-something degrees. Silverton has, if nothing else, three months of great weather.

"Looks like the road is closed already to traffic," Gwen points out, slurping her milkshake. Red lipstick smears the straw.

"No problem, we can see most of the parade from here."

"Oh n-n-no," Gwen protests, wagging a finger. "We're going to stand at the corner of Water and Oak, in front of the Palace Theater. That is the best viewing and where they throw the most candy. We can park here and walk. We got time."

"Sounds like you got this all figured out," I say.

"Not my first rodeo," she replies with a smile, then turns to the back seat, "right Zoëster?"

Zoë looks up just long enough to give that blinding smile, then her head is back down with her attention returned to the game.

We finish up our meals and park the car at the back of the lot before it fills up. We then get the girl some ice cream at the drive-through window. Technically, the girl working the window doesn't have to serve pedestrians at the window, but she is kind enough to accommodate the order. I get a scoop of chocolate for myself, just to make it worth her while.

As we make our way to the tip of the island where the crosswalk crosses over to the sidewalk, I relate how my dad used to work at Boedie's long ago when he was a struggling new father. I have a hazy memory from childhood: Dad, unloading giant bags of frozen French fries from a truck into the walk-in freezer.

"And here," I say with a flourish, pointing to the asphalt at the tip of the island, "are remnants of the old rail lines that used to run up Water Street all the way to Silver Falls State Park, carrying lumberjacks and cowboys. Isn't that cool?"

I'm confident Gwen already knows this, but I hope for more of a reaction out of Zoë. I wait for that thousand-watt smile. Instead, the child coolly observes the pair of silvery metal strips in the street. The asphalt looks like it's melted around the metal, like a receding glacier giving up the bones of some extinct behemoth. Finally, she goes back to licking her ice cream.

"Well, I thought it was cool," I say, chagrined.

Gwen rubs the girl's head. "She's very sedate—part of her condition. Trust me. She thinks it's cool."

She takes the child by the hand, and we cross over to the sidewalk.

"She takes special schooling," she continues, feeling the need to explain. "She's quite smart, really, just has a difficult time expressing herself. There's a word for it, but I don't remember. Every time she is tested, they call it something different. I think they're just making stuff up now, the doctors."

"I can relate," I reply, then point with my chin to the old school we're passing, Eugene Field Elementary. "Why, right in there, I remember Miss Wright telling me I was 'putting my mind in a box,' and I needed to not 'dwell in my imagination so much.' She wasn't mean about it. Actually was very sweet and compassionate. But being held after school because I struggled with things... It was a hard pill to swallow, anyway. So, yeah, I get it."

"Zoë needs more than being held after school." Gwen hugs her girl as we walk. "She needs special attention, above and beyond what the school offers. It doesn't come cheap or easy. It's a catch-22. If I start making too much money, I don't get the state assistance she needs. That's why I don't go back to work full time and stick with the craftwork. Makes a little money, but not too much. It's a struggle to make ends meet." She gives Zoë one more long squeeze. "But my baby's worth it."

I smile, warmed by this facet of Gwen. "You're a good mommy."

She returns my smile.

I look across the street over the heads of the growing crowd. The town's historic, gabled rooftops evoke full-sized dollhouses.

"What's up, handsome?" Gwen asks, pausing at my side and following my gaze.

I look back to the school windows, then to the roofs again—at the row of stout brick chimneys. "Miss Wright," I say, "was always remarking on my imagination. Said the chimney sweeps I saw up there every winter weren't real." I turn to Gwen, look her in the eyes. "You were a year behind me, but I'm sure you had classes in these rooms here. Did you ever see them?"

Gwen purses her lips. "No, but that doesn't mean there weren't any. Just means I never saw them."

I'm glad she phrases it like that. I stick my hands in my pockets, thoughtful, and walk on, confident I'd seen a man and a woman in top hats and scarves, dancing on the rooftops with bristly brooms. Gwen guides Zoë protectively through the crowd. When we arrive at the Palace Theater, the throng makes it hard for the three of us to stick together as we walk. That doesn't stop Gwen, who muscles her way to the front. I follow, muttering apologies, trying not to notice the looks we receive.

Within half an hour, Silverton's population seems to double. Every inch of sidewalk space is occupied. Flags line the streets. Spectators wave flags in miniature. The sun beats down. The air buzzes. It's Homer Davenport Days, and the festival kicks off with the sound of a marching band coming our way.

"Look, there are Dylan and Bailey!" Gwen says, pointing wildly across the intersection.

"And Jeremy," I add. He has a little girl with him, presumably his daughter.

I tense up when I see Jodi a little way away leaning against a telephone pole, sipping on a paper cup I'm sure doesn't contain lemonade. He's scowling at us, but the band arrives, coming between us and the daggers, swallowing up the sensory tide with the noise of horns and drums. The crowd cheers. A young man in an orange-and-black marching band uniform, complete with a tall hat, leads the way, thrusting a baton into the air in rhythm to his high-step gait. The giant gold buttons on his chest, surrounding a silver "S," sparkle in the sun. His tasseled lapels bounce with every step.

Behind this drum major comes an army of musicians similarly dressed, marching in step, swinging and swaying to the music they play. First come the trombone players, shooting their slides this way and that. Then enter the flute, French horns, and saxophone players who jazz up the tune.

The drum major halts and marches in place, thrusting the baton higher and higher into the air. The parade is parked in front of us, as Gwen promised, and the band does a little show by breaking formation, surging and coalescing again before freezing in place, instruments falling silent. The leader is a statue.

The crowd also quiets down, waits in anticipation.

Further back, out of our field of view, we hear the blaring call of tubas playing the opening salvo of the theme to *Close Encounters of the Third Kind*. The flutes in the intersection rouse and answer the tubas, repeating the music but at a lower pitch. The tubas answer. Then the entire horn section joins in. Soon, tubas and the rest of the band are punting the tune back and forth, building impressively. The drum major goes into an incredible display of dexterous twirling with the baton.

The crowd goes wild with cheers and whistles.

Seamlessly, the band transitions to the theme of *Star Wars* and resumes their forward march. The rest of the band marches along, and when the first float passes, I understand why they were so focused on playing space-themed music. Then, a giant foam space shuttle rumbles by with its payload open.

Sitting in a chair in the payload area, flanked by his family, sits Silverton's own Don Pettit, astronaut. He wears the same blue jumper he wears in the mural painted of him on a building in town. NASA and American flag patches, along with an assortment of other insignia, emblazon the suit. He's a tall, thinnish man with a receding hairline, alight with the festivities. He smiles and waves, pitching candy to the crowd.

"Go get it, honey!" Gwen calls to Zoë over the ruckus. Zoë darts like a minnow in the stream, catching it in the air and scooping it from between feet.

With a finale of bottle rockets and sparklers, Don's float glides onward.

"He actually came home for something, huh?" Gwen says.

"Surprising," I reply. "I emailed him, asking him to be the keynote speaker at the writers' retreat I held at the Garden a couple years ago. He never responded. I guess he was busy. Which is not surprising. If I recall correctly, at the time, he really was at the controls of the space station control arm that snagged the Dragon Capsule and pulled it in."

"Dragon Capsule?" Gwen asks.

"The first commercial spacecraft to dock with the International Space Station. Sent up by SpaceX."

Gwen grins. "Neat fact, Professor."

Zoë comes back just as the next band passes, this one playing Bavarian music. Unlike the high school band, this one is the hobby of adult musicians, all dressed in German lederhosen. Following them comes a vintage convertible Chrysler carrying professionally dressed people sitting on the top of the seat in the back, waving to the crowd. The woman in the center is the tallest of them; she sits in the center and wears a button-up dress and pillbox hat that Jackie Kennedy would have loved.

"There's our illustrious mayor," Gwen says, waving and hooting at the car.

"That's right," I say, squinting at the passing car. "The first transgender mayor in the nation."

It had made a splash in the election news cycle, I remember now. Stu Rasmussen, a native of Silverton, owner of the Palace Theater, and the two-time former mayor had come out as transgender before a third run at mayor.

Which brought up a question for me.

"So, pronouns?" I ask. "She/her?"

"Actually, he still prefers he/him around here," Gwen clarifies. Stu caught sight of her in the crowd and returned her wave. "He says everybody in Silverton has always known him as 'Stu,' and it would be kind of unrealistic to expect everyone to change on his account. When he's out and about outside of Silverton, though, it might be different."

"Did you have Miss Kendall-Edens for English back in high school?" I ask.

Gwen shakes her head.

"She insisted that we use a special pronoun that she came up with to use in our writing when it wasn't clear what the pronoun should be, you know, instead of automatically defaulting to the male pronoun."

"Really?" Gwen makes a thoughtful face. "What was that?"

I write in the air. "S/he."

"Interesting," Gwen says, drawing the word out, head tilting to one side while looking at the word hanging there.

"Unfortunately, it doesn't translate verbally, and honestly, I couldn't make it work in my writing, so I'm glad he prefers 'he.' Less of a chance of me to look like an idiot in front of the mayor."

I brush the word with my hand, and it drifts away.

"How do you feel about our mayor being trans?" Gwen asks.

I shrug. "The times, they are a-changin'. How about you?"

"I like that we're progressive enough around here to have an openly transgender mayor," she replies. "Besides, his dresses are to die for! He's still there for every opening night at the theater, and he wears something related to the movie playing. You should have seen him the other night when he had showings of *Alice in Wonderland* and *Gone with the Wind*. Amazing dresses!"

Before Stu's car is out of sight, I note the others in the vehicle.

"Who's he sitting with?" I ask.

"You don't recognize him? That's Goff Sanderson. He's city manager now."

I thought the guy looked familiar. He had been the kind of classmate you'd expect to go on to politics, devoting his life to the student council and the prom committee—where he made sure only the cool kids got crowned king and queen.

Today, he looks at home in an open Chrysler waving to a crowd, but out of place sitting next to Stu with his short, slicked-back hair, three-piece suit, and red tie.

"What is a city manager anyway?" I ask.

"Kind of like the mayor's right hand. He does all the leg-work," Gwen explains.

"Goff never struck me as the kind of guy to play second-fiddle to anyone." The car rolls out of view, blocked by the volunteer firefighters who form a marching bagpipe band.

Gwen scoffs, though she maintains a smile and claps energetically at the bagpipers. "He is sucking up to Stu, riding the celebrity status, prepping for his own run at the office."

I believe it. Meanwhile, the ladder truck follows the bagpipers, lumbering along, blasting out long siren wails. Men in their dress-out gear throw candy from festooned ladders. Zoë runs out to gather as much as she can.

After the firetruck comes another float. Except for a bunch of streamers and confetti, the theme is vague. Something to do with the high school, I think. After that comes another open-top vehicle. This one holds Scott Gragg and his family. Scott played professional football for the Giants and then the 49ers. The giant blond waves to the crowd, throwing another rain of candy. Zoë scores again.

"They say he'll be coaching the high school team soon," Gwen says, clapping. The rising sun starts to glint off her sunglasses.

I shrug an acknowledgment because the cacophony makes anything else impossible. Mainly I'm watching the next wave: a huge mariachi band. The men and a few women are kitted out in black suits elaborately embroidered in silver thread, and they're playing "Si Nos Dejan." Their sombreros cast shade over the hot asphalt as they work the crowd, engaging anyone in the group who knows the music—mostly older women who blush and giggle.

After them come more Mexicans, young girls in embroidered folk dresses, carrying a banner that states, "Legacy Arabians." They are followed by vaqueros on beautiful, sleek, primarily black Arabian show horses. When they ride by, it's in well-disciplined prance, which then breaks into a side-to-side dance, which draws a cheer from the crowd.

No candy, though. Zoë is unimpressed.

Before they pass, Gwen twists up her lips. "Legacy? What's so legacy about the horses?"

"Maybe these horses have something to do with the horses originally brought to the states by Homer Davenport, the guy the festival is named after?" I suggest.

"He brought Arabians to America?" Gwen asks, lips twisting even more.

"Yeah, something like that. The first, maybe?" I shrug. "I heard something like that. I'm not sure about the details. One of the murals around here mentions it."

"Well, they sure are pretty horses," she says.

I grunt in agreement. The topic of conversation passes by and is replaced by a herd of other animals. All kinds of animals. Mostly pets with their owners—dogs, plenty of goats, sheep, even cats. Some farm animals escape attention and wander about, sometimes into the crowd, to mixed reactions. But it is a tradition in Silverton to march in the parade with your pets, even if they are birds and ferrets resting on your shoulder.

A frumpy pile of colorful satin rags comes on the scene, pulling a wagon with a sign stating, "Giggle-Britches and Her Amazing Cats!"

The gal in colored satin, painted face, and blue hair herds a mess of cats around the wagon. She pauses periodically and directs them up a gang-plank that trails behind the cart, having them jump through a hoop embellished with paper flames.

She is actually doing quite well with the cats, considering that they are cats, until she comes to the center of the intersection and someone's dog bounds into the middle of them, scattering them.

As the dog's owner gets the dog under control, Giggle-Britches starts to lose her composure as she struggles to coax the cats back in line. Soon, cats are running helter-skelter. The harder Giggle-Britches tries, the more spooked her cats become. Finally, the parade comes to a halt, backed up.

"Is that Bonnie-Jean Brown?" I think out loud, squinting through the clown's makeup.

"Sure is," Gwen confirms. "Went to clown school and everything."

I am not sure what to think of my former classmate as a clown. Like many people, clowns freak me out (*thanks, Stephen King*). I want to be happy for her, but I'm mostly feeling bad because of the cat situation right now.

Right when I think that, however, I'm relieved when someone comes to her rescue in the form of a honking golf cart. The cart is done up like a miniature green Rolls Royce with a green-and-white striped canopy over the driver's seat. The driver is a paternal fellow in a white button-up shirt with a big green bowtie. A green apron completes the effect. His cottony hair forms a rim around his bald pate like a cloud. Cheerfully, he maneuvers around the intersection and leans to one side to scoop up errant cats. After depositing each in his lap, he honks the cart horn. The crowd cheers. Somehow, none of the cats object to any of this.

Eventually, after a stop at the crowd's fringe to scoop up the last of the cats, he brings them back to the wagon. Giggle-Britches makes a big clown-show of gratitude and moves on with her recaptured herd.

Of course, I recognize the golf-cart driver. Anyone who had grown up in Silverton would. It's Orville Roth, long-time proprietor and founder of the first Roth's IGA Supermarkets, founded in Silverton.

Orville throws a handful of Werther's before moving on himself, making way for his store's float, which is a flower-decked produce bin the size of an entire IGA fruit department. All the riders wear the same green apron and bowtie. Emblazoned on the side in flower petals is a large "Roth's IGA."

After the pets and the IGA float, there are a few more parade marchers. Then comes the cleaning crew in neon-yellow vests, sweeping up flowers, broken candy, lost float parts, and the occasional road apple.

A quietude descends on the scene, and the crowd breaks up. People fill the intersection like sand filling a collapsing hole.

Gwen looks forlorn. "It's so sad when it's over."

"Aw, it's just getting started," I say. "There is the fair in the park, and of course tomorrow, there are the Davenport races."

"Yeah, I guess," she says. "I just wish my girls were here to see it. Damn that Todd!" She doesn't bother lowering her voice, though. Zoë, as usual, seems unphased.

I try to think of something cheerful to say, but as it turns out, I don't have to because she squeals with delight at the sight of Bailey and Dylan making their way toward us. She runs out and hugs Bailey tightly.

"Hey, man," I greet Dylan with a handshake.

"Enjoy the parade?" he asks.

"Yeah, it looks like all the famous people came home to participate," I reply.

Jeremy joins us. We shake hands, and he introduces me to his daughter. She sticks her hand out to shake, too. Then he excuses himself, saying he promises to get her to the park for face painting as soon as possible. "Right, boss?" She bounces a curt nod. Before taking his leave, though, he says to me, "We should grab a beer out at the Wooden Nickel sometime."

"Sounds good to me. Just say when."

"This Saturday, six o'clock?"

"Deal."

Dylan and Bailey also excuse themselves, explaining that some of their older kids were in one of the parade bands and will be needing a ride home to drop off their instruments.

"Not this one," Dylan clarifies unnecessarily, hoisting his young daughter in his arms. "She's not in the marching band yet, are you, pet?"

"No, Daddy!" she agrees with a big smile, then adds on an unrelated note, "Ice cream!"

Dylan groans. "You just had some. Tell you what, get a job, and you can have all the ice cream you want."

"No, Daddy! Ice cream!"

Dylan gives me a deadpan look, and I chuckle. He tugs on Bailey, urging her to wrap up her goodbye kisses with Gwen. While he waits, I ask him on impulse, "Random question, but do you remember the old houses on Water Street across from Eugene Field? Do you ever remember chimney sweeps on top of them when we were in school there?"

Dylan freezes. A strange look briefly crosses his face, but then his eyes widen, and he smiles. To this day, any time he smiles, I still expect to see a mouth full of braces when he does.

"Yeah! Totally. Had the top hats and everything, right?"

"Right!" I exclaim, a feeling of vindication washing over me.

We talk a while longer about other things, and he reminds me that I'm invited over for dinner sometime. So we set that date and time, too.

Bailey finally disengages from Gwen, and their little family disappears into the crowd.

"What's up?" Gwen asks, noting my change in mood.

"Nothing, just feeling good is all," I explain.

She moves us to the sidewalk when the police department moves in to return the street to regular traffic. When we step up on the sidewalk in front of Mac's, another familiar face is there, reviving the past.

"Well, hello there Donnie Bensen," I say, thrusting out my hand enthusiastically.

He takes my hand and smiles a greeting, does the same for Gwen.

If the actor Sean Penn ever needed a stunt double, he could do worse than to use Don Bensen, though in strawberry-blond flavor. From the craggy face to the round-the-clock five o'clock shadow, to the twinkling eyes and showy rings on his fingers, he cultivated a wolfish attitude—even when he had been a shortish, clean-shaven, and chubby underclassman. Now, he outwardly looks like he's grown into the man he's always projected.

After a bit of catching up, it turns out I wasn't too far off from my initial impression. He says that he spent some time in LA as a professional photographer, working for pin-up calendars.

Gwen is quick to point out that he is carrying at that very moment a notably large camera.

"Always," Don growls, patting the expensive item dangling from his shoulder. "The ladies like a guy with a big lens, if you know what I mean."

She rolls her eyes but laughs just the same.

"Hey, how would you guys like a picture together?" he asks.

Before I can protest, Gwen squeals and draws me in, latching onto my arm and digging her nails into my skin.

"Smile!"

The flash goes off and blinds me. A pain stabs the back of my skull. The after-image doesn't go away any time soon, and a static buzz fills my ears, connecting to the pain in my head.

Gwen lets go of my arm as I lean against the nearest building, shaking my head, trying to clear it. I move my jaw, trying to dislodge the static sound. Nothing works. The building that's holding me up is Mac's Place. Even through the after-images, I can see through the open door. The pain stabs my head again, and I mumble that I want to step inside for a drink.

My words disappear in a cacophony of motorcycle engines. A considerable number of them rumble outside with mufflers barking and spitting. Two of them break off and slowly, brazenly, weave their way through the last of the parade crowd. In the process, they bump some pedestrians, eliciting shock and curses that die on people's lips when they recognize the riders.

Everyone recognizes them. They're Regulators.

The bikers, men who are all hair, sunglasses, and brown leather vests, park the hogs on the curb in front of Mac's. When they dismount and make way for the door, Donnie gently takes Gwen by the elbow and moves her out of their way.

They swagger through the entrance after pausing like a dare.

I hear Natalie's voice declare from the direction of the bar, "Actually, there is no smoking on the premises."

The lead biker, a lump of scarred muscles with relatively well-groomed dark hair and beard, doesn't seem perturbed. Instead, he takes another puff, making a show of it. I can see what happens next through the open door. He approaches the bar, trailing gray tentacles of smoke. He peels off his sunglasses, revealing startling blue eyes. He would be handsome if he didn't radiate such intense rage.

The guy who follows is a different story. He is thin, unkempt, with scraggly brown hair and eyes. He looks like he's been used up, thrown out, kicked off the garbage truck, and run over. He walks at a submissive distance behind Black Bart with a bounce in his step. He gives the impression of a Rat Terrier tagging along with a German Shepherd, trying to soak up some of the larger dog's coolness and just looking silly in the process.

It would be funny, except Black Bart is menacing Natalie from across the bar now. Smoke spirals to the ceiling. It's probably been ages now since smoking was allowed indoors. The smell is alien and intrusive.

"I said, you need to put that out," Natalie says. She isn't backing down, but her voice quavers. Instinctively, I step inside, though I have no idea what I can do.

Black Bart smiles at her, lips curling around the cigarette. The Rat Terrier leans against the bar, waiting to see what happens next. Probably so he can tell their other buddies later how *they* put the scare into a girl.

"You heard her," comes a voice from the side, and a tray lands loudly on the bar where Carrie has thrown it down. "NO SMOKING." She stands there, thin arms crossed over her chest. She is a bit older than Natalie and a seasoned bartender who has seen it all. Her dark eyes stare without flinching.

Black Bart makes a quiet snort and quietly puts the cigarette out in a dish of salsa dip.

"No need to get all riled honey," he says, blowing out a gust of smoke from his lungs. "We just stopped by to see if Boomer is around."

"Boomer is—" Carrie starts to say.

"Right here," Boomer Johnson finishes, appearing from the kitchen door at the end of the bar.

In his sleeveless denim vest, he could pass for a biker himself. A scowl makes deep cuts in his craggy face.

"Well, well, well," Black Bart says. "Speak of the Devil, and he shall appear. Well, what do you think of the Fraternity's proposal?"

"There is no proposal," Boomer growls. "Take a hike. Just because Mac's is under new management doesn't mean I'm open to your kind of business. Go sell your wares over at Your Break."

"Yeah, well, Your Break doesn't quite have the reach that your franchise does," Black Bart continues in a friendly like manner and leans against the bar as if settling in for a lengthy discussion.

"I *said*..." Boomer reiterates, and this time reaches under the bar, being slow and methodical about the move and makes it clear that he is gripping something, aiming it now at the big man. "... take a hike."

Any pretense of amicability leaves the biker's face, and he straightens up.

"All right then," he says between his teeth, "but Pops ain't gonna like to hear about this." He turns to his companion, and when he does, my attention returns to the Rat Terrier. The guy is staring at me with a peculiar look: recognition.

"Let's go, Rooney," Black Bart says, catching the look. At first, he seems curious about the exchange, but then turns and leaves, his boots thudding on the bar floor. Rooney is slow to follow, casting a final glance my way as he passes.

Inside my mind, the eternal memory of Johnny's smiling face on a sunny day morphs into a cold mask, eyes closed under harsh electric mortuary lights.

When the door shuts behind them, I realize my guts are tied upside down and sideways. I let out a breath I hadn't known I was holding. Boomer removes his hand from underneath the bar and displays the beer bottle he had his hand on all along. He twists the cap off and takes a drink. Shortly after that, he is consoling the girls in a fatherly manner. I order and chug a whiskey, and after paying and leaving a big tip, I head for the door.

Outside, a police officer is trying to write a parking ticket to the bikers, but they jump and kick their engines on with a roar that quickly turns to a sputtering staccato of industrial mayhem. The police officer stands in their way, and Black Bart stares the cop down. I recognize the policeman: Andy Delaney. He's another blast from the past, but that fact is lost on me while I struggle with the disorientation of the moment.

Andy's blond hair is so slicked with hair product that it's a shade darker. His big glasses reflect the Regulator's face.

After a tense moment, the policeman steps back, looks down and pushes the glasses up the bridge of his nose.

Black Bart and Rooney smile and they roar off, weaving in and out of the motor traffic that has returned since the parade.

My head hurts more than ever. The booze hasn't kicked in yet.

"You okay handsome?" Gwen asks. "You look like you've seen a ghost."

Johnny and Rooney fight for attention in my head, competing with other concerns surrounding me.

Jodi is still in the vicinity, casting a glare at us. The gouges in my skin left by Gwen's nails when Donnie took our picture feel like they're bleeding. I can't seem to breathe. My stomach is still twisting in knots, and my head starts to spin, and I want to lean over on my knees.

I don't. Instead, I make a suggestion to go for a walk. A brisk walk. Away. Away from the crowds filling the sidewalks and every art and antique shop in every direction.

Gwen shrugs and lets me lead the way. She latches on to me to slow me down, though.

I pause at a sepia mural—one of Lori's masterpieces—that depicts the felling of the town's old oak tree in the center of town. It's from the autobiographical book *The Country Boy*, written by Homer Davenport, the man after whom today's festival is named. Bits of trivia begin to register in my brain, which starts a sort of re-orienting process in my mind. Stops the spinning. Eases the pain. Guides the train back onto the tracks.

I look up at the image of Homer striking a pose in his three-piece suit, and it stirs me on some level I can't quite put my finger on. It's like a record needle shifting back and forth on the record, trying to gain a foothold in the vinyl trench so it can commence playing a song. On the other hand, maybe it's just that his sharp features and nineteenth-century mustache are reminiscent of other icons like Edgar Allen Poe and Nikola Tesla.

Regardless, the pain in my head is gone. I feel better.

"Does this say anything about the horses?" Gwen asks. I can almost feel her eyes behind her sunglasses scanning over the mural.

"Pardon?" I ask, then upon realizing her meaning, add, "Oh, the Arabians. I believe that is mentioned in another mural."

"Well, the girl is edgy for some cotton candy," she says. "Shall we go to the park?"

So we do. There is less of a crowd on the edge of town proper, and I can breathe again. Here there is only a steady stream of people coming and going to their parked vehicles. Gwen clings to my arm, and Zoë follows quietly. The whiskey starts to assert itself in my blood, warming my insides. I begin to mellow a bit.

The park is alive with color, sound, and smells, and though it is not quite big enough for full-sized carnival rides, there are plenty of inflatable bouncy castles, games, and food booths. Deep among the trees of the park and concrete paths is a sea of craft tents full of carvings, homemade jewelry, photography, candles, handcrafted knives, paintings, and so forth. A band is playing on a stage near the covered area.

We get Zoë a giant puffy affair of blue cotton candy that makes her happy.

We wander about, and it doesn't take very long to see all that there is to see.

Eventually, we find ourselves on the bridge. We lean over the edge of the rail, watching the children below in full summer-glee, splashing in the water near the buckled walkway along the water's edge.

We comment on how we used to play there when we were young.

"Do you know what that is?" I ask, pointing at the blue-green concrete structure built into the bank. It is a stone-toss from the bridge, hovering over the deepest portion of the water.

"I always figured it's where the pool got its water," Gwen says, shrugging.

"Me too," I reply. "But I think it's much older than the pool. For as long as I can remember, I never really questioned it. Look at it. It's ancient. I'll have to ask my buddy, Jason. He's on the city council. He'll know."

We talk some more about growing up here, pointing to the old piece of rope still hanging from a tree on the cliff next to the mystery structure. How kids used to swing off it into the water. I laugh, confessing I never had the guts to try.

Though I should be happier, an uneasy feeling comes over me. Not the pounding headaches I've been experiencing, but the static sound in my ears. My gaze returns to the mystery structure and then to the bridge I'm standing on. Finally, a thought comes to me: *Something is coming.*

Chapter 33
It's All Theater

On the road to Salem at the intersection of Brush Creek Road, just outside of town, is the Brush Creek School. It sits on the border where the city gives way to manicured farmland and woods.

It is a historic building—a large, single-room schoolhouse from the frontier days, with a belfry on top. A few others like this are still functioning, like the Evergreen School on the road to Stayton. Most have been repurposed. The Brush Creek School is now a theater.

Though the wood structure is sagging in some places, a fresh coat of red paint livens it up, and the white trimmed windows frame opaque boards painted with scenes from past theatrical productions: *Alice in Wonderland. Dracula. The Odd Couple. South Pacific.*

A single flight of stairs ascends to a pale-blue-speckled porch and a pair of double doors that hold a poster for *The Saga of Sylvie Creek*. Cartoon characters dressed in frontier-era clothes surround the text. Through the doors is the single large room dimly illuminated by stage lights to the far right. A red curtain hides most of the stage, leaving only a sliver of wood, like a tongue sticking out.

Where the school desks used to sit is a series of cascading platforms with modern theater seats, complete with cushions and cup-holders. Gwen, myself, and her girl take seats about the center. A couple of groups of seniors occupying the front rows, their hair a line of cottony halos.

"Is that your dad?" Gwen asks, pointing to the framed playbills of bygone years festooning the walls above the original chalkboards. Dad is in many of them, garbed in various costumes from many different plays. The playbills act like a time-lapse series of my father aging, ranging from his skinny youth, with near-Afro dark hair, to the current gray-haired grandfather.

"Yep," I reply. "My dad is one of the founders of this theater troupe. Started it maybe even before I was born. Growing up, my sister and I spent many a rehearsal night here."

"You never wanted to be an actor?" she asks.

I grimace. "Hell no. I like to hide behind a keyboard, thank you very much. My sister did some acting, but not me."

I shiver again. Gwen laughs.

Eventually, a heavyset man in a costume, punctuated by a black fedora with a floppy brim, comes out and stands on the sliver of stage and greets the crowd. He has a neat beard and mustache streaked with gray. Kohl lines his eyes. I nudge Gwen and point out that he is my godfather, Uncle Norman, my dad's friend, and an original cast mate.

He introduces the crowd to the concept of the "melodrama," reminding everyone of those early-era silent films set to frantic piano music. "Remember the one where the damsel in distress is tied to the railroad tracks, with the steam engine barreling down on her? Yes, that's the one! That is what is going on tonight! You are not only permitted—but encouraged!—to hiss at the villain—" he stands straighter, directing his thumbs to himself—"when he does something particularly villainous. Cheer when the hero does something particularly heroic. And 'Awwww' when the heroine does something lovely!"

Gwen and the groups of elderly folks cheerfully acknowledge Uncle Norman's instructions. Zoë and I sit placidly.

"Very well then," Uncle Norman declares in his baritone, removing his hat and tipping it to the crowd. "Without further ado...*The Saga of Sylvie Creek*!"

He exits the stage, the curtains open, and the stage lights flare brighter.

Gwen claps excitedly, making her big plastic pearl earrings bounce.

We observe a modest set of plywood fronts, painted to mimic, in caricature, the storefronts of a frontier Silverton in glorious cartoon colors.

Before the action starts, I lean over to Gwen and say, "I told you my dad wrote this play, right? Well, he and his buddy Frank McNatt. We went to school with his daughter, Jessica."

Gwen nods while craning her neck as the first actors make their appearance.

Like the set, the rest of the production is modest in budget, and the quality of acting runs the gamut. Regardless, they put their hearts into *The Saga of Sylvie Creek*; the story of villainous Waldo Hills, who wants to abscond with the innocent heiress Sylvie Creek and separate her from her true love, Scotts Mills. It's been a tradition for a very long time now for the theater to perform the play during Homer Davenport Days.

As promised, there are plenty of opportunities to hiss at the villain, cheer the hero, and swoon for the heroine, all of whom are named after local landmarks. Dad is playing Grandpa Pudding, named after the Pudding River. The acting is over-the-top-silly, and it's really for kids and the young at heart, like Gwen. She gets so vocal on occasion that I see the actors pause and smile before they regain their footing. Even the other spectators turn and look for the source of the raucous commentary.

I've seen the play enough times, and anyway, hissing and cheering aren't my thing. Nor Zoë's—her mother keeps telling her to put the Gameboy away.

It's after I've turned to watch one of these mild scoldings that I return my gaze to the stage and notice something different. One or more stagehands behind the set-pieces have thrust up two sticks with paper artwork attached to them in the form of pin-wheeling flowers. They bob and weave across the "rooftops" of the storefronts, and I smile at their playful antics, though I'm mystified at what their function is as I'm sure they're not part of the original script.

My eyes widen in wonder when the flowers expand in size, unfolding in elaborate colors and shapes, then just as quickly contract to different geometric patterns only to explode again. I don't see how this is possible on just the simple stick they hang, but I can't help but admire the skill to pull it off. I turn to Gwen to comment on them, but she is in the throes of one of her giggling outbursts, so I turn back to the stage. When I do, my jaw drops.

The paper pieces have transformed through a fantastic act of origami into two chimney sweeps. They cavort with arms and legs swinging from hinged joints in a caricature of dancing. It's not just their arms and legs that are jointed, but their mouths open to reveal nutcracker-like teeth that chatter menacingly as if searching for something to crush or consume. Dark eyes bulge underneath towering top hats, and striped black and white scarves flutter like streamers on a fan. They turn in my direction, and I feel swallowed by the inky depths of the paper eyes. The sounds and actions of the actors on the stage become muted, distant.

A chill comes over me. My hands grip the seat arms as if I'm in a rollercoaster car that has just launched on its track. My stomach grows wings and flees my body as cold perspiration beads my forehead.

Before I can ponder the purpose of the paper characters, I'm distracted by a third flower on a stick that appears a little apart from the chimney sweeps. This transforms into a young boy, blond with enormous blue eyes. An innocent idiot's grin transfixes his face as he bounces a miniature soccer ball, apparently moving on a separate wire invisible from this far from the stage.

The boy loses control of the ball, which pin-wheels up to the chimney sweeps. One of them stops its movements by swinging a hinged leg out to plant its boot against the ball as the boy chases after it.

An alarm goes off inside me, and internally I scream. The chill in my bones turns to ice. The rollercoaster takes a dive, and I want to shout a warning to the boy that something isn't right, but I'm frozen in place. The other chimney sweep fixes those dark eyes on me as if mocking my impotence.

The jaw of the chimney sweep holding the ball drops like a freight elevator, revealing a void from which shoots a wad of paper trailing a ribbon. In the blink of an eye, the wad unfolds into a papery spiderweb, engulfing the boy, and sucking him into the mouth of the chimney sweep by the retracting ribbon. The jaw snaps shut. My breath catches inside me.

There is no indication whatsoever from Gwen and the crowd around me that they have noticed any of this. Instead, they laugh and lurch in their seats, responding to the scene on the stage. Their sounds and movements feel distorted, muffled, and far away as if their reality is the one in question, not the puppetry above the set-pieces.

Now, both sweeps hold me in their mocking gaze. Their mouths extend, ready to consume me, expanding into darkness that eats the stage lights, dimming the room beyond theater-dark to oblivion-dark. A chill accompanies the dark, like a fog. The muffled sounds of the stage and audience fade away altogether.

I squeeze my eyes shut, and my grip on the arms of my chair threatens to unbolt them as the rollercoaster lurches from side to side. My breathing comes in heaving gasps, and the pressure building in my head is going to explode out my ears.

No! Why is this happening? How is this happening?

Anger builds in me, replacing the horror and anxiety. Finally, I decide I'm not going to take this anymore. I'm going to beat back this pain in my head. Squash this buzz in my ears. I'm going to shout at the creatures and show them I'm not afraid. I will fight them. Protest their abuse of my memories.

I open my eyes and lurch forward in my seat, ready to stand and shout.

The puppets are gone. The light has returned.

The rollercoaster stops on a dime, back at the start. Sound and movement are normal. Zoë's Gameboy beeps quietly in the dim light.

"Did you see them!" I hiss to Gwen, grabbing her wrist, desperately needing her attention.

She is startled at my abruptness but smiles just the same. "See what darling?"

"The—the puppets above the storefronts?"

Gwen's eyes widen, and she turns to the stage, searching in excitement. "No! Where?"

By now, my faculties have fully returned. There is no muffled distortion. There is, however, my sister's voice in my mind, echoing from several days ago with her explanation of how creative minds deal with trauma. I cling to this explanation. I tell myself that I do not see things; I'm processing. I meditate on that, repeating it over and over in my mind until it becomes a mantra.

"It was very brief," I answer Gwen apologetically, collapsing exhausted into my seat. "Sorry I didn't point it out sooner."

She makes a pouty face but returns her attention to the current scene.

When the play is over, we exit through the double doors to the relatively blinding twilight. The actors have already exited the back of the school and meet us at the bottom of the porch stairs. We clap and cheer as we descend the stairs and shake their waiting, grateful hands. This simple act helps me reorient myself.

When we come to Dad and my godfather, I introduce Gwen and Zoë.

"What did you think of the show, young lady?" Uncle Norman asks.

Zoë shrugs.

Uncle Normal throws back his head and laughs heartily. He is Portuguese-American and very loud. And hairy. You can see black hair curling over the lip of the collar and the cuffs of his shirt. If this were a movie, he'd probably play himself. He looks like he was born to be an actor, and in his villain getup, he looks the part. But I've never seen him truly angry in all my life.

"By golly! The critics are getting younger all the time!" Uncle Norman declares.

Gwen is staring at my dad and godfather. I understand why. The heavy makeup is the first thing you notice about all the actors when you first see them up close; it seems more like clown makeup.

"It's so the audience can see us better," Dad explains.

"The audience needs to know who's who," Uncle Norman continues. "It helps move the story along,"

"And who to hiss at," Dad adds.

"I had no idea!" Gwen confesses. "It makes sense, though, doesn't it?"

"Yes, yes," Uncle Norman replies. "Wouldn't it be better if all of life were so? We could see the villains coming a mile away!"

They continue their conversation, and because they are Gwen and Uncle Norman, they are shouting. Uncle Norman admires her feather boa, and she snaps his suspenders, eliciting his baritone laugh.

I pull Dad aside and tell him about my encounter with Rooney.

Concern crosses his face but is quickly replaced by an expression I can only call, "It is what it is."

"I think he recognizes me, though I don't know why," I point out. "As far as I know, we've never met. I didn't even know what he looked like until today."

"Son, your picture was in the newspapers for track and field or academics plenty of times long before you were an author," Dad explains. "The upside is now you know who he is and can avoid him."

I grunt. "He looks like someone I'd avoid anyway."

Dad agrees. "Some people don't need stage makeup."

Chapter 34
The Family Man

The following evening, it's time to make good on Dylan's invitation for dinner.

I turn into the Webb Lake Community neighborhood. A metal arch over the entrance off the main road says so in cursive script.

This whole area used to be a ranch owned by a man who raised racing horses, and the dirt path around a tiny lake served as a practice racetrack for the horses. At least on one occasion, I was one of the countless kids to sneak onto the property and try and catch a prized catfish in it. Until recently, the water and track had been hidden behind a wall of blackberry bushes. Now you could see a bit of them from the road since the blackberries mainly were gone.

Some industrial ghosts still live out there too, in the field, as concrete blocks bristling with rebar from past lumber mills. And before that? Probably Indians hunting deer and gathering blackberries.

Now rows and rows of streets wind their way around the area, populated by charming, too-similar-looking homes. I note the addresses clearly displayed on the houses and mailboxes and come to a creeping halt behind Dylan's familiar, white company pickup with rack and utility box in the bed. The door to the vehicle is open, and I see Dylan walking in an agitated fashion in the street nearby with a cellphone glued to his ear. He pauses every now and again to shoot a glare at the interior of the truck cab. Then goes back to having a heated conversation with whoever is on the other end of the cellphone.

I park and get out.

"Just make damn sure it doesn't happen again," he barks into the phone. "I don't care how legal it is, that's not the point. The point is that it's a company vehicle parked in front of *my* house with *my* kids in it...I don't care! Even the smallest chance isn't worth it! My business, my vehicles, my rules! Got it? Good! See you tomorrow."

Dylan stabs at his phone with his index finger and clips it back to his belt.

I've rarely seen him this steamed. His pale complexion is red down to the collar, glowing almost as bright as the pie logo on his shirt.

He leans against the truck door and peers inside. I join him, curious as to what all the fuss is about.

There, inside, the front seat is tilted forward to expose the storage space. A long rectangular plastic case with a handle sits in the area.

"Is that a..." I begin to say.

Dylan leans forward with a huff, opens the latches on the case, and opens the long clamshell. Sure enough, an AR-15 with spare magazines and various paraphernalia embedded in their own foam molds rest in the case. In the streetlight, I can see brass glistening in the magazines.

"Wow," I say.

"Exactly," Dylan says, snapping the case shut and tilting the seat back, covering the gun case.

"What the hell?" is all I can manage.

"That idiot Jodi left it there," Dylan explains, still in a huff. "Said he took it shooting last weekend and forgot about it."

"*Last* weekend?" I say, incredulous. "It's been there this whole time? How'd you find it?"

"When I got off work today, somebody else had grabbed the truck I was using," Dylan says, shutting the cab door and locking it. "It's normal. All the trucks are the same. Leased fleet vehicles. We use each other's trucks all the time—just don't leave your lunch on the front seat. It's normal to drive them home for the night sometimes, too. Unfortunately, Mr. Jodi left more than his lunch in this vehicle."

Typical Jodi behavior. Dylan glares at the truck, shaking his head.

"Gah!" He gives a futile gesture to the sky. "I can't believe that guy. If he wants to use the company vehicle to go shooting in the woods or the quarry pit up the Abiqua on his own time, I'm cool with that. It's one of the perks of the job, the company vehicle. But to leave it in there during the workweek? That's just stupid. Can you imagine the liability if someone had stolen it? Then did something bad with it? Don't get me wrong, I'm no pansy, got my own guns inside, in a *freaking safe* where they belong, but not anywhere near my kids."

"You know Jodi," I say. "He thinks everyone should have one and carry them around like the Old West. Our Constitutional right and all that. I can agree with some of that, but you gotta be smart about it too."

"I know, right? I don't think even cowboys left a fifteen-hundred-dollar piece of hardware rattling around in the back of the stagecoach for their boss to find. Stupid!"

I chuckle sympathetically. It is a rare thing to see Dylan lose his happy-go-lucky exterior.

We hear a screen door's pneumatic hinge open.

"You boys coming in or what? We're getting hungry," Bailey calls from the door.

"Coming," Dylan calls back to the house. It's a beauty. Two stories. It looks a lot like the house to the left, right, and across the street. It can't be more than two years old.

We start walking up the driveway, meandering around the giant blue and red Lego blocks, the pink Barbie car, and the yellow Tonka Truck, but then he stops me.

"Not a word, okay?" he says. "Bailey doesn't need to worry about elephants in the truck."

I give a thumbs up. Satisfied, Dylan turns to take us in the house but pauses and turns back to me with a grin.

"So where's Gwen?" he asks, grin turning mischievous. "You guys like, you know, an item now?"

"Man, I don't even know how that happened. I don't know what's going on, to be honest." I give a confused shrug. "She couldn't come because she's getting her girls back tonight and wanted to spend quality time with them. She said we'll see you guys after the couch races Sunday."

Dylan adds a friendly punch to the shoulder. "You're in trouble now. I love the girl dearly, but letting her into your life is like giving a vampire permission to enter your home."

I snort-laugh.

"Thanks for having me over," I add before he opens the door. "It means a lot to me to have some normalcy right now. Though, that might change after I meet up with Jeremy later tonight for a drink."

Dylan laughs and gives me another friendly punch to the shoulder.

The inside of Dylan's house is every bit as charming and new as the outside. A staircase with a twisting polished wood banister leads upstairs. Comfortable carpet, a kitchen with stainless stove and refrigerator, an island tiled with a beach motif of sand, seashells, and seahorses. Breakfast bar stools line the living room side. Then comes a nine-section couch facing the biggest flat-screen TV I've ever seen.

"Sorry for the toy mess," Bailey apologizes as she goes about the room, picking stuff up. I tell her not to worry about it. The house looks beautiful. Looks lived in and loved.

Whatever's cooking on the stove smells like noodles and Alfredo sauce. Roast chicken. My mouth waters. A teenage girl moves about the kitchen, collects plates, makes a clattering sound, and takes a stack of them into the next room. She is very tall, very blonde, and very much Dylan and Bailey's daughter, grown far beyond my last memory of her. She's taken on Dylan's sharp features softened only a little by Bailey's round cheeks.

"Can I get you a drink, man?" Dylan asks.

"Sure, beer?"

"We got Bud, and Bud Light, and some of the local stuff from Seven Brides..."

"Seven Brides is good," I say.

"Which one? We got a sample pack," he gestures to the shelves in the interior. It's a huge fridge, like everything else in the house.

"Surprise me."

He reaches in, pulls a long-neck bottle out, pops the cap. I sit at the island, watching Bailey and their daughter dish up the food and ferry it into the living room.

"How many kids you have now?" I ask.

"Three," Dylan answers, taking a long pull of his own bottle.

"Quite the age range," I remark, looking at the photos I now see on the refrigerator door among the kid-art in crayon, grade reports, and to-do lists.

"Aw, some of these are old photos, but yeah, we got quite the spread," he says.

We talk for a while about this or that, then Bailey comes in and says the table is ready.

The table is lit up with all its crockery and silverware and evergreen-colored napkins and placemats. The teenage daughter joins us along with her little brother, about twelve, and their younger sister, maybe four. All towheads. All healthy and giggly.

"Do you have any children?" Bailey asks, blowing on a spoonful of soup.

"Not that you know of, right?" Dylan laughs as he hands his four-year-old his keychain. There is a plastic or rubber cartoon character of a starfish dangling from the key ring. The little girl bounces it on the table.

Bailey shoots him a disapproving look, but I laugh too. "No, and I am still pretty sure I don't have any, much to my sister's disappointment."

"Oh, that's sad," Bailey pouts. "Children are wonderful. Don't miss out on them."

It's Dylan's turn to shoot a disapproving look. "No pressure, honey."

"I'm just saying..." She throws up her hands in a *What?* gesture.

"It's okay," I say. "I'm used to it. I just haven't met the right girl, you know? And if I'm going to have kids, I want to do it right."

"Smart man," Dylan says, blowing on his own soup.

"Besides, my sister has had enough for the both of us," I add. "My parents are swimming in grandchildren without any help from me."

"Really, how many?" Bailey asks, reaching for dinner rolls.

"Seven," I reply.

Her eyes get huge. "Seven!"

"Yep."

Bailey straightens in her chair. "I know she had a lot, but seven!"

"Her husband Rod comes from a big family," Dylan explains.

"How does she do it?" Bailey shakes her head in wonder, buttering her roll.

"It just works," I say. "That's about the best as I can explain it. There is a lot of love to go around."

The conversation moves on. We laugh a lot. Talk about school. Talk about how much and how little Silverton has changed. Then, toward the end of the chicken fettuccine meal, Bailey leans toward me and wiggles her eyebrows.

"So," she says. "Tell me about the midget incident with you and Jeremy."

I laugh, pretending to choke on my noodles while hiding that I'm actually choking on my noodles.

"Honey," Dylan scowls at his wife disapprovingly.

"What? I want to know. Don't you?"

"Well, of course, I do," Dylan admits, laughing, "but maybe he doesn't care to share."

"It was nothing, really," I explain. "Just a big misunderstanding is all. But, you know Jeremy, he can either rub you the right way or the wrong way, and there's no telling which."

"So, he rubbed a midget?" Bailey says, just to move the conversation along.

"No, that was a figure of speech...and they were dwarves, or, well, Little People," I correct. "Anyway, my point is, when Jeremy walks up and starts talking to strangers, he can be hit or miss. Why, I remember this time we were in Orlando, Florida? We stopped in a Burger King for a late-night-after-drinking-meal. I'm driving. Jeremy can barely stand. Already passed out once in a club. We finish our food and are heading out the door when he pauses by a couple guys having their meal at a table. He notes one of them is wearing a Chicago Bulls sweater and gets in the guy's face." I lean forward in my chair, do my best Jeremy impersonation, slurring my words and aping it up pretty good, "The Bulls suck..." I pause, realizing children are present. The boy leans over and covers the ears of the little girl, laughing, enjoying my story. The little girl fights her brother off.

"Now, I'm thinking, 'Aw, man, we're totally going to get in a fight and wind up in jail 3,000 miles from home. The guy stands up, and I think it's on, but he spouts off some sports statistics. I don't remember what. Jeremy, all of sudden sober as a vicar, says something like, 'Excellent point, but consider this...' and rattles off some other statistics. The next thing I know, it's two hours later, and Jeremy and this guy have been going at it about sports. The guy's buddy and me, who apparently didn't care about sports either, are just shrugging like, 'What the hell?'"

"Pthht!" Bailey waves the story off. "I want to hear the other story!"

"Okay, fine. But you know, I actually have a better story, which is more family-friendly and involves Dylan here. Whaddya say, kids? Want to hear a story about your dad you've never heard?"

They lean forward on elbows with big eyes glowing in anticipation.

"So this takes place when we were like, oh I dunno, nine or ten years old. We're at our buddy Eric Doolittle's house, just hanging in the yard. It's about sunset, and somewhere in the neighborhood, we hear this woman shouting," I put pull back in my chair and cup my mouth, "'Billy! Time to come home!' So, what does old Eric Doolittle do? He calls back," I pantomime someone shouting again, "'Screw you, Mom!'"

Bailey and the children's eyes get huge. "No!"

Dylan bursts into laughter. His eyes become squints as he rollicks in his chair. He claps. "I totally forgot all about this! Go on!"

"So, this poor woman becomes *very* angry with her son Billy and tells him to get home NOW!" I continue. "But Eric isn't having it: 'Screw you, Mom! I'm running away! I'm going to find a family who really loves me!'"

Bailey and the kids are covering their mouths, not sure whether to laugh or be horrified. Dylan is holding his gut. The only thing funnier than a funny story is watching people's reactions to the story.

"The next thing we know is that the sliding glass door to Eric's house opens and out steps Eric's older brother Richard, shirtless as usual."

"I don't think he owned any shirts," Dylan agrees. "What is he? Something like four or five years older than us? So that would have made him something like fifteen at the time?"

"Yeah, a full-grown adult compared to us, and big," I add. "So anyway, Richard is upset. He's giving Eric the stink-eye big time. He says to Eric, 'Hey, that's not cool! You go find that lady and apologize!' Eric thinks about it, looks at Dylan and me here, then replies, 'Screw that.' Richard completely loses his cool and chases Eric around the yard for a good ten minutes, knocking over lawn chairs, the barbecue. Even the dog got in on it and started nipping at both Richard and Eric when it wasn't barking its head off."

Dylan is laughing so hard he's doubled over. The kids are laughing too at the image I'm painting for them. Bailey is shaking her head. Dylan's laugh has become infectious, and I'm having increasing trouble continuing with the narrative. For a brief moment, I picture Dylan's big mouth open with braces and rubber bands like when we were kids. It makes me laugh more.

"Eventually, he pins Eric down, tucks him under his arm, and starts hauling him down the street. Dylan and I tag along, mostly out of a morbid sense of curiosity. Richard gets about as far as the corner when Eric slips out and makes a run for it. He doesn't get very far when Richard nabs him by the ankles and trips him up. Next thing you know, Eric is hugging a fire hydrant for dear life, looking over at us and shouting, 'Guys! Help me!'"

The dinner table is in hysterics now, and I'm really having trouble telling the story. Tears are coming out of my eyes.

"Dylan and I look at each other, shake our heads, and turn to Eric: 'Ah, heck no. You're on your own!' I think this seriously goes on for twenty minutes. Eventually, Richard throws Eric down and yells, 'Forget it! She's probably already called the police!' and leaves in disgust."

It takes a good couple of minutes for the table to settle down— lots of eye drying and aftershock giggles.

Bailey shakes her head. "Boys."

"You should come over some night when Kevin Shepherd is here," Dylan says. "He's got some great stories too."

"Yeah, he's got some doozies," Bailey agrees. "Mostly not family-friendly."

Dessert is banana pudding, and it's gone in short order.

The kids disperse to go do their own activities. However, before the four-year-old can run off with his keys, he detaches the starfish and hands it to her.

Randomly, I'm reminded of something.

"Hey, I had lunch with Jason the other day. And he's on the city council, right? So I mention what you said about there not enough being done about those girls who got killed."

"Oh?" Bailey says, interest piqued.

"Yeah, he agrees with you," I continue. "He says it's a pretty hot topic right now on the council, trying to get the county or state to throw some resources their way to do a proper investigation. To find a possible connection between the killings."

"That's so sad," Bailey says, beginning the table-clearing process. "I bet at least one more girl has to die before they take it seriously, and that is one too many."

"And even then, it will have to be like we said the other night: she'll have to be white and rich," Dylan points out. "If that happens, then the authorities—no society—will have to take notice. Take responsibility."

I'm deeply saddened at the thought as I glance into the other room where the teenage girl is relaxed on a couch, nose deep in a book. I'm struck by how much she looks like the victims in the news reports. I wonder if Dylan even realizes who he just described.

Bailey frowns at the statement, pausing with her arm full of dishes. "What's that supposed to mean, honey?"

I stand and take some of the dishes from her to help. "I think he's trying to say that serial killers are a product of modern societies, and you reap what you sow. I think, anyway. Is that where you were going with that?"

Dylan shrugs, drinking the last of his beer. "Sort of. People these days let television and video games raise their children. Is it a wonder some of them turn out truly soulless? It's like someone who doesn't watch what they eat. They actually wonder why they turn out diabetic. Their body turns on them. It's the same with kids and being raised right."

"Yeah, but it seems to me it's good people who raise their kids right who suffer the most because someone else didn't do a good job," Bailey says, raising her voice so it could be heard from the kitchen as she dropped the dishes in the sink.

"Well, unfortunately, maybe if enough 'good' girls get killed, maybe society will do something about it," Dylan muses, also raising his voice to be heard. I hand off my load of dishes to Bailey. "And I can tell you right now, they ain't going to be our girls, either."

"Let's change the subject, shall we?" Bailey says, scowling. "How about we put a good movie on?"

I help with the dishes, we pull out some more beers, we take off our shoes, and we spend the rest of the evening watching *Tombstone* on their giant flat-screen TV. We laugh. We quote what the characters will say in the movie before they do it, much to the annoyance of Dylan's kids. The carpet feels good on my toes. The house is cozy. The children are pleasant.

It makes me wish maybe I had settled down, rolled the dice, and hoped it all worked out with any number of relationships I've had.

But then again, I'm no Dylan.

Chapter 35
The Wooden Nickel

The Wooden Nickel is a venerable pub on the edge of town, occupying the same fringe as the Brush Creek Theater, just on a different road. The lighted Indian Nickel Head sign has been greeting people coming home from Salem for as long as I can remember. That logo now adorns a whole series of food trucks, trailers, and industrial-sized combination trailer-barbecues.

Before I turn the engine to my car off, I note the time on the dash. The green digital display just turns to 5:55 p.m.

I don't see Jeremy's vehicle on the premises, nor do I see any WVLC trucks he might be driving. Which doesn't surprise me, Jeremy is the sort of guy who will be late to his own funeral. Me, I will probably be five minutes early for my funeral.

I get the shiver of someone stepping on my grave. I shake it off hard and head for the Nickel's door. It bursts open as four guys in Regulator vests stride out. I do my best to step out of the way of the surge, but one of them still makes it a point to brush against me, knocking me aside.

Black Bart and Rooney are already past, but the guy who bumped me must have noticed the look on my face.

"Problem, buddy?" he taunts.

The guy is hairy and rough around the edges, ably fitting in with the rest of his gang. I don't give him much notice, mostly because I'm still staring at Rooney and Black Bart. Those two have paused to watch the confrontation with curiosity.

"Say, you're that fellow from Mac's the other day," Black Bart says, approaching. He looks me up and down while pulling out a cigarette and lighter. Then, in a single deft movement, he lights the cigarette with the noisiest lighter I've ever heard—one of those large flip-top Zippos.

He looks up and takes such a deep inhale of the cigarette that his cheeks cave in. The tip of the cigarette flares bright orange. He doesn't exactly blow the smoke in my face so much as let it rise out of his nostrils like a double fountain to fill the space between us. His eyes are blazing. His teeth yellow. His breath bad.

It's a wonder I notice any of this because I'm mostly still fixated on Rooney. He's sharing my stare. And oddly, it's not malicious. More curious. Maybe even concerned.

The four guys have me surrounded, but Rooney stands a half-step apart with that weird look. I'd like to think that I'm no coward. A confrontation with a single same-sized man is annoying but manageable. I can handle that.

This, on the other hand, is a different story. Add in an element of personal family trauma, and my stomach is upside-down. The adrenaline pounds. My vision swims. It's basically an out-of-body experience. Yet, the primordial fight-or-flight is still there, lurking in each of us, waiting to show the moment when something as simple as when a bully pushes you into a locker.

None of this is helpful right now. Black Bart revels in my discomfort.

I wish Jeremy would pull up. But he doesn't. He's nowhere to be found.

"Rooney here tells me you two have history," he says. "He wasn't very forthcoming about the details the other day in Mac's, whining something about his parole officer, but he finally told me."

He grabs Rooney about the neck, placing the smaller man in the crook of his elbow.

"Ol' Rooney here got his foot in the door with the Fraternity because he came with some street cred. Murder no less," Black Bart continues, giving Rooney a friendly shake. But, like any Rat Terrier, Rooney doesn't look too pleased by the man-handling. "I guess that was your family, huh? Boy, that must burn you up, seeing Rooney here, huh?"

I don't respond. I still have my out-of-body experience. However, I do feel my hands curl into fists, and my vision darkens.

Jeremy, where the hell are you?

Black Bart takes a step toward me, dragging a reluctant Rooney.

"I'm kinda glad we came across you, really," Bart says, pausing in front of me, giving me the hard stare. "You see, getting your foot in the door of the Fraternity is just the first step. After that, you have to prove yourself in the brotherhood." He gives Rooney an equally hard stare, then after a moment of bouncing the cigarette up and down on his lips, he pushes Rooney at me. "I'm curious to see how he handles this little grudge match."

Rooney stops himself from being wholly thrust into me and just stares at me. It's not an aggressive look, more like a man trying to figure out his taxes, not liking any of the calculated outcomes. I see he's probably not much older than me for the first time, but a life of poor choices has left him haggard.

"Well?" Black Bart urges, taking another cheek-sucking drag of his cigarette.

Gravity feels like it has doubled, and my head is in a pressure cooker.

Rooney takes his hands out of his pockets and prepares to say something.

My fists tighten. My vision tunnels, narrowing to a point where light is cut off and sound too. I have no idea what will happen when the light goes out entirely, and all goes silent.

Despite that, I still hear the sound of a car door slamming shut, which changes the trajectory of the moment.

A bright flash washes over the area, casting our shadows against the walls of the building. I'm blinded by the light, and my ears are filled with an escalating electronic buzz that cuts off just as suddenly as it starts. I'm familiar with the sound: a digital camera's recharging flash.

"Guys, guys, how's it going!" I hear Donnie Robert's voice.

When my vision clears, I see Donnie crossing the parking lot toward us at a brisk pace with that affable, roguish smile that makes him look so much like Sean Penn. His big camera dangles from its strap around his neck.

Judging by the bikers' reaction, they're just as surprised to see him and just as blinded by the flash.

Donnie enters our circle, all smiles, patting the bikers on the shoulders.

"Beautiful night, huh?" Donnie says, inserting himself between them and me. "Great night for a party?"

The look on Black Bart's face is somewhere between annoyed and bemused. He grins and hooks his thumbs in his belt.

"You know what?" Donnie continues, LA-slick, approaching Bart. "How would you boys like a little party favor on me, huh?" He reaches up and stuffs a little plastic baggy of something white in Bart's upper vest pocket. "And well, hey, there you are!" Donnie says, grabbing me by the arm and directing me toward the pub door. "Just the guy I want to talk to!"

As I'm getting dragged off, I see Black Bart smile and give us the double "finger gun" gesture as he backs away.

"Y'all have a good evening," he says. "See you around."

Before the door closes behind us, the last thing I see is Rooney still staring at me with that same haunted look.

Donnie sits me in a chair at a table, and I vaguely hear him ordering drinks. I'm still sinking back into my body when Carrie places a pair of whiskey shots in front of us.

"Intense, huh?" Donnie says, flaring his eyes at me.

I take up the shot glass in front of me and down it, then take up the one in front of Donnie and down it as well. Donnie laughs and orders two more.

"I didn't know you worked here too," I say to Carrie when she brings them.

"Yep, I work all three locations. Here, Mac's, and the pub in Sublimity," she replies.

I can feel my brain processing that information. In fact, I can feel my brain processing all kinds of trivia, ordering my scattered mind. The trivia of the day? Sublimity. A small town, even smaller than Silverton, on the road between Silverton and Stayton. Interesting Sublimity fact? Howard Hessman, the actor who played Johnny Fever on the TV series *WKRP in Cincinnati*, came from there.

"Thanks for that, Don. Great timing," I say. "Were you there the whole time? I didn't hear you pull in."

He takes a sip of whiskey. "I was on my cell phone conducting some business when I saw it all go down."

I grunt, taking a sip of my own, adding its warmth to the two already in my stomach. "Were those drugs you stuffed in his pocket? Not judging, mind you."

Donnie smiles. "Well, you know, I like to diversify my portfolio."

I try to piece it together. "Why would guys who have plenty of access to meth want any from you?"

"Hey now," Donnie says, genuinely offended. "I don't deal in that nasty stuff. I'm old school. Think fun at the club, VIP-balcony kind of stuff. Classy."

I join him in a laugh as we take another sip of whiskey.

"And, I'm sure you've heard the expression 'Never use from your own supply,'" he adds. "Which makes them great repeat customers. Unpleasant people, but great customers. So, what was that all about anyway?"

I fill him in.

"Right! I remember that. Your senior year. Poor Johnny. So, that's the guy?"

I give a long slow nod. He whistles, makes a face, takes a drink. The whiskey in me starts to take hold. I feel mellow and relaxed, and now that I'm settled down some, I look around the bar.

Same, good-old Wooden Nickel. All the furniture is rustic, deliberately left rough around the edges, but with a thick layer of transparent varnish to preserve it from spilled drinks and time. The walls are covered with pop-culture mementos, including Laurel & Hardy, Elvis, and *I Love Lucy* pictures. There is a Highway 66 motif going on, too, with chrome hub caps, traffic signs, vintage car product signs, and even a full-sized 1950s gas pump in the corner. And of course, because Boomer's fingerprints are all over the place, there is music memorabilia as well, including a yellowed flyer for *Commander Cody and His Lost Planet Airmen.*

The Wooden Nickel is so old-school there is still a cigarette vending machine along the railing separating the dining area at the back from the bar area where we sit. Across from it is a jukebox that still plays CDs. The two machines act like gate guards between the two main sections of the Nickel.

Looking past them, I squint at the open door that leads to an outdoor patio area beyond the dining area. I see what looks like a new barbecue and spare propane tanks. Painted on them are rearing stallions. Not the Wooden Nickel's Indian Head logo.

I mention this to Donnie.

"That's probably why those Regulators were here," he points out. "They've been pushing their equipment on the bars in the area."

"Equipment?"

"Yeah, they have a metal fab shop somewhere around Molalla. They make barbecues and stuff."

I frown, taking another drink. "That's an odd business for a drug-dealing biker gang."

Donnie shrugs. "Business."

"I thought all the local places used Traeger Grills?" I refer to the barbecue company that got its start over in Mt. Angel by the same name family.

"Well, the Traegers sold the business," Donnie explains. "That's why you see their units in Lowe's and Home Depot now. I think they're made in China these days. So I figure the Regulators saw an opportunity to fill a local niche."

I'm not buying it, especially after watching Boomer run them out of Mac's the other day.

I shrug it off, and Donnie and I have a good long talk about happier things.

"You going to Bubba's party?" he asks. "It's supposed to be the biggest blowout ever. A party for the ages. Everyone's going. I think it's for his birthday."

I vaguely recall Bubba, the bouncer, inviting me when I first returned to Silverton. I probably should go. It just wouldn't do to turn down the generosity of a giant. And at the mention that "everyone" is going to be there, I think of Jodi again. Then of Jeremy, who by now is definitely a no-show for drinks. I mention that to Donnie.

"Well, if you don't see him at the party, you should see him right back here in a couple of weeks," he says.

He tilts the little plastic notice on the table toward me. Under the WVLC logo, the message states that the Wooden Nickel is under new management and will be undergoing renovations and closed for a week.

I grunt and finish my drink.

"Oh, I almost forgot!" Donnie exclaims, producing his camera and turning the LCD screen towards me. "I got your picture from the other day."

He quickly scrolls through the pictures, apologizing when passing some smiling naked women, then slows down when coming to images of the parade. He finally settles on the photo of Gwen and me.

Gwen's big teeth smile takes up most of the picture. I look like a deer in the headlights, as usual.

"Thanks, man," I say absently. "You can email it to me at... wait a minute. Can you zoom in on that corner?"

He complies until it is clear what I'm looking at. *Who* I'm looking at.

"Crap," I say, wishing for another drink. Todd, Gwen's ex, is in the crowd behind us. He is scowling in our direction—no, more like he's about to come completely unglued. It's a wonder he didn't accost us at the time, and I wonder how long he had followed us that day.

"This story just keeps getting better," I groan.

Donnie is sympathetic but finishes his drink and stands, shouldering his camera.

"Well, I hope it has a happy ending, man," he says, "because you have that look in your eyes."

I narrow my eyes at him. "Pardon?"

He takes a deep breath and absently runs his fingers up and down his camera strap.

"You remember that time in high school when we had a wrestling match, and you, uh, accidentally pinned yourself?" he says.

I bark a laugh. "Yeah, I'll never forget that." I didn't even know you *could* pin yourself. Jay Goin, one of my friends and teammates from back then, is an assistant wrestling coach in Salem now and still uses that story as a cautionary tale when training his kids to watch their backs relative to the mat when trying to pin their opponent. Because, apparently, you *can* pin yourself if both your shoulders touch the mat long enough. "What's that got to do with anything?"

"After the match," Donnie went on, "you didn't throw a fit. You didn't yell. You didn't throw any chairs. Nothing. You just went into the locker room and sat against the wall."

I look at Donnie somberly.

"After a while, I got worried about you," he continues. "So I went in to talk to you. See how you were doing. There you were. Just staring into space. I tried to cheer you up, and you were nice enough, laughing at my lame jokes, but I said, 'Wow, man, you really know how to keep it together. You don't ever get angry, do you?' You turned to me and gave me a look." I don't say anything, and I see Donnie's Adam's apple bob up and down. "You have that same look tonight, and it scares the hell out of me."

Chapter 36
Break

"You've been awfully evasive about Rooney." Homer doesn't mince words. Instead, his gaze is fixed on me with purpose. "You've side-lined his character, relegating him to mere boogeyman status. As a result, we only ever see a glimpse of the monster's claws poking out from underneath the bed. I can understand the desire to avoid him, but I'd be remiss if I didn't present the opportunity here. To take advantage of the cathartic nature of the written word."

I evade his gaze. I fidget in my seat. I can feel the weight of the stares from my two other companions. I raise my beer glass to take a drink, pause halfway, and set it down. Right now, I'd rather avoid the trope of alcohol as crutch.

Instead, I cross my arms and casually look up at the TV above the bar, feigning interest in the news story. On a blustery day, a reporter stands outside what looks like a rural farm, talking pointedly into the camera. The TV's sound is low, but I can still hear the reporter say, "...the insular nature of the Orthodox Old Believer community has added a layer of difficulty in the investigation of the disappearance of Natasha Voslo. Some believe that she is the latest murder victim in the area, escalating concerns that the deaths are not coincidental—or random..."

"There's no need to go into great detail about Rooney," I declare, doing my best to sound dismissive. I maintain my gaze on the TV. "He *is* a boogeyman. An archetype whose sole purpose is to move the story along to what's really important."

The disappointment around the table is palpable.

Stephen leans in, setting his forearms on the table while intertwining his fingers in a clasp. I match his stare.

"He's not just an archetype. He's something deeply personal," he says in a single long breath. "Believe me, I understand not wanting to talk about it, let alone committing it to paper for all time, but Homer is right." He leans back, and there is a glint in his eye. "You can't bury a ghost, but by writing about it, you can put some meat on its bones and turn it into a body, and *that* you can bury."

A long pause separates me from Stephen's words. Then, I glance over to Clark, who doesn't look like he will add anything. However, his expressive face is clear as to what he prefers, though it also says, "The choice is yours."

"Fine," I grunt and snatch up the writing pad and pen. I press so hard with the writing instrument the words become etched in the paper like trenches.

Chapter 37
Between a Bird and a Hard Place

Rooney turned the socket wrench, making that "Crink, crink" sound. He loved that sound. He loved using tools. There was a simplicity to it. A tool did what you told it to do.

Using a tool was peaceful. Especially while working on an engine like now. Down here, on the concrete, looking up into the workings of the truck engine, everything made sense. Everything had its place, and the tool-user had power over the engine. To fix it, to make it go faster, or go slower. Whatever you wanted it to do. You had control of the machine through a tool.

The wrench slowed to a halt, the crinking stopped, and the bolt was as tight as necessary. Rooney set the wrench on his chest, grabbed the truck chassis, and pulled himself to the next bolt by rolling along on the garage creeper that pressed into his back.

After fumbling around his chest for the wrench, he lifted his head to aid in the search. When he did, he saw three pairs of boots walking his way.

He dropped his head back and groaned inwardly.

Not surprisingly, he felt a kick against his leg after he sensed the trio stop at the truck. Not a sharp kick, but stronger than necessary.

"Hey Roonster, we need a word with ya," said Black Bart.

Rooney lifted his head again and saw that Bart had squatted down to peer under the truck at him. No hostility marked Bart's devil-goatee, but it wasn't exactly friendly either.

"Yeah, sure thing," Rooney replied, squashing the butterflies erupting in his stomach.

He grabbed the chassis and rolled himself out to find himself surrounded by men in jeans and leather vests. He told himself these were his people, his tribe, his brothers, and there should be no need for butterflies. Right?

In addition to Bart, there were Chubby and Scruffy.

***

Clark: Chubby?
Stephen: Scruffy?
Me: Hey, this scene was your idea. I'm doing my best here. Just roll with it for now, okay?
Homer: *chuckles*

***

Rooney sat up but remained on the floor, looking up at his comrades while he wiped the grease off his hands with a rag.

"What's up?" he asked.

Bart jerked his head to the side. "Let's get comfortable over there."

"Sure." Rooney complied, standing while stuffing the rag in the back pocket of his coveralls.

Bart's caginess and the formality of the unplanned meeting tore the cap off the lid containing the butterflies.

He followed them to a card table with several folding chairs near the tool cage. Inside the cage, tools hung from a peg-board behind the chain-link fencing. The tools stared back at him, inviting Rooney to put them to use. He wished he could, instead of having this conversation.

Bart turned his chair around and straddled it. He took out a pack of cigarettes and lighter and made his usual show of lighting up. Chubby and Scruffy took chairs opposite each other. Rooney sat across from Bart. His head hung, avoiding eye contact with Bart, but he did it in such a way as to pretend interest in the motorcycle magazines scattered among the ashtrays, coffee-stained Styrofoam cups, and beer glasses lined with weeks old crusted foam.

There weren't that many people in the shop today, so it was relatively quiet with only a pair working on barbecues in one corner and a brother creating a fountain of sparks as he welded on a bike frame in another.

The sizeable open sliding door of the main entrance flooded summer daylight into the expansive shop full of lathes, welding equipment, stacked metal sheets and pipes, grinders, cars, trucks, and motorbikes. Some of the items were shiny and new. Some old and rusty. It was the playground of men who liked to work with their hands.

In between the crackle and sizzle of the arc welder, Rooney could hear birds chirping in the trees outside, and it made him think this would be a nice day if it weren't for the tension in the air.

He counted himself lucky. For the birds, that is. In prison, there had been plenty of stomach-butterflies and tension but no birds. Thank God for the birds.

"So," Bart commenced, sniffing and wiping his nose by rubbing his thumb across its bridge, trailing gray smoke. "That thing the other night at the Nickel. I was only half kidding around, ya know? I didn't expect you to beat that guy's ass right there and then, though I'd been impressed if you had, the point is, you do have an obligation to the Fraternity, see? You've been lollygagging under these old beater trucks, almost as if you're avoiding your duty to show your commitment by doing something more...spectacular."

Bart hung a noticeable pause in the air, and though Rooney wasn't looking at him, he could feel his stare.

Rooney crossed his arms. His gaze moved from the magazines to a notepad with the gang's "legit" business letterhead. The stylized words "Maverick Metal Fab" encircled a rearing stallion logo.

Scruffy lit a cigarette in that moment of silence, and Chubby leaned back in his metal chair, causing it to creak under his weight. In doing so, he grabbed the chain-link of the tool cage's sliding door to balance himself.

Rooney cleared his throat. "It's like you said, you didn't expect me to kick his ass right there, neither did—"

"You see, that's what I'm talking about." Bart stabbed a pair of fingers at him with the cigarette firmly clenched between them. "Lollygagging. Making excuses. The Fraternity expects action. Proof of membership. And just so we're clear, we're not talking about an ass-whoopin', we're talking about something big. Regulators are big time. We expect big-time in return. And don't think because your dad goes way back with Pops, you get a free pass."

"If anything, we expect more from you," Scruffy adds, leaning forward on his elbows. He maintained a hard stare as he slightly turned his head to spit a piece of cigarette filter troubling his bottom lip.

"Yeah, sure, you did some time in prison," Chubby jumped in, punctuating his words by sliding the cage's door in its track, "but rumor has it your time was less than impressive, spending more time keeping your head down, kinda like you are now."

Rooney's gaze shifted to the cage door, rolling back and forth, screeching under Chubby's hanging weight. Rooney winced at the noise. It echoed in his head, joined by other sounds. Screams. It took him a moment to realize they were his own screams echoing inside his head, boiling up from memories of a flurry of arms holding him down while a prison cell door clanged shut. He swallowed hard, and it felt like his body slowly drained out one of his coverall's pant legs. He *wanted* to drain out his pant leg.

A piercing whistle, lengthening and rising in pitch, shattered his trance and damn near burst his eardrums. Rooney's eyes shot up to catch Bart's hand swimming in front of his face with its thumb and forefinger outstretched to mimic a pair of fluttering wings. The whistle, a shrill mockery of the peaceful chirping outside the shop door, didn't end until Bart had Rooney's full attention.

"Earth to Rooney!" Bart's scowl lingered long after his whistle ended. Finally, he leaned back in his seat. "You get the message, or what? We're not messing around here!"

Clang! Chubby shoved the cage door shut, separating Rooney from the tools. Scruffy snorted and looked between his fellow interrogators with a mocking lip curl, gesturing at Rooney as if to say, "...this guy."

Rooney met Bart's eyes and didn't let go. Intrigued by the sudden boldness, Bart's eyes narrowed, and he leaned forward to match the stare. The shop went quiet. Even the activity from the others in the building melted away as if giving weight to this moment. The birds continued to chirp, though it sounded strained as if a momma bird were trying to distract a stalking cat away from a nest full of babies.

Say something, Rooney told himself, feeling the butterflies and panic rise. *Say anything. This is probably the last chance you're gonna get. Play it cool. Use the technique the prison resource counselor taught you when in tough situations. Be water. Flow like water. They can't punch water. They can't choke it. Water squeezes out between their fingers if they try. But if you are water, you can drown them. Drown them with your confidence.*

Rooney became water and let images of slamming prison doors and groping sweaty arms slip past him.

He leaned forward and said, "Look, fellas, I get it." He reached for the notepad and peeled a sheet off, laying it before him. "I owe the Fraternity a debt. My time in prison coulda been a lot worse if it weren't for the brothers I met inside. And I want you to know..." Rooney's hands began to methodically fold the paper into segments while he made it a point to make eye contact with each at the table. With each fold, the confidence in his voice grew. "...that I don't see it as a debt, but a pleasure, because you are my brothers, you gave me a home, a purpose, and I intend to repay that."

Rooney returned his eyes to the paper, making the folds more elaborate with each movement. Chubby leaned forward to watch the work. The expansive skin beneath Chubby's receding hairline wrinkled deeper with each fold and his increased interest.

"So," Rooney continued, "believe you me when I make my move, show my worth, you'll notice. But I gotta be smart about it, right? I can't cause any trouble for you guys. Can't let anything get back to you, so I can't be beating or killing people in public. And then there's my parole..." He shrugged and looked up, and he didn't mind if he looked scared or haunted because he was. "I ain't gonna lie, I ain't going back. No way." Bart straightened, gearing up to protest, but Rooney held up the paper he'd been crafting. It was now shaped like a horse—a stallion. As Bart frowned at the object, Rooney inserted his finger into a slot among the folds and made the horse's head bob while he said with what could only be called a cartoon character's voice, "Don't worry, Mister, I'll make you *reeeeal* proud. I'll do something soon. I'll do something...spectacular."

Rooney pulled on the horse's tail for an encore, and its sides flared to reveal a pair of flapping wings.

Despite himself, Chubby chuckled. "Hey, that's pretty neat. Where'd you learn to do that?"

Rooney reflected for a moment, his brow furrowed. "You know, I don't know. I just started doing it recently. Like it was something I've always been able to do, but I'm just now remembering how. Go figure."

"Who cares," Bart growled at Chubby, then redirected his ire to Rooney. "So, we on the same page? You gonna show us what you got, maybe with this fella we bumped into at the Nickel?"

Rooney bobbed his head slowly, deliberately. "You can count on me."

"Good. In the meantime, I need to count on you for something else." Bart tossed some folded documents on the table. "I need you to go to the DMV in Salem and register that old rental truck we got out back. We're going to need it to transport some of our two-legged merchandise from Portland in a couple weeks, then we'll be transporting those girls across state lines, so the truck needs to be clean, neat, and legal. Can you do that? Because the first rule of committing a crime is: *you don't commit a fucking crime while doing it.* That truck can't be pulled over for not having the proper tags. Also, when the time comes, I want you to be the one to drive the truck because I want to see how you handle the women because I know you get kinda squirrely around them. I want to see you keep your shit together. Finally, when you go to the DMV, take the propane tanks and make the Salem milk run. Got it? Roonster? Hello?"

Bart looked over his shoulder to follow Rooney's gaze.

"You like how them birds sing?" Bart chided.

"Sorry, yeah, I do, I mean...sorry...You can count on me!"

"Well, good," Bart replied between gritted teeth, "because if you fuck any of this up, you'll never hear a bird again."

He made the flying-bird gesture with his hand, his fingers flapping in rhythm with that ear-splitting whistle.

Chapter 38
A Day at the Couch Races

I'm not keen on going to the races, feeling guilty about not spending more time on the computer looking for work, but Gwen once again lassos me with her feather boa and draws me to town to watch.

Homer Davenport Days are not over until adults race actual davenports. And so that is how we end up watching Silvertonians push couches on wheels up and down Main Street. For a prize of bragging rights, large men pushed moderately sized sofas with big, sleek mountain bike wheels and petite helmeted pilots. A few of the davenports are on slow casters and participate just for laughs.

And laugh Gwen does. She still doesn't have her younger girls, as I had thought would be the case, nor is Zoë around this time. I sense something is off but don't ask. Of course, the street is packed, and I don't know what surprises me more: the number of faces I recognize or how many I don't. I'm also surprised to see that news crews are covering the event. I look over my shoulder, but there is no Todd.

I tell Gwen about the picture with her ex-husband in it. She only rolls her eyes, not the least bit surprised, nor all that concerned.

There may be no Todd, but there is a Regulator here and there. Nearby, a pair straddle their parked bikes, making lewd comments to pretty girls as they walk by.

And if that wasn't enough to cast a cloud on an otherwise festive day, I also notice a sad-faced woman wearing a bonnet stapling a flyer to a telephone pole. When she moves away, with her long heavy dress swishing in the oppressive heat, I see the flyer has the picture of a pretty blonde girl with the words, "Have

You Seen Me?" There is a phone number to call and other information about the most recent missing Silverton girl.

I'm saddened by the sight of it, but Gwen pulls on my arm, turning my attention elsewhere.

The races go well, and a team from Scotts Mills wins with their burgundy davenport outfitted with high-tech racing bike wheels. Rumor has it that there had been some serious off-track betting going on this year. In a stunning red dress and hat with a lacy veil, Mayor Stu awards the winners a trophy. They get their picture together on the event stage, though Stu's long legs, chiseled calves, and cleavage steal the show.

Gwen and I decide to go to Your Break.

We find a table easy enough in the establishment; after all, it takes up almost an entire city block. When I was little, it had been Coast to Coast Hardware. Now, it was a honky-tonk with many, many pool tables and a long bar. Unlike Mac's and the Wooden Nickel, this place is bare bones with no frills, aside from some neon beer lights. It does have a shuffleboard table, though, which means my dad is here often with his league.

While waiting for our drinks, I continue glancing over my shoulder.

"You can relax," Gwen says, a bit of agitation in her voice. "Todd is working today, I'm pretty sure. My mother-in-law is watching the girls and keeps calling, asking what kind of cereal they like to eat these days."

The drinks arrive, and Gwen fights her mouth around a parasol in her glass. When she finally gets a sip, she makes a face.

"It's not Todd so much I'm worried about," I say, and when I try to explain to her the whole dynamic history of all things Rooney, she cuts me off with a shout to the waitress.

"Hey, there is waaaay too much amaretto in this!"

As Gwen bickers with the waitress, I sit by, scratching my head, staring at my beer, watching the carbonation bubbles. People have always said that I don't open up enough. That I hold things in. Here I am, trying to do better, and Gwen was more interested in amaretto.

While waiting for a new drink for Gwen, I restart my concerns regarding recent events. Rooney, the Regulators, looking for work, the pain in my head.

Gwen follows along for a while. I notice her pupils are dilated.

After her attention drifts and evidently tired of waiting for her drink, she reaches over and takes mine. She chugs all but the last third of it. When she returns it, her lipstick is smeared all over the rim.

"You think there will be music here tonight?" she asks.

"I...don't know," I say, frowning at my glass. "You know, I've got some things I'd like to talk about. Need to talk about, actually, so..."

"Hey! Any day now!" Gwen shouts, leaning out of our booth. She turns back to me. "What was that again?"

I sigh, turn my beer a hundred and eighty degrees, and take a drink. "Never mind."

The place starts to fill up, and before you know it, day turns into evening, and a band shows up. It becomes so loud that it is hard to hear any kind of conversation, which is fine because there isn't that much conversation.

That is until Dylan and Bailey show up, and there is plenty to talk about. They sit with us in our booth, and I'm incredibly grateful for their presence. I try to talk about my issues over the music, and though Dylan is sympathetic, it is clear there is little he can do to help other than buy me some drinks. Which he does, and the evening goes quite well from there.

Well, for me, anyway.

Gwen drinks much more than usual, and between the hot summer night, the sticky sweatiness, the swirling cacophony of music and a thousand voices, the alcohol, the pressing bodies on the dance floor, she is way past her limit. She runs out the open double doors, knocking over a fan.

"Look out!" Dylan shouts, laughing. "Hot mess express coming!"

Bailey slaps Dylan's upper arm.

We follow and find her hanging from a parking meter.

"You okay, honey?" Bailey asks, approaching.

Gwen waves her off, stands erect, makes as though she is about to make a grandiose proclamation, then turns and vomits into the gutter.

Dylan grimaces. Even my stomach wants to heave.

"That's going to leave a mark," Dylan says.

Bailey shushes him.

Dylan and Bailey haven't been hitting the drinks all day like Gwen and me, so they offer to take her home.

Maybe I agree a little too quickly, but I've had my limit, too—of Gwen.

Chapter 39
The Nothingness

How long have I been here now?

It is hard to tell. It seems an endless cycle of restless sleep with vivid dreams or memories, followed by anxiety-ridden hours staring at a computer screen looking for work, for purpose. Then whole weeks pass, staring at a glass of booze downtown. Sometimes I just stare at the ceiling in my old bedroom. Stare out the window. Hope something will happen on its own.

But nothing comes. So much nothing that it constricts like a snake, suffocating me. Who knew that absence has weight? It threatens to bury me alive. Death would be freedom, but this nothingness, this emptiness, is worse than death. It is like dying without progress, aware of every painful passing second for eternity.

It must impact me on a deeper level than I realize because I start to sleepwalk again for the first time in years. One night, I find myself on the lawn, having jumped out the window. It would have been funny, except for the pain in my head, and it turned out to be one of the few times my parents actually locked the door, and I had to wake up the household to get back in.

I try to relax. Sometimes I sit and watch TV with Dad, even when it does that thing when a live feed comes in from the space station. We watch Don Pettit float around, being an astronaut, going about *his* purpose.

Sometimes I help Mom in her flowerbeds, doing the heavy lifting until fat drops of sweat fall from my forehead onto the bricks of the beds like sprinkles of rain.

When Dad takes his naps and Mom is not in her flowerbeds, we'll take over the TV and watch her favorite shows on the True Detective Channel, where she is always keen to point out she has the case solved before the hour is up. A common element in the shows is that the authorities often leave out specific details of murders when reporting to news networks. This is to help distinguish between false leads and goods ones. It reminds me of the conversation I had with Jason about the chlorinated water found in the women's lungs, and it chills me once again that this is happening in my hometown.

Sometimes I visit Sis and try to be a good Gunky to the kids.

Mostly I go downtown and feed pennies to the hungry parking meters and sit in a bar.

Tonight, Clea has talked me into letting her make me another fruity cocktail at the Grotto. I can't say no to her smile.

I have a notebook with me, and I lie to myself that I will start writing again, but I stare at the pages the same way I stare at the computer screen. It hurts to know I finally have all the time in the world to write the Great American Novel, but these pages are blank. Or are they?

I scrutinize the moisture sliding down the cold glass of my cocktail. I collect some on my forefinger and rub it with my thumb. Something nags at my mind, and I hear that static noise in my ears.

"I'm sorry, what was that?" I ask Clea, vaguely aware she said something.

"Remembering forward," she responds. "That was the plot point at the end of the movie. It was pretty original."

"Pardon?" I can feel red rising in my face. "I was distracted. What were we talking about?"

Clea rests a hand on a cocked hip and gives me a look of disbelief. "You mean to tell me I went on and on about the movie *Arrival* to no one in particular?"

I scrunch up my shoulders, embarrassed.

"I said you, being a writer, would probably be really interested in the movie," she repeats, "because it has a unique twist where the main character, Amy Adams, gains the ability to 'remember' *into* the future. This is because she had been influenced by aliens who have a different thought process." She turns up a hand, like *Well?*

I bob my head. "Cool twist. I haven't seen the movie yet. I'll be sure to now."

Clea playfully smacks me with a bar towel. "Well, we've run out of time to talk about it because it's that time again."

My lips screw up in acknowledgment. I finish my drink, close my empty notebook, and watch Clea's undulating owl as she goes about shutting down the bar. I consider asking her if she wants to join me elsewhere for another drink, with the promise I'll pay better attention.

I lose my nerve and leave.

The evening is quiet. Homer Davenport Days are over.

As I walk, I try to squash a guilty feeling, reflecting on the numerous times Gwen has called and how I have evaded her, citing my need to look for work.

When I arrive at Mac's, the liveliest thing going is the ceiling fan. Music plays from the jukebox, but I can't say what song it is. I sit at the bar and stare at the shelves of booze arranged like stadium seating. The bottles seem to cheer me on.

"You again," Natalie greets me, coming from the kitchen and throwing a towel over one shoulder.

"Me again," I confess.

"What is this, third time this week?"

I shrug. "I have to stay in character. I'd like vodka. Straight. On the rocks...and make sure it's—"

"Potato vodka," she finishes. "Local distillery okay?"

I admit that it would be perfect.

While she turns to prepare my drink, I notice that Jesus has decided to join me. He has a glass of water in front of him. I set my gaze to the mirror behind the bar to note if I can see his reflection. I can't. When I turn back, I see that he has turned the water into wine.

"That one never gets old," I tell him. "Great party trick."

Natalie sets my vodka in front of me. She is frowning.

"What?" I ask.

"You're doing it again," she replies.

"What's that?"

"Talking to yourself. You know you do that a lot, right?"

I swallow hard, apologize, and sip my drink.

"You don't, like, have voices in your head, do you?" she asks, wiping the bar while maintaining a critical—perhaps concerned—look at me.

"Me? Pshaw!" I make a face. "Heck no, but I do have a song in my heart."

I say the last with a smile and a wink, and it seems to alleviate any concern she might have. It even elicits a hint of a smile.

Little did I know that smile is about the only good thing that happens for the rest of the evening. Sitting on the barstool, I try to solve the mysteries of the universe, but the only mystery I progress on is why I had been sleepwalking recently. I squint hard in the mirror, vaguely recollecting dreams of drowning in splashing water. Or was I drowning someone? Fighting someone? Or...?

The pain returns, and rather than try and rub the back of my scalp, I pinch the bridge of my nose and squeeze my eyes shut. When I open them again, I'm in my car driving home, still trying to decipher the dream that sent me jumping out my bedroom window. The road in front of me barely registers. I only see dark water rippling against rocks. I hear a rhythmic splashing noise, and I look up to see a creature lapping at the water with a long pink tongue from a narrow muzzle. Above the tongue, burning into me, are two yellow eyes. They turn red, then blue, then back to red. They're now swirling lights.

My heart jumps into my throat. Police lights fill my rear view mirror.

My heart falling from my throat to my stomach. I pull over, groaning, and do a double-take at the officer who comes to my window. His radio at his shoulder crackles.

"Hey, Andy," I say.

Andy bends over to get a better look at me. He squints, trying to place my face.

"I used to hang with your little brother Reggie," I explain, then say my name. "I lived down the street from you guys."

Recognition crosses his face, and he nods. "License and registration, please."

Despite my urge to point out I just told him who I was, I know futility when I see it. So, I produce the documents.

He looks them over with his flashlight. "Your plates and address are Washington State," he points out. "I've seen your vehicle around town for a while now. Are you moving to the State of Oregon?"

"I'm just staying with my parents for a little while." My heart climbs back into my chest where it belongs. This doesn't sound like a DUI stop. "I'm in between jobs."

"You know you need to register your vehicle and update your address if you're going to live here, right?"

I bristle. I'm angry, outraged.

"Look, Andy," I say, despite his name tag clearly stating 'Ofc. *Andrew* Delaney.' "If I buy a house here, I'll be sure to do that. Otherwise, I have every business being here. This is my *home*. No matter where I go in the world or where I have an address, Silverton is always my home. You should know that."

Andy's face is impassive behind his Coke-bottle glasses. He leans into the window and takes a sniff. "Have you been drinking this evening?"

I freeze just a hair too long. I am committed now. "Yeah, I've had a few."

"What is a few?" Andy asks, straightening.

"Three drinks over four hours," I say. "You can look at the receipts in my wallet to confirm that. Given my weight and height, I doubt I'm over the legal limit." Of course, I don't mention that those drinks were hard liquor.

"Please step out of the vehicle," Andy says, taking a step back and pushing his glasses up his nose.

I almost shout but catch myself. "Are you kidding me?"

"Out, please."

It takes an effort not to slam my car door. Andy's cruiser's lights are still activated, lighting up the entire neighborhood and washing over me like a swirling scarlet-and-blue letter. I can almost feel the neighborhood parting their curtains at this very moment, recognizing either me or my car.

Andy speaks in a professional monotone. "Please extend your arms and touch your nose with the tips of your fingers, one at a time."

I place my hands on my hips. "Andy! You got a breathalyzer in your cruiser or not? Do you really need to make me jump through these hoops?"

"Touch your nose, please," insists Robocop.

Again, I know the futility of arguing, so I comply as deliberately and dramatically as possible. While doing so, I take a good look at Andy. He hasn't changed much. He always reminds me of this Van Halen video, "Hot For Teacher." It starts with a mother putting her nervous son on a school bus on the first day of school, telling him that she hopes he makes friends this year. The boy, Waldo, points out, "Aw, Mom, you know I'm not like other guys. I'm nervous, and my socks are too loose." Waldo wears thick glasses, a bowtie, and so much hair product that it makes a rubbery noise when his mom runs her hands over it. Waldo proceeds to prove his point as he shakes and sweats throughout the video. Yeah, that is pretty much Andy Delaney. Except, rather than shake, he moves around as if there really is the proverbial stick up his butt.

"Please walk this line for three yards, one foot in front of the other with hands extended to either side."

I comply but try to loosen the mood. "How are your folks?"

"They're fine." With his monotone, the answer sounds like a "none of your business" kind of fine. I stand waiting for his next order, still irked that *Andy Delaney* is giving me orders. Finally, Andy pauses to think, covering his mouth with a hand while resting the arm on the other, carefully considering his next move. There is a long moment of silence.

"Well, I'd say I'm nowhere near point-oh-eight blood alcohol level," I finally say.

Andy approaches and takes another sniff. "You've been drinking. Technically, I can arrest you regardless of your BAC, so long as I feel you're DUI and a risk."

Now I'm outraged. "Is this because I used to tell you your sister was hot all the time? Because if that is the case, trust me, I know how that feels now, and boy am I sorry."

Andy is unmoved.

"Or are you compensating for the fact that you didn't write tickets to those Regulator gang members like you should have in front of Mac's the day of the parade?"

His head snaps up, and I see a real reaction swimming behind those heavy glasses. He opens his mouth to say something, and just as I realize I had finally said the exact wrong thing, the radio attached to the epaulet of his right shoulder crackles alive, and a voice calls out a long string of code. The only word I catch is "reservoir."

Andy's jaw drops, and he reels off an answering code as he's rushing back to his cruiser. He slaps my license and registration onto my trunk. In the distance, a police siren wails, getting louder as it approaches. Soon, another cruiser rockets by at light speed, trailing blue and red strobes like a time-lapse photograph.

"This is your lucky day," he shouts. Then, as he ducks into his driver's seat, he fires a parting shot. "If you're going to be hanging out in Silverton, I'd seriously reconsider driving in close proximity to your drinking."

He blasts off in his car, blaring his siren, chasing after his colleague.

When I get home, all hope that the missing Russian Old Believer girl might turn up alive is dashed when the television announces she has been found floating dead in the local reservoir.

Chapter 40
A Party for the Ages

Following handwritten notes while driving in the rural dark turns out to be challenging. Bubba insisted that the party location was not GPS-friendly, and as I try to decode a crossroads from my map of squiggly lines and road names, I find this to be true.

In the distance, a pair of spotlights shoot into the sky, circling. On a summer night, without clouds for context, they simply fade into nothingness. I pause a reasonable distance from the crossroads, letting my car headlights linger on the road sign at the paved intersection. I consult my map and decide I'm at the correct place but do not see the accompanying dirt road that will lead me to the party.

As I coast closer to the source of the meandering beams, what looks like a man on a motocross bike passes through the light. Then I see another dirt bike, then another, fly through the air. I can see them leaping like fleas. I roll down my car window. Even before it's entirely down, I hear the buzz of engines and hard music.

I pull forward a little, and the hillock to my right obscuring my view melts away to reveal a pandemonium of spotlights, generator-fueled floodlights, what look like stage lights, and a multitude of vehicle headlights frenetically roving in a portion of the field. *A party for the ages.*

I now see the mouth of a dirt road. I toss the piece of paper aside, put my car into all-wheel drive and take the road, bouncing gently over the dusty surface.

I park in a vacant spot between two monster trucks tricked out with lift kits. When I get out, I not only hear music and the drone and buzz of vehicles in the distance, I hear the sea-surf sound of a crowd.

Good God, just how many people are here?

I follow some other recent arrivals and we come to a sea of people milling about a stage and a makeshift bar to one side of it. A band there plays thrashing music. Tents of all sizes and shapes pepper the landscape but primarily group in one area. Beyond the stage are the spotlights, and beyond them is a dirt track with little hills evenly spaced out. Here, motorbikes race about to the tune of angry lawnmowers, periodically leaping into the sky to the cheers of onlookers.

I stop one of the milling partiers.

"Hey, you see Bubba?"

"Over there, man!" he shouts over the band, gesturing with a plastic cup in hand and spilling a little of its contents.

Bubba is standing before one of those large canvas hunting tents that looks like a Roman general's campaign quarters. With his bushy beard and shaved head, however, he seems more like a Viking chieftain. He's deep in conversation with several other bushy-bearded guys in jeans and T-shirts. One of them has his shirt sleeve rolled up past the shoulder and offers his tattooed arm up for examination.

Bubba shakes his head. "Nah, man, that's not a tattoo, that's more like a cry for help." Then he sees me approaching and a smile spreads across his expansive face. He brushes past the disappointed tattooed guy and meets me halfway.

I extend my hand. "Hey Bubba, thanks for—oh God!"

Bubba sweeps me up in a bear hug, lifting me off the ground and causes my feet to sway this way and that. I think I hear my back crack.

"Thanks for coming man!" he shouts. He sets me down, and I resist the urge to grab my back like an old man.

"What a party! What is there, like a thousand people here?" I say.

"Fourteen hundred, so far, but who's counting?" he replies.

I notice for the first time who is on the stage.

"Is that Josh Arnold up there?" I ask, noting the shirtless muscular guy on bass. If he had been playing the saxophone, along with that large chain necklace, he would have looked like that oiled-up guy from the concert scene in *Lost Boys*.

"Yep, sure is," Bubba confirms.

"Then, the band must be Floater, right?"

"Right again. I wanted my party to be an all Silverton affair. I tried to get the Dharma Bums to come, but Jeremy Wilson and those guys were busy elsewhere."

"That would have been something," I say.

"Did you know that Nirvana used to open for *them* back in the day?" Bubba asks.

I raise my eyebrows. Of all the trivia running around in my head, that was not one. People who truly love something, whether sports or music, will always out-trivia me in their area of passion.

"No, but wow, cool to know," I reply and add, "that would have been great if Jeremy could be here. I didn't know him really well, but he was the first person my freshman year to show me that not all upperclassmen were dicks. I would have liked to have told him that."

Bubba lightly slaps my upper arm and laughs.

"You can get drinks over there, and there is going to be music of one sort or another *all* night. You're going to recognize a lot of faces, so you'll have a great time. I guarantee it!"

Before he shoves me toward the bar, I thank him again and wish him a happy birthday.

The bar is a series of boards resting on used beer kegs running the length of the side of the stage. There are shorter lengths of boards on more kegs that make tables opposite the bar. Floater is taking a break, and it's relatively quiet. A woman moves back and forth behind the boards, preparing drinks from bottles arranged underneath the bar. Her long sandy ponytail swishes with every movement. I recognize her.

"Hey Krista," I greet her.

The tall woman freezes and upon recognizing me, squeals a return greeting.

"Well, hey there!" she continues preparing a drink while maintaining eye contact. Her expressive dark eyebrows knit over her brown eyes. "I heard you were in town, though I cannooooot fathom why you haven't paid Troy and me a visit yet."

"Soon," I'm quick to point out. "I'm making the rounds, saving the best for last."

"Good save." Her eyebrows release over a big smile.

"Speaking of Troy," I say, "where is your better half?"

"Troy's here, putting his drum kit together." Krista puts the final touches on the drink and hands it to a waiting customer. "He'll be performing on stage soon. First, though, there's going to be a group opportunity for everyone to gather 'round and sing 'Happy Birthday.'"

"Ah, good to know," I acknowledge.

"Make you a drink?"

"Of course."

"Potato vodka on the rocks?"

"You know it."

I watch her in a flurry of activity as she prepares my drink. Her joie de vivre of performing such a simple activity is infectious. When the drink is prepared, she offers up the ice-bobbing cup.

"Hear, hear!" I say, taking the cup and lifting it for a cheer.

"Hear, hear!" She touches my glass with the bottle.

I take a sip, and she takes a breathtaking pull from the bottle, creating bubbles as if a drain plug had been pulled in a sink.

Holy shit, I reflect on the sight, but my attention quickly diverts to a distinct sound, followed by another.

"Are those gunshots?" I ask.

"Yep, over there," Krista belches, gesturing with the bottle in one hand and wiping her mouth with the other. "I set up a regulation firing range."

"You did?" I frown, then remember. "Oh yeah, that's right, you had a scholarship for shooting at AU. I guess if anyone knows how to put a proper firing range together, it would be you."

Krista beams and throws a pair of thumbs at herself.

"You should check it out," she says proudly. "I believe your buddy Jeremy is already over there."

I bristle at the name. "Yeah, I need to talk to that guy."

She doesn't catch my tone as more customers arrive and crowd around me, demanding her services. I pull away from the bar, letting them fill the vacancy.

"Go check it out," she reiterates as she grabs bottles and cups, then adds, "and you better come visit sooner than Halloween or New Year's, you hear me?"

I smile and raise my cup.

I meander in the direction Krista had indicated, and the crowd thins out.

On the edge of the activity is a sculpted regulation shooting range. The same equipment that made the race track probably made its earthen backstop. Cardboard cutout targets of "bad guys" hang from the dirt wall, and a series of metal pivot targets sprout from the ground about halfway between the wall and the firing line. A series of boards neatly rest upon barrels, forming shooting benches, and people are lined up and popping off shots from an armory of weapons.

As I approach, I first recognize Jeremy's tall silhouette among the group. He's with Dylan and Jodi and some others. My stomach tightens at the sight of Jodi, but he's in a passive-aggressive mood tonight and ignores me as the others greet me.

"So, what happened the other night?" I ask Jeremy as I pull up to the bench near him.

"Huh?" Jeremy is in the process of ejecting a magazine from an AR-15. All types of firearms litter the bench, as well as ammo cans and other shooting paraphernalia. Underneath the boards are the various duffel bags and carrying cases. Dylan is presently bent over and rummaging around one of the bags.

I set my drink on the bench. "The Nickel, we were supposed to meet there, remember?"

Jeremy pauses in inserting a freshly loaded magazine into his rifle receptacle. His unibrow screws up in deep thought.

"Oh yeah, sorry, man." He slams the magazine in and pulls on the charging handle, making a hard metallic *clink*. "Something came up. Meant to call you." He turns and raises the rifle in the direction of the firing range. An ear-busting *pop* followed by the distinctive hollow *ping* of an AR-15 fills the air. It sounds like thunder inside a tin can. The weapon's flash lights up the vicinity, etching his and Jodi's profile. Dirt kicks up beyond one of the many pivot targets.

"I could have used your help that night..." I start to say, but a series of *pop, pop, pop, pingpingping*'s shouts me down.

"What's that?" Jeremy says absently, ejecting the magazine and examining its contents.

"Never mind," I grumble, reaching for my drink.

When I do, I see Jesus is there. He has picked up a pistol and is examining it with curiosity as if seeing one for the first time. When he turns it to look down the barrel, I snatch it from him.

"Gimme that before you hurt yourself," I chastise.

"Ah, I see you found my nine-millimeter," Dylan says, standing. "Did you bring yours?"

I hand Dylan his pistol. An old Beretta semi-auto. Blue-black metal with a checkered wood pistol grip.

"No," I confess. "I didn't know half the stuff going on tonight was happening. Otherwise, I would have planned better. My gun is still back in Vancouver."

"That's too bad," Dylan says, inserting the long magazine he had just retrieved from his duffel bag into the butt of the pistol. He pulls the slide, and the weapon is live. He makes sure the barrel points out into the range at all times, of course.

"You still have your Glock?" Jeremy asks, casually feeding long brass rounds into his rifle magazine.

"Nah. I couldn't hit the broadside of a barn with it. So I changed to an H&K forty-five."

"Niiiiice." Jeremy bobs his head in approval. "Which one?"

"The USP sub-compact."

Jeremy bobs his head again. "Like it?"

"Yeah. Ironically, even though I moved up in caliber, I'm much more accurate."

An odd sound follows, like a pneumatic airline that has sprung a leak in its hose but coming in quick bursts. We look over to see Jodi in a wide-legged marksman stance, aiming a Colt 1911 with an extended barrel on it. He pulls the trigger, and the pneumatic sound comes again, accompanied by a suppressed flash.

I realize the extended barrel is a silencer, though it's odd-looking, glittering, and colorful.

"You like Jodi's ultra-cool special-ops silencer?" Dylan asks with an ironic smile.

Jodi is cursing up a storm, his choice of words gravitating toward taking Jesus' name in vain. Every time he does, I see Jesus wince next to me. "The weight of this thing is throwing my aim off."

"Then why did you get it?" Dylan asks, firing his pistol. His weapon has no silencer and is very loud.

"Because it's cool." Jodi scoffs as if the answer is obvious. "Besides, it's not the suppressor that is throwing things off. It's all this crap on it."

Jodi fires again. Curses again. Jesus looks downcast.

"Hey, watch your fucking language," I tell Jodi.

"Bite me," he retorts and shoots his pistol. One of the targets makes a metallic sound and spins. Jodi pumps his free fist in approval and holds up his gun with the other.

I get a better look at the extension, noting what looks like sequins and rhinestones covering it.

"Then you shouldn't have left it in my truck for my daughter to find and bedazzle, you moron." Dylan shoots several angry shots. Dirt kicks up all around the targets.

Jodi sighs. "I said I was sorry. I told you, man, somebody else took my usual truck keys that day and left me with only yours."

Dylan fires his weapon until the slide ejects with the last piece of brass arcing through the air. "Still no excuse for leaving that stuff in my truck."

Jodi mumbles another apology.

"Care to shoot my gun?" Dylan asks, holding it towards me, handle first.

I set my drink down and accept the weapon. Dylan hands me a full magazine. I slam it in the handle receiver, pull and release the slide, take aim, and squeeze a shot off.

Dirt kicks up a good yard before a pivot target. I hear Jodi snort a laugh. I shoot again, and earth flies well beyond the mark, accompanied by some remark from Jodi.

I pause, adjust, and fire repeatedly and rapidly. *Clink! Clink! Clink!* The target spins. The slide ejects, and Jodi shuts up. I hand the weapon back to Dylan, handle first.

"Thanks," I say.

"Nice shooting, Tex." Jeremy smiles. "Want to try this out?" He holds the AR-15 to me—it's technically an M4, the 15's compact cousin. I agree and gingerly take it from him. I raise it to my shoulder.

"Whoa, hey, whatcha doin'?" Jeremy says, reaching for the rifle.

"What?" I bristle and pull away.

"You're holding it to the wrong shoulder."

"So says you," I respond, still bristling. "I shoot rifle left-handed."

Jeremy's eyes widen. "That's right, I totally forgot about that. You shoot a bow that way too, right?"

"Yeah, and pool stick. Actually, about the only thing I do right-handed is writing." I return to raising the rifle and aim.

Jodi scoffs. "Yeah, well, you do realize the shell is still going to eject on the right side?"

Crap, he's right, but I'm not about to let him correct me now. I fire, and sure enough, a brass-colored blur flies out and hits my right shoulder. Downrange, dirt explodes just to the right of one of the cardboard cutouts. Despite having a relatively mild kick, the rifle still stings my left shoulder. This whole experience is going to hurt.

I fire again. A hot shell casing hits my right forearm, burns momentarily. I miss the target again. Jodi is laughing, and I hear him move closer. I fire, and this time the ejected shell clears any part of my body. I feel Jodi to my left, and his mouth is by my ear, invading my personal space with a blast of alcohol breath.

"More proof of your half-breed, cross-wired brain!" he shouts.

I pull the trigger again and miss the dirt wall altogether, and the hot shell ejects into my shoulder and bounces back into my face. It burns so bad I'm sure it leaves a mark.

Jodi is laughing so hard he is doubled over.

I slam the rifle on the bench and come at him. He sobers up just long to take a swing at me. I duck, turning my forward momentum into a tackle. I have my arms around his waist, but he's much more solid than when we were skinny teenagers, and he doesn't go down as I hoped.

"Gotcha!" He laughs and slams his sharp elbow onto my back.

Jeremy and Dylan are shouting. Another blow to my back tells me I won't be able to handle too many more of these, but he's got his free arm entangled in my upper torso and arm, holding me in place. Desperate, I kick one of my legs back, arcing over my back like a scorpion tail. My foot connects with something soft, accompanied by a grunt.

Jodi relinquishes his hold on me, and when I stand up, ready to throw some punches, Dylan's arms nab me. Jeremy is likewise holding Jodi, who is nursing a bleeding nose.

"He actually got me," Jodi says in wonder.

"This guy needs an enema!" Jeremy announces with a laugh, and he drags Jodi off to the bar.

As he's pulled away, Jodi mumbles, "That was actually kind of cool..."

"You all right?" Dylan asks, rubbing my back.

I release a frustrated shout. "Why do I let that guy get under my skin!"

Dylan throws his head back and laughs. "You're not the only one, man. We should have let you guys duke it out. I was hoping you'd kick his ass. My money is on you."

I scream a couple more times until it is out of my system, which, of course, elicits more chuckles from Dylan.

"Here, drink your drink," Dylan says, handing me my vodka. "Wow, you're flexible. Maybe I should get into that yoga thing."

I get the cup to my lips despite the adrenaline shakes. "Yeah, chicks dig it."

"Everything here okay?"

I look over to see a man dismounting a motorcycle right next to the firing range. When he approaches, I see he's a stocky fellow with a shaved head, sandy goatee, and a big hoop earring in one ear. A dreamcatcher necklace hangs from his neck.

"Dave!" Dylan shouts.

I do a double-take and recognize the guy. There are approximately two hundred people in the fraternity of my life whom I've known since childhood. This guy is one of them.

There are hugs all around as we catch Dave up to speed on current events.

"Freakin' Jodi," he says, shaking his head.

Dylan offers his pistol to Dave to shoot, but Dave reaches behind his back and pulls out a compact semi-automatic.

"Never leave home without it," he says with a toothy smile and a glint in his green eyes. "An unfortunate by-product of being a prison guard. I never know when I'm going to run into one of my former tenants."

"How's that?" I ask.

"Prisoners are released all the time, and some carry a grudge," he explains.

"Right," I say. "You work over at the state pen, right?"

"Correct-o-mundo," he replies and squeezes off a barrage of shots downrange. Every last one clinks off the spinning targets. My ears are ringing.

Though not the same, the ringing reminds me of the buzzing that has been recently haunting me, creating an obscure interior darkness that has left me disjointed and confused. A darkness that has coincidentally, or perhaps not so coincidentally, made recent difficult events more palpable: Rooney, murdered women, my relationships—old and new. Dave's presence reminds me he just might be in a position to give context to some of that darkness.

"You've been a guard for a long time now," I observe, angling toward a particular line of questioning.

"And how," he replies. "Going to retire from the state soon. It's a young man's job, and two fused discs later, I'm going to hang up my spurs. Open a shop downtown Silverton like a genuine old person and relax, selling ice cream. Get this; I'm going to reopen the Nickelodeon."

"Get out of here!" Dylan says.

"I've already put a down payment on the space. And you'll never guess what I found in the basement." Dylan and I wait for the answer. Dave sings, "'*Put Another Nickel in the Nickel-Nickel-odeon, Music! Music! Music!*'"

Before he finishes, we're singing along.

"The jukebox is still there?" I ask. This pleasant memory momentarily derails my initial attempt at questioning.

"Yes," Dave says. "Needs a little work, but it still lights up with the oil bubbling through it and everything."

"Nice!" I say. Everyone had loved that place when growing up.

"I'll have to bring my kids," Dylan adds.

"Soda fountains, the whole nine yards. All the ice cream, just like in the old days. And not a moment too soon. I'll be retiring at just the right time and avoid the next monster they catch and throw in my cellblock."

"Who's that?" I ask.

Dylan has already set about to pack up his, Jeremy's, and Jodi's guns and equipment. He scowls when he comes to Jodi's bedazzled silencer before tossing it into a bag.

"You haven't heard?" Dave asks. "The guy running around killing girls? He's gone and done it now. Killed one of the Russian Old Believer women. That's going to attract some attention. It's just a matter of time before he's caught. I can handle killers and thieves, but it's those creepy serial killers that make my skin crawl. Good riddance!"

"You're certain it's one guy? An actual serial killer?" I ask, considering the various points of view I've heard recently.

"Damn straight." Dave asserts. "Prison is like a telephone switchboard for criminals: all the illicit activity in the state is either talked about, ends up, or originates in prison. We guards hear the scuttlebutt. Gang members wield their entire empires from behind bars and much more effectively because most of the information-traffic moves through there. They've got their finger on the pulse of murder in the state, and if they don't know who is committing the murders, that leaves only one option. A lone wolf. A predator. A serial killer."

I'm not so sure I agree, but it gives me something to consider. The discussion of gangs, however, brings up another point for me.

"Hey, wasn't Rooney in your prison?" I ask, trying to sound casual.

"Yes, he was." Dave strokes his chin. "Scrawny guy. He had it rough."

"Well, he must have made some connections because he's a Regulator now."

Dave shakes his head angrily. "Those guys. Ruin the good name of bikers everywhere. They're the reason I get dirty looks when I'm out riding."

I agree and tell Dave about my recent encounters with the gang.

"You'd do well to stay clear of them." Dave levels a dead-serious gaze at me. "Those people ain't no joke. They recently dragged a guy to death because they *thought* he was an informant."

Grimacing, I raise my hands defensively. "Hey, no argument here. As if I don't have enough problems."

Dave tilts his head at that, and I open up about everything else happening in my life, unleashing a verbal torrent uncharacteristic of myself. I didn't realize how much I had needed to unload. I had hoped to do it with Jeremy over beers or even with Gwen, but now it's Dave who patiently listens, leaning against the bench. Eventually, Dylan excuses himself to put the bags and ammo cans in his vehicle.

"Wow, you've got a lot on your plate," Dave says when I take a breath. "It does sound like life is out to get you."

"Funny, that is more or less what my dad said, though he summed it up as 'the Coyote,'" I reply, taking a sip of my vodka.

After another head tilt, I give my dad's explanation of the folklore character putting me to the test.

"I think he might be right." Dave fingers the dreamcatcher necklace around his neck. "Hey, mythology is just ancient man's attempt at making sense of the universe, right? Your mind has a lot to make sense of right now: Rooney. Losing your job. Losing your mind...I mean your memory," he chuckles good-naturedly, "even this Jodi business tonight. Something is making it difficult for you to deal with it all. Why not call that something 'Coyote'?"

My hand involuntarily goes to the back of my head to rub my scalp. The pain is there again but deadened by alcohol. The rubbing seems to elicit the sound of water splashing as if being lapped up by a tongue—a tongue beneath a pair of yellow eyes. I shake the feeling off.

"Or," Dave adds thoughtfully, but also with a shrug, "maybe it really is the Coyote from your native heritage."

"Yeah, how's that?" I try not to sound too incredulous. After all, he is taking the time to listen to me when no one else seems to want to.

"Remember when we were kids? You were always so eager to tell us that you're Indian," Dave explains. "And the rest of us were so jealous because, you know, that made you more interesting than us. But by the time we got to high school, you had stopped proudly telling people about your heritage." I bristle a little at that but can't deny it either, so let Dave continue. "Maybe this Coyote guy took offense to that."

I chuckle, but it comes a little forced. "Maybe it's a little of both. Part psychological, part mythological? I'll take it all into consideration. Whatever the case may be, thanks for listening to me, man."

We are now the only ones at the firing range, and no more shots thunder. There is no music coming from the stage. Only the distant rumble of the generators running the floodlights fills the space between us.

Dave hugs me and slaps my back, hurting the spot where Jodi had been stabbing me with his bony elbow. I pretend I don't feel it.

***

We go to the bar near the stage, where Jeremy has saved us seats. Dave, however, peels off to the bar to get a drink and reconnect with others he hasn't seen in a while. Jodi is off to the side, reclining in a pool lounge chair, surrounded by beach balls. He's immobile and wearing sunglasses. It takes me a while to realize he's passed out.

"Pour enough alcohol down his throat, and he's harmless," Jeremy explains.

"Why, though? That's what I want to know. Why is he such a pain?" I ask, frowning at the unconscious guy pulling a *Weekend at Bernie's*. He starts to snore.

"Hey, he really does have a heart of gold, you know?" Jeremy touches my forearm. "He just has a lot of pride."

"What's that got to do with why he puffs his chest out every time I come around?"

"Think about it. You were always slightly ahead of Jodi in everything. When he was junior varsity, you were varsity. When he was varsity, you were team captain."

"How's that my fault?"

Jeremy is thoughtful. "Okay, how about this? Remember that time we were 'Cruising the Gut' in Salem in your Plymouth Horizon?"

I laugh at the memory: a bunch of nerds joining in the parade of hot rods and street racers in a family economy car on Lancaster Drive.

"Remember we got in that bit of trouble with the locals, and we had to vamoose in a hurry? You kept your cool, went full 'Captain' mode, and directed me and the others into your car to make an escape. Except for Jodi. He completely froze. We were a good hundred yards away by the time we realized he wasn't in the car. We could have got clean away out of that parking lot, but you put it in reverse and backed right back into that mob gathering around Jodi."

"Yeah," I say, reliving the incident in my mind. "I hit some guys just hard enough to send them flying. It took some fast talking to explain to my parents how those cracks got in the window. Defrost never worked again, either."

"Yeah, well, it worked, and we got Jodi in the car and made our escape." Jeremy pauses, searching for the right words. "Anyway, he never talked about it much, but he was really embarrassed. He was embarrassed because he froze at the start of a fight, but mostly because he had to be rescued. By you. It hurt his pride."

"Again, I don't see how what he feels is my fault."

Jeremy sighs. "All I'm saying is maybe you should be more sensitive to the fact that he's, well, sensitive. I don't know if you know it or not, but you can be really antagonizing and intimidating. Captain Writer. And, kind of a dick sometimes, to be honest." Jeremy shrugs as if apologizing for being the bearer of bad news. I can't deny any of it. "Maybe when Jodi tries picking a fight with you, try something different."

"Like what?" I shrug myself. "Breakdance fight? Or maybe *West Side Story* fight?" I back up, crouch forward, and do a little dance while snapping my fingers.

Jeremy laughs. "No man, just use your words or something."

Jeremy turns and gestures to Krista, the bartender, holding up fingers.

"One thing's for certain," he finishes, "he sure learned from that experience. He never froze again. In Iraq, we were in a similar situation but thousand times more dangerous. He backed right over a bunch of enemy fighters in our Humvee to get to some of our guys. Probably should get a medal for that."

I chew my lower lip, pondering that. If nothing else, despite our differences these days, I did hold a tremendous amount of respect for Jodi's service.

Right about then, Dylan joins us, informing us that the guns are safely locked up in his rig.

"That's teamwork!" Jeremy declares, bumping fists with Dylan.

"I thought you didn't want guns in your truck?" I ask as Krista brings over a platter of shot glasses.

"The work trucks," Dylan clarifies, taking up a shot glass. "I put the bags and cans in my personal vehicle."

"What's that?" I ask, also taking a shot glass.

"I bought a junker truck just for tonight." He gestures vaguely in one direction with the shot glass, "Unfortunately, it's more of a junker than I thought. I think the power steering belt broke off. I have to wrestle it just to drive straight. I don't think I'll be mudding tonight after all."

Jeremy picks up a shot glass. "Probably a good idea. Take it back to the dealer before you mess it up further. Get some of your money back."

Dylan agrees, adding, "Never even got a chance to register it. Oh well."

"Speaking of trucks," Dylan says, casting a glance over to the prone Jodi. "Did you grab his keys?"

Jeremy's eyes widen, and he gestures with a finger. "Ah, good point."

Jeremy fights his way through the crowd to the collection of lounge chairs, knocking beach balls out of his way. When he gets to Jodi, he riffles through his pockets and starts to return to our table. Dylan shouts over the crowd, "Get *both* sets of keys."

Jeremy shouts back, "He drove his own truck tonight."

Dylan shakes his head. "Don't care, play it safe."

Jeremy winks and returns to riffling Jodi's corpse and produces a long green object. When he returns to the table, he sets both keychains down on the table.

"What's with the green dildo?" I chuckle.

Dylan picks up the keychain with the rubber green thing and turns it over. It has cartoon eyes.

"That's Peter Pickle," Dylan explains. "All the work trucks have their own key fob so that we can tell them apart." He pulls out his keys and sets them next to Peter Pickle. It's the yellow starfish I saw his daughter playing with when I was last over at his house.

"Suzy Starfish."

Jeremy pulls out his keys. "Harry Hamburger."

He holds it up to my face and squeezes the silly rubber caricature of a hamburger. It squeaks, and its googly eyes roll.

I laugh. "What the hell?"

"They're from my daughter's favorite cartoon. Suzy Starfish is her favorite character," Dylan explains, then adds loudly while looking over to Jodi, "Which is why I rather everyone drive their assigned truck!"

Jeremy sighs. "You know, not that I'm defending Jodi or anything, but each truck is better suited for different jobs. So we do what we have to."

"Yeah, I know," Dylan concedes.

A long-haired man stands at the microphone on the stage. He's stocky and wearing a leather vest over his bare muscular frame. He gives a strum to the guitar hanging around his neck, and the speakers come alive with the sound. The crowd about the stage has grown huge, and they cheer.

"Are we ready!" the guitarist shouts.

The crowd roars. Head and shoulders above the crowd, I see Bubba wading through the onlookers and, judging by how his left arm pulls forward, someone is guiding him to the front of the stage. When he arrives, I see that a small woman is towing him. Also, judging by his face, this part of the night is a mystery to him.

The guitarist riffs on his instrument again, settling to a familiar tune. It's "Happy Birthday," but a rock and roll version of the song. Kind of like Jimi Hendrix's rock and roll version of the national anthem played at Woodstock.

We join in, and somewhere near two thousand voices resonate in the Willamette Valley. Even from our vantage, we can see Bubba's cheeks glistening in the stage lights.

The song ends with thunderous applause from the crowd. Bubba scrambles onto the stage, grabs the microphone, and says a few words. Mostly says thank you but also emphasizes that the night just got started and to enjoy ourselves. We respond enthusiastically.

Bubba smiles and waves and scrambles off the stage to rejoin the festivities.

The crowd disperses to the various activities. Jeremy squints into the milling bodies, and he smiles.

Krista arrives with a tray of more shot glasses and points to an object on the side of the dish.

"There you go, you probably got a little while before my hubby starts his set if you want to get a few in," she points out.

"Perfect timing," Jeremy says, picking up the object.

"Oh God," I groan, realizing what the long piece of plastic and metal is. It has a silver head of metal mesh.

"Yes." Jeremy smiles while scrolling through a tiny LCD screen on the device.

He shoves it into my hand.

"No," I say, which sounds more like a plea.

Jeremy picks up a shot glass and puts it in my other hand. "Drink that. You're going to need it."

He disappears into the crowd.

I groan and throw the shot down my throat. Dylan looks at me in bemusement.

Jeremy returns with a little person in tow. By "little person," I do mean "Little Person." He bends down, picks her up, and sets her on a stool at the table.

"Hi, Staci," I greet the newcomer. She's in a blue dress with a matching blue bow in her hair.

"Hey! Long time no see!" she replies, waving excitedly. She also greets the others at the table.

"How's the Princess of Scotts Mills?" Dylan asks.

"Mostly well," she says in her squeaky voice, and her chubby countenance turns crestfallen. "But that is life."

"Mostly?" Dylan asks.

"I've been fighting with my husband," she replies, putting on an adorable pout.

"This isn't the same guy you dated in school, is it?" I ask.

She shakes her head. "No, but he had the same problem. Like a lot of regular-sized guys."

"He was a douche bag who didn't appreciate you enough?" Jeremy suggests, positioning himself between her and me. Behind his back, he reaches up and fumbles for the thing in my hand. I give it to him.

"You could say that," she admits. "Though specifically, it always comes down to having babies. They're concerned over having babies that are, well..." she sweeps her arms over her form.

We lean forward in interest, our expressions ranging from angry to sympathetic.

"Send him our way!" Dylan announces, looking around the crowd. "Is he here? Is he here? We'll learn him!"

Staci giggles, placing her hands to her mouth. "No, I'm solo tonight."

"Well, it sounds like you need some cheering up!" Jeremy declares. I try to slip away surreptitiously, but Jeremy blindly reaches behind himself and pulls me in, throwing an arm around me. Then, with the other arm, he holds up the microphone to his lips. "Because you know, when you have 'em, you need to know when to hold 'em, and when to fold 'em."

"Oh God," I mumble.

Jeremy smiles and presses the button below the tiny LCD screen. Music starts playing over the stage speakers. *The stage speakers.*

Jeremy looks at me and gives me a squeeze while jerking his head at Staci. She is smiling and looking expectantly.

Inwardly, I sigh but jump in at the cue. And yes, our voices come out over the stage for all the party to hear.

We sing Kenny Rogers' "The Gambler" to Staci. At first, only those around us join in, but soon the entire field is singing.

I do a passable job.

When we're finished, Staci is beaming and looking decidedly happier. The crowd is cheering.

"Thank you," I say into the microphone. "We're here 'till Tuesday."

I can't press the off-button quick enough. I grab up several shots off the tray and gobble them down, hoping to drown the butterflies in my stomach.

"Hey!" I hear a voice coming our way.

I see the crowd around us parting. Individuals are looking down when they do. Eventually, another Little Person is standing before our group.

This Little Person is only little in the sense of height. He's almost as wide as he is tall, all muscle. Actually, with his shaved head, he kind of looks like scale size Dave.

"What did I tell you about being around my sister, Jeremy!" the man says, his bat-like brows crowding over his eyes.

"Hey, big guy, I'm just trying to cheer her up..." Jeremy defends.

"Carl, don't start," Staci says, placing her hands on hips.

"'Big Guy'? Is that supposed to be funny? Am I joke to you?" Carl demands, ignoring his sister.

Jeremy shrugs. "Well, Finnegan..."

Carl Finnegan steps forward and socks Jeremy in the crotch. Jeremy doubles over, and Carl yanks his sister off the bar stool by her arm and drags her away.

Despite his discomfort, Jeremy manages to look up and cough, "Hey, Finnegan, you going to participate in the dwarf-toss later?"

Carl raises his arm as he walks away and gives a no-look-middle-finger. Staci glances over her shoulder, smiles, and waves with her free arm.

Dylan and I are chuckling.

"Way to use your words, Jeremy," I say.

Krista arrives with more drinks.

The guitarist is back on the stage, getting our attention with an opening riff, joined by two separate drum kits. A pretty brunette is behind one, beating away at the skins with her muscular arms. Opposite her is a nice-faced man with a blond goatee beating away at a similar set.

The rest of the night is a blur.

Chapter 41
Coyote

Yes, the rest of the night is a blur.

I vaguely recall seeing many more familiar faces, like Donnie Bensen and his camera. Many were old high school friends, and I had to repeat my story often. I got pretty good at putting a positive spin on the whole being-out-of-work thing. At some point in the night, maybe I even started to believe it myself.

Now, the sun rises on a battlefield.

Bodies lay scattered about, limbs dangling from the stage. Several mud-splattered trucks and SUVs rest idle in the mudding field like dead dinosaurs. The other beasts of the night, the spotlights, generators, and motorbikes, also slumber. The fiery glare of the floodlights is long extinguished, and now their frond-like heads watch over the scene like blind sentinels. Crows circle the area, and bold ones hop along the earth, picking at pieces of pizza and potato chips. An American flag sways on the breeze.

I walk among the bodies and debris, feeling newly resurrected. I had found myself on one of the lawn chairs covered in what I think were packing blankets for musical instruments. Nights are getting chilly, and right now, I'm cold to the bone. My head pounds, and my mouth is dry—I wouldn't call it a hangover, and though I don't remember much after a certain point in the night, I do know that I never got sick. So, there's that.

My feet scatter plastic cups as I walk, and a crow squawks at me. As much fun as the party was, it's time to go home and sleep in a real bed and get warm. I'll probably never drink again.

On my way to the parking area, I come across an empty inflatable kid's swimming pool. I find Jeremy in it, snoring away under a blanket.

I find my way to my car. It's mostly sitting alone now on the stretch of dirt road leading out of the field, covered in a thin film of dust. Inside, the seat is frigid, and I'm quick to start the engine and blast the heat. I fumble around the console for my sunglasses and sigh with relief when I put them on. Then, after soaking in the heat for a while, I pull out onto the dirt road. A short time later, I'm on asphalt, taking the S-curves back to town.

I notice in my rearview mirror a fast-approaching SUV behind me—a gray old-school Bronco or Blazer.

"Geez, fella," I mumble as I pull closer to the shoulder of the road to let the guy pass.

When I do, the SUV matches my move and speeds up, leaving no doubt with its trajectory that the driver's intent is to ram me from behind.

My heart leaps into my throat, and I step on the gas.

I pull hard to the right into the next S-curve, which is probably the only thing that saves me as the hulking SUV is not as maneuverable. It course-corrects after kicking up dust and gravel on the side of the road and resumes its acceleration toward me.

I hit the clutch, put the stick in high gear, and floor the gas pedal, but my six-cylinders are no match for the beast's eight, and soon its bumper touches mine, creating a momentary feeling of free fall. My car lurches forward.

Even though by now I'm having that out-of-body experience caused by extreme duress, I still note that the assaulting vehicle has no muffler or a muffler in such bad shape that the gurgling roar hurts my ears. A quick glance in my rearview mirror shows that the vehicle is a Bronco, maybe from the eighties. Cracks spider across the windshield so densely that they obscure the driver's identity, but I do see that it is a man with blond hair.

The next S-curve is upon us, and I hit the clutch, fight the stick into third, and pull hard to the left. My transmission protests, but the sudden change to low gear slows my car just as quick as if I had hit the brakes, but while maintaining power and control. My car nimbly clings to the inside of the curve. The

Bronco almost overshoots the road and has to slow down and correct its course again.

Back to fourth gear. Gas pedal to the floor. I can make it to the next S-curve. Unfortunately, I know where I am now and know that there is nothing but a long straightaway after this next S-curve. Fortunately, it leads to the crossroads at Central Howell, the tiny village on Silverton Road. If I can make it there, I can pull over into the gas station or school parking lot. There will be enough traffic and witnesses to compel my assailant to move on. First, though, I must survive that long straightaway.

The Bronco roars as it rockets toward me again. I brace for the next S-curve. My gear shifting is much smoother this time, and I traverse the curve efficiently. I come out the other side well ahead of the Bronco, and I see a series of dots moving on the horizon, indicating plenty of traffic and witnesses on Silverton Road. I'm going to make it.

"Ha!" I shout over my shoulder at my assailant.

When I return my attention to the road ahead of me, my heart lurches into my throat.

A strange, long-legged dog is standing in the middle of the road. It stands broadside but looks straight on to me with huge yellow eyes. Even as my motor reflexes take control and swerve my car away from the creature, my mind registers that it's not a dog.

It's a coyote.

My car enters the irrigation ditch at the side of the road at high speed, followed by an explosive crunch. The airbag in my steering wheel deploys so fast I don't see it. It just becomes my next reality, occupying all the senses as it hits my face like a sledgehammer. The car bounces, crunches, bounces. The steering column and dashboard slam into my legs, release, and slam again.

Then, nothing. The car is stopped. It all happened so fast I'm wondering if it happened at all.

But then I smell radiator fluid. Hear steam. The airbag is deflated and pooled around me like a used parachute. Steam rolls out from underneath the Suzuki's crumpled hood. It's a wonder that I can see it at all because the windshield is mostly shattered.

The driver-side door still functions, barely, and my mind is just as cobwebbed as my windshield as I crawl out of the destroyed car. I don't remember taking my seatbelt off or staggering away from the vehicle, but I must have because there I am on the side of the road, holding my nose. It's not bleeding, but it's tender, and my face feels caved in.

The sound of the Bronco's idling engine draws my attention up the road. It's just sitting there facing me from a hundred yards away. I see the driver's hands on the steering wheel. His face is still anonymous.

The hands move, and the Bronco shoots forward. Despite the pain in my legs from the crash, they still function, and I feel them coil, ready to jump back across the ditch. I hope I make it in time. Abruptly, however, the Bronco stops, turns in the road, and shoots off in the opposite direction.

When I turn around, an elderly couple is rolling up to me in an old Buick.

"You okay, son?"

Chapter 42
Glimmer of Hope

The rest of the day is a hornet's nest of activity.

Dad meets me at Clarence's Texaco Gas Station & Garage at the curve of North Water Street. Like Norma Jean's Flower Shop, Clarence's Texaco is an institution of Silverton. As with death and taxes, your car will break down, and you will bring it to Clarence's Garage. Naturally, it's where I have my vehicle towed.

"I wish I had better news for you, young sir," Clarence tells me at the shop, just before Dad arrives. His kind gray eyes regarding me with sympathy. "I'm sure it is no surprise to you that your car is a complete loss. The best I can do is offer a token amount of money to take it off your hands and take it to the wrecking yard for parts. Also, if you're in dire need of a vehicle, I have several here. They're not much to look at, but they're reliable, and the price is right."

He gestures to one side of his property, and there is a line of five or six vehicles. I give them a cursory glance and grimace. Among them are an AMC Gremlin, an AMC Pacer, and a Ford Pinto. The only other vehicles that leave an impression are an old surplus US Postal Service van, another surplus Postal Jeep from maybe the seventies, and a rusty bakery delivery van. None of them look like anything I want to drive, except for perhaps the Jeep, only because someone had personalized it by painting it khaki and mounting a spare tire on its hood to give it the impression of a budget-safari vehicle. The price painted on the window, however, is indeed right.

"Thanks Clarence, but right now I just need to clear my head and get my bearings."

Clarence smiles and shrugs. "They'll be here if you change your mind."

I bite my lip and somberly thank the steel-haired gentleman. He is kind enough to not charge me for the tow, especially after hearing the story of how I was run off the road. I don't mention the coyote, because now I'm not sure if that ever happened.

Clarence is also kind enough to let his shop be the gathering place for the police to interview me. The patrol car is parked in the parking lot, and Dad and I stand at its open driver-side door so one cop can work the laptop inside while the other talks to me.

Andy is not among them, at least. I don't recognize these cops.

They ask in detail what happened, but surprisingly I have little to offer.

"So," the lead interviewer summarizes. "A gray eighties-era Bronco, but you didn't catch the license plate, it's in bad shape, but its engine seems to be just fine, and the driver is a blond male, but you didn't recognize him?"

"I was kind of busy." The scowl I give them hurts my face. My head is killing me.

"Any reason to believe someone wishes to do you harm? Have any enemies?"

I can't believe it. Don't believe it. Still, I mention the incident with Jodi.

The cop at the laptop taps away on the keyboard, and it only takes a moment for him to say, "This Jodi fella has no registered vehicles that are anything like the one you described."

"Any other possibilities?" the other cop asks.

Dad looks at me, raises his eyebrows. I shrug and tell them about Rooney.

"Ah, yes, Mr. Rooney. We know him," the cop in the car says and taps away at the keyboard but comes right back with a similar story. "Nope. No vehicles matching that description."

I insist that it has to be one of them because otherwise I'm a great guy, and everyone loves me.

"You probably accidentally cut some redneck off, and he chased you down to scare you," one of the cops says. "Happens all the time. We'll put out a BOLO in case he shows up on our radar."

"BOLO?" I ask.

"Be on the lookout," the cop explains.

"Is that all you really can do?"

The cop shrugs. "Unless you can remember anything else. We already interviewed the couple who brought you in. They seem to think the Bronco didn't have plates at all. The Wurtzels are very nice people, but very elderly. Not sure I'd trust their memory."

And that was that. They took my information and left.

"I guess I'm minus a vehicle and ready to go home," I tell Dad.

"We'll have to wait for your sister to come get us." He points to his pickup, which is being backed into one of the garage bays by Clarence. "Funny this happened today. I was coming here anyway to get my truck worked on."

"Yeah, funny."

Dad rubs my back. Sis comes and picks us up in her ancient Suburban, which looks like it should be the one in the shop. They take me to the emergency room to get my injuries looked at.

"You know your mother is going to insist on it, so might as well get it out of the way." Dad is correct, so I don't complain as I get examined.

Mild concussion. Lots of bruising on my shins and thighs. I have two black eyes and a swollen nose with a purple welt across the bridge. Ribs are a little sore, but nothing broke.

"What happened here?" the doctor asks, poking at the long pink burn across my left cheek, compliments of the hot M4 shell.

I shrug.

Sis takes us home.

Mom, of course, freaks out. She would have anyway had it been a normal crash, but throw in the fact someone tried to hurt her baby, and it's practically the end of the world. I sit for half an hour on the edge of the fireplace in the living room, getting grilled. A mother-grilling is much worse than a police grilling and takes twice as long.

"Well, will the insurance company provide you a rental?" she asks.

I clutch my head. "When I lost my job, I downsized everything. As a result, I only had collision insurance on my car."

Mom looks upset. "Please tell me you at least have health coverage."

I nod. I do. The bare minimum for a single person, yes.

"Was your car paid for?"

It was.

"Any possibilities for another car?" she asks.

I tell her about Clarence's offer to pick from among his menagerie of oddball vehicles, but my visible cringe keeps her from further questions.

"Well, there is some good news today," Mom says and leaves me hanging with that statement until I gesture for her to share. "The computer in the other room keeps making a dinging noise."

Before she has finished her sentence, I'm bolting for the back office. I wake the computer from sleep, and sure enough, there is a message waiting for me from a job search site. My heart leaps— this time, in a good way.

It's a response from Tesseract Corporation requesting an interview. I pump my arm in the air and generally carry on.

"Good news?" Mom calls.

"Yes!"

I respond to the email, and I call the number in the message. A woman picks up and confirms that they do want an interview. Would the following Monday do? About 10 a.m.?

"Yes! Yes!"

"Good. Do you have our address in Hillsboro? Good. See you then."

I tell my parents the news, and they are just as ecstatic as I am. That is until Mom reminds me I don't have a way to get there.

"What about your car?" I ask.

But her car hasn't driven farther than Salem in years, and even that is a questionable distance anymore. So did I really want to take the chance?

"No," I admit.

The same was true of Sis's Suburban, which she and Rod both needed to get to work and drop the children off at school. I rack my brain. Someone has got to have a car I can borrow.

Mom clears her throat. "Perhaps it's time to swallow your pride and consider Clarence's offer regarding one of his vehicles."

I screw my lips up thoughtfully, weighing options, doing math in my head that involves account balances and credit scores.

"I'm going to try something first," I say, perking up. I take out my phone and make a call. I need to talk to Jeremy anyway.

"Hey," I say when the line picks up. "How are you feeling today? Quite the party, huh?"

We make small talk. Laugh. Then I sneakily ask if he saw what became of Jodi.

"Bum's still here on my couch," Jeremy responds with a laugh. "I think he's only been conscious two or three times all morning."

"Really, you sure? I could have sworn I saw him driving around in a gray Bronco after the party."

"Nah," Jeremy snorts. "He's half-dead to the world. And besides, he drove his Dodge pickup to the party. We have to go back and get it whenever his bum-ass wakes up."

I ponder that for a bit. I do remember that Jeremy confiscated all of Jodi's keys.

"Hey, man, I don't mean to be an imposition, but I got a bit of a situation I was hoping you could help me with."

I explain to him my need for transportation to the Portland area the following Monday. There is a long pause over the phone and then something that sounds akin to a sigh. Not quite a groan, but definitely in the neighborhood of a sigh.

"I'm really sorry, man, but you know the whole WVLC thing is still in a fragile state," he finally says. "We've got contracts and commitments that are riding on a thin margin. We just can't risk taking time away. Sorry."

"Yeah, I get it. Just testing my options," I reply.

Jeremy apologizes again and wishes me the best of luck, and we make small talk a little bit longer. Before we hang up, an idea comes to me, and I ask a final question.

"Hey, does your co-worker Todd by any chance have a gray Bronco?"

"Nah. That guy's personal car is a piece-of-crap Corolla. Bright yellow. Can't miss it."

I thank him and hang up.

Mom and Dad look at me.

"Postal Jeep it is," I say.

Chapter 43
The Reservoir

After a quick stop at the bank to get cash, and by the time I get to Clarence's Texaco, it's late in the afternoon. My face hurts, my head hurts, but I'm comforted by the fact that I'll be buying from a trusted source. I know the process will be stress-free.

Clarence doesn't disappoint. He's a very nice man who almost forgets to take my money as he walks me over to the Jeep while pointing out all the good features of the vehicle.

"The engine is a straight-six cylinder," he says. "Not built for speed, especially with this frame, but it's solid and could pull a heavy weight if necessary. Also, you'll most likely not get stuck in any terrain. The previous owner removed the little government-issued tires and put on full-sized ones with good tread, giving you another inch or two of clearance. It's light as a feather, so gas mileage will be good too."

Where you would expect the passenger side to be, Clarence slides open the door (a flimsy piece of aluminum) horizontally along a rail to reveal the driver's seat. At first, I groan inwardly at the idea of driving on the right side of the vehicle, but decide instead it will be an adventure.

"Yep, if the British can do it, I'm sure you can too," Clarence chuckles, echoing my thoughts. "The previous owner also put in a passenger seat where there used to be the mail storage. That's why the seats look so different from each other."

While Clarence sets paperwork on the Jeep's hood so he can write on them, I give the vehicle a good inspection.

It is one of the most primitive vehicles, a paper-thin cousin to the WWII Willys Jeep with the same iconic grill. Made by the same company, I'm sure it owes its existence to the fact its model line was tacked onto the same federal contract that commissioned the Army transports.

A boxy snout of a hood with flaring wheel-wells extends from flat windshields kept clear by reed-thin wipers. Behind the windshields sits a driver's compartment, and behind that extends a cubicle storage space with a single great door at the back, which hinges open sideways. As noted earlier, the side entry doors slide open like a van and do not allow the windows to roll down. A bracket with a red gas jerrycan is bolted to the rear door. All-in-all, the exterior has a somewhat safari Land Rover look to it, which I dig.

The interior is painted primer white. The flat dashboard is minimalist—Charles Lindbergh would have felt right at home. The radio is a sliver of glass with numbers and a red needle that moves by a knob. The skeletal steering column is classic Jeep. Bolted to the center of the floorboard, just left of the driver's seat, sits a single piece of aluminum, bent into an upside-down "U" shape, with a slot down its center. Printed along the slot are the gear positions. A long stick of a manual-shifter protrudes through the slot, topped with a black knob with a single plastic white button. A little plastic organizer for documents hangs from the lip of the windshield.

"Here you go good sir," Clarence says, his tone drawing me over to the hood. "A receipt for you, and just sign here on the title, and it's all yours. If you hurry, you can make it to Salem's eastside DMV today and make it all official."

I blink at the pen he offers me. He had assumed I planned on registering the Jeep under my name in Oregon, not realizing my residence is in Washington. Until just now, I had forgotten that detail myself. And now, considering the pending sale of my house, this Jeep potentially means so much more. It means I have to make a commitment. I have to make a decision.

My head hurts.

I take the pen and sign on the line beneath his signature on the green form with some trepidation. I fold it up with the receipt and stick them in my pocket.

"I really hope you have good luck with it." His smile crinkles the care lines around his mouth and eyes.

I agree, shake his hand, and climb in.

Immediately it feels alien, but the little PO Box style key starts the engine easy enough, and soon I'm lurching forward. It is indeed a strong engine, and the hula-hoop-sized steering wheel has a lot of play in it, which is why I almost shoot across the street median out of Clarence's lot, causing the passenger-side door to slide open. I panic for a moment when I realize I can't reach over and shut it while driving. Instead, I yank on the wheel and lurch in the other direction, and the momentum rolls the passenger door back into place. I sigh when I hear it click. I'm vaguely aware someone is honking behind me.

Adventure, I tell myself, *it's an adventure.*

With that mantra playing in my head, I make the 20-minute drive to Salem, and by the time I'm turning onto Lana Avenue off of Silverton Road, I'm smiling. The novelty of right-side driving is kind of fun after all, and it turns out, American brains are conditioned to drive on the right side of the road regardless of which side of your vehicle you're steering.

I park a little way down the avenue among other vehicles in a semi-industrial area at a small nondescript building, painted bland white.

My good mood dampens slightly upon entering the building. Salem's east-side DMV may be smaller than its larger counterpart downtown, but it still has the requisite long DMV waiting lines. I take a number from the dispenser and hope enough time remains to get me to the counter before business hours are over.

My hopes come true because, after a relatively short wait in a hard plastic chair, my number scrolls across a digital display, and I approach the window beneath it.

"How may I help you, sir?" the woman with cat-eye glasses asks. Her name tag announces her as Florence.

"I really only have one question," I say, then pause before continuing. "How long can I wait to register a vehicle once I've bought it?"

"Well, sir, it is always best to register under your name and address as soon as possible..."

"Sure, but how long can I go before, you know, it becomes a real problem? I live in Vancouver, but I'm waiting to hear on my housing and employment situation before I can make any decisions on my car."

I realize that nervously shifting my weight from one foot to the other only makes me look, well, shifty.

Florence looks over the rim of her glasses at me. "Sir, like I said, it's best to take care of that sort of thing sooner than later... but," her eyes dart side to side before settling back on me, her voice lowers to a conspiratorial whisper, "as long as you've got the title and it's signed by both parties, you can get away with it for a while. Maybe thirty days, but I wouldn't wait too much longer than that."

My shifting stops, a weight is lifted off my shoulders, and somewhere in the universe, a countdown timer resets.

"Thank you," I whisper back.

As soon as I say that, a disruption a few windows down demands our attention. A long-haired man in a leather vest with a familiar logo on the back has just slammed his fist on the counter.

"Please calm yourself, Mr. Rooney. It was an honest mistake," the woman at the man's window says sternly. "I see now that you're registering the truck under your employer's address, not yours. I'm sorry."

My blood chills in recognition of Rooney only a few windows over. My temple abruptly needs scratching, and my hand shoots up to do so and lingers there while I listen.

"Look, lady, this has to be done right!" Rooney's voice is far north of conversational. "You have no idea how important it is!"

The DMV worker continues to assure Rooney everything will be fine, no need to get angry.

Florence seems unphased. Just another day at the DMV.

"You're welcome," she says to me, then casts a glance at the agitated Rooney. "Too bad we can't make everyone happy."

Wishing her a good day, I slink my way out of the building.

Outside, in the Jeep, my hands fumble at inserting the tiny key into the even smaller ignition. I drop it, which turns out to be a good thing because when I look up again after retrieving it off the floor, I just miss making eye contact with Rooney as he stalks out of the DMV door. His shoulders are squared, and he rocks from side to side while lighting a cigarette on his way to what looks like an old rental box truck with faded paint.

As I remain hunched over, with eyes just over the lower rim of the window, I'm wondering why I'm hiding like this. Can't I be here? Why do I have to be the one who lives in fear? I'm not the one who did anything wrong.

Anger simmers in me, like a pot coming to a slow boil. Not a rolling boil by any means, but more like the moment when tiny bubbles start to appear at the bottom of the pot; small beads birthing sputtering pearls to the surface, coinciding with the mystery static in my ear and the pain in my head.

I don't like this feeling. Maybe I should do something about it. After all, I can be here if I want. I can be anywhere. Perhaps I should just step out of the Jeep, casually lean against it, and make my presence known. Not do anything, mind you, just exist, like I have the right to. Let's see what Mr. Rooney does about *that*.

The bubbles grow in stature and truly agitate the pot now as I reach for the door handle.

When I do is about the same time Rooney opens the door to the truck, and something falls out of the truck's cab.

I freeze at the sight of it.

Rooney leans over to pick it up, and with casual disdain, tosses the object back into the truck. It's exactly what I thought it was when I saw it fall out: a short-haired blond wig. It lands on the passenger side seat, where it joins some piece of purple material embedded with equally purple sequins, maybe a woman's top.

Rooney jumps in the truck and soon is pulling out of the DMV parking lot.

As if by its own volition, the Jeep starts up and moves after the truck, keeping a fair distance between the two. My mind is blank, and I'm just along for the ride. The water has stopped boiling, and only a few wisps of steam roll off the surface. Yet, the static is still there, as is the pain at the back of my head, spiking at the memory of a blond-haired man behind a beat-up Bronco's wheel.

The truck meanders through Salem, mainly taking side streets and passing through lower-income neighborhoods. The Jeep follows. The big steering wheel turns this way and that. My hands rest at my sides, limp as if I were paralyzed. I don't know whether to be terrified or just morbidly curious that the Jeep is following Rooney. I'm just glad that I'm in a daze as we pass through the neighborhoods of sun-bleached telephone poles, knocked-over trash cans, and houses with peeling paint. The Jeep makes all the decisions: everything from taking measures to keep at least one other vehicle between it and the truck and not making too hasty moves after turns to keep up. My eyes are half-closed, and I lazily lean to one side, then the other with each turn, held only in place by the old-school lap seatbelt.

Eventually, the truck comes to rest at the backside of an unfamiliar tavern that has seen better days. The Jeep parks across the street behind a dumpster, but I can still see Rooney exit the truck and move to its back, where he slides open the cargo door. Inside are many propane tanks with the rearing stallion logo painted on them, similar to those I saw at the Wooden Nickel. I think it's odd that the explosive containers are just sitting there, not secured or anything.

Rooney selects one and takes it to the backdoor of the tavern and beats his fist on the door. A man answers, and there is a brief exchange. Then, Rooney hands over the tank and receives an envelope in return, which he opens to examine its contents. He nods, satisfied, and is soon driving the truck away.

The Jeep follows.

This happens several times. A tavern or bar of some sort. An exchange of a propane tank for an envelope. On one occasion, there is a heated discussion about the contents of the envelope. The recipient of the propane tank eventually forks over cash from his wallet. Rooney is visibly upset even after taking the money and adding it to the envelope before moving on.

Finally, the oddest exchange happens just as the sun dips low in the sky, ready to put itself to bed.

At a truly derelict of a bar on the edge of Salem, Rooney performs the ritual of bringing a propane tank to a door and banging on it. This time, a petite woman whose skin is mostly tattoos answers. She backs away from Rooney and his package, making a fuss, which of course, I can't hear from across the road.

They argue. Rooney angrily stabs his finger at her, the tank, and in a vague direction, including someone or something else in the argument. The dispute escalates, and Rooney grabs her by her skinny arm and gives a good shake. Her eyes flare wide, filled with terror.

Just when I start to wonder if maybe I should do something, the girl relents and makes a placating gesture. Rooney backs off. Even from here, I can see he's sweating profusely as if he had been the one assaulted.

The girl bends over to take the tank off the ground as Rooney stomps away toward the truck. She freezes, though, and fear crosses her face when he stops in mid-stride.

He balls a hand into a fist and beats it against his forehead as if trying to exorcise demons tormenting his frontal lobe. It must have worked because a moment later, he's the picture of calm, and he returns to the girl who visibly winces at his approach.

He removes something from his pocket, hands it to her, says some words, and returns to the truck.

My head tilts to one side, and I'm sure the look on my face is just as confused as the girl's as she examines the object in her hand. It appears to be a piece of paper folded into the shape of an animal, a swan maybe. She tugs on it, and a pair of paper wings flutter. Then, she stares in bewilderment at the departing truck.

The Jeep follows.

We're heading back to Silverton. The road between Salem and Silverton is relatively straight, with only the occasional wide-arcing curve, so it's easy to stay a reasonable distance away from the orange and silver truck but keep an eye on it.

Though my hands still rest at my sides with little effort from me to guide the Jeep, my stomach protests the wisdom of this.

Has my curiosity been satisfied? Did any of this help confirm the Bronco driver's identity that tried to run me off the road yesterday? Was it worth the risk of a confrontation? I sense no answers, yet the Jeep follows.

We come into Silverton, and the sun has almost set, washing the bricks of the buildings a bloody red. I'm two cars behind Rooney, waiting his turn at a stop sign at an intersection. I'm searching his scruffy face in his side-view mirror, looking for any hint that he's aware of my presence. I don't see any, but I do see him lean out his open window toward a pair of young blonde girls passing on the sidewalk. He says something to them with a cheesy smile.

The girls pause in their walking, either unsure whether he had addressed them or not sure if they heard him correctly. Rooney removes any doubt by speaking again, and this time the expressions on the girls' faces are disgusted. The taller of the girls replies with her face scrunched up into a mask of derision. Her companion reacts with laughter.

Rooney's response is anything but amusing. Instead, he starts yelling and stabbing his finger at the pair. The girls are no longer laughing and huddle up, concern creasing their brows.

The car at the stop sign has moved on, and the one immediately behind Rooney starts honking. When Rooney turns to direct his anger at the driver, the girls hustle down the sidewalk in the opposite direction.

"Hey! Hey!" Rooney shouts at them when he sees their escape, slapping the outside of the truck door with the flat of his hand.

All cars are honking at him now, and he grudgingly pulls through the stop sign only after the briefest of stops.

I think it would be a good idea to stop following Rooney, but the Jeep seems to have other ideas and follows.

We go down South Water Street, and I'm sure that we're going to take a side street at any moment, until we don't. We pass the last residential housing and businesses and enter the tunnel of trees on the edge of town going uphill that will eventually lead to Silver Falls State Park if you drive long enough. I'm surprised Rooney drives this way, as there are only some homes and Christmas tree farms up that way, but mostly it's wilderness.

Upon entering the tunnel, the already dim light of twilight turns to nighttime. The yellow strips of the road's median become challenging to see, and on instinct, I lean over to pull on the toggle that turns on the Jeep's headlights.

When I do, I can see the Jeep's lights reflect off the truck's side-view mirror, and the truck's brake lights come on as it slows visibly.

My heart leaps in my throat, and I grab the steering wheel and force the Jeep to the right down a side road past a sign that states, "Silverton Reservoir." I pass an idle back-hoe parked next to a large roll of chain-link fencing. There are orange construction flags, but they barely register in my hurry to get off the main road.

Sorry Jeep, but it's time to lay low.

I keep going, rolling down the hill to the lake below.

When I get to a paved parking lot, I'm disoriented, not sure where I am. It's been years since I've been here. It's no longer the rustic dirt patch with a concrete boat ramp that Dad used to bring Sis and me to.

There are public restrooms, official signs, paved parking, and lampposts. A tiny wooden building with a sliding glass window has a sign that says, "Office and Day Boating Permits."

To my left, there are campgrounds with permanent barbecues and firepits. I see a group of people gathered around a dancing fire.

I turn to the right and drive a short distance and come to a stop before some dumpsters.

Despite the presence of the people about the fire, I'm on high alert, already picturing Rooney trundling down the hill after me, demanding to know why I'm following him. I stare in the rearview mirror, counting each passing second in tandem with my beating heart, waiting for the truck.

As I sit there, gripping the wheel, my knuckles turn white as my fists slowly rotate over the black plastic. My brain is on shuffle, like a music playlist, but only discordant violin and cello string scratching plays at each setting.

Typically, trivia steps in to set my mind straight, but not here. I have no trivia associated with the city's reservoir—just memories, and I let one lull me away to distraction.

Straight ahead, well past the dumpsters, I can see the reservoir's water slipping over the spillway. The memory hits me like a dump truck of when I was maybe five years old. I had just learned to swim. Excited, I wanted to show my father that I could without assistance. Unfortunately, I had decided to do this by jumping into the water much too close to that spillway. A terrifying moment almost turned truly tragic as the tug of water pulled me toward that concrete cheese grater. If not for my father's arm shooting beneath the surface of the water in a cloud of bubbles to snag me in time, I would be traumatized to this day. Maybe there would be no "today."

Then again, if I had drowned that day, I wouldn't be here now, jumping out of my skin at the sound of loud rapping on my window.

273

Chapter 44
Russians

A large, bearded man stands there. It's not Rooney. He's shining a flashlight at me, saying something. I move to roll down the window, remember it's not a standard vehicle, then slide open the door. The man watches the door, surprised by how it opens.

"I'm sorry, what?" I say.

"You can't be here," the man says with a deep voice and a vague accent.

"The gate was open."

"The gate is under renovations, but there is a sign."

I look him up and down. He is not in uniform, just a zip-up windbreaker, nor does he have a badge. "Sorry, I didn't see the sign. And you are?"

"Nightwatchman," he replies. "The city hired us to fix the gate and watch the reservoir while the gate is being worked on, to keep people out after dark."

Us?

A voice off to the side calls from a distance. It's in a different language, but the tone is a question. The watchman replies in the same language. It's definitely Slavic, maybe Russian. After an exchange between the two, he turns to me and asks in English, "My friend wants to know if this is a Postal Jeep, like from way back."

I confirm that it is. There is another exchange, and the watchman says, "My friend says engine is straight six-cylinder, but I disagree, I say it is V six. Which is true?"

"I hate to tell you that it is indeed a straight six. Strong, though," I confess.

The watchman rolls his eyes and casts a glance in the direction of the voice in the dark. "I'll never hear the end of it."

There is more talking between the two, then the watchman turns to me. "Come, sit at our fire. We will look at this engine."

He points to the fire I saw on the edge of the reservoir when I drove in. I'm a bit flummoxed, but I agree. I invite the watchman into the Jeep, and he jumps in like a boy who has found a new toy. I drive us over to the fire.

He offers his big hand and introduces himself, "Nice to meet you. I am Ivan Voslo and—whoa!"

The passenger side door slides open, startling Ivan.

"Sorry, it does that," I apologize and take his hand, shaking it as I pull him away from the door. I tell him my name. I park next to a barbecue and fire pit, where at least three people sit about the fire, two men and a woman. There is an exchange between them as we exit, and Ivan asks me to open the hood. I undo the rubber straps holding it down, and hinge it back until the spare tire rests against the big windshield. The two other men join Ivan and me, and they inspect the incredibly simple engine block with spaghetti-work of wires and tubes.

"Told you," one of them says in English.

Ivan rolls his eyes again and makes introductions: Dimitri, Aron, and Svetlana.

"The writer," the woman, Svetlana, says to me.

"Beg your pardon?" I say.

"You're that local guy who wrote those books about knights and stuff." Her clear eyes sparkle from across the fire. She is very tall. Thin. Long blond hair trailing from what looks like a *Little House on the Prairie* bonnet. It's about then I realize who these people are. The bonnet and Aron's and Dimitri's bright shirts tell me they are Russian Orthodox Old Believers.

The Willamette Valley has many communities of these people. I think they came to the area in the 1940s after fleeing Communism through China and South America. Even before the Bolshevik Revolution, they had been on the outs with their own Eastern Orthodox Church, preferring to practice their own older version of Christianity. Basically, between their faith and insular communities, they are similar to the Amish. Except, unlike the Amish, they have no problem with modern technology. In fact, virtually all of them run successful farms and businesses that seamlessly interact with the outside world. Nor do they have any prohibition against alcohol. They just look a bit different, with clothing that leans toward the nineteenth-century. And the beards. Most of the men would give any self-respecting Amish or Jewish elder a run for their money. The women? I'm not so certain Amish women look anything like Kelly McGillis as in the movie *Witness*, but I can tell you that not a few of the Old Believer women look like Charlize Theron.

"Yes, that's me," I respond to Svetlana. "How do you know that?"

"I read your first book," she says, cutting a hole into a watermelon with a knife. There is a stack of them next to the log she is sitting on. "I get it at Books'N'Time. Chuck had a display. I like that kind of story, so I get." She throws the knife, and it sticks point first into the log, and she stuffs an open bottle of clear liquid into the hole in the watermelon. The bottle gurgles its contents into the fruit.

"And?" I ask. Her comrades look at me with renewed interest.

Svetlana shrugs. "You are no Tolkien or Lewis. But it okay."

"If it only 'okay,' then why you read twice, hmm?" Dimitri asks.

She shrugs again. "Had to make sure just okay."

She opens a fresh bottle of clear liquid, takes a drink straight from the bottle, then offers it to me.

Not wanting to be rude, I take the bottle and drink. It's strong vodka.

The men take seats on the other logs, and Ivan gestures for me to join them. I hand him the bottle. Svetlana picks up a different melon and walks to the edge of the water.

We make small talk, mainly about the bruising on my face, and Ivan cuts the vodka-loaded melon into slices. As he passes the pieces around, his coat sleeve rides up to reveal an Old

Believer purple satin shirt underneath. Then it hits me that it can't be a coincidence that this group would be here, at the reservoir, where the most recent murder victim had been found and who had been an Old Believer herself.

I pause in mid-chew of my watermelon, swallow hard, and sheepishly say, "The girl who died recently, you knew her?"

Ivan's head tilts to one side, and even through his beard I can see one side of his mouth curl up into an ironic smile. Naturally, I feel stupid even before he responds.

"Of course, not only do we all know each other, we're basically all related. So, yes. She was our cousin and Svetlana's sister."

My hand droops and the watermelon is in my lap. "Oh my God, I'm so sorry. So, you're not nightwatchmen, after all, just paying your respects." I point with my chin toward the water.

"Oh, we're contractors," Ivan explains. "We won the bid to fix the gate and to watch the property until the job is done."

"Did you get the job before or..." my words trail off after I realize what I'm saying, my curiosity having gotten the better of me. Again, I feel stupid, or insensitive, or both.

Ivan chuckles to ease my discomfort. "After. We didn't let it stop us from working. Also, we needed it for closure. Like visiting a grave, since the county coroner has not yet released...her."

Ivan's chuckle fades, and he takes a bite of his watermelon. Aron and Dimitri sit by somberly, content to let their cousin do the talking. The fire crackles.

"Again, I'm so sorry. I can't imagine how you feel," I say to fill the awkward silence.

Ivan levels a deadly serious look at me. Then, there is a splashing noise, and I note that Svetlana has thrown the melon out into the water.

"Nasty business, this," Ivan states. "Never has such a thing happened. Even when our people were new to the area, experiencing all the prejudices that new people experience, no one kills us."

Right then, there is a thunderous explosion, and I jump up from the log.

Ivan and the others laugh raucously. Several more explosions rock the world. I look over to see Svetlana with a shotgun blowing the floating melon to bits. When she is finished, she sees me on the ground and cackles.

Aron helps me back up onto the log, patting me on the back.

When the laughter dies down, Ivan looks at me again with that serious look.

"I tell you, as God is my witness, if I find this guy, I kill him myself with my bare hands." He holds out his big hands and curls them into fists.

"Not if I find him first," Svetlana states, and she does a Sarah Connor single-handed pump of the shotgun.

"It will be a family activity, yes?" Ivan says to me with a wicked smile.

Chapter 45
A House is Not a Home

The drive from Silverton to Vancouver takes a little longer than usual in the Jeep, mainly because the vehicle's top speed is 55 miles per hour. Even taking the less-traveled and more sedate Cascade Highway through Oregon City, I still have to pull over every now and again to let traffic by. The passenger door frequently slides open on turns, and because there is zero insulation, I have to turn the radio up as loud as possible to get any enjoyment out of it. Unfortunately, the radio's dial keeps slipping, drifting through snippets of Elvis, the Beatles, Aerosmith, Queen, hissing static, and garbled voices. Briefly, an ad-man's voice comes to the forefront, announcing, "Camel cigarettes...for men who know what they want!" I pound on the panel above the radio. It finally settles on a Taylor Swift song just when the sky clouds over and fat raindrops hit the windshield. I turn a knob on the dash, and the thin little wipers go to work, dragging frayed rubber back and forth across the glass.

Fortunately, the portion of my drive on Interstate 205 is relatively brief as I pass through Portland. Despite the turn in the weather, there is little wind to knock me around the Glen Jackson Bridge as I cross the majestic Columbia into Washington State. I take my exit, and within moments I'm in suburbia.

Portlanders like to joke that Vancouver is just a suburb of Portland. They're not entirely wrong. Vancouver has no real skyscrapers and is mostly bedroom communities serving Portland's workforce. But hey, we don't have to pay state income tax, and we can pump our own gas.

My single-story ranch-style house is on a cul-de-sac, and as I park on the incline of my driveway, I note the yard looks like a jungle. The birdbath is surrounded by reeds of dark grass, and the concrete cherub at the center of the water feature looks even more forlorn than usual this gray day, obscured by moss. The cherub's face is nestled in its hands as if crying. What possessed me to buy the melancholy piece is beyond me.

I sling my travel bag over my shoulder and slide the Jeep door shut. The for-sale sign has fallen to the ground. I grumble and wrestle its post into the mud and jam some rocks to brace it. This process causes the shingle to swing on its chains and hit me in the face. I stop its movements and wipe the mud off it to reveal "For Sale" and the picture of a pretty real estate agent. Her smiling face reminds me I need to call her.

I shoulder my door open against a mountain of mail inside the mail slot. Otherwise, the house is now mostly empty. There is only a couch, a few fold-up chairs, some trunks serving as a coffee table, and a sizable mahogany bookshelf in the sunken living room. The bookshelf is still stocked with an array of classics ranging from Hemingway and Bradbury to Tolkien.

A large clock, an imitation of the sort found hanging over Parisian cafés, rests against the fireplace's stone, no longer hung over the mantle. The Latin phrase stenciled in flowery prose on its face stares back at me: *Concupivit Anima Mea Desiderare Te.* "I Want to Want to Believe." The minute hand ticking along the numbers is the only sound besides the rain pattering against the windows.

I throw my bag on the couch, take a seat, and sort through the mail. I separate the colorful junk mail, open the rest, and then peruse the depressing but not surprising statements from my bank, credit cards, and IRA retirement fund. They all tell the same sad story of robbing Peter to pay Paul. The subplot, of course, is that someday the piper must be paid.

I sigh heavily, but my breath stops short when I come across an actual letter. Then my heart leaps when I see that it's from a literary magazine. I tear open the envelope and press the letter flat, only to be deflated by the short message. These form letters all say the same thing: "Thank you for your submission, blah,

blah, blah, but unfortunately this piece doesn't fit what we are currently looking for, blah, blah, blah, we wish you the best of luck in your endeavors."

I throw the letter on the pile, lean back, and cradle a couch cushion on my chest as if it might protect me from the world.

I pull out my phone and make a call.

"Hola, amigo," comes a friendly feminine voice from the speaker.

"Hola, Paola," I say. "¿Cómo estás?"

She tells me she is well and wants to know what I've been up to because she hasn't seen me at St. Joseph's lately. I explain to her that I am well too and that I've been visiting my parents. Have I been going to Mass? Well, I've definitely been spending a lot of time with Jesus.

At this, Jesus raises his eyebrows. I cover the speaker to the phone, thrust my chin at him, and hiss, "Hey, totally true."

I casually direct the conversation from small talk to the topic of my house. There is an uncomfortable pause, and she informs me that there is no news. No bids. The market is still very tight. Would we like to lower the price again? I stare at my pile of bills and statements and do the math. Finally, I say no, no, let's hold off on lowering the price. Let's just hope the next offer doesn't fall through again. We laugh uncomfortably. We make more small talk. Do lunch someday soon? Yes, of course. Let you know the second something happens!

I have the pillow on my chest again, staring at my mostly empty house. Finding a buyer for my home in a recession seems pointless. Selling most of my furniture and unnecessary possessions helped, but that money is now gone. I refuse to part with the bookshelf, so I need to sell the house or get a job soon. Unfortunately, the economy and life are conspiring to keep either from happening. So, time to get to work.

I turn up the thermostat, enter my office, and sit down on the upturned bucket at my cardboard-box desk. I go on the internet and research Tesseract Corporation. I find out as much as I can about them. I reread the job description. Go over my application. Remind myself why I feel I would be a good fit for them. I formulate mini-essays in my mind, little soundbites for the interview: my education, experience, and how it might pertain to Tesseract's mission statement. Finally, I pull out a folder from among many arranged in a milk crate, take out a document, and go over the list of other popular interview questions.

Holding the document, I pace up and down the hall, practicing answers using Toastmasters techniques. I do this until I'm prepared.

By then, it's late. But, for the first time in a long time, I'm feeling hopeful and in control. Soon, my troubles could be a thing of the past. A bump in the road. A character-building experience.

I take from the closet the suit I plan on wearing tomorrow. Subdued colors. Black silk tie. Sharp but not flashy.

Regardless of how the interview goes, I plan on going straight back to Silverton. I pack my travel bag with some clothing I wish I had brought the first time, plus one other thing. Next to the mattress is a metal box tethered by a cable to a bolt in the floor. The imprint of a hand is on top of it with rubber buttons at the tip of each finger. I set my hand in the indentation and press several of the buttons in a sequence, which causes a little panel to pop open. I extract a semiautomatic pistol from the box with the text "Heckler & Koch .45" printed into the black metal. I admire the weapon. It's more like a work of art than a gun, precision-machined into an Art Deco design that gives it an almost science-fiction vibe. I press the button near the trigger guard with my thumb, and the magazine pops out from the bottom of the grip like a snake's tongue. I pull the magazine all the way out, note that it's full, and replace it.

I grab an ammunition box from the hand-safe and stuff it and the pistol into my travel bag. The other night at Bubba's party reminded me how much I enjoyed shooting with friends, and then someone tried to kill me the following morning.

I brush my teeth. Lie on the mattress. My heart is racing as I stare at the ceiling, noting familiar shapes in the plaster. Eventually, the sound of rainfall on the roof lulls me to sleep.

***

I'm up early the next morning. I'm too nervous to eat, so don't bother with breakfast. Even though I've got plenty of time to make it to Hillsboro, I'm leaving nothing to chance. Wet highways in rush hour Portland traffic will not stop me. The frayed rubber wipers are busy the whole way.

Tesseract Corporation sits nestled in a Hillsboro corporate park among many other tech companies. Manicured lawns and arborvitae separate its Borg-like cube of black glass from its neighbors. A winding white sidewalk leads to the front door. I park with twenty-five minutes to spare and debate the merits of being on time versus too early. The Jeep windows fog up. At ten minutes to 10 a.m., I retrieve a leather binder with blank paper and a pen from my bag, so I look prepared.

A classy older woman at the front desk greets me with a smile. I tell her who I am and that I have an appointment. She cheerfully provides me with a lanyard with a visitor pass and leads me to a clear glass cage of a conference room. The interviewing committee will be here soon. I thank her, and she leaves.

I'm feeling hopeful again. Excited. I like what I see. It's a relatively new facility, and the conference table is cherry wood buffed to a high polish. Multiple flat-screen monitors occupy one side of the room. Sunlight streams in from another, seemingly magnifying the light. The rain outside feels very far away.

Presently, several men enter. I stand to greet them and shake their hands firmly, with just the proper pressure. Their attire ranges from polo shirts to button-up shirts without ties. All wear slacks. They range in age as well. All have an entrepreneurial fire in their eyes.

We navigate the small talk. Naturally, I have to explain my bruised face, but the story about being run off the road actually makes for a good ice breaker. They hand me some paperwork with all of today's interview questions and some questionnaires to fill out later.

"We're being interviewed just as much as you," the boss explains. "We'd like your feedback. You can never have too much data!"

The interview starts in earnest then. Starts smoothly. Predictably. I go into the perfunctory description of me.

Nods. Pursed lips. There are glances at my resume and application material before them.

"It looks like you got good grades at...Southern Oregon? Really? Did you know Dr. Binder?"

"Bernie? Why yes, he was my favorite professor, actually."

"Ah, yes? Excellent. Do you know what we do here at Tesseract?"

I reel off what I know: Tesseract analyzes client data, looking for patterns that might yield opportunities for efficiencies...

Right about then, another man enters. He is wearing shorts, sandals, and a relaxed shirt. He has thick hipster glasses. He takes a seat near me, slouching into the cushion. He offers no greeting or explanation to his colleagues or me, though they hand him a copy of the interview materials.

I continue:

"...which, of course, will create synergies down the road. You see, when I called on Weyerhaeuser Corporation, I devised a monitoring program of their process to determine the impact of barium sulfate scale formation on their fiber orientation..."

The newcomer gently rocks in his chair, biting his thumbnail, still looking over my paperwork. Aside from him, the interview goes well, and I'm feeling pretty good about things. I've even shed some of my natural shyness and made jokes, eliciting chuckles. That's when the newcomer sits forward and lifts his glasses on his head, and everyone else falls silent.

The newcomer levels an earnest gaze at me while absently pushing the paperwork aside.

"What do you want from life?" he asks.

Chapter 46
The Bronco

I'm angry.

Very angry.

As I drive back to Silverton, I take Interstate 5, not caring that I'm frustrating traffic with my slow speed. I rattle along in the slow lane, causing even the average slow drivers to have to go around me. Some blare their horns.

When I take the exit at Woodburn, I relax a little but am still angry.

The last moments of the interview keep playing over in my mind.

It was apparent that my response to the "life" question hadn't satisfied the guy in sandals. In fact, he seemed downright disappointed. I had almost lost my cool. What the hell kind of question was that? What did that have to do with data analysis and my ability to do it? Didn't I demonstrate I can do the job? Can't you just give me the damn job and pay me, so I can get on with my life? And who are you to disrespect my interview and ruin my chance?

I stumbled through the rest of the interview, and the interloper left even before it was entirely over.

"Thank you for your time," the others had said, standing, shaking my hand, and ushering me to the door. They didn't even say, "We'll be in touch" or "You will be hearing from us," instead, they just said, "Be sure to fill out the questionnaire! There's a prepaid envelope inside to return it!"

Not freaking likely, buddy.

My knuckles are white on the giant steering wheel as I pass through Woodburn, then Mt. Angel. The radio goes on the fritz again, garbling voices and music until it settles down. Finally, the clouds clear, and the sky is blue. It's summer again.

Just before entering Silverton, I slam on the brakes.

In the road is that long-legged coyote. Its yellow eyes pierce me, challenging.

I scream at it and step on the gas. The boxy Jeep lurches forward and hurtles toward the coyote at a staggering 35 miles per hour. The animal casually disappears into the weeds long before I reach it.

Police lights and a siren surprise me from behind. I curse and pull over.

"Andy," I say when the police officer comes to my open door.

The cop looks my Jeep over in wonder, eyes swimming behind those thick glasses. Then, he asks to see my license, registration, and proof of insurance.

I freeze. Registration? I panic inwardly as I dig in the little file organizer hanging from the flat dashboard. I sigh with relief when I find it and am quick to explain that I haven't had time to take it to the DMV after having just bought it.

"Nice Jeep. Classic," Andy states, ignoring my statement as he scrutinizes the paperwork.

I dig in my pocket for my wallet.

"Yeah, I decided to take your advice and get something with Oregon plates," I say, trying not to sound too sarcastic. "Actually, you must have heard what happened to my other car."

He shrugs, looking over my license and insurance card when I produce them.

"My insurance should cover..."

"I see that," Andy confirms, reading the back of my insurance card, then says, "You look nice." His monotone indicates that it's an observation, not a compliment. "Have you been drinking?"

"No, dammit. I'm coming from an interview." But I'm going to drink up a storm soon.

He returns my documents. "Why did you stop all of a sudden?"

"There was a... an animal in the road. Didn't you see it?"

Andy shakes his head and turns to leave. "Be safe." He pauses, and without looking back, he says, "You asked how my folks are doing." Something about his tone makes me swallow. "Mom's sick," he continues after a long silence. "On Tuesdays, it's my turn to take care of her."

Without waiting to hear a response from me, he climbs into his cruiser and is gone.

I take a moment, gripping the steering wheel until it sounds like I'm making a balloon animal.

Not long afterward, I keep my promise to myself and am sitting on a barstool in Mac's. Natalie says, "Boy, you sure come here a lot."

"So do you," I counter.

"Well, I work here."

"Yeah? Well, I drink here. Two shots of tequila, please."

"Rough day?" she asks as she pours the drinks.

"Not at all," I reply, tipping back the shots in succession without the assistance of lime or salt. I bump my bruised face in the process and wince. "Why do you ask?"

She smirks and decides to change the subject. "You look nice."

"I don't smell half bad either."

"Why you dressed up?"

"When I go out drinking, I like to dress up. That way, it's classy. Two more, please."

She complies.

"You know, you never told me what you do."

"I'm in-between lives," I respond, downing the next two shots. My phone rings in my pocket. I answer, and it's Mom, eager to know how the interview went. I kick myself for not having called sooner. Of course, they would want to know even if it were bad news.

She is saddened and wants to know if I want to talk about it. I tell her there will be plenty of time for that later.

"But right now, I just want to clear my mind, blow off some steam." I want to wrap up the conversation before the alcohol starts to take over. "I'm just going to stay at Mac's a little longer and make some poor life choices."

Chuckling, Mom tells me to be careful and that she loves me.

After I slip the phone into my pocket, Natalie asks what I want next.

"That tequila must have been good," I say, "because I suddenly got really handsome, but I think it's time to change it up. I'll go to my usual vodka."

Gradually, the sun sets, and my mood only seems to darken with the day. The alcohol does numb, though, and the anxiety of the day gives way to melancholy. I start to wax philosophic. Out loud.

"Have you ever done everything just right, but it still just wasn't good enough?" I slur to no one in particular, making sweeping gestures. "I mean, prepared in advance, crossed your T's and dotted your I's, played by the rules...and...it...just...wasn't... good...enough?"

Natalie shrugs and smiles sadly as she cleans a glass mug.

"Right," I say. "'What do you want from life?' Who asks that in an interview? That's nobody's business! I should have told him that. That's it! Maybe it was one of those trick questions. I should have told him to go stick it where the sun doesn't shine. Perhaps then he would have respected me. Given me the job right there on the spot!"

Exhausted, I let my head dip and come to rest on the bar.

"Hey, better not be passing out," Natalie warns.

"I'm not," I protest. "I'm exposing my bald spot to you. In some cultures, that is considered very sexy."

"It looks to me more like you're about to pass out. So don't make me cut you off and kick you out."

I sit up, waver a little. The world is swimming in a comfortable cocoon. "Right then, it is about that time," I confess. "Probably for the best. The bar was starting to hurt my face."

I pay my tab and show myself out to the sidewalk.

"Well, hey stranger!" Gwen shouts, embracing me in a bear hug.

"Ouch," I say, rubbing my nose.

"Oh, sorry, I heard. Crazy!" She pulls back a bit to scan my face. She grabs my cheek and shakes.

"Ouch, dammit," I say, pulling away from her embrace. "Could you just not—"

"Not what?" she asks, stepping back with hands on hips. "Care? Give you attention? What?"

"Just—" I gesture vaguely. "Just this. Everything. Give me some space."

"Space? You've had plenty of space. You haven't returned any of my calls for a while now. How do you think that makes me feel?"

"I've just been going through some things."

"Well, aren't we all!" She crosses her arms. "Don't tell me about 'going through things.' I've been going through plenty too, ya know!" She points sharply to her face, and it is then that I notice that her makeup is heavier than usual about the right eye. Even so, I can make out the swollen black ring there.

"Oh geez, what happened?"

"Todd is what happened! I took that video to the cops of him taking the girls and making threats that morning you were at the house. You know what happened? Nothing! He got a court date weeks from now. Meanwhile, he comes over and does this!"

I bend over with hands on my knees, emotionally exhausted, shaking my head. "I'm sorry. Did you tell the cops?"

"Aren't you listening? Anytime I try something, it gets worse!"

I straighten and apologize again. I'm out of words, out of ideas. My head hurts. I just don't have the bandwidth to cope.

She moves in for a hug. "Let's not argue. Come here, let's just go and forget about this." I put up my hands and back away, but she pursues with a forced and desperate titter. "Why do I always have to be the sexual predator in this relationship?"

"Hey, could we, just not?" The hurt look on her face stops me, but I make myself say it just the same. "Look, I'm sorry. I'm a bad friend. I'm just not in any shape for a relationship, okay? I can barely take care of myself right now."

"You're right. You're a bad friend." She slaps my shoulder. "All I wanted was a little companionship. A little common decency."

She brushes past me. Her platform sandals make a *clump! clump! clump!* down the sidewalk.

"Where are you going?" I call after her, my heart still stinging.

"Home!"

"Let me give you a ride."

"You can barely stand!" She shouts back over her shoulder.

"Well, at least let me walk you home."

"Don't bother. Someone will come along to give me a ride. Someone who cares!"

She disappears into the night, the sound of her shoes following her. I sigh deeply and head to the Jeep. I pause and reconsider and start to hoof it up Oak Street. By the time I reach Hill Street, I'm sweating pretty good, and the alcohol in my stomach feels like a sloshing bag of liquid. I'll probably never drink again.

Movement uphill draws my attention to the side of the road. I freeze. A herd of deer migrates across the street, led by a buck with a magnificent rack of antlers. Their hides shine golden in the streetlight. There must be at least twenty of them, the most I've ever seen this close to town. Their hooves make *clickity-click-click* sounds on the asphalt.

I stand with my hands in my pockets, enchanted. At least something was beautiful today.

They freeze. Their heads jerk uphill, and they tense up, ears and tails flicking. Something about their actions is frightening, more so than if they were just reacting to an approaching car. My stomach folds over itself with dread.

They bolt and are gone, disappearing into the foliage on the opposite side of the street.

I see nothing, nor do I hear anything that could have spooked them. My stomach, however, will not relax, and the dread feeling only intensifies.

Without knowing why, I step down off the street and conceal myself in a juniper bush.

I wait, breath labored in a way that cannot be explained by my drunken uphill walk.

All is quiet. No movement. Not even insects around the lamppost, whose light filters down to me through the shrubbery. But just about when I start to feel silly, I hear a noise coming from up the street.

I recognize the sound of the gurgling motor long before I see the gray Bronco come into sight. It slows down as it approaches as if it knows I'm near.

It comes to a complete stop in the road by my bush. I withdraw deeper into the foliage, breath caught in my throat. When the vehicle starts to back up, I nearly cry out at the sound. I flinch, shaking the branches around me.

The Bronco stops again, its exhaust system gurgling and belching, disrupting the night. I can't see the driver, but I can feel him looking around, searching. Again, that grave-stepping sensation comes over me.

The beast starts to move forward, slowly, prowling. A cold searchlight emanates from the cab, canvassing the area like a nightmare radar system.

Without warning, the light goes dark, and the Bronco revs forward, heading toward town.

When it does, I note that it has no license plate.

Chapter 47
Salamander Island

When the Visitor comes to town, the streetlights dim.

With every passing step, his wing-tipped shoes go *tap, tap, tap* on the sidewalk, and the light of each lamp post dims further as he approaches until he is just underneath, and it goes out altogether.

In this way, he leaves a trail of darkness.

Even the flowers wilt as he passes, and each blade of grass bends with its evening dew turning heavy with frost. The song of insects goes silent. The nighttime breeze settles like a held breath, and a stillness descends like a funeral shroud. It is not, however, an unnatural silence.

Tap, tap, tap.

He comes to a bench under the last working light, which does not go out. A dusting of tiny, kicking insects surrounds the lamp's base. The Visitor takes a seat on the weather-worn bench, leans back, spreads his arms along the backrest, and crosses a leg over his knee.

Absently, he removes the red silk handkerchief from his coat breast pocket and polishes the toe of the dangling shoe.

He then hears the sound of footfalls: not wingtips, just soft shoes of the modern era. Soon, a form materializes out of the gloom and stands in the wan puddle of light about the park bench.

"Good evening," the Visitor says.

"Isn't it, though?" the Killer replies, taking a seat on the bench, leaving a respectable space between them. Though it is August, his breath comes out in icy puffs. "Imagine seeing you here tonight."

292

The note of whimsy in the Killer's voice does not go unnoticed by the Visitor, who concedes, "You *have* been busy, I'll grant you that."

The Killer looks up at the flickering light, ponders. "Yes," he says at last. More puffs of vapor from his mouth.

The Visitor taps his fingers on the backrest. "Which begs the question: Why?"

The Killer scrutinizes him. "Is that a note of consternation in your voice I detect? I didn't realize it was your place to ask."

"Careful, boy. There is an order to things. A natural order. And you are dangerously close to tipping it."

"Says who?" The Killer does not like being called *boy*. He leans back, crosses his leg over his knee. He repeats himself, this time directing his gaze at the Visitor. "Says who? The stars? You? What if I tip the balance? What will happen?"

"Tip away, and we shall find out," the Visitor replies.

The Killer's lips twist into a smile. Just short of mocking. "You know what I think? I think you're afraid. Afraid that you're an antiquated notion. Unnecessary. Redundant. The likes of me can do your job just as well."

"You?" The Visitor looks down his prodigious nose, irritated. "You're not 'Death.' You're not even 'death.' You're just murder. What makes you think you're so different from the untold legion that has made my presence necessary?"

"Ah, but how many can call you at will?" the Killer asks, snapping his fingers for emphasis, becoming bolder with each passing moment.

"More than you might think. It is not an extraordinary feat to call me. *You're* not extraordinary."

"Oh, but I am," the Killer insists. "I know when you will be coming long before you do. I lay the groundwork for you, making you possible. What are you without me? What could you possibly accomplish without me? I give you purpose. You sneer at me as if I were some sort of tool. An instrument. Does the gardener sneer at the trowel? No, he is happy for the trowel. It makes his work easier. Sure, you can argue that the gardener can always dig with his bare hands, but the question is...would he?"

"The Garden has always been tended," the Visitor states calmly. "Always will be. With or without trowels." And now, perhaps a bit amused, he asks, "What is curious is that a trowel feels so special. Why?"

The Killer stands, looks again to the flickering light.

"Because I can sense them," he says. His eyes are vacant. Though he stares at the lamplight, he is staring past it, through it. "I know when they are ready to go. When they need to go. It's like I said, I know it before you do."

The Visitor spreads his hands. "Perhaps a self-fulfilling prophecy."

"Oh, no. You smell that?" The Killer sniffs the air, turns about, turns his attention to the darkness. "I can smell the dying, ulcerating for release from miles away, long before they even know it. Mostly the slow dying. Those dying an incremental death, which burdens those around them. They call me, whether they realize it or not, and I oblige them. *I* bring about your precious balance." The Killer again looks to the Visitor. "Admit it."

The Visitor merely chuckles.

The Killer jerks his head back to the darkness, sniffs, and then cocks his ear.

"Smell. Listen," he commands.

The Visitor humors him and complies. He inclines his head at the sound of footsteps, going *clump-clump-clump* in the darkness, subtly changing in tone as the walker moves from concrete to asphalt.

The Killer returns his gaze to the Visitor, a glint in his eyes. "Time for me to do my job and you to do yours."

"Indeed." The Visitor laces his fingers behind his head. "Go on. I'll be along shortly."

"Yes, get comfortable," the Killer says. "You're going to be around for a while." He turns and takes off at a leisurely jog into the darkness.

Sniffing the air, staring at the Killer's back, the Visitor grins.

"More than you know."

***

The Visitor stands on the edge of the flowing water. His black wingtips make a sharp contrast against the gray volcanic rock of Salamander Island. He notes a spot of muddy moss on his left instep. He removes his handkerchief from his breast pocket and crouches to clean it off. When he does, he sees a little friend in a small pool of water among the many hollows in the rock formed from lava bubbles eons ago. He reaches down to pick him up and lets the little fellow crawl over his fingers. The colors are so vibrant they almost glow.

"*Taricha Granulosa Skilton,*" the Visitor says. The rough-skinned newt, affectionately known locally as the bumpy back salamander. The Visitor puts up his other hand, offering it as a bridge for the creature to continue its crawl. It is chocolate-brown or black in color; with an underside that is bright orange-red. The skin is leathery, with a granular or warty texture, and can release a milky white poison.

The Visitor sets the creature down, and it wiggles away in the water. He follows its progress, and when he does, he notices the white feather boa snagged in a tree branch downstream.

The Visitor stands and looks into the gently swirling pool just off the edge of Salamander Island. Gwen is there, floating on her back. Her face is blank, and looking skyward with empty eyes. Her skin is pale. Though her polka-dotted dress clings to her in its wetness, she looks naked without her boa. In its place is a necklace of purple bruising.

The salamander exits the water, crawling up Gwen's cheek and into her mouth.

Chapter 48
The DA Pays a Visit

My sleep is full of fitful dreams. I feel water dripping out of the darkness and landing in my eyes. There is that static sound again. When I wake up, my mouth is dry as a desert, and my head is pounding. It's the static noise that wakes me, but by the time I'm fully awake, the sound has gradually shifted to that of sizzling bacon. The smell confirms it.

I make my way down the hall to the dining room and kitchen. Mom is moving about the kitchen, and Dad is reading the paper at the dining room table.

"Blow the steam off?" Mom asks, handing me a glass of orange juice.

I laugh, taking the glass. "I suppose so, for now."

"That must have been some steam," Dad says, turning a page. "You came in awfully late. I'm glad to see you decided to walk."

I frown. "It couldn't have been too late. It wasn't that long after dark."

Dad snorts. "In another time zone, maybe."

I chug the juice. My last recollection was making my home by crossing the street, jumping from bush to bush, trying to stay out of sight, much as Eric Doolittle and I used to do when we were kids, pretending we were fugitives on the run. Still, it couldn't have taken that long. Did I really stay that late at Mac's?

"Dad, we got company," Mom says, looking out the window above the sink. Her voice denotes that something is out of place. I hear car doors slamming. The surprise in her voice escalates. "For heaven's sake, is that who I think it is?"

She moves from the kitchen to the family room in such a hurried fashion that Dad and I follow, worried. When we gather at the end of the bar facing the carport door, I can see out the window that there are at least three police vehicles in the driveway. A blue-and-white Silverton cruiser, a brown Marion County Sheriff's SUV, and an all-white sedan with the acronym HART stenciled on the side in large red letters. Below the acronym, in smaller letters, it is spelled out: *Homicide and Assault Response Team.* A multitude of officers in their different agency uniforms exit the vehicles. Andy Delaney is among them. My stomach tenses into knots, and my skin crawls. Something is definitely amiss on a grand scale. My first thought is that the police have come to tell me that they found the driver of the Bronco, but somehow I don't think that would merit a convoy of cops in our driveway.

A civilian in a nice suit is among the arrivals, and he makes his way for the carport door. He looks familiar, and he is indeed going to the door that only friends and family know to enter.

Mom and Dad collectively call out for him to come in.

The man enters with Andy and a deputy sheriff.

"Well, hello, stranger!" Mom says, coming forward and embracing the man. He kisses her on the cheek. Then, he turns to Dad and shakes his hand.

It finally dawns on me. The summer before I left for college, I worked in my mom's office in Salem, filing paperwork for the district attorney's office. Great job. Good pay. Got to dress nicely. There were always a handful of law students acting as interns, usually from Willamette University's School of Law. Walt Beglau was one of them, often employing me as his runner to feed coins into his parking meter so his VW Bug wouldn't get towed. "I know lots of pretty girls, and maybe I'll introduce you to some," he would promise as repayment with a wink.

Years later, that intern became the district attorney for Marion County. And now, here he is, smiling with that friendly face. He is wearing a beige suit with a light-pink button-up shirt, dark-purple tie, and gold-wire-framed spectacles. His blue eyes sparkle.

He pumps my hand vigorously. "There's the guy I want to see! How are you?"

I'm flummoxed but stammer a greeting. I feel lightheaded, and my anxiety doesn't know what to do with this blast from the past. But his easy manner brings out some humor in me as I make an obvious examination of his head.

"Hey, what happened to the mullet?" I ask.

He laughs and tugs at the spiky hair on top of his head. "Where do you think I got the hair to make this weave?"

"Speaking of which, the eighties called: they want their gel back."

There are chuckles all around except from the two law enforcement officers who have taken positions near the door. Their radios make occasional crackling noises.

"So, to what do we owe the pleasure of this unexpected visit?" Mom asks.

The friendliness gradually flees Walt's face, and his demeanor turns businesslike, with a note of apology. "As you know, in my position, I'm bombarded by information constantly," he starts, addressing my mother. "I start my mornings with a sit-rep with my staff."

"Situation report," Mom clarifies for us.

"Right," Walt confirms. "We go over the most recent events, crime stats, etc. Well, first thing this morning, a familiar name comes across my desk, and it brought back all kinds of pleasant memories," he glances at me, "but unfortunately, it was tied to some unfortunate news. News I felt demanded my personal attention, considering those involved."

Walt pauses, and my stomach twists anew. Again, I can't imagine where this could be going, and it's ominous.

"I'm very sorry to tell you that your friend, Gwendoline Thompson, has been found murdered this morning."

My legs go to rubber underneath me. I feel like I've been socked in the gut and the air driven out of me. I lean heavily into the bar, almost falling. Mom and Dad catch me and guide me to the edge of the fireplace, where I sit hard.

"That can't be," I mumble to no one in particular. "I just saw her last night." I look to Walt. My tone is pleading. "This can't be right. You must have the wrong girl."

Walt takes a seat next to me. "I'm sorry, but we're certain. A couple of kids found her in the creek at Salamander Island."

The words create a hurricane in my head. How could something happening in the news, happening to other people, be in my living room? I can't fathom it. But then, all at once, I can.

And I'm furious. "Todd, her ex-husband. He did this."

"He was our first suspect," Walt explains. "We already paid him a visit. He was with his daughters at his mother's in Albany at the time of the murder."

"I don't believe it."

"Well, we will follow up on all alibis. But I, um, have to ask…" Walk looks first to my mother, then to me. "Where were you between midnight and two of this morning?"

Mom gasps, and it all suddenly comes together. The visit from Walt, the DA himself, and the numerous officers present. I'm a suspect.

"Wait. What? Seriously?"

Walt's gaze is focused on me, professional. "The bartender at Mac's says you were with her last night," he spells out. "Says it looked like you two had a disagreement of sorts. That's how your name came across my desk this morning."

"Well, yeah," I argue. "I was trying to convince Gwen to go to the cops because her ex had assaulted her. Instead, she basically told me to mind my own business. I offered to give her a ride home, but she turned me down. That was the last I saw her. Walking toward Mill Town."

Walt scrutinizes my face. "About what time was that?"

"Around 10 p.m.?" I reply.

"And he was home by ten-thirty," Dad offers, stepping forward.

I look at him, surprised, but Mom is quick to agree.

"His Jeep is still downtown," Andy adds. "I ticketed his vehicle just before the call about the murder. The parking meter had run out."

I look at him and spread my arms in a *what the hell?* gesture. He shrugs apologetically.

Walt is contemplative as he measures every inch of my face. Even under the most ordinary circumstances, I'm not an eye-contact kind of guy. It takes every ounce of self-control to not squirm under his searching gaze.

Finally, Walt slaps his knees and stands. "Okay then. I had to ask, you understand. I have to follow through on these things."

"Of course," Mom says and laughs nervously.

"I do need to ask your permission to search your Jeep. That okay with you?"

I exhale the knot out of my throat. "Yeah, no problem."

Walt stays a bit longer, questioning us thoroughly. His manner is friendly and respectful, but the questions don't leave any stones unturned. We tell him everything we know. I make a point of the Bronco, convinced that it's still somehow Todd. The deputy sheriff furiously scribbles down all that I say in a notepad.

I ask just as many questions. Walt points out he can't divulge too much because it's an ongoing investigation. However, he tells me what he will say to the news: Gwen was strangled sometime between midnight and 2 a.m., and her body was found in Silver Creek at Salamander Island.

After that, we make more small talk and promise of getting together for lunch sometime. Then, as Walt begins his farewell, he snaps his fingers.

"Oh, I've been meaning to do this forever," he says and gestures to the deputy. "I'd like you to do something for me if you don't mind?"

The deputy struggles a brick of a book out of the side pocket on his utility pants. He hands it to Walt, who gives it to me. It's a copy of my first book.

"Um, could you sign it please?" Walt asks sheepishly. "I'm long overdue in asking."

"Uh, sure, man," I reply, setting the book on the bar. I flounder around for a pen, and Walt hands me a fancy gold one from his breast pocket. I sign the inside title page with a flourish, along with some kind words about "old times."

While I do, Walt watches carefully. "You're right-handed."

"Oh, c'mon," Mom says, crossing her arms. "Did you really just do that?" To my confusion, she says, "He did that on purpose, just to see what hand you use. I'm guessing the strangulation ligature marks suggested a certain handedness. A deeper bruising on one side of the throat than the other. I'm right, aren't I, Walt?"

Walt smiles meekly as he clicks the pen shut and returns it to his breast pocket.

"I always said you would have made a better investigator than a legal secretary," he confesses. "But I really was killing two birds with one stone. I got my autograph...and determined he's likely not a suspect. Trust me, you want that. Though, as I'm sure you know, nothing is certain until it's certain, and the investigation has concluded."

Mom grudgingly nods.

We say a few more goodbyes, and Walt leaves, taking his posse with him.

When he does, I turn to Dad and say, "You didn't have to tell him that. About what time I got home."

"Yes, I did, son. There is no way you did this. I just saved the taxpayers a load of money by keeping the cops from investigating a false lead."

My hand goes to my heart, but I frown deeply as I hold up my hands, examining them like they might belong to someone else.

Chapter 49
Reflection

"I don't like this story anymore," I say. I'm near tears. "It's not what I thought it would be."

A hand grips my shoulder from behind and gives a long squeeze. The size of the hand tells me it's Clark. It's very warm, his hand, almost hot.

We're sitting among the pews in Mt. Angel's Abbey church. It is dark, serene, and empty except for us—and the riot in my head. I can't see Clark, Homer, and Stephen sitting behind me, but I can feel their presence. They are comforting.

Jesus is there too, moving before the altar. He has a mop and bucket and is busy cleaning the floor. I've long ago stopped trying to fathom why he does what he does and when.

"I don't mean to give you platitudes," Homer says. His voice is quiet and kind. "But I would be remiss if I didn't point out that this does happen. Stories often go in directions we didn't expect... or even want. The stories more often than not write us, rather than the other way around. I know it's small comfort."

"It's true for all artists, whether painters, sculptors, or actors," Clark adds.

I nod despite water starting to brim in my eyes. I bite my lower lip.

"God is an artist," I muse. "Does He feel the same? Was He surprised how His creation turned out? Did the Fall in the Garden of Eden surprise Him?" I wipe my eyes. "I guess it's a circular argument because God can't be surprised, right?"

"I believe He knew it would happen," Homer offers, "but decided it was worth the risk. Imagine, to love something so much that it had to be created, despite the outcome."

I nod again but let my chin come to rest on my chest. Another hand grips my other shoulder. This one is smaller and cooler.

"My advice?" Stephen suggests. The cool hand squeezes. "Continue onward. Everything happens for a reason. Serves a purpose. Let the story take you by the hand and draw you down strange alleys and wondrous avenues, full of light and dark. Joy and terror."

I reach up and squeeze the hand.

"Nothing risked, nothing gained," I say.

Chapter 50
Funeral of a Movie Star

On the day of Gwen's celebration of life, you would think the real Marilyn Monroe had died.

Unger's Funeral Chapel is standing-room-only with a large extended family and a plethora of friends and acquaintances whose lives were touched by her outrageous personality. Cars line the streets in every direction. By the time I arrive, I have to sit in one of the side galleries, peering through the decorative wood bars that separate the gallery from the viewing area. Of course, these days, no one has a viewing anymore. Instead, people choose an economical cremation, followed by a celebration of life, entailing a parade of speakers at a microphone next to an urn.

I don't think I could handle a viewing and seeing her one last time. I'm sure she would reach up and pinch my cheek and declare, "This was all your fault, handsome!"

I bunch the fabric of my slacks with my fists, trying to gain some measure of control. My mind is scattered in all directions as I try to piece together what happened. How could I have prevented it? Could I have insisted I walk her home? Did the Bronco driver have anything to do with it? Was it Todd behind that wheel, despite what the police say? If so, would my urn be next to hers right now if I had insisted on walking her home? Or was she really the victim of a serial killer?

Like Clarence's Texaco Garage, you will eventually come to Unger's if you live in Silverton. The chapel hasn't changed at all since Johnny's funeral. A darkened room with pink walls and sizable crystal chandeliers hanging low from the ceilings. By their dusty appearance, they're probably not crystal. Maybe not even glass.

Gwen's family is in the first row—but her younger daughters are not. I expected Todd to be absent, but their girls too? What kind of man doesn't allow his children to say farewell to their mother?

Zoë sits with her numerous aunts. She plays with her video game player, intent on preserving that bubble around her.

I see Jesus at the back of the room and a distinguished older gentleman with blazer and wingtip shoes. Before I can ponder who he is, I'm distracted by the light above me as it begins to flicker. I look up to see a moth beating against its glass housing, but it doesn't explain the flickering. When I look back to Jesus and his companion, they are gone. The light stops flickering, but now there is a dead moth on my leg. I brush it off.

Bailey emcees the occasion, inviting people up to the podium. Behind it are several picture boards with montages of photographs of Gwen's life, many from her cheerleading days, her eighties hair taking up a lot of room in the frames. It seems hundreds of people speak at the mic about Gwen's zest for living, her larger-than-life personality, and her unfulfilled potential. Their voices become muffled, distant, and blend together.

The temperature in the room rises, or is it me? I pluck at my collar. Sweat beads on my forehead. The walls start to move in, and the air smothers. My eyes squeeze shut, and inwardly I ask myself, would it have been better with an open viewing? Would closure have been more likely? When I ask myself this, I remember Johnny's open casket. He had looked at peace, but he had also been very pale, and it was pretty obvious he was no longer there.

The temperature is stifling. The walls are touching me now, pushing me in my mind toward Johnny's face, which is as big as the moon.

I abruptly get up and race for the door at the back of the chapel, praying that I make it in time.

I get out on the porch just in time to lean over the railing and vomit.

I stay there for a while, leaning on shaking arms to ensure it is all out of my system. It is, but I don't feel better. In fact, I tense up at the sound of a growling engine coming up the street. It sounds like a motorcycle.

I nearly jump out of my wet skin at what sounds like a gunshot.

Before I can duck or jump, I realize it's just an old car driving by, its engine backfiring. I let out a long, rattling breath.

The door squeaks open behind me, then a hand rubs my back. It's Gwen's sister Beatrice, who looks very much like her, but much more adult in her pantsuit and conservative hair.

"You okay?" she asks.

I wipe at a spot of vomit on my suit. Part of me distantly ponders how fortunate I am to have a suit for her funeral because of the failed interview.

"I'm fine," I say. "Thank you."

"It's not your fault," Beatrice says, clearly reading my thoughts.

I return her gaze, shrug, and almost break down into tears. She hugs me.

"I told the police everything I know. I hope it helps," I mumble on her shoulder. She shushes me. After a moment of rocking side to side with her, I say, "I don't think we've talked since the fifth-grade Christmas program. You cut a huge chunk of hair off my head with scissors."

Beatrice laughs on my shoulder. "Well, you were pulling my hair earlier that day. I had to teach you a lesson."

Lighter, we go back inside just as the celebration ends, and people stream into the foyer. Soon we will all be walking down the street to the aged Majestic Rose Event Hall for a reception. But first, there is something I must do.

Sitting in a series of chairs along the wall is Zoë, surrounded by Dylan and Bailey's kids. I note that Dylan's daughter is again playing with his work keys, but the giant yellow starfish is missing.

"Hey, what happened to Suzy Starfish?" I ask Dylan.

He bares his teeth. "One of my employees lost it. No one owned up. I should just get a separate Suzy for her."

"Look, dear," Bailey says, gesturing with her chin at their girl playing with the keychain. "It wasn't the stupid starfish she cares about. It was the fact that those are Daddy's keys."

I take a knee before Zoë, who is clicking away on her game player.

"Hey, buddy," I say lamely. "I'm very sorry about your mom, but you're going to be all right, okay? You have some great aunts, and they are going to take real good care of you..." I glance at Beatrice. "Just don't let them cut your hair."

Clickclickclick.

My heart hurts. I sigh and move to stand, but Zoë stops her playing and extends her tiny fist.

I bump it with my own.

Chapter 51
Press Conference

When I go to City Hall to pay my parking ticket, a crowd gathers in the parking lot. News vans are disgorging news crews armed with cameras and microphone booms like D-Day boats disgorging soldiers to Omaha Beach.

A temporary stage has been erected with a podium and a semicircle of folding chairs behind it. The crowd stands before the stage, buzzing loudly, waiting. Meanwhile, it looks like every city official is in the foyer of City Hall, prepping like rock stars in a green room. Directly behind them is a sign on the wall: "Pay Parking Fines Here." The cashier's window is inaccessible.

I sigh and stuff my ticket in my back pocket, and head for the old police station blockhouse kitty-corner from the stage. There I lean against the corner and wait for the show to start, curious.

As the city officials take the stage, I feel a tap on my shoulder. Lori from the Grotto gives me a hug hello.

"What's going on?" I ask.

"Haven't you heard?" she replies. "It's been all over the news. They're going to make it official today with this press conference. We have a for-real serial killer in our midst. After today it should be national news."

I grunt. "I've been avoiding the news."

Mayor Stu Rasmussen takes the microphone as the other officials take their seats. I recognize Jason, Walt Beglau, and Goff Sanderson among the group.

Stu is in a solemn blue skirt suit. No hat today, just long curly hair pinned back in a no-nonsense pearl comb. A tap with a gloved finger tests the microphone and draws an answering thud over the loudspeakers. The journalists' cameras click incessantly.

"Good morning, my fellow citizens," Stu says, scanning the crowd and smiling at the cameras. "It is with a heavy heart that I make this statement today. That statement is this..." The cameras click. "Our beloved and ideal community of Silverton has gathered storm clouds of an unprecedented nature. This past year, and escalating in recent weeks, that storm has increased to a magnitude that can no longer be ignored. Namely, four local women have been murdered: Luisa Maria Lopez, Mariposa Angelica Rodriquez, Natasha Alexandria Voslo, and less than a week ago, Gwendoline Michelle Thompson. All were taken from us before their time, in relatively rapid succession, and in a violent manner that is too similar in nature to pass off as coincidence."

Stu pauses, scans the crowd with a serious gaze, and continues. "The Marion County District Attorney's Office officially recognizes this as a serial killer situation, and as such, will allocate all appropriate attention and resources in resolving the situation." A murmur ripples through the crowd. "Designating this a serial killer scenario also affords us access to federal resources." Stu gestures to two individuals in suits, a tall man and a red-headed woman with short hair, sitting among the city officials. "Special agents from the Salem FBI Resident Agency have been assigned the case. Furthermore, we are making this public statement with the expectation that the perpetrator is aware that we are on to him and that he will think twice before acting again. I assure you this individual's days are numbered and that he will be brought to justice. This is Silverton. We will not tolerate the sort of sickness that afflicts other places in the country with such sad frequency. I urge you not to fall victim to the terror but go about your normal lives, though, of course, be aware and vigilant. Report anything that might be pertinent to the investigation but be judicious in what you report. We are smart folk. We know when something is out of the ordinary and when it is not. I will now field questions from the press."

I note that Stu is already calling the killer *him*. Seems like some of the facts of the case are already known or presumed.

"Why did it take so long to recognize this as a serial killer?" a reporter from Channel 2 asks, shooting up his hand.

Stu explains evenly, "The victims all were involved in previous domestic violence incidents, or were involved in high-risk environments, which overshadowed the possibility of recognizing a pattern sooner."

"You mean, you overlooked it and messed up!" someone shouted from the crowd. "These women could have been saved had you acted sooner!" An agitated murmur from the public indicates that the angry man isn't alone in that sentiment.

The news cameras swivel to the citizen, and Stu calmly addresses the accusation. "I'm confident we did everything within our resources at the time—"

"You shouldn't be confident!" the citizen interjects. "Your town has a serial killer!"

Goff Sanderson launches out of his chair to the podium and leans into the mic, declaring, "I just want you to know that I have been pushing for a more detailed and coordinated investigation from the start..."

The cameras swivel back and forth. Stu calmly detaches the microphone from its holder and pulls it away from Goff. "As I was saying... The county and state forensic and investigative teams have performed in an exemplary manner, as is always the case, and no significant amount of time was lost before a serial killer designation was..."

Goff reaches for the microphone again, and Stu bops him in the face with the foam tip, causing a percussion sound over the loudspeakers. Jason and another councilman gently but sternly guide their colleague back to his seat. There, Goff crosses his arms, and his too-tan face turns beet red.

Stu fields more questions coolly and professionally, but it is apparent that citizens of Silverton are unnerved and unwilling to be mollified. Finally, the cameras and questions have reached a fever pitch. I sense Stu is about to curtail statements—but just then, a school bus with the name "West Harbor Trinity Church" on its side pulls up on the street and discharges a long line of people, like clowns from a clown car, carrying signs and shouting slogans.

Many of the signs read things like "God Hates Fags!" "Reap What You Sow!" and "There Are No Innocents in Silverton!" Their shouts echo the sentiments. They move up to the crowd about the stage, and within moments, altercations start. Eventually, police move in to break up the fracas.

Almost as if on cue, the noon siren on top of City Hall begins to wail. Stu pauses, waiting for the horn to finish its business.

"What's up with these assholes?" I ask Lori, gesturing with my chin to the sign carriers.

"That's the same church that protested Stu's election last year," she explains over the wail of the siren.

"West Harbor Trinity? I never heard of them."

"That's because they're from the East Coast. They're not even local. It's funny, no one around here ever had a problem with Stu, but these guys make it a point to protest anything remotely controversial all over the country. They even protest soldiers' funerals, blaming America's problems on American involvement in foreign wars, or something crazy like that."

"Oh, *them*," I say, recalling hearing about the group on television.

"Yeah," Lori confirms. "I guess they are blaming all the murders on the fact we elected a transgender mayor."

I shake my head, watching the circus ensue. The wailing stops.

"Well, I got to get back to work," Lori says. "Don't be a stranger, okay?"

She punches me in the arm and leaves.

Despite the disruption, Mayor Stu wraps up the press conference by announcing a toll-free number hotline for tips.

Chapter 52
The Mayor in the Dress

I leave the pandemonium behind and walk down the street. I'm still dazed. Have been since I got the news. Paying a parking ticket seemed like an invitingly ordinary errand. Something to tether me to reality—but now, it's my hunger that grounds me.

There's a ground-floor café in the Wolf Building on the corner of Main and Water. Approaching, I decide the wolf silhouette on the weathervane looks more like a coyote. After placing an order, I take a seat at one of the outdoor tables on the sidewalk. My mind wanders, and my head hurts. The static buzz is in my ears. I keep going back to the moment I found myself on the bridge. What was I doing there? How did I get there? I don't remember leaving Vancouver or even making plans to. It wasn't unreasonable that I did. I'd been in a rut, an inefficient routine that wasn't getting me anywhere. But when did I depart, and why?

I squeeze my eyes shut, and I have visions of water. Wetness. Dripping. I rub the back of my head. Move my jaw to clear the static in my ears.

Deep down inside, I feel disturbed by it.

The waiter comes and delivers a coffee.

Its strong flavor helps me think. The night on the bridge wasn't my only episode of discombobulation. It happened again just the other night after leaving Gwen and after running from the Bronco. I could have sworn I had gotten home not long after sundown. Dad says otherwise. Where was I during that missing time? How many other times have I lost time and just don't know it? How many other visits had I made to Silverton? Technically, I had lost time when I had punched out that customer the day I lost my job.

I look at my fist, reminded of what I did to that customer's face during that disembodied moment. What else am I capable of?

My gaze shifts from my fist to a long line of protesters marching from City Hall to the center of town, carrying their signs and chanting their slogans. They form a frothing river of sound on the sidewalk across the street.

My ear static increases, and the sensation of water dropping in my eye sends a chill down my spine. I shiver.

Before losing my job, I had been experiencing episodes of forgetfulness, which I had attributed to stress. No blackouts or time loss—just plain forgetfulness. But maybe that had been the start. Maybe it got worse the day of the incident that cost me my job. Maybe when that filter lid had burst off under pressure, it had hit my head.

I take another drink of coffee and set the cup down; I used my left hand to pick it up.

I'm reminded of the exchange between Mom and Walt after signing a copy of my book for him. I have doubts. Deep down inside, a horror lurks, begging to ask a question I don't want to answer.

Another customer steps outside with coffee and bagel in hand.

It's Mayor Stu, looking for a place to sit.

All the places on the sidewalk are taken. When Stu's gaze sweeps in my direction, I gesture to the empty seat at my table. An open seat is an open seat. The mayor shrugs and walks over, high heels making a sound reminiscent of Gwen's.

"Why, thank you, kind sir. You are a gentleman and a scholar."

"I don't know about the gentleman part," I reply, taking a sip of coffee, "but I might fit the scholar part."

Stu squints at me while tearing open a sugar packet, trying to place my face.

"Recognize me yet?" I ask.

"Maybe?" Stu has a winning, honest smile and eyes that glitter with alert intelligence even when hunting for a memory.

"I thought you knew everyone in this town," I say. "From the Palace Theater, if nothing else. Everyone passes through there. Then again, you only had to yell at me and give me the famous evil-eye once when I was growing up."

Lines crinkle around Stu's brilliant blue eyes. "Only once? You must have been an exceptionally good boy."

The spoon clinks in the coffee cup as Stu stirs in slow, steady circles. There's an effortless grace in the gesture, impossible to ignore—flagged by long fingers tipped with immaculate red nails. Stu's voice is a smooth, gentle baritone that belies the hair and double D's under the dress. I've only ever met a few other transgender people that I'm aware of, and it seems to me that they always altered their voice. Not Stu. That voice is comfortable as it is. In fact, I've never met anyone so comfortable in their own skin.

"Nah, I was just really quiet and sneaky," I confess.

Stu props an elbow on the table and settles chin in hand. Takes a sip with the other, scrutinizing. "Now I know where I've seen you before. You *are* a scholar of sorts. Your picture was in the window of Books'N'Time. You're the writer." Sits back, looks up as if reading a theater marquee, and makes a sweeping theatrical gesture. "'Local Boy Makes Good.'"

I laugh just as my food arrives.

"I must say, though," Stu continues, "you looked much happier in your photo than you do today if you don't mind me saying so."

"I don't mind," I reply, shaking salt onto my omelet. "Pretty dang accurate, actually. I was close to Gwen. The latest victim, of the..."

Stu's eyes widen. "I'm very sorry to hear that."

"Thank you." I slice my omelet up.

"How are you handling that, if you also don't mind me asking?"

I pause with a chunk of omelet dangling from my fork. I feel the need to speak, but I also feel the need to guard what I say, especially to the mayor of Silverton. Stu's easy nature, however, tugs at me. That tug pulls on a frayed string, widening a tear in a bag full of roiling emotions that need to come out.

"I feel...guilty," I start. "I saw her the night she died. I feel like if I had just said something different. Done something different, she might still be alive. We argued. About something stupid. I don't even remember what now." Stu leans in as I blather, eyes focused on me. "I told the police everything I know, but I have this feeling like I know more. A nagging feeling. Like somehow I'm involved more than I know. Weird, huh?"

Stu sips, is thoughtful, then says, "Survivor's guilt. It's not uncommon. Not surprising, if you were as close as you say. Trust me, it's perfectly normal and nothing to be ashamed of."

I shift uneasily in my seat. Take a half-hearted bite of my food.

"Maybe," I follow, "but that's not exactly what I'm trying to say."

The long line of protestors is mostly past, but a lone straggler's head does a double-take in our direction, zeroing in on Stu. The man puts on a determined mask of self-righteousness and starts to cross the street.

"Go on, then," Stu says. "My job is to listen."

While maintaining a watchful eye on the protestor, I say, "It's...complicated. I'm not even sure what I'm trying to say myself." I pause, searching for words. "Have you ever thought something about yourself, but weren't sure?" Stu's head tilts to one side in sympathy. The protestor closes in. "There was this time when I was a kid, my sister had this five-dollar bill that turned up missing. She told our dad that I had taken it. I hadn't. I really didn't know what had become of it, but boy did I get the third degree. So much so that by the end of the day, *I* was convinced I had taken it. Turns out, she forgot she'd used it as a bookmark. But by then, everybody had already convinced me of this thing about myself, and it was like I couldn't shake it." I pause again, not sure if I was even using the right example. Stu patiently follows. The protestor stops just short of us on the sidewalk. He grips the wooden handle of his "God Hates Fags" sign, and he takes a deep breath as if struggling with his own internal monologue.

"Anyway," I continue, "it's like that. A sense of doubt. Of two things being true at the same time." I sigh, sit back in my chair, drained. The protestor takes a final step forward, and a hush falls on the cafe's patrons on the sidewalk.

Stu becomes aware of the protestor and gives him an eye roll.

"The righteous shall know the blessings of the Lord!" the man shouts, bouncing his sign into the air. "The wicked shall know only the afflictions of the Devil!"

Aside from the eye roll, Stu ignores the man. Instead, delicately adjusts the saucer and bagel on the table. "It sounds like you are indeed struggling," Stu states, reaching down for the blue velvet clutch leaning against the chair's leg, "and it sounds like you question the veracity of that guilt..."

"Satan has been given free rein!" the protestor continues. "As with Job..."

"My advice..." Stu rummages through the clutch, extracting various items. A compact. A tube of lipstick. Each goes onto the tabletop in a neat row, hitting the table with increasing force. "... before you make any big decisions, ask yourself first all the questions that need to be asked. Take inventory, so to speak, of all the facts..."

"...loss of his sons, his home, his cattle...until he was full of disease and pestilence! Yes, the Lord our God allowed this!" By now, the protestor is in such an agitated state that spittle is flying from his mouth.

"...get your ducks in a row first." Stu extracts a small pistol. I tense up, and I'm sure my eyes are bigger than the saucer on which Stu's bagel rests. The protestor skips a beat in his ranting, but he puffs his chest up and continues. Stu doesn't miss a beat either and slams the pistol on the table. The weapon has a mother-of-pearl grip, and though about the size of a derringer, the giant bore indicates a large-caliber gun.

"By performing your own search for your truth," Stu continues, returning to rummaging. "You may find that your concerns are completely unfounded...ah, here we go."

Stu withdraws a slim black device, holds it up while admiring it, and a blade flicks out. A very long blade.

The protestor is much quieter now but continues, a bit unsure with his pacing. "Yea, though I walk through the valley of the shadow of death..."

Stu uses the knife to bisect the bagel—then to absentmindedly gesture at me with the point. "Ultimately, you will have to decide for yourself. No one else can do it for you."

"I fear not the arrow of the enemy..."

Stu slowly, deliberately spreads cream cheese on the bagel with the blade. "I do know, however, that when it comes to important personal matters, it is always best to approach them with conviction. Don't let fear get in your way. Attack them with confidence!" Stu gestures pointedly at the protestor with the knife. "Wouldn't you agree?"

The man pauses in his rant and considers the knife. Yet he puffs up his chest again and starts into a new round of quoting.

Stu regards him as he slowly wipes the blade clean.

The protestor's words catch in his throat. He looks nervously between Stu, the knife, and the gun. He ambles away.

Officer Andy Delaney comes jogging up to the table about then, huffing.

"I'm sorry Mayor, I just got the call from the cafe owner...are you okay?"

"Though I'm certain that I *look* fabulous," Stu says, still fiddling with the bagel, "I must admit I'm a bit perturbed. Isn't there anything you can do about these *people*? And where are the rest of them?"

Andy pushes his glasses up his nose. "They are, uh, gathering in front of the Palace, doing their thing there."

Stu's lips press into a line. "I guess they aren't as dumb as they look. Targeting my businesses now." Sighs, looks at me. "Well, was I at least helpful to you, young man?"

I smile. "As a matter of fact, you were."

Chapter 53
Private Eye

I sit at home and stare at the computer.

The right thing to do would be to hunt for a job, but there are bigger things on my mind right now. I pull the chair closer to the computer and start typing away in the internet search bar. I enter the name of the first murder victim. A dozen news articles pop up, and after skimming them, I find the information I'm looking for: the medical examiner's estimated date and time of death.

Relief rushes through me. The death was long before I found myself on the bridge in the park. Clicking on the Google Maps link shows where the girl's body was found. In a section of Abiqua Creek out in the middle of nowhere. A farmer had gone to check on why his irrigation system wasn't sucking water from the creek. A body obstructing the intake will do that.

The second girl was found by hikers floating in the pool of Butte Creek Falls. I don't need to click the map link because I know where that is. My stomach knots, however, when I read the medical examiner's time of death. It is about the time I found myself on the bridge.

I tap away on the keyboard, and the results for the third girl come up. The Russian girl. She was found at the reservoir, near rocks on which people sun-bathe. I remember the night when Andy pulled me over, and he got the call about her body being found. Just before that, I had been...where? I can't remember. The days had run together at that time. Lots of job searching online. Lots of drinking.

Then there was Gwen. Found at Salamander Island, a former mill site on Silver Creek, families took their children to swim and catch salamanders there for generations.

Except for the first girl, all were found in well-trafficked places. The inquiry suggested all four were victims of domestic abuse. But when did this start to look like the work of a serial killer? Surely before Gwen.

I shake my head. As I stare at the Google map of the Silverton area on the computer screen, I try to add it up. Bodies dumped in water in a mostly circular pattern around Silverton. Gwen's site was the closest to town, just upstream from the city park and the bridge where I had started this adventure.

Using the program's tagging feature, I place digital pins on the map at each location. No pattern that I can see. Maybe there are more victims to be found in other bodies of water. If so, perhaps they would complete a design. Aren't serial killers supposed to do crazy stuff like that?

I consider the map. Anyone can tell that the Willamette Valley is alive with blue arteries and capillaries running in every direction across the green terrain. You can't throw a rock from anywhere and not hit a body of water. Silverton is surrounded. So what might a crazy Satanic serial killer do? Pentagram? Hexagram? Hell, I don't know.

Nothing makes sense. No pattern lands on water. This is probably a good thing because if I were a crazy serial killer, I'd probably be obsessive-compulsive about it, and there would be a pattern. So not seeing one makes me feel confident that I'm not crazy but doesn't bring me any closer to solving the murders, which would really ease my mind.

"Hard at work, honey?"

I jump five feet off the chair.

"Mom, don't sneak up on me like that!"

"Sorry, geez," Mom says in the doorway. "You hungry?"

I breathe past my racing heart and shrink the browser window. "No, but thanks."

She gives me a long motherly look. "You know if you ever want to talk..."

"I'm fine, Mom, really. I'm okay. In fact, I was about to take a breather and go downtown and see who's out and about."

I stand, kiss her on the cheek, and run out the door.

Not long afterward, I'm on a barstool in the Grotto.

I haven't been back to Mac's since Walt Beglau paid me a visit. I'm sure Natalie had done the right thing by telling the cops she had seen me arguing with Gwen the night of her murder, but I was in no big hurry to see her or revisit memories of that last argument on the sidewalk.

Besides, Clea is easier on the eyes. I'm currently arguing with her over getting a "normal" drink rather than getting one that looks like something from a Dr. Seuss story. Not today. Not in a box, not with a fox, not on a house, not with a mouse, I will not drink the concoction she is offering up.

"Well, what do you want?" she asks.

"For starters, how about you turn the heat up." The air conditioning must be on full blast.

Clea, not wearing much of anything, as usual, lifts one corner of her mouth. "Seriously? The thermostat is set to seventy. You feel cold because you just walked in from a ninety-degree day outside."

"Is this bar wet?" I ask, running my palm over the marble surface.

"No. Now, what do you want, mister?" she asks in mock seriousness.

"How about a warm drink? That's not out of the question, is it?"

"Sure. Weirdo. Hot toddy? Bailey's and coffee?"

I ponder the choices, then perk up. "A Minerva."

"Never heard of it."

"That's because it's my own invention. Named it after a girlfriend. It's Mexican hot chocolate with a shot of tequila," I explain. I really am shivering now.

"Mmm." Clea's eyes light up. "Sounds good, and we have all those ingredients." She sets about to make the drink. "Minerva, huh? Pretty name. What became of her?"

I sigh. "Same thing that's happened to everything in my life. I can't seem to decide what I want. And I couldn't tell you why. We were at her sister's wedding in Mexico City when it came time for us to talk about getting serious. I was a coward and basically ran away. I know, I'm a douche."

The corner of Clea's lip turns up again as she hands me the finished drink.

I thank her and take a huge, warming sip.

When Clea returns the bottle of tequila to its storage location, I notice for the first time that it was held in a slot in a miniature Mayan pyramid. The sort of ceramic thing tourists buy in Mexico. This one was obviously meant to be a promotional tool by the tequila manufacturer.

"Of course..." I murmur.

Chapter 54
Altar of Sacrifice

The climb to the top of the pyramid is much more challenging than I thought it would be. It is very steep, the stairs are narrow, and it is hot and muggy as hell. It's jungle humid. Yucatán humid.

I've decided I'm never going to travel anywhere hot and humid ever again. Warm is good, but the constant moisture attacking my armpits and crotch is demoralizing. And the insects. The occasional horsefly taking a bite out of my skin every now and again is tolerable, but the mosquitoes and their lingering itching bites are not. I'm still itching from two days ago.

When I get to the top, I try to forget about my discomfort and admire the temple. Its architecture is simple: stones set one atop the other with very little mortar holding them together. Figures are carved into small alcoves, weathered to the point of barely being recognized as human.

The little doorway mounted by a single massive stone lintel leads into a dank room with a formless altar stone that may have been perfectly square at one time. I stare at the thing. It's nothing. Had I come across it in the jungle, I wouldn't think twice about it. Just another rock. But because it's here, it has a particular menace. A certain malevolence staring back at me with its drooping crevices, chips, and grooves. Surely people died on it. The stone is drenched in pain.

Moisture drops from the ceiling and lands on my cheek near my eyes. Besides the stone and my discomfort, there is nothing else here. Just moisture. Dirt. Mildew. I know there is historical value to the place. I should appreciate it more. But I've been caught on a bad day. I'm in a foul mood.

I return to the daylight.

Beneath me, a sprawling canopy of trees covers a flat countryside of packed limestone dirt. The day is overcast, which makes the humidity all the more aggravating. A cloudy day should mean coolness, not oppressive heat.

I shake my head, squeeze my eyes shut. Cobá, Mexico, is one of the more exciting places on earth, but I can't shake how bitter I feel. I've never felt so alone. There aren't even ghosts here to keep me company. I've traveled from one end of the earth to the other. Sometimes with another person, sometimes with a group, but many times alone. I used to be okay with that. Others found it strange, but I had liked it. But not today. Today the loneliness is as crushing as the atmosphere.

Lightning flashes across the sky, a brilliant arc worthy of a horror movie. Rumbling thunder follows.

My cup of loneliness is full. Funny, I should feel this way so close to the sky, within touching distance of God. Instead, I feel like Adam in Michelangelo's *Creation*, reaching out and almost touching, but not quite.

I reach up to the sky, extending my fingers as far as they will go, but touch nothing.

I let my arm fall and hang loosely at my side.

Even the stones feel weak beneath me. The pyramid looks like its stones are about to crumble, fall in on themselves, slide this way and that, and take me down the mountain.

I don't care. It would be something. Something to fill the hole in my soul.

I look out across the jungle again, as far as I can see to the horizon.

I'm not sure if I'm even looking in the right direction, but out there somewhere is Mexico City. And in that city, a girl named Minerva is with her family while I continue with my vacation. I didn't invite her on this leg of my journey because I wanted her to spend quality time with her family, so I told myself. So I told her. Truth be told, I wanted to be alone. Now I wonder. Wonder why I keep people at arm's length, embracing solitude instead.

No answer comes to mind. The only thing that ever happens is the sensation of a needle caught on the scratch of a broken record, repeating *why, why, why?*

I shake my head.

Why does anyone do anything?

Not too far away is an opening in the jungle canopy. According to the tour guide, the ancient inhabitants of this city had bound and thrown sacrificial victims into the cenotes, the watering holes, in the jungle's limestone floor. There was still much debate as to why this had happened. What wasn't up for discussion was the number of skeletons that had been found.

I shake my head again.

Not knowing what I want has hindered my friendships. My relationships. My career. Minerva.

I love her name, her beauty. She had dark skin, Kardashian eyes, and a cute little witch's cackle of a laugh. Why didn't I want her more a part of my life? Why hadn't I wanted any number of other women a part of my life? Why was I here alone on top of a pyramid in the middle of the jungle?

I reached for the sky one more time. Nothing is here. Not even lightning and thunder.

But there is rain. Big, fat drops that land on me, soaking me through and through with water warm like tears.

Chapter 55
Holy Places

"What did you say?" Clea asks, breaking my reverie.

"I'm sorry, what?"

"You were talking to yourself," she answers, giving me a funny look.

"I'm sorry, I do that."

Clea shrugs it off and continues about her work. I stare at the little ceramic pyramid. Altars. Water. Holy places. All the locations where the bodies were dumped weren't just public places where the killer could make some kind of statement—well, maybe they were that too, but they were also unique places in the public consciousness. So, in a sense, holy places. Not just some random stretch of creek. Well, the first girl was, but I'll ignore that for a moment.

The killer probably fancied some sort of connection to nature and possibly even made the killings some sort of ritual. I wonder if the FBI has picked up on that yet.

Water, altars, and rituals.

I feel a stab in the back of my skull. I realize I've only proven what was already running around in my head.

I need to take a walk. I need to clarify some things.

"Thanks, Clea," I say, laying some money down. "Catch you later."

It isn't that far a walk to Salamander Island. A dirt trail in the park leads to an embankment, which leads down to the creek and the island. The place is really more like Salamander Peninsula. It is an outcropping of volcanic rock jutting out into Silver Creek, creating a couple of eddy pools, followed by a series of natural water slides. Significantly, though, there are the concrete-and-rebar remnants of an old flour mill here. The ruins pepper the landscape, embedded in the volcanic rock of the creek so seamlessly it's hard to tell where concrete ends and geology begins. They might be toppled stones from Stonehenge or blocks from a tumbled Egyptian pyramid to the imaginative mind.

Perfect altar stones.

I clamber over them, inspecting the more horizontal of them. There are no bloodstains. No chicken feathers. No melted wax from ritual candles. No crazy serial killer detritus. Just moss and bird poop. I don't know whether to be relieved or disappointed.

As far as I know, it's been years since I've been here.

From my vantage, I gaze at the nearest eddy pool. My stomach turns when I think of Gwen floating there. I feel compelled to leave, so I bound across the concrete foundation and climb the opposite bank to the city trail there, then follow the bark dust path upstream until it comes to a paved side street. I walk for a while until I come to a wood bridge.

I cross it midway and gaze out over the swimming hole here.

The Luti. Or is it the Lootey? I've only ever heard it by name, never seen it in writing. Its water is deep and slow-moving. A bulge of the same volcanic rock forms a low bank on one side and a sheer cliff on the other. An old rope swing dangles from a nearby tree. Nothing gives the impression of sacrifice. It's been forever since I've been here, or so my conscious mind tells me.

I stick my hands in my pockets and walk back to town, deep in thought.

I'm not about to drive the long winding gravel roads up to Butte Creek Falls. I've been there before and know there are no manmade structures as there are at Salamander Island. There are plenty of rock outcroppings. Same story as the reservoir. I had pinned my hopes on Salamander Island, with its ruins, as holding some answers.

What kind of answers, though? Clues of some sort? Closure? Absolution?

I'm not finding any of that.

Soon, my thoughts are a riot again, and I find myself past the park and behind the library, almost back to town. But, to my left, if there ever was a place in Silverton that looked like the haunted ruins of a bygone era, a place one could perform sacrifices, it is right here. Situated behind the library, set into the creek's embankment, is the weathered foundation of another old flour mill. Or was it a wool mill?

Either way, it is more intact than the slabs and low walls at Salamander Island. This is a proper ruin, with two stories exposed on one side to the elements as if an explosion had taken place. The top ramparts are garnished with crenellations, giving rise to what we liked to call it—the Castle. Unlike the gray concrete slabs at Salamander Island, this edifice is made from dark concrete mixed with smooth river rock. It's really not that big a place. Just a squat ruin the size of a house, but it has charisma. And it's next to the water. I don't know why I hadn't thought of it sooner.

Its moss and weed-covered roof is level with the top of the embankment and incorporates a mini-park with a picnic table. A wood railing separates the park from the ruins with a warning sign to not cross or climb on the structure. Which, of course, is an invitation to children to do just that.

I take the side path down the slope to the park. There, I stand near the railing, looking this way and that with my hands in my pockets. Then, when I'm confident no one is looking, I jump the fence and land on the mill's roof and quickly jump down into the second-story room. It's maybe an eight-foot cube with the one side blown out. The rusty four-foot diameter pipe embedded in the floor is the most notable feature, forming a shaft down to the lowest room.

The rusted holes in the pipe let in daylight, revealing nothing but leaves, branches, and some garbage. The floor at my feet has about the same. Nothing out of the ordinary. Even the graffiti on the walls is quotidian.

I jump down to the ground room, which has uneven dirt and bowling ball-sized rocks for its floor. Nothing here, either. Walking along the creek, I come to a stone arch that is half-buried in the earth. Peer inside. Just mud and rocks.

"I'm missing something," I say out loud. "I'm certain I'm on to something."

"I believe that you are too," Homer says to me at my side. I hear him snap his pocket watch shut. "You're very close. Just not how you might think."

"What is it then? I've looked everywhere. Can you tell me what I'm missing?"

"I can only offer hints from the recesses of your mind," Homer replies. "And you haven't looked everywhere. Ask yourself this: compared to all these places you've searched, what, if anything, is special about the suction side of a farmer's modern irrigation system?"

I frown. "Nothing."

"Precisely. So why would she be there?"

My eyes widen. "Because she floated downstream from someplace else."

"Very good. Now, what is upstream?"

I recall the map in my mind, the landmark at the bend in the creek

"Another bridge," I whisper. "A special bridge."

"You best hurry," Homer suggests. "It's getting dark."

I turn, and no one is there.

Chapter 56
Gallon House

Gravel and dust spray as I wind my way down Gallon House Road in the Jeep.

I don't have a good flashlight with me, so I'm racing the setting the sun. I want a good look at the area when I arrive. Something tells me this is a lead. An answer. Good or bad, I want to know what it is.

When I arrive at the bridge, I pause and then drive across. The sound of the Jeep's tires changes from gravel to wood planking, echoing off the rafters inside.

Once upon a time, virtually all bridges were covered. Not just in the Willamette Valley but all over the nation. Nowadays, the few covered bridges that are left are assigned historical significance and maintained with reverence. Like a church. Like a holy place.

Gallon House Bridge is no different. The white siding glimmers in the twilight. The shingles on the steepled roof are neat and orderly. A plaque just over the entrance dates its construction in 1916, though its name came later. The mural in town depicts men transferring crates of Prohibition booze by the gallon between vehicles at this covered rendezvous point in the wilderness.

Mist is gathering in the hollow beneath the structure, extending up and down Abiqua Creek. I find the parking place I'm looking for, a dirt turnabout, and by the time I make my way to the edge of the bridge, the gloom has set in. I take out my phone and find the narrow path that leads under the bridge.

I curse as I fumble my way down among the weeds. I don't want to go home and get a real flashlight. I don't want to come back tomorrow. I want answers now. The sensations that start in my gut and bunch up around my shoulders tell me I'm close.

My free hand trails along the concrete pylons, which are the only modern addition to the bridge.

The mist thickens. It is moist and clammy against my skin. Not exactly pea soup, but it impedes how far I can see.

The sound of crickets soon gets lost in the creek's gurgle just as the ground levels out, and I'm standing on a sandy bar. The light of my phone reaches impotently into the dark, and I decide it is probably best, for now, to turn it off and see what my eyes can see on their own.

As my eyes adjust, I can see the outlines of the bridge above me, the brush, and the trees. The mist obscures everything, warping them into fantastical shapes. Presently, I wonder if coming here alone was such a good idea. Especially considering my mission. I squint into the darkness at the creek's edge. My heart skips a beat when I realize someone is standing there.

"Hello?" I call out, taking a tentative step forward. My feet sink in the sand.

The person doesn't react. Doesn't respond.

I call out again. My heart's pounding. I pull out my phone again and click it on. It lights up the individual at the water's edge, and instantly I feel silly.

It's a cairn of rocks, stacked singly on top of each other, smaller stones on top of larger ones. The topmost is a warped piece of river rock that looks like a shrunken head, complete with a twisted face as if an entombed soul struggled to escape. I turn my phone off and let my eyes readjust. The moon is up now, glinting off the mist, and I now can see that there are more stone sentinels. They are of varying heights, populating the shore and extending into the creek like a silent army disappearing into the mist.

There is a word for it when people stack stones like this, but it escapes me. It's supposed to be a Zen sort of thing, but many critics also call it a form of graffiti. I don't know about that, but right about now, I just find it pretty damn creepy. I shiver, feeling just as chilled as I did not too long ago in the Grotto.

To my left, light flares. A fire has been lit, and the fuel is something highly flammable. Through the mist, I can see a bearded man sitting a little way away on the sandbar. He is dousing the fire again with liquid from a can, and the fire flares and growls.

I recognize him.

"Willy?" I approach, announcing myself well before my arrival so as not to startle him too much. He looks up briefly at my voice but otherwise seems unperturbed. When I reach his makeshift circle of rocks and fire of driftwood and trash, I ask if I may join him. He shrugs agreeably and gestures to one of the larger pieces of driftwood in the sand. I take a seat. I can smell alcohol from here. His movements are a little unsteady, but otherwise, he seems entirely lucid. Much more so than when I last encountered him. I scrutinize him, seeing him in a new light after what dad told me about him. His dark eyes sparkle with intelligence that escaped me before.

"Evening, Willy," I greet him.

"Evening, young sir," he replies, peering at me over the flames while poking the burning wood with a stick. "How is the runner this night?"

"Honestly, I've been better."

"Must be true because it looks to me like you're still running." Willy vaguely points around our surroundings, "Why else would you be here at night, alone? Or maybe it's that your quantum entanglement has become more entangled in the web."

"I'm looking for something." I try to redirect him to a more rational conversation.

"What might that be?"

"Willy, are you aware that someone has been killing girls in Silverton?"

He doesn't seem surprised. "I reckon I am."

"Well, one of them was a friend of mine. I believe whoever killed her is doing the killing in places like here. I'm not sure why. Something to do with water, or location, or wanting people to find the victims to make a statement, I don't know, but I was hoping to find something, anything, that might help explain things."

Willy purses his lips, tilts his head thoughtfully. Then, absently, he reaches inside his rumpled old army jacket and withdraws a bottle of booze, removes the cap, and takes a swig.

"Find anything?" he asks, wiping his mouth.

"So far, just...you."

Willy snorts a laugh. "You don't think I'm the killer, do you?"

I grin nervously. "That's not what I meant."

Willy laughs and takes another drink. "Well, I could be, I suppose. Most folks think I'm homeless, especially the tourists. I guess I'm homeless enough to know that homeless people are invisible, you know? People look right through me, especially when I'm right in front of them, trying to strike up a conversation...to be acknowledged." He stares into the flames, then regards me. I feel a sting of shame for having once thought he was homeless myself. "With a superpower like that, I could sneak right up on people and do them in!"

While sitting on his log, he goes into an exaggerated pantomime of someone sneaking along. He laughs heartily and takes another drink. The liquid sloshes loudly in the bottle.

A thought crosses my mind, jogged by what he said.

"Willy, no offense, but you spend a lot of time under bridges, and as you say, you're invisible. A fly on the wall. What have *you* seen? Anything out of the ordinary? Anything that might help stop these deaths?"

Willy goes quiet. He hugs his bottle of booze and looks to the sky, examining the darkness. Gradually, he makes a noise, like a low moan from the back of his throat. Though his mouth doesn't move, the smell of alcohol intensifies from across the fire. He wavers on his seat, almost tips over, catches himself. His eyes turn glassy, and the fire dances in their reflection.

"Tiddleywinks and fiddleywinks," he says distantly. "Snufflewumpuses and catawumpuses. A feast of crows. A murder of crows. Scavengers and coyotes..."

"What," I say, leaning forward, "was that about coyotes?"

Willy turns his attention to me as if realizing for the first time I'm here.

"Coyotes, raccoons, deer," he says, brow furrowing as if explaining the obvious. "They've all been pushed out of their natural habitat. That's why we're seeing more of them in town. That's the real tragedy. The real murder. All the development going on around here."

He takes another drink. I try to contain my impatience and frustration.

"What does that have to do with murdered girls?"

Willy offers the bottle to me across the fire.

"I'm really not in..." I start to say, but Willy shakes the bottle impatiently. I take the bottle, and he chuckles when I wipe the bottle's mouth with the tail of my shirt. "Go on," I say, taking a drink of the liquid. It tastes like straight spirits. Ninety proof, at least. There is a hint of something else, but I can't put my finger on it. It's cringe-worthy.

Willy's chuckle turns to a full laugh, and he takes the bottle back and drinks.

"Murder. Girls," I say, waving to get the conversation back on track and to vent the excess sensation caused by the liquor.

Willy turns somber again, looks around as if he's about to divulge secrets.

"Spirits. Demons. The incarnation of nature unbalanced. Call it what you want," he says in a conspiratorial tone. He sees my expression. "Don't believe? Don't understand? Here, this will help. It's my own concoction."

My gaze shifts between him and the bottle. His eyebrows lift. I take it and take another tiny sip.

"It started when they cut the Old Oak Tree in the center of town," Willy continues. "That moment has been recorded in

Homer Davenport's biography, which can also be seen in a mural downtown. That moment signified when nature started to disappear, replaced by buildings, sewer lines, pipes corralling and enslaving the water, power lines, television and radio towers..."

My vision starts to swim. The liquor is hot in my stomach. I feel it begin to spread to my extremities.

"Nature doesn't like it," Willy goes on. "When you cut a plant down, kill it. It rots and leaves a stinking residue. Sure, it eventually returns to the earth, becoming new nutrients to continue the cycle of life, but for a while there, it stinks like evil. Especially to those who did the killing. And what if you are constantly cutting? Constantly killing without a plan? Don't properly tend the garden? Just leave a constant, rotting mess? Eventually, it saturates the ground, and everyone walks through it, tracking it into their homes like dog poo."

I wobble on my log. I wave a hand in front of my eyes, and it leaves a trail.

Willy reaches inside his coat and pulls out a little brown bottle with a rubber-eyedropper cap. He uses this to place some drops under his tongue.

"Told ya, it's my own concoction." He laughs.

Oh, boy, I think, but oddly, his words seem to make sense so far.

"What does this have to do with the girls. What have you seen?" My tongue feels too big for my mouth.

"So much of this self-inflicted rottenness saturates the blood, gets into some individuals, and it makes them see things...do things," Willy continues.

Right about now, a reasonable person might be genuinely concerned, but Willy is the one who is upset. He is frightened.

"Did you know there is a wasp that attacks ants, leaves a stinger in their brains, which makes it possible to control them like zombies?" Willy asks, shiny eyes drilling into me. "Nature at its most wondrous. Most deadly."

I teeter on the log. I feel like I'm about to float out of my skin. I resist the temptation to flap my arms.

"Girls, Willy, what about the girls?"

Willy hugs his bottle again, peers into the night, truly afraid.

"You're right," he confesses. "I see things. Sometimes darkness descends on me like this mist. When that happens, I know bad things are afoot. One night, here, the darkness was thick, like a blanket. The crickets died. The moon stopped. Death sat right where you are now."

I shift under his gaze. I feel that grave-stepping chill run up my spine. I see what he saw that night. The night grows heavy around us. The pearly mist is no longer glowing with moonlight; it is dark and oppressive. The moon is full, standing still in the sky, pale as a corpse.

"That night, I heard a truck on the planks above." Willy gestures up. "A monster of a truck, belching smoke, an un-muzzled dog. Then, a door opens, and..."

He gestures to the creek. A heavy object splashes in the water after having scraped between the bridge's railing and wall covering. Something like a pale lily floats downstream.

Willy is now rocking back and forth on the log, hugging himself. Tears are on his cheeks.

"I froze when I saw a pale creature come to the corner of the bridge..." he gestured to the spot of the railing where the bridge cover ended, "...watching the body float away. Watching his handiwork. I didn't dare move in case he saw me. I looked at Death sitting across from me. I was expecting the worst, but he just put his fingers to his lips and whispered, 'Sshhh.' He put me at ease." Willy looks up at me, terror in his eyes. His face is questioning like *he* is the one desperate for answers right now. "Who or what is so horrible that *Death* is comforting by comparison?"

My head is beyond spinning by now. The world is tilting. Images are warping.

"A pale creature? You mean a pale man?" I croak. "The loud motor on the bridge—who was driving? Please, I have to know, do you know who it was?"

As I start to teeter forward, Willy nods but doesn't answer. His nod leaves trails like time-lapse photography.

My face hits the sand hard, and darkness engulfs me.

I have restless dreams, if you can call them that. I can't call them nightmares. I dream of Arabian horses, sleek and black as night, galloping down Water Street. Their hooves spark, their eyes are blazing, leaving red trails. I'm standing in front of the Palace Theater under the blinking marquee lights. One of the horses pauses long enough to rear and kick at the air. Flames shoot from its nostrils, flaring a good three feet. The herd moves on, and the earth shakes.

My jaw drops at what I see next. Mammoths. The great shaggy beasts lumber along, tossing their heads and tremendous tusks this way and that. Their trumpeting is deafening. I have to duck and step back when they pass, as one of their tusks has hooked the "W" from the "Wonder" in "Alice in Wonderland" off the marquee. Sparks fly in all directions, as the herd has also snagged many of the power lines, dragging destruction behind them. When they have passed from sight, I turn to the theater's box office.

Stephen is sitting behind the glass, looking ridiculous in a theater uniform, complete with a pillbox hat.

"Stephen, where am I?" I ask.

Stephen levels a dead-serious gaze at me. "Somewhere between memory, imagination, and madness."

Sparking downed power lines draw my attention back to the street. When it does, I see Coyote glowering at me with his yellow eyes.

I wake with a start. I'm on my back, looking skyward. It is daylight.

A pair of faces are looking down at me: a tall man and a red-headed woman.

"Well, good morning there," the woman says.

Chapter 57
Interrogation

It started as a short conversation under the bridge this morning. The FBI simply wanted to know who I was and why I was passed out in the sand. When I told them my name, however, it turned into an "invitation." I ended up following their sedan back to Silverton.

"We may as well get this over with now," the man with floppy curly hair had said.

"We should do this back at the situation room," the red-headed woman had added. "To make your statement official, of course. We were going to call on you soon, anyway."

Their tone had implied that it wasn't a suggestion. Their tone also suggested that they knew I could say no and walk away, but it was in my best interest to comply. Otherwise, I'd look suspicious.

So here I sit, in a room in the basement of Silverton's City Hall. I didn't know City Hall had a basement. It's concrete, dusty, and dark despite peeling white paint. The paint is so old it is probably full of lead. Probably a holdover from when the building had been a Cold War-era fallout shelter. I'm kind of disappointed, really, as far as interrogation rooms go. There is a mirror on one wall, but a quick examination proved that it really is just a mirror hanging by a wire, not a two-way mirror in which I can shout, "I want to talk to who's in charge now!" Television has ruined me.

When I sit back down at the card table, I see a small black device with a glassy eye and a red LED light in the corner of the ceiling. So, someone is monitoring after all.

I try to calm myself and make an effort to not think out loud. Now is not the time to come across as a crazy writer.

After parking my Jeep in the parking lot, they had directed me here, stating that they had to take care of something first, then they would ask some standard questions, and I'd be free to go. That had been half an hour ago. Of course, I can guess what they are doing, especially considering the camera in the corner. They want to get a handle on my nature. You can learn so much from how someone handles irritation and discombobulation. Being a writer has taught me that much.

The question is now, would an average person display some amount of nervousness given the circumstances, or would he show calmness? Will too much calmness make them think I am a psychopath? I decide I'm overthinking it and just try to be myself, drumming my fingers on the table opposite the two empty chairs. I'm nervous. Under any circumstance, sitting across from my fellow humans causes discomfort. The Tesseract interview is a case in point. There, I had to sell them on the idea of why they wanted me. Now, I have to sell my interviewers on why they don't.

A frown at that thought. Why am I so sure they think I'm a suspect?

My finger drumming escalates. My knee bounces.

Eventually, they return and take the seats across from me. They place several manila folders on the table. Both agents are in their mid to late thirties and professionally dressed. Him in a dark suit. Her in a similarly dark pantsuit.

The man is lean, brown-haired, brown-eyed. He looks more like someone from IT than a field agent. The red-headed woman, on the other hand, is tall, big-boned, and athletic. Her face is hard as if carved from white marble. Very masculine. I'm confident she has more testosterone coursing through her veins than her partner. Her hair is thick and cropped short. None of this is to say she is unattractive, but her impassive face and cold green eyes make it hard to see her as anything but intimidating.

"Sorry for the unconventional introduction," the male agent says, then extends a hand across the table. "I'm Special Agent Ted Johnson. Normally we would have called first, but since we came across you at a potential crime scene... This is Special Agent Amanda Johnson."

The woman thrust her chin at me in a curt greeting. *Johnson and Johnson?*

Ted adds, "No relation."

"Speaking of the crime scene, why were you there?" Amanda asks.

I've already told them back at the bridge, but I guess we're talking for posterity now.

I reiterate what I told them earlier about seeking closure to Gwen's death at Salamander Island, which led to Gallon House and a hope of finding clues. My whole theory about watery altars. I attribute the idea to my writer's imagination, but the agents are unimpressed. Even less impressed that I'm a writer.

Amanda shrugs. "The bridge as a location to dump a body is a no-brainer. There is nothing special about it otherwise."

"Well, you keep referring to it as a crime scene, and you were there. Did you find anything of interest?" I return.

"Just you," Ted replies. "Someone coincidentally close to one of the victims."

He opens one of the manila folders and looks over a printed document with a header *Marion County Sheriff's Department— Interview Report.*

"I explained why I was there," I say.

"And you were sleeping because...?" Amanda opens a folder and scans some documents.

"I told you, I was talking to Willy. I drank enough of his liquor that I passed out."

"Who is Willy? We found you alone," Ted states.

"He's a homeless guy. Sort of."

"A homeless person in Silverton, Oregon?" The agents raise eyebrows at each other.

"Yes."

"We have no record of a Willy," Ted says.

"He's been a fixture around here for ages," I explain. "Ask anyone."

"How often do you drink with homeless people at night? Once a week? More?" Ted sits back in his chair, crossing his arms.

"I was trying to get information. Willy might have seen something that others didn't," I explain.

"Did you?" Amanda levels those cold peridots at me. "Get information, I mean."

I rub the back of my head. Willy had told me something. Something important, but it was all a blur. The only things that came to mind were horses and...mammoths?

"I don't remember," I admit. "His booze had quite the wallop to it. But ask him yourself. I felt what he told me was important."

"Right," Amanda says, writing in a notepad. "Ask Willy."

The way she says it, you can almost see the quotes around the name Willy.

"Well, we should get down to the real business," Ted says, placing a piece of paper before me. It's dense with text and has the blue-and-gold FBI logo on the header.

"Sorry for the formalities, but any time we have an official conversation during an investigation, we are legally obligated to inform you that, according to Federal statute Title 18, United States Code, Section 1001, anything you say is a permanent record and taken as truth." Ted waves his hand over the document. "Just to paraphrase."

"By signing this, you're basically acknowledging that this conversation took place, and it was factual and accurate," Amanda adds. "Just sign anywhere."

There is no signature line. In fact, this document doesn't look like it was meant to be signed. I feel the corner of my lips rise. Then, taking a page from my mother's playbook, I take the pen offered me and sign the document with a flourish while maintaining eye contact with the agents.

As I suspected, they watch with great interest.

"You see, I'm right-handed," I say.

"We know," Amanda says, pushing along the surface of the table a printed copy of my driver's license at me. It has my signature.

"Then, why the theatrics?" I ask.

"There is right-handed, and then there is right-handed," Ted explains. "You're the latter." At my confused look, he clarifies, "Some people are born left-handed, but in school, they are forced to learn to write right-handed. Their writing looks like a right-handed person's, but watching them write right-handed is painful. You're a natural."

I am in no hurry to reveal that I'm ambidextrous.

"Studies are suggesting those poor kids who are forced to write with their opposite hands lose their creativity in life. It disrupts their natural brain functions. It 'breaks' them, so to speak. Lord knows what else it does to them," Amanda points out.

"So, the killer is left-handed," I state. My stomach tightens. My left hand clenches under the table. "What else do you know?"

The Johnsons exchange a glance. "We can't really say in an active investigation."

"We're more interested in what you know," Amanda says.

"Like?" I ask.

"You were with Mrs. Thompson the night of her murder. You claim you were stalked by a Ford Bronco that night, the same Bronco that forced you off the road a week earlier," Ted says, glancing over a Silverton police report.

"Yes, that's why I think it was her ex-husband."

"Except he has a pretty solid alibi," Ted says. His eyebrows rise while reading the report. Then, poking the paper with his index finger, he slides it over to his partner. "Which rules him out."

I remember how my father was quick to provide me with an alibi, so I point out that Todd's mother could have lied for him. Ted purses his lips and shrugs.

"You've had a run-in with the Regulator biker gang?" Amanda asks while scrutinizing the Silverton incident report.

"Yes."

"You think it's possible that this Rooney guy was driving the Bronco and that it's somehow related to Mrs. Thompson's death?" she asks.

I think about that, then give a condensed account of the murder in my family and the night Black Bart goaded Rooney into doing something to me.

The Johnsons agree that forcing new members to commit acts of violence is the standard practice for gang initiations.

"There you go," I point out. "It's possible that Rooney was behind the wheel of that Bronco. He might have been looking for me that night and settled on the woman he'd seen me with."

"If so, then it's a big coincidence that it looks like the serial killer's doing," Amanda says.

"Maybe he *is* the serial killer, and he was killing two birds with one stone with Gwen," I offer.

Ted shakes his head. "If he has multiple kills under his belt, then the Regulators wouldn't have bothered pushing him at you."

I'm stumped. I reassert my original belief it was Todd, suggesting he killed the other girls too. I catch their brief exchange of glances, and before I can comment, they cut me off and go in another direction.

"Gwen's ex has a history of violence toward women," Amanda says. "How about you?"

"Come again?"

Amanda leans forward on her forearms, levels an impassive gaze at me. "You ever get angry with women?"

Ted adds, "Or ever get frustrated with your relationships? You know how women can get, all that drama. You ever want to hit them?"

I can't believe what I'm hearing. "No."

"That's hard to believe," Ted says, leaning back in his chair. "Especially when you are dealing with the frustrations of being unemployed..."

"...because you assaulted a customer..." Amanda adds.

"...and don't forget, your writing career isn't exactly taking off either..."

"...that's gotta be frustrating..."

Now the agents aren't even addressing me; they are fielding ideas at each other, letting me witness their insulting narrative.

Ted continues, "Then you get bullied by the guy who killed your cousin. That's gotta make you feel weak."

"Right," Amanda says. "Runs you off the road. Wrecks your car. You feel helpless. You need to lash out."

"Then there's this girl in your life. Loud. Opinionated..."

"She says the wrong thing at the wrong time. She needs to be shut up. Just wrap your hands around her throat. Maybe this has happened a couple times, and it's been your go-to solution for shutting girls up."

I see what they're doing. I'm not falling for it. I'm fuming, but make sure I don't act out.

"Sure you never hit a woman?" Amanda asks, eyebrows raised.

"Actually," I divulge, leaning back in my own chair with back erect. "Wendy Watkins. I smacked her good."

The agents lean forward, interest sparkling in their eyes.

"We had a disagreement," I continue. "I walloped her in the side of the head so hard it sprung my entire arm. When I did, she just looked at me like I was an idiot because I had hit her with the side of my fist at the thumb, and she's a stocky girl. I spent the rest of the class curled up under my desk, cradling my arm and crying. The teacher told me it served me right and just went on with class. Wendy spent the rest of Fifth Period reaching over every now and again and giving me a good kick."

After that, the Johnsons wrap up the interview, thanking me for my time.

When they escort me out of the interrogation room, Ted veers off and enters a door just before the stairs. Before the door closes behind him, I catch a glimpse of what they must be calling the situation room. There is a table with many documents and a dry erase board with pictures of the victims. Gwen's smiling face stands out. It has a circle around her throat drawn in red marker, emphasizing the left-hand side. In the corner of the board are the phrases "Chlorinated water" and "Hot tub?"

Amanda steers me away to the glass entrance of City Hall. I see Svetlana, the Russian girl from the reservoir, sitting in a chair, waiting in the lobby. Her bright eyes narrow at me.

"Leave the investigation to the professionals from now on," Amanda advises. "Just because you self-published a few books doesn't make you an investigative journalist."

She turns on her heel and leaves. As the door swings shut, I see her greet Svetlana, and together they head to the basement stairs. Svetlana looks over her shoulder at me.

"I prefer 'indie-published,' thank you very much," I say to no one.

Chapter 58
The Russians Are Coming

I'm standing at the street corner, waiting at the crosswalk. It's not a great place to be deep in thought, trying to make sense of a swarm of information. A headache hatches between my ears, along with that recurring static noise. Vaguely, in another reality, a vehicle at the stop sign is not moving on. In fact, it pulls closer, and an electric window hums open.

When I look up, Svetlana's alluring face is smiling from the passenger-side window of a huge four-door truck. It's a shiny new Dodge.

"Hey, handsome," she says. "Need a lift?"

My idiot grin evaporates when the back doors open and several large men with beards and the characteristic Old Believer bright-colored silk shirts jump out and buffalo me into the backseat. There, they flank the middle seat, and to make room for me, one of them picks up the potted ficus plant that had been previously occupying the spot and sets it on my lap.

Reflected in the visor mirror, Svetlana is staring straight ahead—stoic, disinterested. Ivan is at the wheel, and he lurches the truck away from the curb.

"Hey Ivan," I say, blowing ficus leaves out of my face. "What's up?"

"Hello, storyteller," Ivan replies, glancing into the rearview mirror. "I'd like you to tell me a story."

"Sure."

"Svetlana here tells me you were with the FBI today," he says. "Tell me that story."

His tone now is not so friendly, and a firm knot forms in my throat. "Yeah, they wanted to talk to me about my friend Gwen. She was the fourth victim. They wanted to know if I knew anything that could help their investigation. Pretty standard stuff. Who she hung out with? Had she felt threatened by anyone? That sort of thing."

Ivan touches the brakes just hard enough to cause me to lurch forward. Because I'm the only one not wearing a seatbelt, my face crashes into the seat in front of me, and my almost-healed face bursts into pain.

"What the hell!" My cry is muffled in my hand as I examine my nose. I feel a trickle of blood.

"I don't like this story," Ivan says matter-of-factly. "You see, Svetlana had interview today also with FBI, as you know. Is update on investigation into sister's death. While there, she ask about you, because she saw you with them. They are cagey in their response. Say they can't say, because—"

"It's an active investigation." I finish. I use a leaf from the ficus plant to wipe the trickle of blood from my nose.

"Hey! Don't use ficus for tissue!" Ivan admonishes, glaring at me in the mirror.

"Hey, bite me! That's what you get for hurting my face," I retort, then add while shaking the plant. "What's with this thing, anyway?"

"Was my cousin's. Svetlana's sister," Ivan explains, his tone calming down, turning almost sad. "Was wedding gift for her and her piece-of-shit husband. He is the reason she is dead. He is non-Believer. Into drugs. Got her into drugs. Exposed her to wrong crowd. She would be alive today if he hadn't. He doesn't deserve ficus, so we take back! Didn't we?"

This last was directed to the others in the cab, who agree enthusiastically.

"I didn't think you guys married outside the faith."

"Not supposed to. Rare. Is why she is dead. Now—" Ivan touches the brakes again. My face lurches into the seat again. "Tell us what you know. What is the FBI hiding from us? You aren't suspect, are you? That would be most unfortunate. Would upset Svetlana, because she likes your books, and we'd have to kill you."

Pain keeps blooming in my face. Ivan confirmed that the FBI didn't tell Svetlana much more than me regarding their personal theories on the serial killer. He also confirmed that they didn't tell her that I am a person of interest.

"I am *not* a suspect! And I couldn't get them to listen to any of my theories, and they wouldn't tell me any of theirs. So I'm in the dark just as much as you!"

Ivan grimaces in disbelief. What he does next is predictable now—and sure enough, he touches the brakes again, and I brace my forearms against the seat. My head is buried in the ficus branches and leaves.

"Dammit, Ivan!"

"Hey! Gentle with the ficus!" Ivan warns.

I grip the main branch of the plant with both hands and bring it near its breaking point.

"All right, knock it off, or the ficus gets it!"

Ivan's eyes widen, and there is a collective breath drawn in the cab.

"Okay, okay, let's not get crazy now," Ivan soothes, gesturing with his hand for me to be calm.

"I'll show you crazy!" I put on my best wild eyes. Whatever it takes. "Pull over! Now! Or this bush is going to be in a thousand pieces!"

Ivan puts up a hand in a gesture of compliance.

"All right, it's like this, see? You pull over and let me out—with the ficus—when I'm safe on the sidewalk, I'll give it back." When he hesitates, I shake the bush at him, and soon he is pulling to a stop. "Move it, *comrade*," I say to the big guy next to me.

The man lets me out. When I'm on firm footing, I shove the pot into his hands and think about running. But Ivan's voice is congenial again. "You will call if you hear anything, yes?"

I don't respond.

The man and the ficus return to the truck, and as they pull away, Ivan casts a final look while putting his hand and fingers to the side of his head to make the universal sign of the telephone.

I give him the finger.

He smiles.

Chapter 59
The Serpent's Lair

When Mom sees my face, she freaks out more than usual. She demands to know what happened. I tell her I accidentally walked into the glass door of the Grotto, and the only reason it looks so bad is that it wasn't quite healed from my earlier car wreck.

"What's the big deal?" I ask.

"Your father tells me you had a run-in with Rooney, that's what," Mom retorts, arms crossed. "Why didn't you tell me?"

The sheepish grimace my dad gives me from his recliner tells me he let it slip.

I try not to roll my eyes. "Because I knew you'd get upset, and you'd attribute any little thing that happened to me to Rooney... like walking into glass doors."

Mom is not entirely buying it. Her arms stay firmly crossed.

"I did talk to the FBI today," I say, looking to assuage her fears. "They don't feel Rooney has anything to do with it or me."

"What do they think?"

"They wouldn't tell me more, just took my statement on what I know, such as it is."

Out on Oak Street, a long rumble of motorcycle engines shakes the air so much that the windows actually rattle. Mom jumps and squeezes her eyes. I see the bikers through the kitchen window. It looks like the whole gang is headed to Silverton. They toss a beer can or two, which land on either side of the road near our house.

When they've passed, and it's quiet again, Mom lets out a long rattling breath.

"That's daily now," she says, pouring herself a cup of coffee. "Noisy bastards. Leaving trash all over the neighborhood, too."

"A friend of mine says the Regulators have a business somewhere near Molalla," I say. "Unfortunately, that means we're right on their commute."

"Ha," Mom scoffs, sipping at her coffee. "'Business,' huh? I wonder what that could be."

"They say it's a metal fab shop and garage," I explain. "They supposedly make barbecues and work on...old trucks." *Like old Broncos.*

Wheels turn in my head. Mom looks at me funny.

"Ya know, speaking of Molalla," I say, putting on a smile. "I need to head out there and...see Dylan. I've meant to pay him a visit at his work and see what his operation looks like."

"Sure, honey." Mom shrugs and grabs the funnies from the newspaper off the kitchen counter. "Tell him we said hi." Then, as an afterthought, she adds, "Don't be running around too much. We'll be having a family get-together this weekend, so plan on being home then, okay?"

"I will," I reply. "Wouldn't miss it."

Not long afterward, I'm eastbound on Oak Street, well past the point it becomes Cascade Highway, following a map on my smartphone. I have my dad's binoculars stuffed in my mailbag.

I'm not familiar with the stretch of country between Silverton and Molalla. The route meanders through wheat, corn, and beet fields. Occasionally there's what looks like an abandoned turn-of-the-century gas station, waiting its turn to be placed on the National Historic Registry. After about half an hour, phone service evaporates, and the map freezes in place.

While sitting at a crossroads, speculating on which way to go, a dark sedan eases into the rearview mirror's field of view. It pulls to the side of the road a good quarter mile back, where it sits as if watching me, nudging my senses into high alert. The car looks too similar to the one the FBI drive, reminding me of the uncomfortable conversation I had had with the agents earlier today and how I don't want another.

I pull the Jeep's steering wheel to the right and put the gas pedal to the floor. The sedan lurches into action from the side of the road. Around the next bend, a dirt road spurs off the pavement. I yank again to the right on the steering wheel and head down it—a path, really, leading into the forest. The Jeep clears the ruts and branches. A patch of blackberries grows halfway across the dirt, and from behind it, I can watch the paved road through the trees. The sedan shoots by like a missile. It might have been the same model the FBI agents drive, but at that speed, it's hard to tell.

Maybe it's paranoia, but I return to the road and head in the opposite direction, past the crossroads. Miraculously, there's a sign ahead stating, "Fab Shop." An old warehouse is to the right, surrounded by a rusty chain-link fence. A peeling bulldozer and backhoe sit at the back, and brush and trees obscure the front.

There would be a clear view from the road in a perfect world, something for the binoculars to see. Turns out that doesn't suit the Regulators' purposes. If I want a better look and answers, I will need to step onto the property. Sweating coldly, I slow down at the property's driveway. A narrow corridor of brush leads to the shop. The shop's hangar doors are open, and people move about. The occasional flare of sparks suggests welders and grinders. If I can barely make out the people, then likewise, they would have a hard time noticing me at the end of their driveway. I hope.

I dig the binoculars out of my mailbag and scan the structure. Just a quick look.

A lot of the guys wear their signature leather vests with the cowboy skull on the back. I'm in the right place. A series of motorcycles are lined up outside the shop. Apparently, there are more Regulators than just the group who rides into town, and fortunately, I don't see Rooney or Black Bart among the guys smoking outside.

A row of vehicles sits to one side of the shop. Trucks, SUVs, trailers, landscaping equipment like the bulldozer and backhoe.

All older models, but many of them obviously still serviceable. The row extends out of sight beyond the corner of the shop. There very well could be an old Ford Bronco back there—it would fit right in. Movement in the corner of the lens draws my attention to the far side of the shop's backlot. It's Rooney. He's rolling up the back door of the truck that I saw him driving from the DMV, and soon after, a procession of women hops out of the vehicle's storage. They are all young, thin, attractive, and wearing clothes and shoes better suited for a cocktail party than a fab shop. Sequins and rhinestones glitter in the sun, reminding me of the articles of clothing I had seen on the front seat of the truck that day at the DMV. The women look lost, unsure where to go, and Rooney tries to herd them like cats toward the shop, impatiently waving his hands. Through the binoculars, his mouth moves in silent but angry bursts. A redhead seems to take offense to something he says and pulls up, waving her hands in an equally agitated manner at him. Rooney grabs her by the elbow and shoves what looks like a blond wig in her chest. When he does, her hands automatically enclose around it, and he pushes her toward the shop. Soon, the group is obscured by the corner of the building.

Lowering the binoculars, my imagination goes into overdrive, assembling a narrative that would put this entire story together. Say the women are a part of the Regulators' portfolio of businesses. Sex workers. Maybe against their wills. Trafficked? When trafficking humans, you are bound to have difficulties. Like women who fight back or resist in some other way. Women who need to be dealt with so they don't create a problem. Rooney, the newest member of the Regulator family, is tasked with the dirty work of dealing with them. And disposing of the bodies.

No. Gwen was no sex worker. So how does she fit into this?

Maybe what I had initially postulated to the Johnsons is true. She had been seen with me. And Rooney, who had been tasked with targeting me, settled on her instead. Because he had experience hurting women? This thought stabs me in the heart because it then really does confirm I'm at least partly to blame for Gwen's death. My breath comes out in a shudder.

Why dispose of the bodies so publicly? Maybe Rooney isn't the sharpest tool in the shed. Or maybe, he needed undeniable proof for his brothers that he had accomplished his tasks.

But what about the writing on the dry-erase board in the situation room? Something about chlorinated water. The binoculars are no help here. Though there is plenty of discarded equipment on the property, none of it is related to water. Maybe inside the shop where I can't see? A hot tub? Unlikely.

I'm so engrossed I don't notice the rumble of motors coming up behind me. By the time I do, they're right on top of me, pulling over to my side of the road.

The rest of the Regulators have come home to roost, and I'm blocking their driveway.

My heart leaps into my throat. The binoculars drop to the floor of the Jeep, and I try to put the vehicle in gear like a half-frozen mannequin. When I do, I kill the engine. My mind becomes mush, and I start stomping on the floor with my left foot, looking for the clutch. A panicked moment later, I realize I'm not in my Suzuki SX4 with its stick shift. Instead, I'm in my manual transmission Postal Jeep that can go 55 miles per hour at best.

I look up in the rearview mirror, and I see Black Bart at the head of the pack, waving an arm in disgusted exasperation. A colleague next to him is dismounting.

I turn the ignition, making that God-awful noise ignition switches make when you've gone too far.

"Play the part," I hear a voice from the back compartment.

"What?" I squeak, looking up in the rearview mirror.

I see Clark's handsome face staring back at me. "Go with it. Play the part."

I turn in my seat and see that the compartment is empty, but I can see through the back window that the Regulator who had dismounted is walking my way. He is short and chubby with a receding hairline of curly blond hair, plus the obligatory biker beard. The ignition still isn't cooperating. By now, I'm sure my heart is pulsing through my shirt like a Looney Toons character.

The chubby Regulator comes to the driver's side door and raps on the window. I woodenly open the sliding door without making eye contact.

"Hey, you going to deliver the mail or what?" Chubby makes a sweeping gesture over my Postal Jeep, then points to my mailbag on the passenger seat.

Play the part. Without looking, I reach over and grab one of the envelopes under my bag. It's been there since I returned from Vancouver.

"Is this Tesseract Corporation by any chance?" I ask, reading the self-addressed envelope meant to return the questionnaire from my interview.

"Nah, man," Chubby replies. "This is Maverick Fabrications. They're probably in the industrial park down the road."

"Sorry," I reply with a sheepish grin. "My mistake."

"No problem. Could you move, though? We gotta get back to work."

I apologize, start the engine on the first try, and rocket off at a staggering 55 miles per hour.

Chapter 60
Evan's Valley

Those yellow eyes penetrate me, unblinking, even as the long pink tongue laps at the water.

Like everything else here, the water is dark. There has to be a light source, other than those blazing eyes, otherwise how could I distinguish the water, the rocky shore, and the pair of boots standing next to the Coyote?

The boots belong to cousin Johnny. They fit in with his usual worn jeans and holey T-shirt. His hair is curlier than I remember, and his mustache is bushier. His eyes convey a sadness that I usually don't associate with him as he returns my gaze.

"There is a time to fight and a time not to," he informs me. "I learned that lesson too late."

A chill comes over me as the Coyote takes one final slurp from the slow-moving creek and turns to Johnny. They exchange a look, and the Coyote trots away into the darkness. Jonny turns and follows.

Reaching out, I shout.

I'm still shouting when the darkness evaporates and I'm bouncing down a gravel road in the Jeep. Sunlight bursts inside my field of view, and it's a bright summer day all around me. Slamming on the breaks, the Jeep skids to a halt along the rural road.

I grip the steering wheel, breath coming out in huge pants. Sweat beads on my face.

This is the first time, I think, that I've actively caught myself in a blackout. The next closest time had been when I had viciously lashed out at my customer, which had effectively ended my sales career.

In a panic, I turn wildly in my seat to get my bearings, and gradually the disorientation fades, revealing my location: Evan's Valley, a hilly country just east of Silverton, full of poppy fields, horse pastures, and a mixture of evergreen and oak forests.

I'm guessing in my emotional distress and my desire to escape the Regulators, should they have realized who I was, I had left the beaten path of Cascade Highway. Or maybe I had just needed a peaceful place to compose myself before going home.

As my breathing calms, I look around and realize the latter theory definitely fits the bill. Poppy fields paint the hills with bands of stunning purple, crimson, and yellow.

I take a final calming breath, but in the rearview mirror is the face of a panicked man. White as a ghost. A sheen of sweat on his cheek, one of which still bears the burn scar from the firing range at Bubba's. Both eyes are blackened, and a purple welt accents the puffy bump on the bridge of the nose.

"What are you doing?" I ask the image in the mirror.

I know the answer, or rather, Johnny had given it to me.

The latest encounter with the Regulators has given me perspective. Scared me straight. It's time to let go. Let the FBI draw their own conclusions. An obedient streak in me wants to call the Johnsons and clear the air over the car chase, but what would I tell them? *Hey, remember when you told me to stop poking my nose around? Well, guess what? I didn't. Oh, and the Regulators might be sex trafficking...then again, it might have just been strippers for a birthday party. Anyway, why don't you look into it based on my lame theories so I can really piss you off?*

No. It's time to let go, get out of town, and stop being a target before it hurts the next person I care about. Or before I become the next Willy.

I step out of the Jeep to get fresh air. When I do, my spaghetti legs collapse under me, and I fall to my knees. That's fine because I still need to gather myself. The bright sun, cobalt sky, and poppies sway gently in the breeze. Bees buzz among the flowers. I focus on a lone tree on a hill among the swatches of poppy paint and the marshmallows floating behind it in the sky. Next to it is another hill with what looks like a statue on an island of green. The landmark pinpoints my exact location, and I wonder that perhaps none of this is a coincidence.

I sigh deeply, pick myself up, and begin the long walk up the hill, stepping off the gravel into the poppies. I do my best not to crush them, trudging along until I come to a manicured lawn. As I continue, the occasional tombstone appears. First, there are the flat ones, then the standing monoliths of every size and shape. Many have dates from the 1800s. Finally, when I come to a statue of the Virgin Mary, I pause. There is no reaction from her, just outstretched welcoming hands. She's about as talkative as her son.

I move on until I find a rose-colored marble gravestone with a bugling elk engraved in it. I kneel before it, letting the plush grass cradle both my knees.

"Hey, Johnny," I greet. "I just want you to know that I heard you loud and clear. I'm not going to fight anymore, even though it doesn't always feel like I've got a choice. It's been the toughest time ever, and I've been too stubborn to reach out for help. Maybe I should have spoken up sooner, especially when the wheels started to come off. And they're off plenty good now. So, I'm going back to Vancouver soon before someone else gets hurt." I run fingers through my hair. I'm not sure if I'm trying to convince Johnny or the Coyote. "I just hope it's not too late because if one more thing happens, I feel like it's going to push me over the edge like I'm going to do something crazy. Unredeemable. The wheels won't ever go back on."

I pause, plucking at the grass. Of course, there is no response. Not from Johnny, the Coyote, Mary, or Jesus. Just an echoing silence inside my head.

"I guess that's all I wanted to say." I rise to my feet. "It was good seeing you again. I'll be sure to stop by more often. Love you, cuz."

Taking a deep breath, I turn and leave. I don't get very far when I notice a figure on a bench nearby. Immediately I recognize Willy and freeze, thinking maybe he had been watching me all along, but now I see that his gaze is firmly fixed on the gravestone before him, lost in his own thoughts. Apparently, I wasn't the only one today with a date with the past.

Not wishing to be intrusive, I move along, but again don't get very far before pausing when I recall my last encounter with him and the subsequent conversation with the FBI. Willy had told me something important that night, but it never took hold in my memory. Maybe his presence now is also no coincidence, but an opportunity to reclaim that memory. To help find justice for Gwen and the other girls. To find the truth, regardless of where it leads.

No, no, stick to your original plan, I tell myself, feeling the weight of a pair of yellow eyes on me. *Let the FBI figure it out.*

I take a few more steps away but stop. Gears grind to a halt inside me. The yellow eyes are replaced by a pair of balancing scales, like the kind held by the blindfolded statue of Lady Justice. They hang askew from each other, out of balance.

Abruptly, I stomp over to Willy as if my legs had a mind of their own. His army jacket looks excessively warm in the heat of the day, but he seems perfectly comfortable. His hair is combed back, revealing a receding hairline, and an effort had been made to tame the unruly mass of his beard. Crow's feet spider away from his staring eyes.

"Willy, I'm very sorry to disturb you right now," I say as respectfully as possible, casting a glance at the gravestone he watches over. The woman's name on it, along with the birth and death dates, leave no doubt that this is his mother's final resting spot. "But I need your help."

Willy doesn't budge. I do, fidgeting.

"The other night, when we talked under the Gallon House bridge," I recommence after an awkward pause, "I believe you hinted that you might have seen who threw a body off the bridge.

Can you tell me please? These girls could use your help. Find peace. If you're worried about having to deal with the authorities, maybe we..."

"The universe is still out of balance," Willy says without removing his eyes from the gravestone. His tone is not reproachful for having been disturbed. In fact, it's conversational, if only a bit distant, as if he were reciting poetry. And in that brief space between his opening statement and what follows, in a gravelly voice sounding as if it comes from a place of cosmic wisdom, the wind rests, and the birds and insects quiet to listen. "The stars turn and turn. They expect to return to the same place, only to find themselves slightly off track. There, they create a wave pattern whose frequency peaks and valleys magnify the original white noise amplitudes, deepen their troughs, and create a new noise, a new song, a new...story. This is not wholly un-pleasing, but it *is* an aberration. So what is one to do?"

The wind resumes, the birds chirp, and the insects buzz. I hang my head and fidget some more. This is not what I had hoped for. I say as much.

"Willy, please, of all times, I need a little more clarity than that." I give sufficient pause for a response. When none comes, I'm afraid he won't respond at all, let alone with puzzles. "Say something, anything, please. You're making me feel like Bruce Willis in *The Sixth Sense* here."

Enough time goes by that I'm sure he's said all that he is going to, and I turn to leave.

"Mammoths," he says quietly.

"What?" I say, looking around, uncertain if he had actually spoken.

"Over there, in Evan's Valley, a farmer plowed up mammoth bones. Some of the few to be found in Oregon..."

I wait for more, for clarification, but nothing comes.

I recognize the look in his eyes. The turning of wheels, looking for trivia to suppress pain, or an attempt to make order of chaos. Maybe this was his way of saying that he struggled with so much in his interior that he could not help. That he, too, had decided to not fight today.

Eventually, I wring my hands one last time and leave, respecting his choice and his privacy.

Chapter 61
Gears and Water Colors

For the next couple of days, I do an excellent job of hiding in my room. All I have to do is wait a couple more, stay out of trouble, and make my escape. The FBI then can conclude their investigation, arrest Rooney, or Todd, or whomever, and the world will be back to normal. Easy peasy, lemon squeezy.

Unfortunately, I'm sure the walls in my room are several inches closer, and the second hand on the clock is sweeping backward.

I go to the kitchen. I have cravings, but not sure for what.

Rummaging around the pantry and refrigerator, I find nothing to eat. I go out onto the deck where I hear music. I see Mom and Dad dancing to the portable turntable, which is playing something romantically folksy.

"Hey, son," Dad replies. "We're just enjoying the deck before the weather turns. How about you?"

"Just looking for something to eat."

"Sorry, the cupboards are empty," Mom apologizes. "I'll go shopping tomorrow before the gathering. That way, everything will be fresh. Why don't you go downtown and eat at Chan's? You haven't seen Eva since you've been back, have you?"

"I haven't yet," I confess, "but there's plenty of time for that. I can just snack for now."

"Nonsense," Dad scoffs. "You've been cooped up here for days now. Why don't you give your mother and me some quality time?"

He swats Mom's butt.

"Ew." I grimace, horrified. "How about you guys act your age?" This, of course, only elicits chuckles from them. "Fine, I'm outta here. I'll take my time too."

"Don't disappear for days, though," Mom cautions. "It's tomorrow evening. Your Uncle Norman will be here, and so will your oldest niece, Sarah."

Assuring them I won't be that long, I leave them to their dancing.

I decide to walk to town, leaving the Jeep parked behind the house out of sight from prying eyes. I don't need the Regulators seeing it and putting two-and-two together. I'm glad I've made that decision when I bend over to pick up a piece of trash at the head of the driveway. It's a piece of origami among the beer cans and other litter the Regulators have been depositing in the neighborhood.

I analyze it for a while, sure it was the sort Rooney had given that girl he had intimidated in Salem. I crumple it up until it matches what my stomach feels like, then toss it aside.

By the time I find myself in front of the red-tiled faux pagoda that makes the entrance to Chan's Chinese restaurant, I've convinced myself Rooney had thrown the origami aside along with an empty beer can and had not been staking out my house. Yet, despite this self-assurance, there is a tremor in my hand when I open the door to the restaurant.

Inside, I find Eva's smiling face be-bopping between tables, serving the few customers here this evening.

The room has changed very little over the decades. Rows of booths with red leather cushioning take up most of the space, but there are also tables. Elaborate Chinese lanterns hang from the ceiling. I'm sure they're plastic, but they do an excellent job of simulating image-painted rice paper stretched between wood frames with dragons carved into them. Jade-colored rings hang from the dragon mouths by red tassels. When I was little, I always thought those rings were green LifeSaver candies.

When Eva sees me, we hug, and she shows me to the booth I've sat at since my dad has been bringing me here since I was six years old.

After I lie about why my face is beaten up, she takes my order.

"Number Six?" she says. It's more of a statement than a question.

"Of course."

Soon, she brings me my plate, along with a ceramic teapot and cups without handles.

She looks over her shoulder and shouts something in Chinese to the kitchen. When she does, I nearly jump out of my skin.

"What?" she asks while taking a seat opposite me.

"It always catches me off guard when you do that," I explain, digging into my plate. "You're so quiet when you speak English, but when you switch to Chinese, you turn up the volume and are more...animated. It's like you're a different person."

Eva laughs her happy laugh.

"Miss Fox explained that to us in French class, remember?" she says. "The part of the brain that is responsible for language is responsible for other things too, like expression."

I wonder what else the brain can compartmentalize.

"Someone else told me something similar recently, about left-handed kids being forced to learn to write right-handed, destroying their creativity, or worse."

"I believe it," Eva agrees. "It's good something like that never happened to you. You would never have written your books. How's that going?"

I sigh. Not my favorite topic. "Far from rich or famous."

"You will be," she assures, her smile brightening the room. "You and everyone else from Silverton."

"How's that?" I ask.

I pour several packets of sugar into my cup and dissolve it with hot tea. It's sweets I've been craving, I realize. I wonder if that has anything to do with not drinking for the past couple of days since I generally don't drink at home.

"Seems like everyone we grew up with is doing something creative," she explains. "Maybe it's something in the water, or maybe it shouldn't be surprising if you think about it. How could we not be creative, having gone to schools all our lives in buildings named after poets and writers?"

"Yeah," I say. "I forever associated 'Eugene Field' and 'Robert Frost' with buildings, and not famous people."

Eva joins me in drinking tea. She uses no sugar.

"Did you see Heather Downey was the model for LL Cool J's fitness book?" she points out. "Open almost any page, and there she is. She looks great."

I nod, sipping.

"Oh, and you missed Stacy Mulligan during Homer's when she came into the restaurant. Did you know she's a librarian? Not just any librarian, but the Resource Officer on Air Force One. I guess she was there on 9/11, and President Bush relied heavily on her when he prepared his speech. How exciting is that! Remember Ellen Lewis? She's won awards for the plays she's written. She was interviewed on NPR. Jason Cortlund? He's making indie movies; I guess he's won all kinds of awards too. Amy Temple? Writing books, I hear they're pretty good. Heck, even Jason Rappé's little brother Eric is writing books, and...hey... why are you beating your head against the table?"

I stop my slow rhythmic head butting of the tabletop. I didn't realize I was until she said something.

"No reason," I say, rubbing what I'm sure is a red spot on my forehead.

She smiles sympathetically and takes my hand. "It will all work out for you. I just know it."

"Tell that to NPR or LL Cool J."

We talk more, reminiscing as far back as kindergarten. We share some laughs. Her bobbed haircut bounces with every giggle, and beneath the straight bangs, her eyes almost wholly close when she really gets laughing.

For a moment, I feel good. I forget my troubles. I forget origami. Eva's positivity warmly spreads from the hand she is holding up my arm. For the first time in a long time, I believe everything just might be okay.

But then a familiar sound out on the street shocks me back to reality. I turn in my seat.

"What?" Eva asks, looking over my shoulder out the window.

"Did you see the truck that just now went by? The one that made all that racket, like it's missing its muffler?"

Eva shrugs and shakes her head.

I remove my hand from hers like someone realizing they're crushing a flower. The warmness in my hand and arm recedes. A stabbing pain hits the back of my head, and I grab the base of my skull, squeezing my eyes shut.

"You okay?" she asks.

"I...just have a headache," I reply.

"There is some aspirin in the kitchen. I'll get you some if you like?"

"Sure."

She leaves, and I stare at the hand she had been holding. It's turning pale as if the blood is draining away, not just the warmth.

Abruptly, I get up and leave.

When she comes back and finds my seat empty, she might be upset, but if that is the worst thing to happen to her because of me, then I'm happy.

Outside, I creep down the sidewalk, trying to be invisible. In my mind, I'm sure I look like a cartoon character hugging the buildings like an escapee trying to avoid prison searchlights.

I jump at every loud motor vehicle that passes by, and at one point, just to be safe, I step inside a coffee shop and peer out the window. The vehicle that rounds the bend is a truck—Todd parks the white WVLC pickup on the curb and steps out. He locks his door and walks down the sidewalk in the opposite direction. As I follow his movements, my eyes are drawn to the window of the restaurant he passes. There, sitting at the counter in the window is Svetlana staring back at me. She has a cellphone to her ear, talking earnestly into the handset.

I step back, out of her view.

"Sir, can I help you?" The girl working at the register gives me a funny look. "Sorry, didn't mean to startle you. Coffee?"

"No, dammit." Shit. "I'm sorry," I apologize. "I...I don't need coffee. Obviously, I'm plenty jittery, but I am craving something sweet, so I'll take a hot chocolate. Plenty of foam, please."

She smiles and sets the espresso machine to hissing. I look out the window again. The WVLC truck is still there. Svetlana is gone. I don't trust any of it. Silverton is small, and it just got smaller. I should never have left the house.

I turn back to pay for my hot chocolate, thank the girl, and ask if there is a back door. Giving me another funny look, she points, and I follow her finger, thanking her again.

There is a patio with shop goers enjoying their coffee at little tables, including a familiar pair wearing sunglasses outside the door.

"Really?" I mutter.

"Well, what a surprise to see you," Agent Johnson says. It doesn't matter which one speaks because they're both Agent Johnson, and they're both there.

"Agent Mulder, Agent Scully," I greet them. "Still following me, I see."

They exchange a look, make a face. "Don't know what you're talking about. We're just enjoying coffee."

"Right..." I say and briskly walk away. Their sunglasses follow me, with no expression on their faces.

I round the corner and orient my way toward home. I decide to take Main Street rather than Oak Street, thinking it's less traveled when leaving town. With my shoulders bunching up around my ears, I continue until I'm at the base of Main Street Hill.

There, perhaps portentously, is a red diamond-shaped traffic sign that simply says "Danger." It sends a chill down my spine.

Pausing, I slowly sip my hot chocolate while staring at the sign, telling myself I'm just silly. This sign has been a fixture of Silverton for so long that Main Street Hill is more commonly known as "Danger Hill." A well-deserved name, considering the incredibly steep serpentine hill that has been the cause of more stitches to bike-riding boys and girls over generations than all the sports at Silverton Union High School combined. It has nothing to do with my current predicament.

"Screw it."

I begin my trek up the hill's sidewalk, leaning over and huffing. At least I'm not drunk today, so there's that. As I climb, a Silverton Police car comes down the hill. Officer Andy Delaney is behind the wheel.

I give him the finger.

Without skipping a beat or even looking my way, Andy returns the gesture while extending his arm out the window.

I have to admit, my respect for him just went up.

When I crest the hill, I sigh with relief. Just a short straight away, then it's all downhill to my parents.

Right when I'm thinking this, a white truck comes up behind me and brushes so close when it pulls over it almost hits me.

I stiffen when I see the WVLC logo on the side of the truck. I just can't believe how this day is going, and I really wish I had stayed home.

I relax with gratitude when I see Jeremy's head and arm pop out of the driver's side window.

"Hey buddy, need a ride?" he asks with a big smile full of teeth.

I exhale, open the passenger side door, and jump in.

"Thanks," I say.

"No problem." He pulls back into the road. "Geez, what happened to your face?"

"This is what happened after Bubba's party, when I got run off the road," I tell him.

"Right." Jeremy bobs his head. "Sorry, I wish I could have been there."

"Me too. There, and at The Wooden Nickel before that."

"What's that about the Nickel?"

"I had a run-in with the Regulator biker gang while waiting for you," I explain, finishing off my hot chocolate. "I really could have used some backup, but you never came."

Jeremy makes a face as if something actually broke in his brain while deciphering what I said.

"We were supposed to meet that night?" he asks.

My eyes roll so hard in my head it's a wonder they don't bust loose and bounce onto the dash.

"Yes!" The paper cup in my hand crushes.

That came out much more forceful than I meant. Or maybe it came out just right. It felt good, but it also felt like a can of worms just exploded all over the cab of the truck.

The gears in Jeremy's head are smoking, and after a beat, he says, "How about I make it up to you. Let's grab a drink later tonight. I have to wrap something up first, but then I can meet…"

"Oh, for fuck's sake, really?" I explode on him. The can of worms just keeps going like silly-string now. "I don't want to wait on a bar stool for hours for an alleged friend to show up while I'm getting my ass kicked by bikers!"

"Hey man, I'm…"

"I don't want a drink! You know what I want? What I really want?"

"What?" Jeremy tries to divide his attention between me and his driving but not succeeding very well at either.

My brain locks up. What do I want? I recall my graveside confession to Johnny about not reaching out to others, yet here I am, having an opportunity to do just that, but I'm at a loss of words to make it happen. I feel like someone is offering me watercolors and brushes for the first time, along with a blank canvas, but no instructions on what to do next.

What do ordinary people want from their friends? It's the simplest of things, so why can't I paint a picture, let alone find words?

My own gears are now grinding inside my head, and smoke coming out of my ears fills up the cab of the truck, obscuring matters more.

Jeremy waits patiently with his unibrow scrunched up in befuddlement.

"I dunno, man, just pull over please." I finally say.

"You sure?"

"Yeah."

He reluctantly complies, and I get out. Outside the truck, on the side of the road, Jeremy maintains his gaze on me as if expecting me to say something profound.

"I'll see you around, I guess." That is all I can manage.

He gives a casual salute, puts the truck in drive, and pulls away.

When he had put the gear in drive, it had made a distinct "clunk" noise. Just about then, a similar gear engages in my head, and somewhere inside me, a blank canvas has a splash of paint thrown against it.

As the paint runs down the canvas, it spells out *I just need someone I can rely on.*

Chapter 62
Home is Where the Family Is

The morning of the family gathering starts off with a dark note. The television announces that another girl, McKenzie Hughes, is missing in the Silverton area. Another young, pretty, and blonde girl. In an interview, her dentist father states he was a little concerned about her partying while at college, but other than that, she did not fit the profile of the other murdered girls. It is for this reason the authorities are reluctant to connect her disappearance with the serial killer. Yet, my gut tells me they should.

By late afternoon, the family starts to show up. First Uncle Norman with his long-time partner Elaine. He is quick to give me a hug and tell me how sorry he was to hear about Gwen.

Next are Sis and her family, who always fill up the house pretty well. Usually, Aunt Cathy and that side of the family come up from Eureka to visit during Homer Davenport Days, but for some reason, they can't make it this year. Regardless, we have the annual summer family gathering anyway, before another summer runs out on us.

Steam rolls off the stove in the kitchen, and smoke billows from the barbecue on the deck. Toy trucks scrape along the carpet. The television is set to one of those channels that play music, so classic Johnny Cash and Hank Williams fill in the background sounds, tangled up with children's squeals and Uncle Norman's booming laugh. Jesus plays with the younger children by rolling a ball back and forth across the floor. It was making for a better day.

As I help Mom in the kitchen, cutting some carrots, I hear an uptick in activity in the family room. The carport door has just opened and closed, and the children's squeals escalate to a new pitch.

"Sounds like Sarah has arrived," Mom says. "Why don't you go say hi to her. I don't think you've seen her since you've been back."

By the time I finish up what I'm doing and go out to greet her, she has already moved out to the deck and is seated on a deck chair, smoking a cigarette. She has a few more tattoos and piercings than the last time I saw her, and she has dark rings under her eyes. A family trait, but they are darker than usual. Her hair looks good, though, long and silky and getting darker with every year. She's a pretty girl, if a bit tough looking around the edges.

She's wearing a piece of jewelry that is like a delicate tiara across her forehead. It's slightly askew, like a crooked halo. The white plastic fiber tarp that usually covers the barbecue is draped over the back of her chair. A breeze has kicked it up, making it dance behind her like a pair of frayed wings.

"Gunky!" she cries when she sees me, sets the cigarette in the ashtray, and runs to me, and gives me a big hug. She is almost as tall as me, and her honey-scented hair almost suffocates me while she rocks me from side to side. She hasn't hugged me this fiercely since when I came back from a year-long stay in France. Now that I think about it, I probably haven't seen her for close to a year.

We sit, and she tells me about her adventures and her sorrows. Her husband had recently passed away, dying in his sleep from complications related to cancer treatment that he received some years before. She still struggled with his death because they had been fighting just before his passing. Being married to a rock'n'roll musician came with its challenges.

I had missed the funeral, being away on business.

"When they say, 'Never go to bed angry' in your marriage, you better believe it," she finishes, exhaling a long stream of gray cigarette smoke and murdering the butt in the ashtray.

I have no words for her. All I can do is hold her.

Right about then, Mom comes out and announces that dinner is ready. So we move inside and crowd around the much too small table and load our plates.

During the dinner, Sis addresses us both. "You two better put on your schedules that Marie is having her First Communion next month."

"Yeah, they're going to drown you in holy water," Little Joey says to his sister Marie.

"Mom!"

"Now, now," Sis admonishes her boy with a frown. "Nobody is getting drowned. Besides, that's baptism. She already has had that, just like you. This is different."

"Why do we drown people in holy water?" Joey asks, fighting his mouth around the giant corncob in his hands. Kernels get everywhere.

Sis rolls her eyes. Everyone else at the table chuckles.

"For the last time, nobody is getting drowned, but you do die, just like how they teach you in Sunday school. When you're submerged in the waters of baptism, you die to Sin and are reborn in Christ."

Joey struggles with the concept as much as he struggles with the corn. He gives up on both when his sister sticks her tongue out at him.

Something about Sis's explanation nudges a thought loose. Something about water and rituals. It makes my head hurt. I give up thinking about it when Mom announces desert.

As she serves the pie, she asks the kids, "Hey, you guys want to hear something funny about your Gunky and holy water?"

Of course, they squeal with delight.

"Well, when your Gunky was little, and we were at church, and the priest would come around to sprinkle holy water, every time Gunky would shout as loud as he could, 'Mom! Look out! Holy water! You'll melt!'"

The kids laugh. Mom loves to tell that story.

After eating, we migrate back to the family room just as the sun is setting. The TV channel is changed to an old *Rambo* movie. The younger kids watch while hanging all over their big sister.

"This is really cheesy," Sarah says, wrinkling her nose at the action on screen. "Kinda over the top, isn't it? With all these explosions?"

"That's just how it was back in the eighties," I explain. "It wasn't considered a good action flick unless it had massive and frequent explosions. And snappy one-liners."

Sarah is not convinced. Her younger siblings seem entertained enough.

Uncle Norman falls asleep while sitting on the couch. Soon his baritone snoring is shaking the rafters while the rest of us settle on conversations. Mom and I sit on the edge of the fireplace while she talks to Elaine, and I speak to Dad while he bounces Joey on his knee in his favorite chair, telling him stories of ancient Indian folklore.

His doing so triggers my memory of recent events involving the Coyote, especially my conversation with Dave at Bubba's party. The part where Coyote takes offense at my denial of my heritage.

When there is a pause in Dad's storytelling, I clear my throat and speak.

"There is something I've been meaning to say," I begin, and Dad waits, giving Joey an extra bounce. "You know, it must sometimes look like I don't care about my native heritage," I glance over to great-grandmother's picture on the wall. "I want you to know that's not true." I squirm on the rocks of the fireplace. "I admit that in high school, there were certain... people...who delighted in their racism, and after a while, I just didn't feel like fighting it anymore. The same is somewhat true today. But by the time I learned to not care or stick up for myself, I had stopped talking about my Indian side. Never showing an interest in going to the powwows with you. I'm sorry about that. I let others direct me down a path I'm ashamed I took. Maybe not a denial of my heritage, but not exactly embracing it either."

Dad is thoughtful for a while. It is hard to tell what he's thinking, whether he is agreeing or because he's bouncing the boy on his knee.

"It's okay, son. Your grandfather knew the risks taking us off the reservation," he replies eventually. His tone is sad but understanding. "Losing touch with our past, that is. It was a risk he was willing to take, seeing the benefits outweighing the costs. It is unfortunate to see you, your sister, and her kids lose touch with the traditions. It was inevitable...but then again, you're alive and healthy. Not everyone can say that. We didn't all entirely escape Coyote." I know he's referring to more than just Johnny. Other family members also hadn't been so lucky. I nod somberly.

Dad gives Joey a bounce and asks, "Something in particular happen to make you think of this?"

I chuckle. "What *hasn't* happened lately? I thought maybe I should confess, in case my denying my heritage is why Coyote has been so hard on me lately. Maybe by doing so he'll back off."

Dad shares my chuckle. "Could be, could be. But Coyote is a trickster. Sometimes he doesn't know when to quit. Sometimes he goes too far."

"He's a trickster too?" Joey asks, apparently following the conversation.

"Yessiree," Dad says in a sing-song fashion, kissing Joey's head. "He's not all bad, really. He's no worse than a storm that knocks a tree on your teepee or when your water hole dries up— just a part of life. In fact, his role sometimes is to keep a balance in nature or to teach lessons. He often does this through tricks."

Joey wriggles on Dad's lap. "How?"

"Well," Dad begins, "there's the time all the great dogs of the world gathered to go swimming and frolic in the water. They wouldn't let Coyote join them because he was not powerful like Wolf or beautiful like Fox. 'Go away, you ugly scavenger!' they told him and went to play in the water. When they did, they all took their tails off so as not to get them wet. Angry, Coyote took up all the tails where they had been neatly set in order and threw them in a pile. When the dogs came out of the water, they did not know whose tail was whose and had to put on whichever they could find. That's why to this day, you see dogs sniffing each other's butts because they're still trying to find their own tail. And that's why you should always be humble and not discriminate against others, because Coyote will come and play a trick on you."

Joey giggles up a storm. Briefly, I forget darker things.

Until that is, the rumble of motorcycle engines shakes the house as the gang drives by the house toward Silverton. Mom flinches, and her drink shakes when she next puts the glass to her lips.

"Look, Sam," Marie says, drawing my attention to them in front of the TV. "It's you."

A news announcement has interrupted *Rambo*, re-broadcasting the news of the missing McKenzie Hughes, showing a picture of her from what looks like one of her social media accounts. She is standing with other young women, smiles on their faces and drinks in their hands.

"Nah, that's not me," Sarah assures Marie.

Marie purses her lips and tugs on Sam's hair. "But that's your hair."

That grave-stepping sensation comes over me when I realize that Marie is correct; the two girls look remarkably similar.

The chill intensifies when a gut-wrenching noise draws my attention to the windows overlooking the driveway to the highway.

There, the Bronco has slowed to a crawl on the highway before the house. I stand and jolt to the window, trying to get a look at the driver in the waning daylight before it launches down the road toward Molalla.

I stiffen. I'm beyond angry. I feel violated that the Bronco would make an appearance this close to home. A home, I'm keenly aware, that is very exposed to the road and exposed to a drive-by. I'm reminded of the origami I found at the head of the driveway.

Rooney. It has to be him.

It will never end.

I turn to look at the family gathered here. Mom is still shaking. A girl who looks like Sam is on TV for the most tragic of reasons.

Something snaps inside me.

"No," I growl.

Chapter 63
Showdown at the Wooden Nickel

I go to my bedroom and upend my travel bag.

Clothes fall out, plus a heavy object.

I pick up the heavy object, the pistol, and hold it sideways to contemplate it. Eventually, I eject its magazine and confirm that it's loaded with as many bullets as it will hold.

Satisfied, I slam the magazine into the butt of the handle and pull and release the slider to arm the weapon. After engaging the safety, I slip it into my waistband at the small of my back, hidden under my shirttail.

When I announce to the living room full of family that I'm going to the store for something, there are groans of disappointment, and Mom heads me off at the door.

"Stick around, you can get whatever, whenever," she says, a hint of unease in her voice. Apparently, her mother's intuition sounded an alarm.

I look at her long and hard. I feel my Adam's apple bob heavily with a slow swallow.

"I gotta go, Mom," I say, placing my hands on her shoulders. "I love you." I hug her and use the gesture to move her aside.

Moments later, I'm in the Jeep, driving across the lawn, popping apples as I run them over. I hit the highway and am racing toward Molalla. If I catch up to the Bronco, great; if not, I know where it's going. And I don't care what waits for me at the shop. My intention is set.

There is no gate to the facility. Probably just a bunch of guys sitting around drinking beers, welcoming their brother Rooney from his latest round of terrorizing people. The last thing they'll expect is a Postal Jeep rolling up the driveway with a special delivery.

Just step out, smile, and *Pop! Pop! Pop!*

Whatever happens after that, I don't care.

"I know what you're thinking," I say to Jesus in the passenger seat. "'Turn the other cheek' and all that. 'Thou Shall Not Kill' and whatnot. I know. You're right. I want to be sorry...but I'm just... not. It will never end. More girls will die. Sam can't be one of them. Maybe the FBI will catch up to him, but not until it's too late. Sure, I can go to the police, but with what proof? My gut? No. Even if they detain him, they probably won't be able to hold him for very long. Just like last time, with Johnny. And now, he's with the Regulators. Even if Rooney goes to prison forever, his support group will do his dirty work outside. I have to do this. I gladly take responsibility. Take the sin. Happily, if it means those I care about will be okay."

My grip makes creaking noises on the steering wheel. My jaw hurts from clenching.

Jesus doesn't say anything, just stares out past the headlights into the night.

"Would it hurt to say something every now and then?" I almost shout, turning on him. "Just once? Something? Anything?"

Silence.

I wipe my eyes. "Okay then."

I come to the intersection just before the shop, ready to blow through it before losing my nerve and covering the final distance up to their driveway.

Ahead, a single headlight comes at me, the rumbling of an American motorbike coming with it. It slows and drifts to my left as it approaches, then turns and passes me the way I had just come.

"What the...?"

I turn in my seat and watch Rooney go by. Then I work the wheel around and follow after him. He's hauling and, well, I'm in a Postal Jeep, so I almost lose sight of his single red taillight before reentering Silverton. I pass home, not giving it a single glance, and catch up to Rooney at the top of Oak Hill in front of Circle K.

We dip over the other side of the hill and approach downtown.

Even from far away, the mob filling the intersection in front of the Palace is visible. People are carrying protest signs. It looks like the West Harbor Trinity Church is out in force tonight, picking fights with moviegoers in front of Stu's theater. A police car has rolled up with its lights flashing.

Rooney sees this too and cuts between two buildings through a parking lot. I curse, not sure what to do. I can't turn left against a one-way street, and if I dart through the parking lot after him, the pursuit will be obvious. So I turn right and circle around, hoping to catch up with him on the other side of the block.

Precisely that happens, and I step on the gas and follow Rooney, screeching around corners, zigzagging now through neighborhoods with wooded lanes. Then, up ahead, Rooney makes a final turn and rockets down Hazelgreen Road toward Salem. I curse again, worried I'll lose him, worried I'll catch up.

He is outdistancing me at first but then slows and drifts almost to a stop as he turns to the right off the road.

So, this is where he's going. I don't know if it helps my plan or not. And what is my plan? My hands tighten up on the wheel again. An uneasy feeling causes me to glance up in the rearview mirror. There are bright headlights, and I realize they've been following me as I sped through the last neighborhood. While debating what to do, the truck veers to the right and disappears down another road.

A relief. I idle along, drifting up to the darkened sign of the Wooden Nickel. A temporary one is slapped over the top, stating that the establishment is under renovation and will be open in a couple of weeks.

Yet Rooney parks out front, detaches something from his bike, and carries it through the door.

Killing the lights on the Jeep, I creep into the parking lot. A light comes on in the main room, revealing my good fortune: running into a building full of gang members is no longer necessary. Most chairs are flipped upside down on the tables, and plastic tarps cover most everything else. My target is right here. All alone. Why? Who cares? This is the final chapter in his life. Heck, I'll have plenty of time to dispose of the body, too, if I want. Maybe I take him up the Abiqua and bury him deep in that Oregon jungle. Maybe I stuff him in a plastic bag and take him to Oregon City Paper Mill, where I happen to know where a drum of hydrofluoric acid sits in an isolated corner. Drop his corpse in and —*fizz!*—no evidence. The Regulators will scratch their heads for who cares how long, speculating on what happened to the Roonster.

Stepping out of the Jeep, I approach the door and lighted window. My legs aren't as steady as the conviction in my brain.

I peer inside, and Rooney's back is to me, the prominent cowboy skull insignia facing and mocking me.

He's at the jukebox, pressing the buttons on the old school interface, flipping through the songs. Tools and power cords occupy the floor. At Rooney's feet is a white metal propane tank with the rearing stallion logo on it. To his left, the other dining room is partitioned off by a dark plastic tarp. Perfect for wrapping a body in.

I step away from the window.

"You ready for this?" I whisper to myself. "No going back. You commit." I take the H&K from the small of my back. Its solidness is reassuring. Real. I take deep breaths, puffing my cheeks out with each exhale. *Ready? Ready.* I exhale until my heart slows down. The puffing stops. I close my eyes. I calm. A single word comes to mind. *Commit.*

Opening the door, I glide in, taking a few long strides right up to Rooney as he's prepared to drop a quarter into the jukebox. I place the gun to the back of his head behind his ear. Rooney freezes, the quarter hangs on the lip of the slot.

The quarter rattles against the slot. "Uh...?"

My fingers readjust on the grip. My hand is suddenly slick with sweat. "You know who I am?" I ask.

I tell myself I want him to know why he died. But, truth is, I'm probably just stalling.

He slowly turns his head just enough to look at me from the corner of his eye. Otherwise, he doesn't move.

"Yeah," he says, swallowing. "I know you. Of you."

The gun presses harder against his head. He squeezes his eyes shut. It feels oddly powerful. The opposite of what I've been feeling for weeks now. It's liberating, which is its own kind of frightening.

"Then you know why I'm here."

His head moves up and down stiffly.

To my left, the plastic partition opens like a shower curtain pulled aside with the quickness of someone late for work. Chubby, the Regulator, stands there with eyes wide, holding the plastic in one hand. Despite my shock, I manage to maintain the gun pressed against Rooney's head, and we all freeze in place.

The room beyond the tarp is filled to capacity with bikers. I'm guessing if I'd parked on the opposite side of the building, I would have noticed their fleet of motorcycles. As it is, here we are. Black Bart stands at the side of an older man sitting at a table, who regards me with raised fuzzy white eyebrows. Next to him, tied to a chair at the same table, sits Boomer Johnson. His face is bloody and bruised. Near the trio, a Maverick-labelled propane tank rests on the floor with its top removed, revealing that it's brimming with plastic bags of white powder.

Collectively, the standing Regulators withdraw an arsenal of handguns. One points a Kalashnikov automatic rifle.

Boomer chuckles. "Tough luck on the timing, kid."

To my right, casually leaning against the jukebox, Clark advises, "Play the part. Don't show fear. Follow your own advice and commit to the role."

I glance at him, distracted, but turn my attention back to the room when the older Regulator speaks. "Well, well, well, what do we have here?"

"Remember," Clark continues his instruction, "stay in character to..."

"Yeah, okay, got it!" I growl under my breath at Clark, returning my attention to him and making eyes.

The old Regulator and Black Bart exchange a glance. "Wow," the old guy exclaims. "Looks like we got a real live one here." He gestures to Chubby. "I'm afraid we're going to have to ask you to put that gun down and have a seat."

Chubby takes a step toward me and reaches for my weapon.

"Ah-ah!" I warn, pressing the metal into Rooney's scalp until he squawks. "Just back off porky, or I'm going to make a Pollock out of the jukebox screen."

Chubby hesitates, also looks confused.

"That's Jackson Pollock," I explain. "Makes art from splattered paint? Like brains, splattered?"

The old man rolls his eyes. "Still going to need that gun."

"H-hey, Pops?" Rooney says under the weight of the gun. "Could we not antagonize him?"

"This is your dad?" I ask.

"No, that's just my name," the old man sighs while removing a pipe from his vest. He lights a match and sets it to the pipe bowl while puffing slowly. The rest of us fidget. Then, in between clouds of pearly smoke, he says, "Pops Montgomery. I'm the leader of this merry band of outlaws, and you're seriously hindering negotiations here. You mind telling me why?"

He throws the spent match into an empty coffee cup on the table.

"You know this is a no-smoking establishment, right?" Boomer points out.

Pops levels a languid look at him. "Really, Boomie?"

He then squints at me, leaning heavily on an elbow, evidently still waiting for a response. Under other circumstances, the man probably would make a great Mall Santa.

Chubby and most of the gang seem to be amused. Black Bart doesn't. His grip on his gun is steady and pointed right at me, just waiting for permission. The only reason I'm still alive is probably that this Pops guy is curious.

The quarter on which Rooney still has a death-grip rattles in the jukebox slot.

"Well," I begin, summoning the courage Clark suggested I display. "I'm truly sorry for having troubled your business. To be fair, I really did think Rooney here was alone. We have some things to...discuss."

Pops raises his eyebrows. His lips purse around the stem of the pipe.

Black Bart leans over and explains the situation.

"Ah," Pops grunts, stroking his beard. "Good old-fashioned family feud. Which I can appreciate, but of course, it's interfering with things."

"It's more than that." I feel a confidence I've never felt before, almost as if I had crested the peak of known morality to see what lies on the other side. I've come to the dark side of the Moon, and ahead is I don't know what, and I don't care. "He just didn't kill my family, but my friend, a lot of other women, and it wasn't going to stop there. I think you put him up to it. I won't let that go on."

Pop's eyebrows are halfway up his forehead now, and he exchanges another look with Black Bart, whose frown conveys both irritation and confusion.

"Now, I'm familiar with the family affair," Pops explains, "but what's this talk about friends and women?"

"The killing going on in Silverton," I say. "Women you couldn't get to go along with your operations? You eliminated them. Had Rooney do the dirty work, dropping their bodies off.

The last victim, Gwen Thompson? She got in the way when Rooney was set after me by him."

I gesture to Black Bart with my free hand, whose frown only deepens.

Pops chuckles, somewhere between genuine amusement and consternation. "Not likely. Though I admit our, ahem, portfolio involves ladies of certain moral flexibility, it would be just plain bad business to kill them, let alone leave their bodies lying around for the whole world to find. And if such a thing were necessary, I certainly wouldn't assign the job to this idiot—no offense Rooney."

"None taken, Pops," Rooney rasps.

Pops levels a *Well?* look at me. The pistol is starting to feel really heavy. The look Pops gives me, his tone, his manner; everything points to the fact that he's not lying. He has no need to. I'm not getting out of here alive, and he knows it. The gun dips a bit.

I have to force it back against Rooney's scalp.

"There's still the matter of you following me around. I can't have that. Can't have you hurting my family."

"Man, I don't know what you're talking about!" Rooney all but screeches, and his following words come out like an embarrassed confession. "I've actually been avoiding you. These guys want me to rough you up, minimum, and I've been wracking my brains how to get around that."

Pops seems to retract whatever decision he was about to make. Instead, he looks curious again, if a little angry.

"Is that what you told the judge? Is that how you got off?" I seethe. "When you shot Johnny in the back of the head. 'It wasn't me'? 'The Devil made me do it'? 'I didn't want to do it'? Was that how it was?"

Rooney turns his head slightly to me. "Look, man, you gotta understand, your cousin Johnny was a badass, okay? He used to smack me around for nothing. That day, when we argued, he got that look in his eyes, and when he turned around to go into the house, I just knew he was going for a gun. He was going to kill me! It was either him or me! Even if I had turned tail and run, he would have just chased me down! It was self-defense!"

"Shut up!" I shout, pressing the gun so hard that his face hits the jukebox screen, fogging it up.

My world is upside down. I don't know what to think, other than it's too late. I've made a terrible mistake to cap off a summer of mistakes. My only tether to reality right now is the gun pressed against Rooney's head, which is a horrible reality. Pops just crosses his arms, pipe clenched in teeth. He's clearly run out of patience.

"Time to hand the gun over, son," he says around the pipe, gesturing again to Chubby.

"Hey, Bad Santa," I growl, mustering a last ounce of confidence as I stab the finger of my free hand at him. "I'm not handing anything over. I'm going to walk out of here now, and you're going to let me."

The amusement is back. "Is that so?"

"Yeah, I—"

The door on the opposite side of the bar, the side where the bikes are probably parked, bursts open, and a long line of people with bright colored shirts march in. The shirts are silky and so shiny in primary colors they look like an Away Team from the old *Star Trek* series.

"Would it hurt if someone were to lock a door around here?" Pops shouts.

Russians form a line along the bar facing the bikers. Ivan is there along with Svetlana, who looks like an angry Laura Ingles Wilder with her bonnet and shotgun.

I'm caught in the middle.

"Good work, storyteller," Ivan says. "You do good job finding killers of girls."

"You were following me?" I ask.

"Da!" Ivan nods triumphantly.

All eyes are on me. Recognition dawns on Chubby, who points and declares angrily, "Hey, you're the mailman!"

The Regulators raise their weapons, emphasizing their feelings on recent developments. Naturally, this causes the Russians to do the same.

In the tense silence that follows, the creak of the central door opening again sounds almost deafening.

"I told you we'd have limited access to 220 voltage here," Dylan says, carrying a loop of power cords through one arm.

"I thought for sure the kitchen would have some," Jeremy counters, huffing along with Jodi while they carry what looks like a generator.

Todd walks behind the trio, carrying a box of power tools.

All four stop and stare wide-eyed at the scene before them. I can only imagine what they're thinking. Perhaps that they've stumbled upon an argument over who has the best beards? Their jaws drop when it registers that it's me in the center.

"What'd we miss?" Jeremy says ironically.

"You see what I mean?" Pops cries. "Doors! They have locks! Simple concept!"

Rooney makes a run for it, stumbling toward his group, catching me off guard. The quarter he had been holding rolls into the jukebox, sounding thunderous as a bowling ball.

Someone fires a gun.

The room erupts in a conflagration of thunder and fire. It's deafening, setting my ears to ringing.

Instinctively I duck as wood slivers explode in the air. Russians duck behind the bar. Todd simply curls up into a fetal position under a booth table. Jodi pulls a pistol from an ankle holster and joins the fray even as Jeremy and Dylan yank him back. Clark remains leaning against the jukebox, not only calm but smiling. Music starts to play. Even in the cacophony of gunfire, I discern it's Nazareth's "Hair of the Dog."

I've never been shot at. Never been in a gunfight. Of course, I've been to plenty of gun ranges and shot plenty of weapons, but this is some other planet. My only preparation was an article I once read in a magazine about the psychological impact of being involved in a firefight. The article's writer interviewed military personnel, law enforcement officers, and victims of gun violence, particularly a group of people involved in a hostage situation of a US embassy. All had similar stories of how the mind behaved during their experience, especially the "surreal" quality and "slowness of time" caused by an adrenaline overload. One police officer distinctly remembered that after each shell ejected from his gun after firing, that not only did they fly through the air in slow motion, they looked as large as barrels, and he had time to read the writing on them.

I didn't expect the smell. Spent gun powder stings your nose. It feels asphyxiating. The one good piece of movie advice I recollect I fail to follow. Gene Hackman, in *Unforgiven*, had astutely pointed out that it wasn't the fastest gun that won; it was the steady hand. Me? I just start shooting anything that moves.

People yell. Glass explodes. Wood splinters fly.

Still tied to the chair, Boomer hops as best he can across the floor, crying out, "Shit! Shit! Shit!" as bullets whiz around him. It would have been comical if not for the seriousness of the situation.

The jukebox takes a few hits, and each time it rocks back and forth the song changes. "Hair of the Dog" skips to The Eagles' "Life in the Fast Lane," to Madonna's "Like a Virgin," to *ABBA*'s "Take a Chance on Me," to The Supremes' "Reflections" before returning to "Hair of the Dog."

Or maybe it's because Clark is rocking and kicking it, stabbing at the keys, shouting, "Is there no good music in this infernal age?"

I crouch-run for the door where Jeremy, Dylan, and Jodi have almost made their escape.

Time slows down. A bullet grazes my leg, parting the fabric of my jeans and leaving a red channel. The bullet doesn't even *touch* me, but it doesn't have to. Its shockwave alone feels like a sledgehammer side-swiping my leg. Somehow, next, I'm on my back. Jodi's eyes are seeing me, then the door closes between us.

I fire a wild shot. My gun's slide ejects and mocks me with an empty chamber. I'm out of bullets.

It's about then that Black Bart catches my eye and takes a slow, steady aim at me.

***

Out in the parking lot, Jodi is frantically pulling on the handle of one of the locked WVLC trucks.

"Who's got the keys to this one!" he shouts.

"Who cares, let's get out of here!" Dylan responds.

Jodi hands his pistol to Jeremy. "Keys! Now! Who's got them?"

Dylan and Jeremy fumble out their keys, and the three of them juggle them around until they find the right one. When they do, Jodi flips back the front seat and pulls out a familiar-looking object.

"Are you kidding me?" Dylan shouts.

"Can we not talk about his now?" Jodi removes his M4 from its case, slaps in a full magazine, and pulls on the spring-loaded charging handle. He then looks to Jeremy. "You good to go?"

Jeremy smiles, hefting the pistol. "Hell yeah."

***

Back inside, I'm sitting in near shock. I am both feeling the worst pain I have ever experienced, and it is also oddly numb and unable to support my weight. I can't stand and can barely crawl. My emotions are split, too. I'm frantic and scared, but things are also happening so fast they can barely register.

Black Bart gives a contemptuous smile, ready to pull the trigger, but suddenly blood sprays from his upper arm, and he goes over sideways. A new sound enters the room. More gunshots, but from a different weapon. The distinct sound of the M4 carbine.

At the entrance, Jeremy and Jodi charge in. Later, I will swear they were in desert camouflage, geared up in their complete Iraq equipment, helmets and all. But it's just them in their khaki-colored WVLC uniforms. They surround me. Dylan, who has come in behind them, grabs me under my armpits and wastes no time dragging me toward the door.

Of all the gunshots, I hear one in particular, followed by a metallic "clink!" and there is a staggering, ear concussing explosion out on the patio beyond the Regulators, where a bunch of real propane tanks sit. A rolling fireball pours in our direction, and heat washes over me.

Break, I think. *Break.*

***

"I say," Homer comments over the rim of his teacup. He's frowning with disapproval. "An explosion? Don't you think that is a little much?"

"I have to agree," Clark says, looking over his shoulder as he continues to wrestle the jukebox. "It's over-the-top. And *I'm* from Hollywood."

"Pussies," Stephen scoffs at his colleagues. "I say it's fine. Go with it."

With that, Stephen turns to me and gives two thumbs up with a cheesy smile.

***

Whoosh! Clack!

In the center of Mac's dance floor, there are the weavers at the loom.

My image in the tapestry is near complete, and a chill comes over me when I consider what might happen once it is. Something tells me that the weaver at the loom will not move on to the next scene of my life.

The crone hovering over the thread cackles as it frays on the blade of her shears.

Break.

***

We tumble out the door and fall in a heap.

Flames and smoke boil out behind us.

392

Jeremy's pistol has ejected its slide. Jodi is examining the empty magazine from his rifle.

Inexplicably, Dylan runs back into the building.

Before any of us can protest, he comes right back out carrying Boomer, chair and all.

He drops him among us, panting and coughing.

Next, Todd leaps out of the building, runs past us, and jumps into the nearest WVLC truck.

"Hey!" Jeremy shouts after him as the truck backs out.

Todd ignores him as police and fire sirens fill the air.

A Silverton police cruiser flies into the parking lot, almost hitting the escaping Todd as it comes to a sliding stop. Andy jumps out, and the door to the Wooden Nickel bursts open again. This time a smoldering and pissed Black Bart appears and aims his gun at my group.

Gunfire explodes, and Black Bart's head snaps back, and he drops like a sack of potatoes.

We turn to see Andy standing there with an open mouth and a smoking gun. He pushes his glasses up his nose.

More police cars enter the parking lot. Fire engines come to a crawl out on the road, fighting to get to the building. And meanwhile, Todd is flooring it in the other direction, ogling the mess of Black Bart's face, so he doesn't even see the incoming lights. He slams his truck headfirst into the next cruiser.

Garbage cans and yard debris containers fly from the bed of the maintenance truck over the cab and onto the police car's hood.

One of the containers bursts open, spraying grass clippings everywhere. In the mess of debris, the container also ejects the body of a young girl.

Chapter 64
Aftermath

Things happen fast. Real fast. I get a front-row seat, though on the sidelines with my hands zip-tied.

The place is soon crowded and crawling with uniforms of every color: Silverton Police, Marion County Sheriffs, Oregon State Police, FBI, firefighters, and ambulance personnel. Not long after their arrival come a fleet of vans disgorging a multitude of technicians in colorful coveralls bearing an alphabet soup of acronyms and initials. Most saying something to the effect of "Forensics." The Marion County HART team is there. Even though the action is over, plenty of personnel "tac-ed out" in paramilitary garb and weapons, ready for World War III.

It appears that the Johnsons are in charge, directing logistical traffic, telling technicians where to set up the command tent, the medical tent, the interrogation processing center, and where to set generators and floodlights. Everyone deferred to them immediately. There was no moment like in television when a cigar-chomping detective argues with the feds over jurisdiction. It just happened.

I hear Agent Ted Johnson comment, "I haven't seen this big a mess since the mass shooting at Umpqua College."

Agent Amanda agrees. "Amazing, isn't it? How much blood the human body holds."

The fire is put out, and most of the firefighters have pulled away from the scene. A single lanyard-wearing fire marshal sifts through the debris with technicians from various agencies.

The area is cordoned off with yellow police tape and metal barriers like those used at music events. A convoy of news vans is lining the road outside the cordons. Emergency lights glitter in every direction.

In the beginning, the police didn't know what to make of things, and they rounded up all the survivors and made us kneel or sit with our hands zip-tied behind our backs, regardless of whether we were good guys, bad guys, or indifferent. Except for Todd, that is. He was cuffed and taken away and hasn't been seen since.

Jodi protested loudly that he knew his rights and wanted his guns back.

They took our wallets and the contents of our pockets. They also tagged us with plastic bracelets with barcodes like the sort you get when in the hospital. Some guy in civilian clothes, wearing a ballistic vest with "FBI" printed in giant yellow letters, now scans these with a handheld scanner, which sends Jodi into another diatribe on government overreach.

They place us in separate groups based on our apparent demographics. There aren't that many bikers left. Rooney is among the survivors, and briefly, before they move him on to his group, he is on his knees at arm's length in front of me. His arms are just as zip-tied as mine. We're eye to eye. His are wide, scared. I realize, no matter how this shakes out, any surviving Regulators will never forget him as the guy who started the chain reaction that led to this. Rooney has been scared probably all his life, but if anyone will be on the bloody end of vigilante justice, it's him.

Probably me, too.

I feel a warm hand on my shoulder. I look over, and Jesus is staring at me. He is actually touching me and not some old couple acting as a go-between. And for once, he is looking me directly in the eyes, urging me.

I scowl. I want to shake his hand off, but it is firm and comforting.

I turn back to Rooney. Swallow hard. Tears are brimming in my eyes. I can't breathe. I realize I haven't been able to breathe for a very long time. For years.

"Look," I finally choke out to Rooney. "I wasn't there that day. I don't know what really happened. You had your perspective, I'm sure Johnny had his, and if I'd been there, I'd probably have mine. I don't know if this means anything or if you care, but I got to say this for my sake. Maybe for yours too. Maybe I can make the world a slightly better place today by saying so." I pause. "I forgive you."

The scruff on his neck undulates with a big swallow. He nods, and oddly, his attention is jerked to nearby trees where birds are chirping. Then he is gone, taken away by county sheriffs to his group.

I can breathe again.

The warm hand on my shoulder squeezes, and a gentle and melodious voice says, "If living were easy, everyone would be doing it."

I turn to Jesus. "What?"

A commotion draws my attention away. Svetlana is viciously struggling and bilingually cursing up a storm between Andy and another cop.

"Woo! Get some, girl!" Jeremy proclaims.

Me, Boomer, Dylan, and Jodi chuckle.

"Hey, keep quiet!" Andy shouts to us, and when he does, this distraction allows Svetlana the opportunity to land a foot to his groin, which of course, only elicits more chuckles from us.

I look back to Jesus, but he is gone.

Svetlana is escorted to her group and left writhing on the ground, bound hand and foot.

"This man is wounded," Agent Ted says to a colleague while standing over me. "Get him to the medical tent pronto."

The bleeding stopped long ago, but my leg throbs more as the adrenaline wears off. It's not life-threatening, and I expect to be triaged as such in the newly erected tent in the Nickel's expansive parking lot. Before they drag me off, however, I get a better look at my group. We say nothing, but I'm sure to make eye contact with each of them, lingering especially on Jodi. For once, his features soften, and we give each other a long knowing look before I'm escorted away.

In the tent, my escort removes my zip-tie then presides while I'm situated on a gurney, and a technician with blue latex gloves and medical scissors cuts an opening in my bloody pants. He then injects the meaty gouge in my thigh with a needle three times. By the third injection, I'm no longer wincing, and it's completely numb.

While the tech sets to cleaning and sewing the wound closed, another one fingerprints me, takes my photo, and swabs my hands with a tingly chemical that turns them pinkish.

I've plenty of time to think.

Things like: Todd.

And: Todd?

It must be true because the latest missing girl's body fell out of his truck. Was it him driving the Bronco this whole time? I hope the FBI finds it parked behind his house, or whatever. That mystery needs to be put to rest. How could I have had it so wrong? I guess I must have been so prejudiced against Rooney I was blind. But what else did I get wrong? Something is nagging at me. I can't put my finger on it.

I look at my pink hands.

"GSR," Agent Amanda says, entering the tent, followed by the other Johnson. "That would be 'gunshot residue.' Which means you've been firing a weapon and have some explaining to do."

Agent Ted scans my bracelet with a handheld scanner like grocery clerks use and holds up an electronic tablet with a stylus. He and Agent Amanda interview me in a clinical manner that is as sanitized as my surroundings. He jots away on the tablet as I speak.

I tell them I had left a family gathering earlier that evening to go to the store. I had decided to surprise my mom by getting her some of her favorite vinegar fries from the Nickel. I didn't notice that the place was closed for renovations because the lights were on. When I went inside, I walked in on an assault in progress. The Regulators had Boomer tied to a chair because, as rumor had it, he had been refusing to be pressured by the gang into allowing them to use his network of pubs to distribute drugs and launder their money. While there, a group of Russian Old Believers came in, heavily armed, and confronted the bikers. Weird, right? There I was, caught in the middle. That's when the renovation contractors came in, and all hell broke loose. I had a gun on me because, as you know, I've been threatened lately by someone in a Bronco and felt I had no choice but to defend myself. And now I can't remember very much after that.

I'm quiet after my explanation, and the only sound in the tent is the slapping noise caused by the technician removing his latex gloves.

Ted makes a final note on the tablet. Amanda's raised eyebrow threatens to crack the plaster of her face. Her green eyes drill into me.

"That's quite the story," she says. "And so convenient."

I shrug.

Ted sets the tablet down and scans my wrist again, saying, "Considering that you're a writer and your job is making stuff up, I'm going to take everything you say with a grain of salt."

I say to Amanda, "Well, considering I'm only a 'self-published' writer, how good a story can I make up? Truth is stranger than fiction, as they say."

I ask them about Todd, particularly what happened to his "rock-solid alibi" they had told me about earlier.

"We're working on it," Ted dismisses.

I want to press, but I'm bone-tired, and the nagging in my mind can wait.

"Can I go now? I'm sure my family is worried sick."

"I've got them up to speed," I hear Walt Beglau declare.

I look to the tent door, as he is entering, peach-colored suit and all.

"He can go, right?" he asks, looking at the Johnsons.

The agents nod.

"Don't leave town; we'll probably be in touch again," Ted warns and holds a card out to me. "If you remember anything significant, or if there is something else you'd like to say, or if you have questions, don't hesitate to call."

I take the card even though I already have one from my first interview with them.

They leave, and Walt escorts me across the parking lot to another tent. On the way there, we pass a canopied area with a series of tables and chairs. Every person involved is sitting before a cop with a tablet, giving a statement.

My leg is still numb, but I can feel the sutures pulling on the skin.

"Your mom, of course, is out of her mind," Walt informs me, "but I've calmed her down pretty much. I sure hope you had no real part in this."

"Thanks," I reply, genuinely grateful for his aid.

Inside the tent is a series of folding tables with an array of manila envelopes with names on them. Walt takes me to the table with the package with my name on it. He speaks with the attending officer to expedite my out-processing.

"Are you coming over?" I ask Walt.

"Not tonight, at least," he replies. "Too much left to do here."

I thank him again, we shake hands, and he leaves. It's then that I see Dylan and we make eye contact.

"Hey, you okay?" he asks.

I lift my leg and grimace. "I'll be all right."

We stare at one another.

"So, you, uh, going to tell me..." He stops, and we both feel the weight of all the ambient police attention in the room. "...when you are finally going to come meet me for a beer?"

I grin. "Of course, but I gotta get home first and check my calendar."

"No kidding. Bailey and the kids are probably going nuts."

The attending officer interrupts and wants me to sign some paperwork. As I do, he upends the manila envelope to pour out my keys, wallet, and other effects. He also tells me I have to leave and not linger.

"So, Todd, huh?" I say, ignoring the cop while returning my belongings to my pockets.

"Crazy." Dylan makes a face. "Just when you think you know a guy."

When I slip the last item into my pocket, that nagging sensation hits me hard, and something clicks.

"Hey," I say to Dylan. "Todd had access to the pump station in the city park, right? Because of the contract you guys have with the city? Well, doesn't the city swimming pool water circulate through there?"

Dylan shrugs. "Yeah, I reckon so. Why?"

"Well, if I'm not mistaken, all the victims had chlorinated water in their lungs, despite being found in swimming holes along the creek. I bet if the FBI looks into that station, they'll find evidence. Something to clinch Todd's conviction."

The attending officer scans my wrist, and an LED on the scanner turns green. He also hands me what looks like a grocery receipt with a barcode on it.

"You're free to go now," the officer says. "Your vehicle is in the pound area, near the road. Show the receipt to the pound attendant, and he'll let you out."

Dylan purses his lips and looks like he is about to say something when a plainclothes FBI agent enters the tent and addresses Dylan.

"I'm sorry, sir, but Agents Johnson and Johnson would like to see you again before you leave. They need you to sign a release for the suspect's work history."

"Sure, I'll be right there."

"Hey, can I come? I need to talk to the agents again," I ask the plainclothesman.

"Sir, you've been processed out; you need to leave the crime scene," the attending officer reminds me.

"Hey, I'll talk to the agents," Dylan assures me. "Call me tomorrow. We'll get that beer."

We bump fists and part ways. I wade through the crowd of emergency personnel to the head of the parking lot. A tow truck sits like a dinosaur among a sea of vehicles. A cop approaches me for my receipt. He guides me to my Jeep, removes a piece of yellow plastic ribbon over its door, and points the way to the road designated as an exit. The cop on the street with a red-colored cone over his flashlight stops traffic for me and motions me through. I crawl through the area eerily lit with sputtering red flares until I come to the first stretch of road free of activity. That's where I step on the gas to leave it all behind.

When I reach town, I slow down.

Despite my exhaustion and the midnight hour, my head is whirling with thoughts. The pain in my leg is resurfacing. I can barely drive straight. I wouldn't be surprised if Andy pulled me over for "drinking and driving." I turn on the radio to help keep me focused.

Something is still nagging at my mind.

My head hurts with pain at the base of the skull, and when the static noise engulfs my ears, I pull over.

I squeeze my eyes shut, grab my head.

Then it hits me.

Todd. He's a rage character. Impulsive. Angry to the point he loses his mind and acts out. Prone to beating women. Had he killed Gwen, his ex, he would have beat her to death like every douchebag perpetrator of domestic violence since the dawn of time.

But Gwen was killed like all the other girls. Ritualistically, meticulously, with intense precision and slow deliberateness. Not at all what I would expect of Todd.

Was it possible Todd, as a killer, could turn off his rage, filter it, modulate it? Did serial killers switch gears?

I reject that notion, because again, even if he were capable of that, I doubt he would be capable of maintaining the clinical kill for his ex, for whom he felt a tremendous amount of rage.

But what do I know? I'm no expert. I'm just someone feeling a crazy, obsessive need to understand. So I dig out Ted's card and call him. I turn the radio down.

"Special Agent Ted Johnson," he answers.

I tell him it's me, apologize, and point out that he did ask me to call if I had any questions. With that, I ask him about the possibility of serial killers switching gears.

Surprisingly, Agent Johnson is accommodating. "It's not common, but it's not unheard of. Anything else?" he asks.

"Yeah, is Dylan still there?"

"We cut him loose, probably home now," he replies.

"What did you think about my theory of the pump station?"

Silence.

"He didn't mention it," he says. "Like everyone tonight, he's exhausted, and we relentlessly ran him through some paperwork. Our fault. Probably slipped his mind. I'm sure he'll bring it up the next time we see him."

Rather than wait for that, I float my theory now. Ted doesn't seem too excited.

"Sure, we'll look into that," he replies, and I can almost hear his eyes rolling.

"When?" I urge.

"Soon. Let the professionals handle this. Don't go and do anything stupid. If you are right, then if you go messing up a crime scene, that would be a shame. We'll see you again soon, okay?"

I hang up.

My head hurts. The static is driving me crazy.

I reflect on how the processing officer and pound-lot officer hustled me out of the area. I'm sure the same happened to Dylan. And even if Dylan did mention it, I don't have much confidence in the FBI remembering and taking it seriously. These are the same people, after all, who didn't see 9/11 coming, and they never did find D. B. Cooper.

I grip the steering wheel, creaking my hands back and forth on it. I'm no longer tired. I'm wired. I need answers. I need to put my mind to rest. I need the nagging to go away. What I really need is the pain and static in my head to stop.

I wrench on the wheel and turn around.

I'm going to go do something stupid.

Chapter 65
The Pump Station

When I bring the Jeep to a rolling stop in the empty swimming pool parking lot, I stare long and hard at the gate and wire fence. It cordons off the concrete platform forming the upper deck of the pump station. The light of the lot's lone lamppost glints off a chain and padlock securing the gate. Barbed wire is there to keep out vandals and stupid wannabe writers.

I lean over to turn off the engine, and that's when I hear the radio is still on, still turned down low from when I was on the phone with Ted. Something about the indistinct music draws my attention, tickling my memory, but I can't put a finger on how. I turn up the volume—Peter Gabriel's "My Body is a Cage." Lovely song, but otherwise not ringing a bell. It does calm the pain at the base of my head. When it does, it reminds me that I'm going to need more to comfort me going forward than a song, so reach up and remove the rosary from the rearview mirror and stuff it in my pocket.

I leave the Jeep and peer through the chain links. The concrete pad is about ten feet by ten feet and is level with the parking lot. At the center is what looks like a submarine door or perhaps a bunker or fallout shelter entrance. It doesn't appear locked or even secured, needing only some wheel turns to hinge it open like a can of soup. Surrounding the portal are banks of piping, valves, meters, and analog gauges. Some look modern. Some look as old as the turn of the century. A hum permeates the structure, indicating it's alive with power.

After looking around to make sure I'm alone, I place my hands as best I can between the barbs of the wire and pull myself up, sticking the toes of my shoes into the links of the fence for assistance. Though there is ever-increasing pain in my wounded leg, I'm healthy and athletic enough to struggle my way over the fence with some comical acrobatics that eventually plops me down inside.

There, I turn on the wheel of the submarine door, and despite its antiquated look, it turns smoothly on greased threads. It hinges heavily open with little sound, exposing a ladder leading down into a pit. I descend into damp air, gripping the rough metal rungs.

When I alight some ten feet below, the air is thicker, and there is a hint of chlorine, ozone, and mildew in my nostrils. Motors and electric-driven equipment hum in my bones. There are no lights, no indicators, but the far wall is basically open to the outside, with a broken-down stretch of old chain-link fence between crumbling concrete pillars. Light from the lamppost bleeds into the chamber.

As my eyes adjust to the dimness, I can see several pumps. Some flat on concrete mounts, some vertical, which extend through the ceiling and floor. A glance down the crumbling space around where the pump disappears into the floor shows me its intake pipe. It extends down into a grotto of the bank where Silver Creek's water is sucked up. The water in the little cave below is partitioned off from the rest of the creek by more chain-link fencing to keep driftwood and adventurous children out.

In the chamber's center is an old pump-mount whose mechanical apparatus was removed long ago, leaving a concrete slab about three feet off the ground, two feet wide, and about as long as a coffin. Something about it is disturbing, especially how everything seems to revolve around it. Its cold, hard edges tell a story of unyielding discomfort. Silent screams. Desperation. Tragedy and hopelessness taint its surface every bit as much as the moisture and the lichen covering it. A chill wells up inside me from the darkest recesses of my soul. Repeated episodes of terrible pain and sorrow occurred on that piece of man-made stone—I know it.

I know this feeling. I know this place. I've been here before. Or a place very much like it.

A drop of moisture from above lands on my cheek.

I had this same sensation in the chamber found at the top of the Mayan pyramid on the Yucatán Peninsula.

It's an altar.

For sacrifices.

Another drop hits my cheek as I approach the concrete block, and I wipe it away. There is a depression in the surface where the pump motor had been set at one end. The hollow is filled with water, which smells vaguely of chlorine. About two feet above the block is a rusty pipe six inches wide that runs the room's length. A valve and spigot are situated right above the hollow. I turn the faucet, creaking with every turn, and water pours out, filling the depression. It smells strongly of pool water.

Even after the flow is off, the action must have triggered some process. One of the pumps in the room groans to life, humming and spinning. I hear water flowing in the pipe works, and a gushing noise reaches my ears, alerting me that water is pouring outside the building out into the creek. I see a stretch of pipe from my vantage, corroded to the point of forming a jagged canoe of rust, extending past the chamber's lip. It's from here the water flows. It stops gushing after only a few moments, and the pump comes to rest.

I look back to the depression, now reeking of chlorine. Spidery strands are floating in the water, agitated by the recent movement. The wispy threads are caught on a rusty bolt sticking out of the concrete. With a sinking feeling, I pull one loose and examine it. They're long silver-blonde hairs.

Gwen's hair.

I shouldn't be surprised, but I still feel gut-punched.

I gently return them, aware that I am definitely disturbing a crime scene.

Leaning heavily on one of the crumbling concrete pillars at the edge of the platform, I stare out into the darkness of the city park, breathing air in gulps. I hear the gentle roil of the creek. Below are jagged rocks about the station's firmament. I return my scrutiny into the darkness, letting my heartbeat calm me. A thousand beats pass. Maybe two thousand. Long enough to understand what Nietzsche meant when he said, "And if you gaze long into the abyss, the abyss gazes also into you."

What did I expect to find here? Perhaps in the back of my mind, I wanted clarity. An answer. I'm tired of everyone else always having the power and choosing when to act. It was too easy an explanation for Todd to be the killer, and I wanted to be right about that hunch. Sure, I had wanted it to be him at first because that was the obvious explanation. But wouldn't Gwen have been one of his first victims? No, he had only turned his attention to her when she had angered him with the video I urged her to make when he came to the house that day. Because of my idea, Todd had to face a real possibility of losing custody of his girls. If he had intended to kill her someday, my involvement put her at the head of the line.

My stomach feels as though it falls entirely out of me, and I turn my gaze down to see if it might actually hit the rocks below. When I do, my attention snags on a colorful object caught in the rusty discharge pipe. Something familiar.

I crouch and fumble for the thing while bending the broken fencing outward. After a few attempts, I find that I have to basically lie on my stomach and stretch as far as I can with a flailing arm. I almost cut myself on the jagged piping, and just when I'm wondering in the back of my mind how long it's been since my last tetanus shot, my hand grasps something palm-sized and made of plastic or rubber.

I struggle back to my feet and hold out my hand to examine my prize.

My heart stops.

I'm so shocked that I don't notice the sound of scuffing feet behind me until it's too late.

Chapter 66
Coyote

I'm at the crossroads of Main and Water again. "White Rabbit" is playing down the street to my left.

My head hurts tremendously. Nothing vague or distant about it. It's searing. My hand comes away from the back of my skull wet. Well, I'm wet all over, but my fingertips are covered in blood.

I look behind me and see my wet footprints. This time they are mixed with red.

When I turn back around, Coyote is there. Baleful yellow eyes menace me from twenty feet away. His jaw drops, and that static sound comes from his muzzle.

Even though it's dark and nowhere near noon, City Hall's noon siren blares to life just down the street to the right.

Chapter 67
Amnesiac

My eyes open to the noontime siren wailing in the background, drowning out the beep of the hospital equipment and the radio gently playing "White Rabbit" next to my bed. Dylan is standing over me, holding a pillow. His eyes are wide as saucers. He turns and shouts, and a woman in hospital scrubs rushes in and pries my eyes open, examining me.

"I was adjusting his pillow, and he woke up!" Dylan explains frantically.

The nurse scrambles among the equipment to check monitors. Others rush in, more staff in scrubs. One pries my eyes open even further and blasts a penlight into them.

"Turn that radio off." She motions, and Dylan complies. Then, to me, she asks, "How do you feel?"

I try to swat the light away. "I'd feel better if you'd get that out of my eyes."

Satisfied, she stands up and slips the light into the breast pocket of her lab coat.

"Concussion," she assesses, "but dilation is improving. I think you're out of the woods."

Woods? What woods? A rolling wave of exhaustion pounds through my head, eddying at the base of my skull. The bandage over my head feels too small. Dylan tells me they found me at City Hall and the police station ringing the emergency button, soaking wet with a bloody gash in the back of my head. That was several nights ago.

Or weeks, gauging by how I feel. My arms feel full of sand. My mouth feels like a herd of squirrels crapped in it. Dylan asks what I remember, and I can't answer him. I tell him I remember something about the pump station, and he confirms that the lid was found open when the FBI went to investigate. He also says they didn't find anything.

My head hurts with the effort of trying to remember. The doctor shows me a series of CT scans of my head. She's talking, explaining things, but she sounds like she is underwater. Or I'm underwater.

She points to the images. "You have multiple head injuries, some older than others."

I shrug. "It's been a rough summer."

She tells me that my memory loss is not unexpected and can clear up if I keep trying. "It might not even be very long."

"How long?" Dylan asks. "We did as you suggested, taking turns, playing the radio while he was out to keep his mind engaged. I don't think there wasn't a moment that someone was here doing just that, especially his family."

"Just depends," she explains, now examining my leg wound. "Considering you were also in a highly traumatic violent situation, you might be experiencing some PTSD. That could complicate recovery."

"I don't have PTSD," I object. "That's just silly."

"Denial is generally the first symptom of PTSD," she replies with raised eyebrows. "I'll be back to check on you soon. We'll schedule you with a neurologist and some counseling."

"I said I don't—" I want to explain to her she's making a huge mistake, but her brusque manner shuts me down, and my head hurts too much to fight.

She leaves, and then everything happens. Dylan makes phone calls, and a long list of visitors comes. First are the Johnsons. I'm glad I'm still in a fog because it makes their barrage of questions and admonitions easier to take. They say things like "possible legal action" and "tampering with a crime scene" and other threats that just hurt my head further. I can't tell them much, and they leave in a huff. But before they do, they at least fill me in that Todd stringently denies everything. He's blaming everyone and everything else.

Next, come Mom and Dad. Mom alternates between being angry, relieved, and distraught. Mostly she is hugging and kissing me, but then at one point, I swear she is choking me out like Homer Simpson does to Bart, upset that I hadn't been candid about my encounters with Rooney and that I'd been "bottling myself up," and who cares that I hadn't wanted to worry her. I swear I had only gone to confront Rooney to tell him to leave the family alone. Which is mostly true. Everything that happened after that was beyond my control. She is only partially placated by an apology and wants to know what happened at the pump station.

I tell her the truth that I don't remember, only that I had wanted to confirm for myself that Todd was responsible for the murders.

She goes quiet, a struggling sort of quiet. Then her whole attention is on me so closely that it is suffocating. "Tell me the truth. I won't judge; I just need to know. As your mother. You didn't jump off the bridge, did you?"

My eye roll is so severe it might be causing another concussion.

"Mom, if I wanted to hurt myself, there are much higher bridges than Silverton's city park bridge."

When they leave after a good hour's visit, my mind starts to clear up some, and I begin to ask myself the same questions being posed to me. What had happened? Why was I wet? I remember something about standing on the edge of the pump station, staring out into the darkness, feeling absolutely awful and guilty about Gwen. Pain stabs my head at the memory. The words spell out visually in my mind's eye: *She. Is. Dead. Because. Of. You.* Then I ask myself, So was it a suicide attempt? Had I jumped head-first into those rocks below the station?

Sis comes then with her tribe before I know the answer.

It's probably the only truly happy moment I've had in a long time. Nieces and nephews are crawling all over me, and despite the obligatory knee to the crotch as they clamor on the hospital bed, my heart is full.

"Look what I made you, Gunky," Marie says to me, holding out a piece of shaped paper.

"Ah, what do we have here?" I take the paper and pull it apart, revealing a chain of paper angels. "Thank you, sweetie!"

They too stay for a good long while, then leave, promising to come back tomorrow.

Even before the glow of their visit wears off, a familiar head pops around the corner of my door.

"Hey buddy, how ya feelin'?"

"Hey Jeremy, okay I guess, considering."

He's all smiles and pulls out a bottle of beer from his pants after looking around.

"Snuck it past the nurses," he explains cheerfully.

I laugh but wave it off. Despite my dry mouth, the idea of alcohol makes me nauseated.

He shrugs and drinks it himself. He also has a small cardboard box.

He tells me most everyone involved with the shootout at the Wooden Nickel basically got a slap on the wrist except for the Regulators. Boomer told the police the whole story about them trying to pressure him into moving drugs for them. If we hadn't shown up when we did, they probably would have killed him. Jeremy repeats expressions like "legal indemnity," and "mutual combat clause," and "Stand Your Ground law" while talking to me. I don't understand half of it, and I don't think he does either.

After we clear up some particulars about how the whole confrontation had started, he tells me I've been out for at least three days and repeats what all everyone knows about showing up at City Hall. He tells me many people have already visited me, watching over me while unconscious. Says Jodi had been one of them.

"Well, it's not like he held your hand or anything," he explains when I scoff, "but, yeah, he was here."

I fill him in on what I remember, plus what the doctor told me about my condition, which throws a wet blanket on my mood.

"Like I didn't already have enough to worry about," I grumble, making a general sweep of the room with a limp arm. "Like I could afford any of this in the first place. Now they want to add weeks of specialists on top of it?"

Jeremy looks about the room in silent agreement. The frustration in his face tells me everything I need to know; he wants to help but doesn't know how. Neither do I.

The wet blanket smothers me a little more.

I don't know about PTSD, but I'm plenty depressed. Gwen is still dead. I'm still unemployed. And despite what Jeremy says, I don't see a mere slap on the wrist in my future.

"Oh, I brought you this." Jeremy's smile returns, apparently realizing he can at least do one small thing. He produces the box and opens it. "Talked to Boomer the other day. He found this kicked under what was left of the jukebox before any of the cops could. It's in perfect shape. I even reloaded it for you. Don't worry, the safety is on. I figured even in the hospital you may need to protect yourself. After listening to your story, it sounds like I might be right."

Sitting up in bed, I peer in the box. My gun is there. I have mixed feelings about it.

"Uhm, thanks, man," I reply and steer the conversation away from it. "How is Boomer taking all this?"

Jeremy laughs. "He's actually happy as hell. He got the Regulators off his back. Insurance is paying for all the damages, plus the renovations we'd been working on."

Outwardly I smile, but inwardly the wet blanket constricts a little tighter. It seems everyone but me is making out well. The beeping hospital equipment next to my bed sounds more like a cash register tallying cost, with no end in sight.

We talk until the sun starts to dip outside the window.

Before he takes leave, his happy-go-lucky smile fades. "That PTSD is no joke," he says. "Go easy, okay? Take it from me, I've known more than a few Iraq vets who didn't...and it cost them... and the families they left behind."

I've already made up my mind about my next move. But, despite that, I put on a brave smile.

"I will."

Chapter 68
Break

A drop of water splashes on the table. The puddle grows, spilling onto the floor and creating a pool under the bottom rungs of the stools.

I don't mean to, but my head lolls with fatigue. "I'm exhausted. I'm not sure how much more of this I can take. I feel hollow inside like all the blood has drained out of me."

Drip.

"This is precisely where you shine, though," Stephen replies. He's not looking at me when he says this but listlessly swirls the ice around in his soda. His thousandth soda. Doesn't that guy ever take a piss? "You persevere where few else do. The finish line is in sight. Hang in there."

Clark examines the jukebox. Homer draws on his pad.

Drip.

Why am I the only one getting wet? I lean forward. My sight swims. My pint glass tilts over. What little beer there was in it spills on the table and mingles with the water, complicating the mess.

"S-sorry," I mumble.

"Clark, isn't there some song on that contraption that will get him through?" Homer asks.

"The music has run dry for the moment, and I don't think that is a coincidence."

The back of my head is throbbing. I look down at the puddle on the table. The beer mixed in with it is red, turning redder. So is the puddle on the floor. Much more red than the spilled beer can explain. I see wet footprints leading from the door to the pool.

At least that damnable electrical hissing noise is no longer issuing from the speakers, but a steady heartbeat is now starting to emerge.

I start to lean to the side. "My mind holds the key," I say listlessly and go over.

From the floor, I hear the panicked movement of my companions.

Chapter 69
Concupivit Anima Mea Desiderare Te

When I pull into the driveway of my Vancouver house, the lawn is even more overgrown than my last visit. The thought of finding a way to mow it is exhausting, depressing, and overwhelming because I sold my lawnmower at a garage sale. A neighbor might lend one to me, but I shove the idea out of my head. I have pride.

I slide out of the Jeep, dragging my travel bag loose from the gear shift. The "For Sale" sign has fallen over again. The flyers in its little box have flown out and are strewn all over the cul-de-sac. Entering my house, paper scrapes along the linoleum as the door plows the pile of mail aside.

Inside, nothing has changed. Still the same, big, empty house. A bit more dust. The ticking second hand on the clock is a bit louder. I sit on the couch. Sunlight streams through the window above and behind me, but who knew sunshine could be so depressing? Its rays are bent and warped and have lost their luster. They are pale, diluted, like cheap watercolor paint. It is, at best, the sort of sunlight you find in the farthest corner of a dusty museum that has no artifacts of interest, no art, no masterpieces. Just a public ashtray with a smoldering half-extinguished cigarette whose gray smoke adds to the day's dishwater haze.

I realize why I had left Silverton without telling anyone. I don't want them to see me like this. I don't want to have to explain myself. To hear their pity anymore. I need to sort this out alone. If it can be. If not...? I guess I just keep running from one place to the other to escape the same kinds of pain. Running until I have nowhere left to run, having returned to the starting place. Like now.

I shake my head, try to snap out of it.

To change the narrative, I lean over and start to sort through my mail.

Mostly junk mail, of course, but then there are the inevitable account statements. Breaking open the seals reveals that my IRA is almost empty and my credit cards maxed out. I toss them aside. I come across a letter from a magazine. A response from a submission for another short story. My stomach churns. I'm afraid to open it. I'm scared to hope. I know the answer already, but by not opening it, there is the suspended possibility that it could have been accepted. It's like Shrödinger's cat, both alive and dead, both accepted and rejected.

It's a useless ploy, I know, and of course, I eventually open it to reveal the trite form rejection. The cat is dead. I toss the letter aside.

It lands on top of the last un-opened envelope, which piques my curiosity. It's from Tesseract Corporation. Again my stomach goes sour, and I'm afraid to hope. A callback? It can't be, but... I tear the envelope open, and it's a copy of the same damn survey they sent home with me the first time. Apparently, they really want me to fill it out.

I throw it on the trunk with disgust, and it lands facing up. The last question of the survey mocks me: *What do you want?*

I lean back on the couch and cradle a pillow over my chest as if it might protect me from the horrors of the world. The sunlight bleeds away its color before my eyes, and the sound of the ticking clock echoes inside my head like someone beating a stick inside an empty trashcan.

I pick up my bag and go to the other end of the house, to my bedroom, to escape the constant ticking. I stand over my bed and stare at the corner of the room where the blank walls meet, and it dawns on me that I've run as far as I can. I could curl up in that corner, I guess, but that would just be a formality.

This is it—the end of the line.

As I stare at the corner, I realize that I'm kneading my travel bag in my hands, distantly aware it isn't that full. I had only had the briefest of moments to sneak into my parents and retrieve what I could.

I do feel something hard in the bag, though.

I unzip it and upend the contents onto the bed.

My gun falls out.

I pick it up and pull on the slide just enough to crack the breach and see brass glint at me.

I slowly release the slide, easing it back into place, letting the weapon hum with power in my hand.

I take a deep breath. I stare at the corner. I note how white it is. How blank. All angles of the wall running to a point with finality.

The clock in the other room ticks on relentlessly, moving toward inevitability.

Corpse Pose is the hardest pose to maintain.

The cat is dead.

The metal of the gun feels cool against the skin of my temple.

"Hey, Jesus, you there?" I throw one final and desperate call to the universe.

Silence.

The gunmetal is ice cold now. It touches the skin alongside the bandage around my head. My index finger slowly, gradually tightens.

Ding-dong!

I exhale explosively, and my gun hand drops to my side.

Of course, my doorbell doesn't go *Ding-dong!*, but it might as well have for the way it's echoing in my head. It's been ages since I've heard it used, and I've forgotten what sound it actually makes. But it's ringing now.

My body feels clammy with sweat. I walk briskly to the door and look through the peephole. Dylan is there on my doorstep, looking awkward with hands in pockets.

Jesus is standing behind him, and he reaches around Dylan to ring the doorbell again. When he does, Dylan jumps and looks at the button.

I'm half surprised, half upset, all grateful.

I move to open the door, but I realize I'm still holding my gun. I curse and look around to find a place to hide it. I end up stuffing it behind the cushions on the couch and rush back to the door.

"Hey, buddy, what's going on?" I ask when I open the door on him, startling him with the suddenness of the gesture.

He throws his arms up. "I could ask you the same thing. What's with the disappearing act?"

I invite him in, close the door behind him. Jesus is gone.

"I just needed some...space."

"Well, people are worried about you," he explains, brow furrowed in exasperation. "Concerned for your state of mind and all that. You should really still be in the hospital. I can't believe they just let you check yourself out."

I sigh. "I know, I'm sorry. I'll go back to Silverton soon. I just need a moment to breathe."

Dylan takes a look around, assessing the environment, the emptiness.

"How you feeling?" he asks.

"Head still hurts like a mother—"

"Remember anything yet?"

"Not really."

"Good."

My blood goes cold, and my following words catch in my throat when he places the bedazzled silencer end of a pistol against my forehead.

"Have a seat," he says.

Chapter 70
The Stagger

Suzy Starfish stares back at me from the palm of my hand, wide cartoon eyes just as surprised to see me. Then, as the implication of her presence sets in, a scuffing noise behind me alerts me that something is coming.

I start to turn, but before I can, pain explodes at the base of my head, sending stars shooting across my vision. They have silly eyes like Suzy.

Stunned, I fall forward, and in that brief moment, I catch a glimpse of the silhouette of a man holding a shiny, metallic object in one hand. Then I'm falling headfirst into the water below, gasping in anticipation of the cold. My breath is still lodged in my lungs when it closes over me, shocks my limbs so numb I can't surface to take a breath. Instead, I float up like a dead man, arms splayed out, staring into darkness from the cold mountain runoff.

Eventually, my eyes figure out how to blink. *Somebody had struck me from behind.* A somebody, not a something. My skull feels shattered. How I'm conscious at all, I don't know. My brain feels like it's swelling like a balloon. As the numbness and shock subside, I flail, trying to swim or at least roll over to get air.

Before I can, however, a fish swims out of the darkness into my view. A fish with eyes so intensely blue they can't be real.

The fish is a white-and-gold koi.

"Don't move," the fish instructs me with Jade's voice. "Play dead. Go dormant, as the koi in your country do in winter."

Just the effort of listening hurts my head, and I float, resting, waiting. Finally, the fish darts out of view, and the creek flow drifts me into the shallower area beneath the bridge illuminated by the city pool's parking lot light.

The muddy rocks look yellow in the light. The water is heavy with suspended sediment, leaves, and twigs. My shadow drifts just ahead of me, rippling over the rocks with its arms spread as if crucified. The shadow of the bridge slowly comes into view, and someone standing on it. The shadow is holding a gun.

I brace myself but don't move.

Play dead.

There has been a sound in my ears this whole time until now. Until my heartbeat had calmed, I hadn't been aware of it. Currently, it attacks my inner ear, keeping pace with the pain in my head, which aches with every surge of blood pulsing through the wound.

It is a crackling, static sound.

I recognize it from countless childhood summers spent swimming in this same stretch of the creek at the city park. It's what the hum of electrical power from the pump station sounds like underwater. Drifting to the tune of that sound, I see the shadow on the shadow-bridge move back and forth in agitation, trying to scrutinize my prone body floating away.

It raises the shadow-gun. Panic surges in me. *Dive! Swim! Do something!* But before I can act, Brent the yoga instructor's voice comes to me, cutting through the static. "You are dead," he informs. "Be like a dead person, relax and let your worldly concerns drift away. What can they do for you, anyway? I know it's difficult. Corpse Pose is the hardest pose to maintain. The dead have it the hardest."

The shadow remains poised with shadow-gun. My lungs start to burn. My head starts to ring with hypoxia.

Corpse Pose. I am a corpse, I tell myself.

I accomplish stillness, but my eyes flutter, struggle.

Whoosh! Clack!

I'm standing in the upper room of the tapestry shop, with the loom.

I'm staring at the crone with the shears in her hand. The thread is fraying even more, making a *phssphss!* sound against the metal.

Over at the table, Jade is having tea with our guide.

A newcomer is sitting with them. A well-dressed older gentleman in Western garb, particularly a scarlet handkerchief in his breast pocket. As he greets me by raising his teacup with a smile, I recognize him. He's the stranger from Gwen's funeral. Something about him is comforting. I'm tempted to forget the loom and join him at tea. I then understand the call for prayer that has been resonating throughout the city outside the window. Not the words, but the meaning. It is truly a call, an invitation, to let go.

Phssphss!!...Whoosh! Clack!... phssphss!

The call to prayer is louder now.

I'm back in the water. My lungs are bursting. My eyes are bulging. The shadow-gun is still aimed at me. Brent's instructions reach me through the static, the prayer, and my throbbing heartbeat. "Six...Seven..." He counts toward ten when the pose will be finished. "...Eight...Nine...Nine...and a half..." I can hear his smirk. *Not funny, a-hole!* "...Nine...and three quarters..."

Glancing to the shadows painted before me, I see the shadow-man relent, lower the shadow-gun, and leave. I pass out of the illuminated area into darkness, approaching the little spillway.

"Ten!"

I'd sigh, but I'm underwater. My feet can't touch the bottom, and worse, the suction of the water going over the spillway is pulling me down. My arms flail, burning up the last of my oxygen. Unable to lift my head, panic sets in.

Phssphss!!...Whoosh! Clack!... phssphss!

The flow grows more turbulent as it rushes into one of the gaps in the retaining wall, overpowering my body. Panic escalates to hysteria, my flailing wilder. My toes occasionally brush the bottom but gain traction nowhere. I can feel the blood vessels in the whites of my eyes bursting. I've never been this close to passing out from lack of air, and it's just as horrible as I imagined.

Whoosh! Clack!... PHSSPHSS!!

Ahead, in the darkness, in the turbid water, a hand shoots down in a cloud of bubbles. It's my father's hand, young and strong with his favorite wide leather watchband from the seventies. I grasp it, and it pulls, struggling against the current.

Clack!

I'm back in the upper room. The thread about the closing shears has frayed to its final strand. She narrows the gap between the blades of the shears. Without thinking (I'm past thinking at this point, it's all survival instinct now), I reach out to stay her hand. It's ice-cold, emaciated.

Her head jerks up, and she looks at me with one good eye. Surprise is there.

She looks at the tea table. I follow her gaze.

The distinguished gentlemen's eyebrows are raised. He looks to the crone and gives a nod of concession.

The crone lowers the shears.

My head bursts above the water, where I'm pressed against the retaining wall.

Vast gulps of air enter my lungs. I sound like a walrus.

I'm in my yoga studio, lying on my back, staring up. Brent's bearded face comes into view as he leans over me, blocking my view of the ceiling. His glasses are fogged over, and he has the biggest, stupidest grin.

"See, that wasn't so hard, now was it?" he says.

Water streams down my face and torso as I lever my way onto the retaining wall. Gradually, I scoot along the V of the wall to shore.

At least I think I do. I'm not sure what happens next, but I find that I'm standing on the corner of Main and Water in front of the Ames Building. Wet footprints leading up to me from across the bridge. They are pink in the lamplight. My head hurts as if my scalp has been flayed off. It's not just the back of my head. It's all of it. It just doesn't feel like my head is about to explode. It feels like it already has, with my brains leaking out my ears and out a crack in the back of my head. It feels true.

My vision swims. I can barely see. Despite the warm night air, I'm chilled to the bone. My arms and hands are pale, as if the color is leaking out of me.

Music floats to me from my left, from up Water Street to the North. The rhythmic drumming and low bass drone the familiar tune of "White Rabbit." It's enticing, luring me. I want to go that way, to the warm sugary depths.

Coyote is there, watching intently, licking his lips. He stands to the side as if waiting to guide me to the music.

I take a step in that direction.

However, when I do, a Collie darts out from behind me and confronts Coyote, barking at him until he grudgingly saunters away, casting one final hungry gaze at me.

The Collie worms around my ankles, edging me in the opposite direction. It goes to my right, gives a bark. I want to turn back the other way, but the Collie isn't having it. It barks again, walks a few steps to my right, looking over its shoulder. The barking hurts my head. I want it to stop.

"Okay, fine." I shuffle after the dog. It leads the way, its toenails clicking away on the pavement.

My steps are labored. I'm almost falling forward with each one. The night grows narrower. The dog, the street, the streetlight start to look a million miles away down a tunnel. My head and neck throb. I want to die. I want it to end. But the dog won't let me stop. Instead, it urges me on, barking if I stop.

Reaching out to the wall to my right, I steady myself. My hand leaves an ochre-colored streak. I realize I'm holding my breath, which seems to increase the pressure in my head. I let it out in a long rattle and wonder if maybe that was the wrong thing to do because now it feels like not just my brain is about to fall out of my head, but my entire soul is going to slip right out of my mouth if I'm not careful.

Taking another breath, my head fills like a balloon. Do I hold it? Do I let it out? It's so confusing.

Ahead is City Hall. And above the double glass doors to City Hall is the blue neon sign that says, "Police."

Something tells me the sign is my destination. If I can just reach that sign, all will be well. No pounding headache. No pain. Just get to the soothing blue light. Let its balm cover me in peace. The dog urges me on.

It's not just a raspy breath coming out of my mouth. Long phlegmy red strands dangle from my lips. My steps stutter to a stop.

"Not much farther, handsome." I hear Gwen say.

I look up, and there she is, bathed in the glow of a streetlamp. Her hair is more silver than ever. Her lips are very red. Her dress is very white with black polka-dots.

I cry a little. "I'm so sorry. I should have been a better friend."

"Don't you worry your pretty head off," she says with a smile, slipping her arm into mine. "You were a better friend than most, and besides, no one is perfect. Take it from me. Now, come on, just a few more feet."

With her aid, I stagger a foot forward, then another, and another.

Music fills my head again. Not coming from any bar but from inside. From some unknown place. It's Peter Gabriel's "My Body Is a Cage," reaching its orchestral crescendo. Mounting and bursting to its finale. I realize it's been playing this whole time.

I'm standing underneath the neon police department sign. Its blue light bathes me in a soothing glow, but it's not stopping the sensation of slipping away. My soul is detaching. It's trying to shrug off its mortal coil.

I pull on the door handle. It's locked. There is a black box on the side of the building next to the door. It has a large button labeled, "Press for Attendant Afterhours." A handwritten note is posted next to the button: "No prank calls! Premises under video surveillance!"

I look around, wanting to thank the Collie and Gwen, but they are gone.

Swaying, I reach up and press the button.

A shrill shriek escapes the box, rising and falling in tone. When the noise goes away, it is replaced by what could best be described as a vacancy. I stare at the box, thinking I've just been pranked into listening to another noise that hurts my head. A desire to just lie down overwhelms me, and for a moment, I believe that I am. I'm in Mac's Place, on the floor staring up at the ceiling fans and the network of belts connecting them.

My head is cradled in Clark's lap, and he's holding it. Homer is on his knees, holding my hand. Stephen is down here too. They all have concerned looks and appear to be arguing. Their voices are garbled, coming from a thousand miles away.

"He's going to be okay," Stephen assures when I can finally make out their words. "We know how this ends."

Clark's response is harsh. "Do we? You're the one who told him to go nonlinear! Anything can happen! Many artists have died from their art!"

"And many have willingly died for it," Stephen counters.

"Gentlemen, please," Homer says. "We need to be calm. Let him finish the story...however it ends."

A woman's voice comes as if from deep inside the box. "State the nature of the emergency."

I sway and respond, "...my mind holds the key."

Up to my left, a video camera on the corner of the building clicks on and points at me like a gun, its little red laser light drilling me.

"Oh my God."

Chapter 71
...And Your Enemies Closer

"It was you," I say, sitting on the couch, holding a pillow before me as if it might protect me from the horrors of the world.

Dylan sits opposite me on a fold-up chair. One leg is crossed over the other, bouncing a little. His foot brushes the edge of the Tesseract questionnaire, and one arm rests on his knee. The other is balanced on it while it casually points the gun at me.

His face is blank, void of emotion. Void of everything, really. I almost don't recognize him.

"Oh, so now you remember." It's a statement, not a question, in response to my comment. "I knew Suzy Starfish would eventually rat me out if I didn't pay you a visit today."

My mind is reeling. I'm trying to not only piece it together but fathom the fundamental "why" of it all.

"I tried before," Dylan explains. "Like at the hospital, but I just couldn't get you alone long enough to smother you. The moment I got the chance was the moment you woke. Go figure."

"That was you in the Bronco all along..."

"Yes," he admits. "I got it for Bubba's party to go mudding. I hadn't registered it yet. No license plates. The perfect tool to mow you down. But you just wouldn't die. Lucky bastard if there ever was."

"Why?" The question is more significant than just the simple word. "Why Gwen? Why any of them? What the hell, man?"

A corner of his lip curls up, the first indication of personality since he whipped out the pistol.

"I have a gift. A mission," he explains. "The women, they call out to me, whether they know it or not. They suffer silently, begging for release. I give it to them. I ease their pain, and

428

ultimately, in time, the people nearest them are free of the pain they caused."

"A 'gift'?" I raise an eyebrow.

"Well, we can't all be writers, now can we?" he says. "I am an artist in my own way."

It's disgusting. "The manner of killing. The positioning of the bodies. The 'ritual' of it all..."

"Yes. So, you do understand."

"I understand you're pretty screwed up."

Both corners of his mouth turn up this time. "Now, now. You of all people know the sting of a critic."

"Why Gwen? She was your friend."

Dylan draws a long breath. "She had been calling me for a long time. Long before you came along. She's in a better place now. Her kids will be with her sister, especially now that Todd is out of the picture. And there you have it, the world is a better place, compliments of me."

I shake my head. "Why me? Have I been 'calling' to you too? I guess I should be flattered, being the only dude on your list."

"It was the chimney-sweepers," he says, and his smile expands at my confused look as he continues. "When you mentioned them to me the day of the parade, the fact that you saw them too told me that you're special. Like me."

I lean forward slightly. "No one else can see them?"

Dylan nods.

My attention is drawn to the side of the room, near the fireplace. The distinguished gentleman I saw at Gwen's funeral is standing there, looking with intense interest between Dylan and me.

Whoosh! Clack!

"You see?" Dylan adds, also glancing at the Visitor. "You can see them. But unlike you, I can *hear* them too. They talk to me. Tell me I'm special. Tell me I have a gift. A mission."

I lean back, return my gaze to Dylan. He blinks, and his eyes turn solid black. Their oily depths reflect no light. In fact, they suck in the light of the room.

...the hell? I want to crawl out of my skin.

He blinks, and they're his human eyes again. "Between you being able to see *them*, that photographic memory of yours, and your nosy-writer ways, it's just a matter of time before you put it all together. The pump station proves it. I can't have that."

"So, that's it?" I say. "This town ain't big enough for two creepy bastards who see things?"

"Oh, there are more," Dylan confesses. "I have my work cut out for me. Willy? He sees things, too, doesn't he? And even though people generally don't take him seriously, who's to say that they might someday? Can't have that."

I stiffen, clench the pillow.

"And speaking of work," Dylan continues. "Many women are calling to me. Your niece Sarah? She's been calling awfully loud lately."

My whole body coils with tension. I sit up, clenching my teeth so hard they hurt.

"Why bother telling me any of this? Why haven't you just killed me already?"

"Oh, trust me, if it were possible, I would—purge you with sanitizing water while I looked you in the eyes, so you knew who did exactly what to you." Dylan squints at me. "As it is, I have to settle for looking you in the eyes as I pull Jodi's trigger. Killing two birds with one stone, so to speak. That idiot has left his guns in my trucks for the last time. My kids are everything to me. Works out, though, because the police will find his gun on this floor after your neighbors have seen a blond guy in khaki uniform come and go in a WVLC truck. They'll probably put him in the same jail cell as Todd."

I notice for the first time that Dylan is holding the gun in his left hand.

"You're not left-handed," I point out, maybe trying to buy time.

"Oh, but I am," Dylan responds. "In Eugene Field, Miss Smith —remember that old bat?—she forced me to write 'correctly.' I had to become someone else to make her happy. Put myself in a different box to get things done. But as you now know, I bring out the other me from the other box to do other things." He blinks, and his eyes are black. He raises the gun. "Now, it's about time we wrap this story up."

Whoosh! Clack!

"I guess so," I say, shifting the pillow between us. Sadness hangs from my words.

His brow churns over those oily pools. He opens his mouth to speak, but before he can form a word, the gun thunders, and the pillow on my lap explodes into a cloud of feathers.

A red dot appears between those black eyes, and a crimson spray fountains behind his head as it snaps back, tipping his whole body and chair over backward.

His foot snags the mail on the trunk and sends it flying into the air.

I stand pointing the Heckler & Koch at Dylan's supine body. It's not necessary. He'll never move again.

Feathers and mail fall all around me.

I snag a piece of paper out of the air as the Visitor drags Dylan away by the collar.

It's the last page of the Tesseract survey. Not surprisingly, the question, "What do you want?" stares at me.

I ponder that for a moment.

"I want to live."

Chapter 72
Curtain Call

We're in the Brush Creek Theater. The four of us are all in a row in the back. I'm seated between Homer and Clark. Stephen is on the far side of Homer. We're clapping along with the full house as the curtain closes.

"It will open again soon," Clark whispers. "The players will come out for their bow."

"Yes, Clark, we know," Homer says, setting down his play program and picking up his copy of the *Silverton Appeal Tribune*. "We're not unfamiliar with theater."

"It's not quite over, though, is it?" Stephen points out.

"No, no, it isn't," I respond.

Homer summarizes from the *Tribune* as he reads, breaking it down to the main points. "After an extensive investigation, it was found that Dylan claimed the lives of five victims. The fifth was initially attributed to Mrs. Thompson's ex-husband, Todd, who was later exonerated and is facing lesser charges of assault. The FBI declined to offer a motive as to why Dylan, the Silverton native, and the family man went on a killing rampage, other than the crimes were premeditated. The FBI asserts there are no other victims and concedes that it was likely he would have killed again."

Homer trails off as he adjusts his spectacles and studies the poorly lit print. "And so on, and so forth. We're left to assume ownership, and control of Willamette Valley Land and Craft went to Jeremy and Jodi. Oh, look, they used my drawing of you."

Homer turns the paper for us to see. There is a picture of me, a reproduction of a hand-drawn image done initially in charcoal.

"Very nice likeness," Stephen compliments.

Clark agrees.

"So, that is what you were working on," I say.

"Indeed, it's how I got my start, if you recall," Homer replies. "Making images for the newspapers."

"I recall." I study my own face, as the whole community must see it in the pages of the town's newspaper. "You know, on paper, I'm almost interesting."

Homer gives me a paternal smile. "You're not half bad in real life."

I smile, maybe blush. "Did they mention my books?"

Homer scans the article, then says apologetically, "Afraid not."

"Of course not."

The curtains open, and the crowd rises. Uncle Norman comes out in complete villain getup. The set is still the Dr. Seuss-esque caricature storefronts of old-time Silverton used in the *Saga of Sylvie Creek*.

"Ladies and gentlemen, give it up for the players!" Uncle Norman steps aside and sweeps his hand toward the cast, then joins the applause himself. The crowd is generous with their affection, sending waves of appreciation to the stage as actors come from the back of the set, stepping out from behind the storefronts.

First, come Lori, Manny, Carrie, Bailey, and many who appeared in the first act. They step aside and take a position in front of the storefronts. Next, come Sis, Mom, Dad, Officer Andy, Ivan, Svetlana, Clea, and Natalie, and others who stand in front of the first group, but in a staggered fashion so the audience can see them all. Then come Bubba, Mayor Stu, Dave, a group of Little People, Todd, Boomer, Rooney, Black Bart, Pops Montgomery, and the Johnsons (wearing sunglasses). The Visitor is there too, quietly standing by (though everyone gives him a wide berth).

Jesus is lowered from the rafters by wires. However, whoever is operating the winch is obviously struggling because his descent is not all that smooth. Nevertheless, in his dangling, Jesus manages to turn to the audience to smile and wave.

There is a brief pause, and the crowd parts as Jeremy and Jodi come to the front of the stage.

Dylan comes out next. Egged on by Uncle Norman from downstage, the crowd boos, and hisses. He throws up his hands and shrugs. But the crowd returns to clapping, letting Dylan join the ranks onstage. The cast parts one more time.

From the gap in the crowd, Gwen comes striding downstage in true movie star fashion, feather boa trailing behind her as she blows kisses to the audience. The response is thunderous. The few people who had been still sitting are now on their feet.

They all hold hands, collectively lift their arms overhead, and take a bow.

A Collie runs loose on the stage, turning in circles and barking.

Don Bensen is at the bottom of the stage, washing the players with flashes from his camera.

After a few more bows and blown kisses, the curtain comes down. The room quiets, and people start to shuffle to the aisles.

"Well done, well done," Homer says, still clapping.

Epilogue

"Excellent." Stephen raises his soda in approval.

Homer and Clark agree.

We're in Mac's now, seated at our little round table. It's full of empty and half-empty glasses, plus Homer's teapot.

The darkness is wearing off the sky. The sun is rising outside. I'm dry now and feeling much warmer. My clothes have changed too. I'm dressed more like Homer in a shirt, tie, and vest, complete with a dangling watch fob. The pain in my head is a faded memory, as is the static noise.

We push back our chairs and stand, pausing to examine each other.

After a beat, Clark is the first to break the silence.

"I must be getting back," he announces, pulling on his suspenders. "The boys will be waiting for me at camp. We have many trees to get to today." As he walks to the door, a trolley car pulls up on the tracks on Water Street outside the pub window.

"Thank you, Clark," I call to him. "Your advice to put on a performance at just the right moments probably saved me."

With a hand on the door handle, he looks over his shoulder.

"You're welcome," he replies. "And thank you for including me on this little adventure. Thank you for remembering me, for the only true death is to be forgotten."

He leaves then and climbs aboard the red trolley. It's a smart little car with gold filigree trimming and artwork on its side: cascading falls and flourishing letters: "Silver Creek Falls! It's Heaven!"

With a *ding! ding!* the trolley moves on, and I can see across the street to the Palace Theater. Behind the glass of a theater display case is a poster for *Gone With the Wind*. An older version of Clark is bending Vivian Leigh over for a kiss.

"I guess it is that time," Stephen says.

He takes one last sip of his soda, shakes my hand, and turns to leave.

I can't let him go just yet. "I bet if you think about it, you can offer up one last pearl of wisdom."

Stephen thinks about it. He gestures at me with a finger. "If I've learned anything in life, it's that sitting on a park bench with a good book is a lot less creepy than just sitting on a park bench." He nods assertively, satisfied with his response.

I give him a look. "Okay. Thanks."

He leaves, and through the windows, I see him get into a glossy red '58 Plymouth Fury parked along the curb. He drives off in the wrong direction, a victim of Silverton's infamous one-way streets. A long angry honk follows as a car passes him going the other way.

I shrug. He'll figure it out.

I turn, and Homer is assessing me.

"So, what pearl of wisdom have you garnered from all this?" he asks.

It's my turn to get introspective. "It's all about the journey. The end is not near as important as the people you meet along the way." I gesture with my chin to the windows, the outside. "There are many people out there, and I need to put that principle into practice because before you know it, the end is here."

Homer's eyes radiate a joyful glow, and he gives my hand a solid shake.

"Thank you," I say to him. "Your spirit is a part of the DNA of this town. I'm certain it has infused many of us, and you live on because of it."

Homer takes his leave of me then, pausing at the door to retrieve his walking stick and bowler hat from the coat rack. He passes through the door, and before it swings shut, he consults his watch.

He looks to one side and says, "Come, boy."

He turns and leaves, and a Collie trots after him.

When the door closes, the lights come on full inside Mac's. I turn to the table and reach for a beer glass. I stop just before grasping it and instead take up the teapot and pour myself a cup of tea.

I take a sip of it, consulting my own pocket watch.

"You were talking up quite a storm with yourself tonight," Natalie says to me from behind the bar. She's wiping the counter. "More than usual."

I smile. "I know." I set the cup down and return the watch to its pocket.

"Where are you headed to now?" Natalie asks.

Out the window, the dawning day is full of possibilities. The weathervane above the Wolf Building shifts in the breeze. Soon it will be autumn. There will be a chill in the air. The leaves will turn. The constant rain will come, and children will have boat races in the ditches. Smoke from chimneys and leaf-burning piles will mingle with wispy fog filling the hollows. The fields will be stubbled from harvest. Oktoberfest will come, then bright-orange jack-o'-lanterns will gallop through neighborhoods.

There will be new stories to tell.

I take a deep breath.

"I don't know just yet," I respond, "but whatever I do, I'm going to enjoy it. Appreciate every minute of it."

Natalie smiles, bobs her head, returns to wiping the counter.

I open the door. If I had a fedora like my godfather, I'd probably slip it on with a flourish and wink.

But I don't.

Let's not get crazy now.

The End

February 23, 2020
7:13 PM

About the Cover Artist

Lori Rodriques was born and raised in Central Oregon. She took up art as a child and it remained the one constant throughout her varied professions. She worked on horseback in Sunriver, OR, Palm Springs, CA and Yellowstone National Park before becoming the Naturalist at Silver Falls State Park near Silverton, Oregon.

Under the business name, LL Webb, Rodrigues began painting murals in 1995. Her mural projects can be seen in several Oregon State Parks, at the state fairgrounds, in the cities of Saint Paul, Silverton and in Valladolid, Mexico. More about her, and her work, can be found at https://www.silverstreamstudio.com/

About the Interior Artist

Jeremy Kranz is the proprietor of "Digital Illustrations by Jeremy Kranz Art" and graduated from the art institute of Seattle with a degree in visual communications, worked as a free lance graphic designer for 15 years, and now lives back in his hometown of Silverton creating fine art.

Adam Copeland is also the author of works of historical fiction, the two-part "Tales of Avalon" series:

Echoes of Avalon

Patrick Gawain knows monsters. He's seen plenty of the human sort in the Holy Lands, and as he sails home from The First Crusade, a hooded apparition begins to stalk him. Convinced that he's lost his mind, he holes up in a monastery to convalesce and, if recovery proves impossible, to hide his demons from the world. But a stranger comes to find him and presents a barely credible invitation: travel to Avalon and serve with the Avangarde, an order of knights sworn to protect young scholars from around the world.

Thinking it will be a fresh start, Patrick agrees, and soon discovers that Avalon is more than a myth; it is the site of a vibrant secret academy - and it's also full of ghosts, goblins, and talking wolves. He can capably protect the castle from the island's supernatural beasts, but in the relative peace of the academy life, his hooded demon returns and his troubled heart causes him to sabotage the love of a young woman, Katherina. When an ancient being with sinister designs for the island infiltrates the academy, Patrick is the first to suspect its true nature when it begins its quest by seducing Katherina.

Patrick soon learns that before he can defeat monsters, he must first defeat his personal demons.

Ripples in the Chalice

The Holy Grail is found! Sir Patrick, the Irish knight who brought the cup to Greensprings on the Isle of Avalon, never intended for it to stay there. He had only wished to save his love from the clutches of death with its miraculous abilities. Now, Roman Church officials, politically ambitious nobility, and ancient supernatural creatures fight to lay claim to it. In the resulting battle, it is not enough to be strong—one must also be ruthless. To live with the consequences of his act, Sir Patrick assumes the burden of leadership to protect his comrades and the woman he loves. But in his struggles to set matters aright, he risks losing that love forever. Patrick must grow stronger in body and soul to keep the chalice out of the wrong hands, and to keep his world intact.

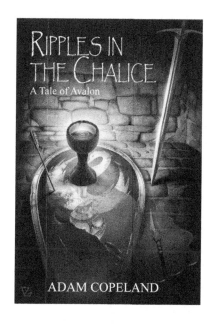

Made in the USA
Monee, IL
14 September 2022

13983197R00246